Crossing the Lines

Books by M.Q. Barber

Playing the Game

Crossing the Lines

Healing the Wounds

Crossing the Lines

M.Q. Barber

LYRICAL PRESS
Kensington Publishing Corp.
www.kensingtonbooks.com

For all of the encouraging voices that pushed me to believe in myself, but especially for Dee, who read every word along the way.

Chapter 1

Weaving through cubicle farmers streaming from white-collarville, Alice fished her buzzing phone from her pocket. "Hello?"

"Alice." Henry, *telephoning?* "I hope I'm not disturbing your workday."

She hustled to beat the crowd. "No, no, I'm done for the day." Maybe a sweet Henry-surprise waited at home. "Headed to the T stop." Not a handwritten note, or he wouldn't be calling. "What's up?"

"Jay was in a scrape this afternoon, and I didn't wish you to worry in the event you came looking for us this evening."

"Just a scrape?" Bullshit. They'd be at home. "Where are you?"

"Perhaps more than a scrape, but not so urgent as to demand immediate attention, apparently." Detached. Rattled, for Henry. The clipped distance in his voice blazed a trail for her fears. "I expect we'll be at the hospital a while yet."

No wonder he'd risked disturbing her at work.

"Which one?" She elbowed through the churning sea of laptop bags and bulky winter coats. *Move, damn you.* "I'll come wait with you."

"Unnecessary, my dear. Jay is rather short-tempered at the moment, as you might expect. Too much waiting, and no pain medication until they receive the results from the scan. But I will keep you informed."

"They're worried about concussion? What happened? Is that his only injury?" She couldn't get the questions out fast enough.

"A delivery-truck driver opened a door into traffic at the wrong moment and clipped his bike. I believe once properly medicated, he'll be ecstatic with the scar he can expect on his right leg, though the wrist will be a problem, as it's his dominant hand. They're calling the damage a sprain for now. They've taken X-rays to be certain he hasn't broken any carpal bones. He's a bit bruised, of course, though that will worsen tomorrow. His nose is already a ghastly shade."

Jesus. Jay rode through the streets at maniac speeds. Body slamming a door equaled rapid deceleration, redirected momentum, *fuck*.

She needed to see him. Tonight. She'd never sleep otherwise. If Henry didn't consider her family enough to join them in the emergency room, fine. "You'll both be exhausted by the time you get home. It'll go easier if you have dinner waiting and a hand getting him situated for the night."

God, she'd gotten fucking sick of eating neighbors' casseroles in the weeks after Dad's accident. The same damn nightmare every day. Walk her little sister home from school. Fix dinner. Supervise homework. Wait for Mom to stumble in from the hospital with her broken smile. "Two people wrangling one doped-up injured person is a lot easier than one."

Her phone dug into her hand. Too blunt and pushy. She'd assumed a place in their lives she didn't warrant.

He sighed, and his voice lost its Henry-ness. He sounded tired. "That would be lovely, Alice. I would . . . greatly appreciate your assistance, thank you."

"You don't have to thank me. We're friends." He couldn't argue with such a safe statement of fact.

"I'll call the super and instruct him to let you into the apartment, my dear. Make use of whatever you like." His voice regained its brisk control. "I'll inform you when we're on our way."

"Call me if you need anything else. I can get to the hospital if you need me." If he'd let her.

They hung up on good-byes, and she caught the train. The lumbering journey of creaks and groans and passengers nursing winter colds differed little from the hard seats and anxious undercurrents of a hospital waiting room. She resisted the urge to call. He had his hands full with Jay. Pestering wouldn't help.

She grabbed her mail before knocking on the super's door. An

older widower, from the ring on his finger. On the handful of occasions they'd met, he'd been unfailingly courteous.

"Hi, Mr. Nagel."

"3B. Miss Colvin. You're here about the key for Mr. Webb's apartment? He called a bit ago."

"You got it. I'm giving Henry a hand with dinner tonight. I just need to get into the apartment."

Mr. Nagel gestured her toward the stairs. "Yes, he mentioned young Mr. Kress had been injured. Nothing serious, I hope."

She made small talk as they climbed the stairs and ventured down the hall, where Mr. Nagel unlocked the door and excused himself without a fuss. Fifteen minutes of poking around in the kitchen turned up the makings for a decent meal. She darted across the hall and changed into yoga pants and a long-sleeved tunic.

Fuck if she'd serve a lackluster casserole. Assuming the men came home. Maybe the hospital would keep Jay overnight for concussion monitoring.

Henry's pastry bag worked like a charm to pipe a cheese and Italian sausage filling into softened manicotti noodles. Measuring an equal amount for each tube took steady hands, a discerning eye and plenty of concentration.

Maybe Jay slumbered through surgery for nerve damage in his wrist.

She punched dough into shape for garlic bread. Her phone kept its silence on the counter. Maybe a superbug had infected Jay's wounds and Henry sat digesting words like bacteria and amputation and mortality rate.

Mom had cried over those words.

The plastic wrap stuck to itself and tore three times before she got the pan into the fridge. The dough rose under a damp towel. A salad waited for last-minute dressing.

She wiped down the counters. Leaving Henry's kitchen as clean as she'd found it would show him her respect. No calls yet. No car coming around the corner as she stood at the window and twisted the kitchen towel around her hand like a boxer's tape. The constriction heightened the thump of her pulse rushing under her skin.

Henry's hands would've felt better.

Settle the fuck down. He'll call.

Anxious wandering deposited her outside Henry's bedroom. Nary a wrinkle disturbed the bed. Clothes hung over the back of a chair, ready for a trip to the dry cleaner.

Three steps inside, she jerked to a halt. Trespasser.

No. She had every right to be in Henry's bedroom. Every other Friday. Not on a Wednesday. Not when he wasn't home.

The mattress welcomed her as an old friend. The pillow crooned a faint lullaby of dark leather and light citrus. Curling on her side, she hugged the pillow to her body and clutched her phone.

A tug pulled up the comforter with its gentle warmth, and she dozed in its embrace. The bread's need for the oven prodded her from her nest. After straightening the sheets and replacing the pillow, she haunted the kitchen.

Her ringing phone jolted her.

8:47 p.m. "Is everything okay?"

"Hello, Alice. I apologize for the delay. They're about to let Jay go. I expect we'll arrive in half an hour or so. It will be . . ." A quiet sigh puffed from his end of the phone. "It will be very nice to be home. You were able to get in all right?"

"Yeah, everything's fine here. Don't worry. I'll be waiting."

"Yes. Thank you, Alice. We'll see you soon."

He ended the call, and she sprang into action, heating the oven and extracting dinner from the fridge.

The doorknob rattled. She flicked off the burner under the extra sauce. Thirty-four minutes. Her rush came to a dead stop in front of the gaping door.

Jay's huge doped-up eyes with a grotesquely swollen and discolored nose between killed her. He'd look full-on raccoon in the morning.

"Alice!" Left arm slung across Henry's shoulder, Jay shuffled through the doorway. "I got doored. Wham! Fucking truck. You should've seen it." He walked like an old man but babbled like a kid on a sugar high. "S'been years since I got doored. Like, at least two years."

They must've given him something fantastic for the pain. *Please not Oxy.*

"That's a long time, Jay." Was it? Who knew. An air cast gleamed white as exposed bone on his forearm. "Sorry the truck got in your way."

His bright smile dropped into a mournful frown. "Weeks, Alice. They want me off the bike until the wrist heals."

Dried blood spotted his cargo pants. He'd lost the shorts-converting bottom halves somewhere. "S'not fair. Stupid driver should hafta stay out of his truck for weeks. He's the one who parked the wrong way."

The gauze encasing the lower half of his right leg and dotting the left itched at her. She should be something. Moving. Doing. Anything.

"Is that marinara I smell, Alice?" Thank God for Henry.

"I raided your freezer." She slid herself under Jay's arm and helped Henry balance his weight between them. "Figured you'd rather defrosted homemade than stuff from a jar. Couch?"

"The couch first, yes. He'll need to eat something. He's had nothing since lunch, and the medication on an empty stomach has had a rather predictable effect."

"Hey, I'm not pre—preda—predacable."

Charming. He'd be a handful. "No, you're totally *un*predictable now, which is why Henry wants you on the couch."

"Couch is good," Jay said. "Or bed. Bed is better. I like it when Henry wants me in bed."

Hoo boy. Two handfuls. Her commiserating glance at Henry went unreturned as they lowered their patient to the couch. Jay's casted hand ran over her breast as she disentangled herself, and his goofy grin suggested the move wasn't clumsiness. "You're sure they got his dosage right?"

Nodding, his face solemn and distracted, Henry stretched Jay's legs along the cushions. The charcoal-gray fabric dipped, the couch more soft than supportive. A stiff accent pillow added a dot of dark mustard beneath Jay's calf.

"He's a lightweight for his size—with alcohol as well—and particularly susceptible to the euphoric effects of narcotics." Henry straightened and offered a shadow of his usual smirk. "And, of course, he has no sense of boundaries. You'll have to excuse him, I'm afraid. I doubt he even recalls that it's Wednesday."

Did he mean to say her presence confused Jay? Maybe her being here was improper on a day other than Friday. He'd had plenty of time to rethink his decision to let her help. The longer she stayed their sometime sex partner, the more she risked their friendship.

"I made manicotti. It's under foil in the oven to keep warm."

Distance. She needed distance. "There's garlic bread, too, and extra marinara for dipping on the stove." The kitchen and its sparkling clean counters beckoned. "I can just—"

"Alice." Henry encircled her wrist. "Would you make a plate for Jay? We'll need to feed him first and get him tucked away in bed before we can sit down to our meal, my dear. If you haven't eaten yet, of course. I realize it's quite late."

She slipped her wrist free, squeezing his fingers before letting go. "You bet. One plate of pasta coming up."

She cut everything into bite-size chunks, even the bread, because chewing would hurt, judging from the bruising across Jay's face. One plate, one water, one Alice-ass on the coffee table once she'd dragged it closer to the couch where Henry sat behind their patient and propped him up.

Jay fumbled for the fork as she lifted the plate. "I can do it. M'not a baby."

"Jay." Henry used his firm tone outside the bedroom. "You'll sit quietly and let Alice help you, my boy. No arguments, now."

She jettisoned the spirit-enlivening childish mealtime ideas. No airplane or funny sounds. With older sisters, Jay'd probably had his fill of being babied. She stuffed him with technical details about her latest work project. Grade-A adult snooze-fest material.

His euphoria dulled into drowsy boredom with drooping eyelids. He'd finished three-quarters of his plate and half his water, but he wouldn't stay awake long enough to have the rest.

Henry mouthed a silent, "Thank you."

Exultation. He appreciated her help. Pushiness had been the right call. Shrugging off his thanks, she set the plate down and slid the table aside. Coordinated movement got Jay on his feet.

"Bathroom and then bed, Jay." Henry supported him on the left, and she undertook the right.

"Your bed," Jay said.

"My bed," Henry agreed.

She suppressed a flash of jealousy.

Leaving them at the bathroom door so Henry could assist alone, she turned on the bedroom light and pulled back the sheets. When they returned, Henry steadied Jay and she stripped off his clothes. Even if the blood came out, the ragged slashes made them unwearable.

God, the bruising and the scrapes. Bad, and they'd be worse in the morning. Purpling lines across his chest probably marked where the handlebars had hit him. The bruises along his left side from his ankle to his ribs had scattered patches of raw, red skin. Gauze hid larger scrapes. Road rash.

She tried to picture it, the door opening into his face, eating his forward momentum and knocking him back. Him tilting and putting the bike down. Sliding on the filthy street under the door as it gashed his right leg open.

Jesus. If she'd seen him howling in pain for hours, she'd have gone fucking crazy. Thank God Henry knew how to hold it together.

Henry lowered Jay to the bed, and she pulled the covers up to his underarms, leaving his arms on top. She picked up his hand. Unblemished, his palms and knuckles exposed an oasis of pristine beauty. She traced his fingers.

"Quality biking gloves," Henry murmured. "That and a good helmet. And all that concerned him was whether a backup messenger had arrived to courier the package."

Jay's eyelids fluttered. His breathing slowed and evened out.

Relief manifested as a magnetic charge drawing her toward Henry. He leaned in. The charge strengthened, promising the answer to everything waited in his kiss. But he only pressed his face to hers, rested his nose above her ear and retreated far too soon. "If you'll sit with him until you're certain he's asleep, I'll get our plates ready, Alice."

She claimed a place beside Jay's hip as Henry left. A few minutes later, she turned off the light and slipped out, leaving the door cracked in case he woke and needed them.

Henry had laid out their meal on the breakfast bar, a cozy setting ensuring they'd sit elbow to elbow. If his hunger rivaled her own, the quiet they settled into wasn't surprising. She cleared her plate. Henry started his second helping.

"Have you called his family?" Jay boasted a big, blurry web of family—parents, a gaggle of siblings, a herd of young nieces and nephews. The way he talked, he bore the "cool" uncle title.

"Not as yet, no." Henry set his fork down and wiped his mouth on his napkin. "I didn't wish to worry his parents. We'll call them tomorrow, perhaps, if he's coherent enough to reassure them himself.

He'll likely want to impress his nephews with his scars when next he visits."

His halfhearted smile raised a matching weariness in her. Maybe he didn't want to think about what Jay's family would say. Or about the scars Jay would have. Blood and crunching metal. Her stomach turned.

She carried her dishes to the sink and rinsed them before loading the dishwasher.

Henry, his plate empty, stared in her direction. Distance clouded his eyes. Leaning on his elbow, he rubbed his index finger across his lips.

She reached across the breakfast bar for his plate.

"Finished?" She softened her voice, in case he didn't want to be disturbed.

"Yes, thank you, Alice." He blinked and stood. "You put together a lovely meal. A favorite?"

"One of the few staples I know how to make." Fucking up pasta took effort. She rinsed his dishes and loaded them beside her own. Beside Jay's, too. Henry must've collected them while she'd sat in the bedroom. "I'm glad it turned out okay. I haven't done a lot of cooking lately."

Years, more like. Not since she'd lived at home and Mom worked late and Dad couldn't and Olivia needed a hot meal. She and Ollie had been culinary explorers, the half-trained teenage chef and her untrained assistant.

Henry swaddled the leftovers in foil and loaded the refrigerator.

She wiped down the countertop.

He rummaged through a small drawer with the assortment of clutter kitchens collected—pens and notepads, novelty bottle openers, scissors, aspirin. Everything with no other home. Organization apparently did have limits. Even Henry had a junk drawer.

Metal clinked. Henry slid his hand across the counter toward her, palm flat. Raising his hand, he left a key behind.

He cleared his throat. "In the event you have need of it again, Alice. The spare key hardly fulfills its function residing in the drawer."

The bronze key gleamed, a miniature mountain range to unlock the tumblers between her life and theirs. No ad nauseam discussion about his intentions necessary. Common sense and neighborliness, that's all. Like the McCaskeys, who'd lived across the street from her parents since forever. They'd had a spare for emergencies.

The key chilled her palm.

"I'll take good care of it, Henry." And of him and Jay, too. Tonight, at least. She slipped the key into one of the front patch pockets of her yoga pants.

Henry exhaled in the silence. A long day, and longer still if he meant to watch over Jay all night.

If it were her, she'd want to decompress first. Midnight loomed, but she couldn't leave him alone. Not unless he asked. "Do you want to sit down?"

His abrupt nod conveyed his preoccupation. "Yes. Of course. Please make yourself comfortable on the couch. I'll just be a moment." A hint of a frown crossed his face.

She gentled her voice. "He was sound asleep when I got up. The door's open. You won't disturb him by looking in on him."

"Thank you, Alice." Closing his eyes, he swayed toward her. A wisp of sterile antiseptic clung to the deeper note of his sweat. Intrusive. Needing her hands to wash it away in a relaxing shower. But he opened his eyes, clasped her shoulder and hurried down the hall.

She curled up on the couch. Throw in dessert, and this might've been their Fourth of July dinner. A late night with Henry, Jay's absence an ever-present thought in her mind.

Classical music often helped Henry relax, but she didn't turn the stereo on. Tonight he'd only wonder if he'd missed a sound from the bedroom. If Jay needed him.

He'd lost his frown and the tension in his shoulders when he returned, but he sat heavily beside her. His usual grace, in word and deed, had faltered. The oddity unbalanced her.

"Jay still sleeping?" They sat side by side, staring across the room, a small span of inches between them on the wide couch.

"Yes. Yes, he seems fine for the moment. The narcotic effect of the painkillers, undoubtedly." He brushed at his pants.

She wove her fingers through his. Warmth and life under her hand.

He squeezed their fingers together. "The wait for them while the medical staff assessed his injuries was very long." His quiet laugh cut. "The injuries weren't as bad as they'd appeared, which made him less of a priority once he reached the hospital."

"Minutes feel like hours in a hospital." Olivia's hand in hers had been small and cold. Mom's had trembled like a baby bunny. But Henry's grip radiated strength even now. "Especially when someone you care about is hurt."

He lifted his head. "You've had some experience with this, Alice?"

Too much. Tonight wasn't about her.

"My sister took a line drive to the shoulder at softball practice once. She sat out the rest of the season with a busted collarbone." She wouldn't detail her father's accident or his lengthy hospital stay. But sharing would show Henry he wasn't alone. "I was doing homework on the bleachers when I heard it. Just this god-awful scream. I spent hours with Ollie at the hospital. It was terrifying."

"How old were you?"

Nope, not happening. He'd dominate the discussion if she let him. Guide the talk toward her experiences and away from the fears he'd hidden from Jay today.

"Sixteen. But it doesn't matter, does it? It's terrifying at any age. All that uncertainty. The noise and confusion, and nobody has time to give you answers. You want to make things better but you can't. You sit and pretend you know everything's going to be fine, because maybe it will be if you fake it hard enough."

Silence. Shit. Henry would take an alien invasion in stride. Respond to news of a hurricane-force nor'easter with the comment that the weather might be breezy. Maybe he hadn't been terrified.

He let out a long, shuddering sigh.

She curled her arm around his shoulders. The scant pressure reeled him in as if she'd accessed some preset reflex in his muscles. She leaned against the back of the couch, and his head came to rest on her chest. The sort of thing she'd do for any friend. Well. For her sister. And now Henry and Jay.

Refusing to examine the thought, she rubbed Henry's back as the silence settled. If he didn't want to talk, she'd stay while he worked the problem through in his head. He was a thinker. An analyst, like her.

She wanted to lay her cheek against his head. Pull him farther onto the couch and lie down beside him. Pure presumption.

Minutes ticked by as his muscles relaxed under her hand. A quarter-hour. Seemingly asleep, he might not notice if her fingers strayed to his hair and slipped through the short brown strands. Maybe.

"Jay lost consciousness at the scene. The authorities called me from his phone." Her shirt half swallowed his soft words. "I admit, I feared the worst when the voice was not his."

Her chest ached with the urge to strip away his pain.

Stressed and vulnerable, he confided in her out of convenience. Unwise to read more into it. He could've lost his lover today.

"He's home now." She couldn't stop her fingers from smoothing his hair, but she fought off the desire to kiss him. "And he'll be fine." Calm reassurance, like he'd given her on their last night in bed together. "You know that."

If the action was appropriate for him as her friend and dominant, reciprocation had to be appropriate, too. She wasn't crossing any lines or taking advantage of Jay's injury to manufacture a bond with Henry. "You can lie next to him and watch him sleep all night if you need to, Henry. I don't think he'd object to that, even if all he had was a paper cut."

He shifted, his nose rubbing the side of her breast. Heat prowled down her ribs and took up residence between her thighs. She stiffened and stifled a gasp. For God's sake, she damn well wouldn't jump the man on his couch while his lover lay hurt in his bed.

Henry lurched upward, forcing her hand to drop from his hair.

"No, no, of course. I'll do that. Of course." He cleared his throat, and his voice smoothed into fluid Henry-speak. "You've work in the morning, Alice, and I've monopolized entirely too much of your time this evening."

He took her hand and helped her to her feet.

"Thank you for your assistance with Jay, my dear." His chaste kiss mimicked the sort she'd gotten from her grandmother. "Shall I walk you to your door?"

Done. Gone. His vulnerability hidden away, maybe for good. The rejection squeezed her lungs. He was still in pain and struggling to cope. He had to be. "I could stay a while—"

"No." He lifted his chin. His chest broadened as he inhaled. "You'll go to bed and be well rested." Glancing at the antique wall clock, he shook his head. "Partially rested. I shouldn't have kept you so late."

The clock hands neared one in the morning, but tired didn't describe the ache in her bones. "It wasn't any trouble, Henry." She felt adrift. Inadequate. "I'm glad I could help. If there's anything . . . you'll let me know?" Unable to identify what he needed or how to offer it. Jay, safe and healthy, probably. If she stopped delaying him, he could go to bed with his lover. "Or I could stop by tomorrow. Whatever you and Jay need."

He'd been steering her toward the door, and he pulled it open now. "It's fine, Alice. Your friendship is much appreciated."

She mumbled something, an acknowledgment, a denial—she wasn't sure, and it didn't matter. The door closed behind her. The empty hallway chilled her. No radiator. No Henry.

She'd let things go wrong somewhere, but the catalyst eluded her. A failed trial, and Henry would keep watch at Jay's bedside alone.

Sleep, when it found her, offered little rest at all, and she walked through Thursday like a zombie.

Chapter 2

"Your weekends with us are intended to be about you and your needs, my dear. My attention this evening would, I'm afraid, be unduly focused on Jay's needs. You are not obligated to spend that time—"

"Wait." She almost never interrupted Henry. Damn straight he wouldn't skip out over the phone on a Friday afternoon. She'd tried that maneuver. Once. He hadn't let her get away with it. Fuck if she'd let him get away with it, either. Not when he always pushed her so hard to share her needs with him. "What if I feel I need to help care for Jay?"

A nosy Nellie strolled past the corner of her desk.

She lowered her voice. "It's supposed to be my time, right? So if I want to help . . ."

His silence sent a prickle down her spine. Surprising him would be okay. Offending him, not so much. If she only ranked as an occasional playmate, he might tell her to stay out of their relationship.

No. He'd welcomed her assistance on Wednesday at first. The sexual benefits might be segregated, but the friendship endured.

"*Do* you feel that way, my dear?" The curious note in his voice defied interpretation.

"He's my friend. I care about him." If Henry felt awkward about saying yes now, then he thought her needs conflicted with Jay's. That he couldn't balance them as he usually did. "You haven't had a break since he got hurt. Why not let me take care of you both for the night?"

"Would that please you, Alice?"

"Yes." Hell yes, and yes again, no hesitation.

"You're quite certain?"

Disbelief. How insulting. "Of course I am. Why wouldn't it please me?" She hunched over her desk with her cell phone and whispered. "You tell me what you want done, and I'll do it. How's that different from our regular Fridays or not focused on my needs?"

Her heart battered her ribs. The hum of the office lights swelled like a discordant soundtrack for her life.

"Very well. We will see you at the usual time despite the unusual circumstances."

She wasn't at all certain what to expect when she knocked Friday at seven.

Henry had left a note on her door. Following his terse instructions, she'd dressed in casual clothes as she had Wednesday, yoga pants and a worn henley, and forgone eating dinner. As though she'd curl up at home with a frozen meal for one and watch mindless videos. Fridays were Henry's time. If that's what he told her to do, that's what she'd do.

Henry answered the door. Him performing Jay's usual task with Jay at home struck her like a hammer. Jay couldn't perform those tasks, because he could've been dead or comatose instead of hobbled.

The beaming smile she meant to offer him faltered.

He gave none in return, his face a flat mask. "Good evening, Alice." He ushered her in, and she slipped off her shoes. "Jay is resting on the couch. Go and sit beside him, please. I've placed a pillow on the floor for you."

On the floor. She'd been demoted. "Yes, Henry."

Henry's agitation didn't manifest in fidgeting the way Jay's often did, but his tension bled into the air. Distracted and stressed after two full days of caretaking. He'd warned her she wouldn't get all of his attention, and she'd signed up for it anyway.

She settled into the floor pillow's cushy depths in the waiting pose Jay favored, her legs curled beneath her. Close to, but not crowding, him in his half-propped perch at one end of the couch.

The television emitted brightness and low chatter behind her. The heavy, rich scent of meat and potatoes flowed from Henry's post in the kitchen. Homey. Comforting.

Henry called to them. "Jay, you may give Alice your greetings now."

Grinning like a fool, Jay reached for her. "C'mere, Alice! He's been promising for hours you were gonna come visit. It seemed like forever."

Pain-med euphoria. Must be.

She raised up on her knees and leaned in, searching for safe places to touch. The swelling of his nose didn't seem too terrible, but the bruising across his eyes spread broad and deep. The map of his bruised body from Wednesday pressed at her, a mental inventory impossible to shove aside.

Even awkward and one-armed, Jay hugged her tight. Tape and gauze rasped against her shirt. When his grip loosened, he fumbled for her lips. His painkiller-delayed coordination and her surprise merged in awkward harmony. Muscles readied for Henry's voice, for a command that never came.

Once Jay aligned their mouths, he kissed her like a lover he hadn't seen in months. His desperate, hungry kiss conveyed passion and affection.

She tried not to bump his nose.

"I missed you," he said after he let her lips go.

She didn't doubt his word, even though they'd already spent more time together than they did in a normal week.

"I'm glad you're back." He had to be stoned. Sure, Jay was an open, happy sort of guy, but not that open. Henry must've given him relaxed boundaries because of his medication.

His right arm, splinted in its brace, lay across his stomach. His legs extended sideways down the couch, leaving the thinnest space beyond his feet in their thick socks.

"I missed you, too," she said, because it seemed the right thing to say and it wasn't a lie. "I was worried about you."

"You helped. The other night. I remember." He planted a smacking kiss on her cheek, the sort a child might bestow. In his T-shirt and sweats, he resembled one who'd stayed home from school. "Henry says it's okay if I thank you." He kissed her other cheek. "Thank you, Alice."

Jay. Making her eyes itch. So goddamn sweet, and a fucking truck could've killed him. "It was my pleasure, Jay."

He nodded, a serious expression overtaking his face. "Henry's in charge of your pleasure. That's how you know it'll be good."

Amusement tingled in her mouth. No laughing. Not at the earnest sincerity proving Henry and sex never left Jay's mind. Five bucks said he'd skipped undershorts today. "That's true. He has a gift."

"Oh! But I have a gift for you. Wait—" He struggled to turn. "Henry, can Alice open her present now?"

"I don't see why not." He'd paused his work in the kitchen to watch them, it seemed. "We've time yet before dinner."

Jay settled back against his pillows. "It's in my bedroom, on the dresser. It has your name on it. I picked it out special for you."

Leave without Henry's permission and root around in Jay's private room. Yeah, right.

"Go ahead, Alice." Henry answered before she'd gotten a question out. "You know which room is Jay's."

She walked down the hall to the second door on the right. The first, always closed, hid Henry's studio. The next stood half-open. Slipping inside, she sidestepped the messenger pack threatening to trip her.

Neat, organized Henry permitted Jay to keep things as haphazardly as a teenage boy. Impossible. The unmade bed and clothes strewn about demanded she believe. Half a bike stood upside down in the far corner with a bare rim and tools spread nearby.

Dresser. Sure. Probably the clothing-draped lump on her left.

She picked her way across the floor to the lump. Nothing labeled *Alice* jumped out.

The door swung farther open, and Henry stepped inside. "Jay isn't the most organized. Do you need assistance, Alice?"

The pile atop the dresser and the biking gear tossed on the bed ignored her vigorous gestures. "How does he live like this?"

"He doesn't, generally." Henry crossed to her side and pulled things off the dresser. "It's the one place where he knows he needn't answer to me. Consequently, you'll almost never find him here."

"He doesn't like that kind of freedom." She tested the hypothesis in her mind, fitting the idea into her Jay-puzzle. "Knowing you're in charge comforts him."

The feeling wasn't so different for her. Sometimes, at least.

"Mmm. You're alike in that way, you and Jay. But he needs it more than you do, I think." He paused, gaze flicking toward her. "You find it more difficult to admit to or allow what you need. Ah. Here we are."

He lifted a brown paper bag with her name scrawled in black marker. No shiny paper, no bow. No wonder she hadn't spotted the gift.

"Not to worry, it's neither alive nor edible. I did make certain he'd selected an innocuous object. Nothing you'll find disgusting, shocking, or offensive, I trust. But Jay was rather secretive on the subject." Henry gestured her out of the room in front of him.

"You let him get away with that?" she teased. He'd relaxed since she arrived, and he hadn't made any sexual overtures. His behavior said friend, not dominant.

"He was uniformly cranky yesterday." Henry had a gift for understatement. If he thought Jay'd been cranky, the day must've been awful.

"I may have suggested he think on how he might thank you for your assistance Wednesday. He happily informed me this morning he had just the thing and did not require my help in acquiring it. Thinking about you proved a suitable distraction from his injuries. I wasn't inclined to question him."

Wow. He'd proffered a fuller answer than she'd expected, especially on a contract night. He wasn't obligated to explain himself to her.

Maybe he'd forgiven her for whatever she'd done Wednesday night to make him tired of dealing with her. Pushing for an emotional bond outside a contract night and making him uncomfortable. Trying to force him to accept comfort. Tonight would be different. Contract time. She'd comfort and relax him with her body once they'd taken care of Jay.

She settled back on her pillow with a greater certainty the night would go well. Whatever Henry had planned, she'd be allowed to take care of them both. She had a purpose, a function, in the mechanism of their relationship.

Henry handed the lunch bag to Jay. "Here you are, my boy. This is what you picked out for Alice this morning?"

Grinning, Jay nodded. "That's it. Alice, you have to open it now, okay? You're gonna love it."

His enthusiasm, drug-induced or not, infected her. He pushed the bag into her hands, and she slid a finger under the tape holding it closed. "I'm opening it. Gimme a minute here. It has an expert wrapping job."

"I did it myself. Henry didn't help at all. It's *my* thank-you. I bet Henry will give you something else. But it won't be as good as mine."

Lifting out a pair of binoculars, she pinned her perplexed smile in place. Jay's pharmaceutical cocktail must've skewed his estimation of a good gift. "They're nice, Jay. I, umm, haven't really used binoculars before."

Not really. Or at all. Maybe he wanted them to catch a baseball game at Fenway?

"It's okay. They were mine first. I can show you how to use them." Jay hadn't stopped grinning.

"So, umm, what do you use them for?" She peered through them. Oh. Right. Lens caps. She pulled the binoculars away and fiddled with them.

"Me an' Henry go camping in the summer sometimes. On weekends. He likes to bird-watch on Saturday mornings. But that's so not for me. Too boring."

Henry cleared his throat. "Well. That's—"

"I'd rather bike. Or kayak. Or anything other than sitting still for hours. Being hurt? It's totally like bird-watching. But I thought, an' I thought, an' I thought, and the perfect gift came to me."

"Jay, perhaps—"

"I'm giving you the binoculars 'cause now you'll camp with us, and you can sit still for hours with Henry. It's perfect."

Henry sucked in a breath like he might choke.

Oh my God. She couldn't look at him. Summer was five months away. Jay expected she'd not only still be in their arrangement but that she'd join them on trips? No way did he have that authority.

"You might have mentioned the purpose of your gift in advance, my dear boy." Utter neutrality left Henry's voice almost unrecognizable.

Would he ask her to go with? Or arrange their camping weekends on Fridays she didn't spend with them? Great. Now she'd host a daily parade of worries about something that wouldn't be a question for months, if it ever was.

Jay's smile dimmed. "Are you mad at me?"

Henry exhaled, his soft puff rippling as though it held back a storm. "Never for long, my boy. It's a fine gift, and I'm certain Alice will find a use for it."

"Absolutely." She faked a cheerful tone and a matching grin. "It'll be great for spotting architectural details. I'll take you on a tour downtown sometime."

Henry excused himself to attend to dinner, his back rigid as he walked away. Maybe he thought she expected an invitation from Jay, on drugs, no less, to be binding. The math added up to Henry not wanting her to join them.

Jay patted her shoulder. "Don't you wanna go camping? If you don't like bird-watching either, it's okay. We'll make Henry stay in bed later."

"No, I like camping fine, Jay." She launched into a story about camping with her sister on their aunt and uncle's ranch, ending with two screaming girls fleeing a flash flood after a leaky water tank burst open.

She figured he'd laugh. Not enough to hurt his ribs, but a chuckle. Instead, he eyed her with solemn intensity. "Don't worry, Alice. Henry would never let that happen. He'll take good care of you."

She forced a laugh of her own. "He takes excellent care of you, that's for sure. Tell the truth—the warm socks were his idea, right?"

He wiggled his toes. "Yup. You want some?"

From his chaotic bedroom? "Umm, no. Thanks, but my socks are warm enough. Not so stylish as yours, of course."

"But you could have some like mine. Henry would give 'em to you. Just ask." He shouted, "Right, Henry?"

She winced along with Jay. The movement must've aggravated his ribs.

"Please don't shout, my boy." Henry's voice carried easily from the kitchen. "It's not good for your health."

"But you'd give Alice socks if she wanted, right?" Jay didn't quite shout, though his voice rang in her ears.

"Are your feet cold, Alice?"

"No, I'm fine. I don't need anything." She mock-glared at Jay. "Jay is teasing me, I think."

"He does enjoy teasing. I would hope he's minding his manners at least somewhat, however. Jay, you recall we discussed appropriate boundaries for this evening. Relaxed does not mean nonexistent. Alice is being very generous with her time tonight."

"I know, Henry." Jay sighed. "I just said if she wanted something

I have and she asked you for it, you'd give it to her, too. Like . . . comfy socks."

The lengthy silence roused her curiosity enough to bring her up to her knees. Henry stood at the kitchen island, facing their direction with his eyes closed. Doing nothing. Just breathing. She hunched back down.

"If and when Alice decides she wants socks, Jay, I will provide them." Weariness bled between his words. "Until then, please stop trying to force her into them. I doubt she appreciates it."

"It's okay, Jay." She squeezed his good hand. "I'll be sure to ask for socks when I want some, all right?"

He rolled his eyes, a petulant child missing only the tongue sticking out. "No you won't. Your feet are cold. You need socks. You'd be happier if Henry would just tell you to put them on, and so would he." He wriggled his toes. "I am."

"Jay." Henry's sharp tone cut off in an instant.

Her desire to comfort Henry warred with the understanding that he hadn't wanted her to see him upset on Wednesday. She didn't want to disrespect Henry. He was the only man she'd ever met who was so worthy of respect.

Jay's shoulder made an excellent blind. Henry had his back to them. His bowed head and slumped shoulders resurrected her concern. One hand rested on the far counter beside the stove, as if he couldn't hold himself up. He'd raised the other to his face.

She launched herself halfway to her feet before indecision caught up with her. How far did relaxed boundaries go? He hadn't gone over safewords. She could say she wanted a glass of water. Lie. To Henry. *Not gonna happen.*

"Enough, please, Jay." His voice had regained its lightness. "Alice is likely as tired of hearing about your sock obsession as I am."

She didn't buy it. Stressed and upset, he'd tried to cover with humor. But the moment passed as Henry moved. She dropped to the pillow in a flash.

"You'd be happier," Jay grumbled.

Henry hadn't been kidding about Jay's moods. Worse than her little sister with a cold. Not as bad as her father, thank God, but bored, cranky and turning every conversational topic into a battle. Henry deserved a break.

Swallowing her annoyance, she tried light chatter, avoiding the growing list of Things Not to Mention, which now included socks and camping, of all things. Jay's short responses and turned-away face made her effort meaningless. She should've agreed to put on some fucking socks.

"Alice," Henry finally called. "Come and fetch a plate, please."

She smiled at Jay and rose to her feet. She'd explain to Henry he didn't need to worry, because she hadn't taken the camping invitation any more seriously than she'd taken Jay's babbling about socks. Sweet Jay, wanting to make things fair. Henry didn't need to take her camping just because he took Jay.

"Come back soon, okay?" Jay gazed up at her with sad eyes. "I'm hungry."

She squeezed his good hand. "Quick as I can."

When she reached the kitchen and started to speak, Henry held up his hand in a "stop" motion. He studied her with an unfathomable expression. Pained, almost.

The desire to hug him hummed beneath her skin. But not if she'd make him uncomfortable. Break his in-charge image with too much vulnerability.

"Alice, do you recall what you told me this afternoon when we spoke?"

"Yes, Henry."

He raised an eyebrow and gestured for her to elaborate.

"I said I needed to take care of you both tonight."

"You also asked how such a scenario might not focus on your needs. How such submission might be different from other nights." Resting his hand flat on the counter, he tapped his thumb in rapid, minuscule rhythm.

The night's nonsexual start already marked a difference. Friendliness didn't bother her. It was nice. But Henry's uncharacteristic motion bothered her. She wanted to do more. She nodded.

"I think you need to appreciate that difference more fully."

"Like Jay thinks I need comfy socks?" Maybe teasing would draw him out. Get him to tell her to drop to her knees. A blow job would cure his stress. "So you're going to provide some?"

He frowned. "I don't expect you'll find these socks comfortable. But I would like for you to think about that difference. Can you do that for me?"

"I'll do my best, Henry." Uncomfortable socks. Was this still about the camping thing?

"Thank you, Alice." He pointed to the counter. "Load the tray and bring it to the living room, please. I've made enough for three."

"We're all eating now?" Feeding Jay first on Wednesday, they'd had time to sit together with their meal and talk afterward. "I thought—"

His hand, palm front, stopped her cold. "Jay has been granted relaxed boundaries tonight because of his circumstances, Alice. You have not."

He'd praised her for her initiative before, even if he controlled their activities.

"Your independent thought is not required, only your obedience. Surely you didn't mean to question my instructions. Perhaps you feel I was unclear?"

Holy shit. Throat tight, she rushed to shake her head lest he take her silence for insubordination.

Beyond different. Callous, dismissive words from Henry's lips confused her. But his tone lacked anger. He prodded. Like reminding a puppy to sit and stay.

"No, Henry." His tired vulnerability had morphed to distant dominance. As if her ability to listen and obey defined her purpose. Bewildering. "I'm sorry."

"If you've already eaten, contrary to my instructions, simply bring enough for two." He gestured at the counter. "Shepherd's pie. No side dishes required. Water will suffice for everyone to drink. You know where the cutlery is. I'll be with Jay if you have further questions."

He ignored her as he strode around the far side of the kitchen island. She rated no higher than a servant. A piece of furniture. Kneeling with swift precision, he nuzzled Jay's cheek and whispered in his ear, a tableau of tenderness. For two.

The starry granite counter invited her to fall into the void. He hadn't looked at her sexually or called her his dear. He wasn't planning to dine alone with her. He didn't care if she dined at all, unless it meant she'd gone against his instructions.

Except he hadn't once sounded angry with her. If the gift upset him because Jay believed Henry owed her something or her miserable failure to comfort him Wednesday bothered him, he wasn't punishing either of them for it. He intended to teach her something.

"Alice, don't dawdle," Henry called. "Jay is waiting."

She loaded the tray with three bowls of shepherd's pie. They had a name, the round serving-size ceramic dishes that went in the oven. Henry would know. *For God's sake, don't ask him. That would be independent thought, and we can't have that, now can we?*

She added glasses and poured water from the refrigerator. Snatching three spoons from the drawer and napkins from the holder on the counter on her way, she carried the tray to the living room. Her floor pillow had gone missing.

"On the coffee table, Alice." Henry sat behind Jay, providing support, and Jay seemed content despite the turned-off TV. Of course he did. He had Henry's arms around him. What could hurt him there?

The table had been pulled closer to the couch. Round impressions in the rug marked where it belonged. She set the tray down.

"Leave room for yourself to sit, Alice."

She pushed the tray over and sat.

"Alice always gets to be on the table." Jay's laugh vibrated with nerves. "It's 'cause she tastes so good, right, Henry?"

"You've often said so, my boy. But Alice won't be your meal this evening. She's simply serving it." Henry's formal nod and empty eyes painted a portrait of exile. "You may begin, Alice."

She picked up a bowl and spoon. Cuddling with Jay, watching her with disdain, Henry didn't extend a hand to take it.

"I, umm, did you want to take yours while I help Jay?" Fear of a reprimand seized her. Unquestioning obedience fail. How dare she try understanding his needs.

"No. If I had wanted to do that, I would have told you, Alice."

They'd lost something beyond the sex. Where was her spark of joy from obeying Henry? He didn't seem pleased with her, and she wasn't pleased with herself. Taken together, the displeasure left her hollow.

"Do you find my instructions lacking? Perhaps you're incapable of following them?"

Prodding her again. With disappointment? Disapproval? Boredom? She opened her mouth to answer, and he waved a hand.

"Never mind. When I wish to hear your voice, I'll tell you so."

Avoiding her gaze, Jay lowered his chin to his chest.

"You'll feed everyone tonight, Alice. It's more efficient, and you'll fulfill an important function." Henry tilted his head, eyes narrowing as they bored into hers. "That *is* what you need, isn't it, Alice? The efficiency of a clear chain of command and the satisfaction that you have a proper place, a function to perform?"

Her fingers shook around the spoon handle. They'd had this conversation long before having sex. Harmonious function. Fulfilling a function tonight struck her as far from harmonious. Wedged and grinding, she waited like a gear with a stuck tooth. The force of the machine might shatter her, and the shards wreck the whole thing.

"Alice is gonna perform?" Jay peered at her with curious intensity behind his raccoon mask of bruises. "I wanna see."

"Of course, my boy. This is all a performance for Alice. A bit of fun every other week. She attaches no deeper meaning to it." Henry tossed the words off casually.

Six months ago, he would've been right, too. But not now.

"You and she are not the same, Jay."

"Nope." Jay rolled his head against Henry's chest, staring straight at her as his expression turned sad. "'Cause I know you love me. I don't hafta wonder. You tell me all the time."

Henry's breath hissed out.

Fuck. The difference between her and Jay slammed into her with blunt force. Henry loved Jay. Didn't love her.

She wriggled her toes, breaking the deep yellow line in the patterned rug. A blip in perfection. Her emotions had become way too involved. *Really fucking uncomfortable socks, Henry.*

She didn't want to usurp Jay's place. She just wanted more than every-other-week sex and playacting. She wanted enough that Henry would've let her hold him Wednesday night instead of sending her away.

The tail end of a wince flashed by on his face. Panic?

"Dinner, please, Alice." A smooth expression accompanied his brisk tone. "Jay is less likely to say something dangerous when his mouth is full."

The bowl heated her hand. By telling Henry she needed tonight, she'd taken advantage of him, of his sense of responsibility toward her. Pushed him to the verge of a breakdown in the kitchen. What the fuck was wrong with her?

He tipped his cheek against Jay's hair, the brief touch twisting the knife. God, just, just fucking *that*. She'd never craved anyone's attention like she craved Henry's.

"Though nothing is guaranteed," he murmured, more to himself than her. "He's such a risk-taker."

Taking her sister's suggestion to find another guy would break the emotional misfire and let her go back to enjoying the hot sex. Except she wanted the friendship and the lust both, and she hungered for part of what Jay had. The knowledge that Henry desired her submission, not as a game but as a symbol of her respect for him.

She fed them in unnerving silence, every motion a potential mistake. An object of pity for Jay. A burden to Henry. She'd asked for the chance to take care of them, and he'd let her, but the reality proved an ill match to what she'd wanted and needed.

Then what do I need?

She gave Jay another bite and turned back to the tray for water.

"Alice."

Please, God, let Henry show her the answer.

"You haven't tried your supper yet."

Nope. Fucked up again.

"Eat. I insist."

The hearty fare delighted her taste buds, savory and baked to the perfect texture. Henry's kitchen would produce no less. His acute, unwavering scrutiny as she ate jangled her nerves. Was the glint in his eyes satisfaction? Aside from her silence, nothing else had seemed to please him.

She cleared the tray and set the room to rights at his direction when they'd finished. Standing beside the couch, she shifted her weight and reminded herself not to fidget.

"Undress, Alice." Nuzzling Jay's ear and pressing gentle kisses to his head, Henry spoke without acknowledging her. "Jay asked to see a performance. I expect your nudity will suffice."

Relief and distress warred in her. He hadn't ordered her home, but he wasn't watching her, either.

She grasped the hem of her shirt. The wrongness of the whole situation screamed at her. Henry's face and voice revealed no tenderness, no desire. Not even lust.

Boredom.

He'd disengaged. As if their nights had become routine.

She yanked the shirt over her head before she could talk herself out of it.

Her hands wrapped around the soft waffle cotton, the henley she'd chosen because Henry said to dress comfortably. She'd thought he meant they'd relax together. Twisting the material, she held it to her breasts.

She could say her word. Her word. Henry hadn't gone over safewords tonight. She hadn't forgotten hers—her mind unhelpfully chanted *pistachio-pistachio-pistachio*—but why hadn't he reminded her? He always did near the beginning of the night.

"Alice."

She jumped at Henry's voice, not distant or bored now but soft. Tender.

"Stop."

Thank God.

"You're anxious, my dear. Tell me why."

Relief swept in like fresh air filling her lungs. He'd called her his dear.

"I don't know what you want, Henry." Tonight's wrongness wouldn't shatter the machine. He'd fix it, a patient tinkerer at the gears until they worked in smooth motion again. "I don't know how to please you tonight."

Jay shifted, mumbling about making Henry happy, and Henry shushed him, steadying Jay with his arms around him.

"I've given you instructions, Alice." His gentle voice failed to accuse. "I've told you precisely what you were to do. Yet you haven't enjoyed following those directives, have you?"

"I . . ." Her shirt bulged between her knuckles. Fabric spilled as uncontained as the chaos in Jay's bedroom. "No, Henry."

"No," he echoed. "You haven't found pleasure in fulfilling my needs and Jay's tonight, not as you did Wednesday night nor as you've done on our other nights together. Isn't that so?"

"Yes." The truth stung more than the lingering confusion.

"Do you know why, Alice? Do you understand the difference?"

Not a chance in hell. Failing grade for this one. "It doesn't feel right. It's empty."

"Because a full-time domestic submissive relationship is not something you want, my dear. You've been wondering about it, perhaps, about the things you sense Jay has that you do not."

Panic swamped her. Oh God, did he pity her the way Jay seemed to? Henry was an honorable man. Even if he wanted her submission, he wouldn't take it if giving him that control damaged her.

He lifted his hand in a calming wave. "Shhh, that's fine, Alice. It's natural you might compare your situation with Jay's and be curious. But it's important to realize that the things we believe will make us happy are not always the things that do make us happy."

She wasn't good enough, and she never would be. Paralysis gripped her.

"If submission itself made you happy, you would have enjoyed your tasks tonight. You would have taken my instructions at face value."

The rug grated like ground glass under her feet.

"You would not—as I suspect you have been doing—have devoted your mind to considering what I might mean by such instructions, beyond cataloguing the differences as I asked you to do. You would not have been angry or confused. You would have been pleased to serve in whatever capacity I deemed fit."

Henry didn't want her mishmash of deeper feelings because he didn't return them.

His smile seemed off. Tired. Thin. "It's all right not to want those things, Alice. Simply because Jay has beliefs about summer vacations and about . . . about *love* . . . it does not constitute an obligation. One cannot force a feeling that is not present."

Stand straight. Smile. Nod. A performance, like he said. Like his. He didn't want her reading meaning into his act, but he'd make allowances for her substandard submission. He'd anticipated her disappointing performance. Knowing she wouldn't like submissive socks, he'd let her try them on and learn for herself.

If she could get him into bed, she could salvage the night. She excelled at letting him lead there.

Jay squirmed and tipped his head against Henry's chest. "Time yet?"

"Not for another two hours, my boy. We'll have a bath first, and you may take your pills once you're snug in bed."

"But it hurts now."

"I know, Jay. I'm sorry. Two hours." Henry's bleak gaze met hers. The inability to make everything better tortured him.

"Alice . . ." He sighed. He clasped Jay's left hand, the distinction between comforter and comforted blurry at best.

"If you wish to go, my dear, I'll dismiss you from your obedience for the rest of the night. You've seen . . . more than I intended to show you, I expect." Lips tight, he searched her face. "There's no need for you to be unhappy and uncomfortable in a situation you've discovered you don't enjoy."

She hated his distance, not the situation. Henry had fed her on her first contract night, and she cherished the memory of intimacy and sweetness. He'd bathed her on the night he'd spent alone with her. Same deal. She couldn't play the full submissive and pretend to be happy, not when it made Henry cold. Maybe he should get socks, too.

Agree, and Henry would push her out the door, hide his vulnerability and leave her feeling like a failure. Fuck that.

"Do you want me to go?" Perfect. Enough brazen challenge to draw Jay's attention, too. C'mon, c'mon, please let him be her ally here.

"Alice, the decision—"

"I want her to stay." Jay bulldozed over Henry's request, something he'd never do without the excuse of the drugs to hide behind. His lip curled in a smirk Henry wouldn't see. "She's pretty and soft and she can make the pain go away."

"You want to forgo your bath and rest here on the couch with Alice for the rest of the evening, my boy?" Speaking to Jay, Henry held her gaze.

She gave a slight nod. She'd sit with Jay if he wanted. Chatting with him had been the highlight of her evening so far, and events damn well didn't seem headed for improvement. If she'd had a chance to comfort Henry with sex, she'd missed it.

"Why can't Alice help in the bath?" Jay's smirk widened. "She's seen it all before."

"Alice is not a bath toy, Jay." Henry's weary voice carried a sharp edge. "Ask for something else."

"But I want Alice."

"It's okay." She jumped in before Henry could quash the idea. "I'd much rather help you give Jay a bath than sit at home by myself for the rest of the night."

"Alice should be naked."

"Jay." Henry's warning tone. Either Jay'd hit the limit of the night's relaxed boundaries, or Henry suspected he was being played by a mischief-maker. Probably both.

"She should. Baths are wet." Good God. The look Jay gave her. He knew his game to the last nanometer. "Don't want her clothes all wet, too."

He wanted her to stay and he wanted her naked. Whatever his reasons, they lined up with her own goal to perfection.

"I'm halfway there anyway." She let her shirt fall to the coffee table. Nudity didn't feel wrong now. Henry's distance had done an about-face to vulnerability.

She and Jay played for Team Make Henry Feel Better. He held the only playbook, but she'd follow Jay's lead. He loved Henry, and he liked her. He wasn't likely to steer her anywhere she didn't want to go.

"And I'll need dry clothes to go home in later." She unhooked her bra, pushed the straps down her arms, and dropped it on the shirt. Her hands went to the waistband of her yoga pants. Henry didn't say a word. *This can work.*

She stripped, pants and underwear at the same time, pulling socks with them as she stepped out of them. Fewer chances for Henry to object. She laid the bundle atop her shirt and bra. "Ready for bathtime whenever Jay is."

"Thirty seconds," Jay said. "I'm always ready for naked Alice in thirty seconds."

Her lips twitched. He wasn't kidding. His baggy sweatpants showed signs of movement underneath. Maybe arousal would distract him until he could take more painkillers.

Henry extricated himself from the couch in careful silence, laying Jay back against the pillows. "Wait here, my boy, while Alice and I prepare your bath." He gestured her toward the hallway. "If you please, Alice."

He didn't sound angry, but leaving the room meant losing her partner in crime. If Henry planned to take one of them to task for pushing things, it'd be her. Flipping on the bathroom light, she stepped inside. Henry crowded her, close but not touching. Christ. Lust raced through her at warp speed even as she feared his words.

"I gave you the option to leave, and you chose not to take it. Why?" Incredulity colored his voice. A demanding accusation, as if he couldn't believe she hadn't dashed out the door.

No problem. Vulnerability prompted defensiveness. Classic.

"The long or short answer?"

"Short first."

"Jay wants me to stay."

"Yes, I'm aware." The dry amusement in his voice sent relief crashing over her in a wave. "Jay is always happy to spend time with the people he cares for deeply. But as the short answer tells me nothing I do not already know, I'm afraid I must ask you for the long one."

He stepped past her and started running the bath. "I've orchestrated enough scenes to know when I'm being manipulated, my dear, and you and Jay are not the most subtle coconspirators. Why, after all of the discomfort you've felt tonight, would you wish to remain in our company?"

A tendril of doubt crawled beneath her skin, invisible in the Alice reflected in the mirror over the sink. With previous guys, she'd have said fuck it and walked out. With Henry and Jay, the possibility never reached the menu. "You were right about submission being hard for me tonight. I didn't like being told what to do and feeling I wasn't getting anything out of it."

Despite her nudity, Henry hadn't ogled her. He hadn't looked anywhere other than her face. That he respected her as more than a sex object calmed her even as it relit her fear he'd lost interest. "I felt unwanted. But that's not how you make me feel on every other night, Henry."

He watched her, gaze fixed on her face. "Oh?"

"I wanted to stay because—" She wasn't trying to claim something that wasn't hers. "I don't like distance between us. I don't want to leave tonight like I failed some test I didn't expect to be taking." She could settle for less than what Jay had. "I value the time we spend together and the way you make me feel. I don't want to stop playing the game even if the board has places I can't go. Socks I can't wear."

Henry straightened. Gaze skipping to the floor, he delivered a slow nod. "You're certain there are places not meant for you? Socks that don't fit?"

"I am," she said. "Jay and I have some overlapping squares, but we aren't the same players. I'm not trying on his socks."

Henry turned away and tested the water. He took a long time to be happy with the temperature before shutting off the taps. "All right, Alice." He flicked water off his fingers, tiny drops breaking the calm surface of the water. "No socks. We will carry on as we have these last six months."

The water he found so fascinating refused to yield its secrets to her. The shallow depth suggested Jay's bath prioritized a comforting touch over soaking. She wouldn't mind one herself.

Standing to face her, Henry snorted softly. "You realize your presence—nude, no less—will give Jay ideas beyond the relaxing bath I had planned for him."

"I know." Should she apologize? She wasn't a tease. She wasn't unwilling to give Jay what he needed.

"Intercourse is out of the question. He cannot support his own weight. He needs to let his injuries heal. His bruising is too extensive to allow you on top either."

"He likes blow jobs," she offered. Henry's laugh warmed her cheeks.

"I doubt there's a man alive who doesn't, my dear." His chuckle trailed off. "In the bath would be awkward. We'll need to keep his right arm and leg dry because of the splint and the sutures. After his bath, then, once we've gotten his bandages replaced and settled him in bed. If you would?"

Finally, an easy question. "That's a direction I know how to follow."

Henry studied her face. The seductive tang of leather and citrus surrounded her as he cupped the back of her head and squeezed her to his chest. The first time he'd truly touched her all night. She embraced him in return, comforted more than she could explain by his touch.

"You do very well, my dear girl." Her hair muffled his voice. "You give all that you're able, and I'm so pleased that you do."

She basked in the feeling she'd been missing all night, their hollow distance erased. Even if she couldn't play all of the games and be the perfect submissive, her effort pleased him. He'd still give her what she needed. His attention. His comfort. His praise.

He pressed his lips to her head before he let her go. "Come along, my dear. Let's fetch our wayward boy before he goes stumbling about and finds trouble."

They stripped Jay when they got him up from the couch. She'd been right about the lack of underwear. Steadying him between them, they shuffled to the bathroom. Jay cracked no jokes, his bruising worse since Wednesday, a deep blend of colors across his rib cage.

She waited outside while Henry helped him use the bathroom.

The two of them lowered Jay into the tub. The water was lukewarm rather than hot, in deference to his road rash. His bandages had been removed, aside from the stabilizing wrap on his right wrist and one covering the stitched-up slash on his right shin. His leg hung over the tub's side, safe from the water.

Passing her a washcloth, Henry poured bodywash with a familiar woodsy scent. His hand grazed her back. "Go ahead, Alice."

She knelt on a towel by the side of the tub and worked the cloth into a foamy lather. Leaning over, she touched Jay's lips in a light kiss. He stroked her side and breast with his good arm.

Jay's mass of bruises provoked an all-consuming protective, almost maternal, instinct. Arousal skated away. But she allowed his explorations. His reach didn't extend far, and any distraction from his pain merited indulgence.

"You're quite lucky this evening, Jay." Henry's voice floated over her shoulder.

He'd seated himself on the lip at the far end of the bathtub, holding Jay's right leg in a secure grip across his lap, out of her way. Back straight, not slouching against the tile. Thumb probing at the ball of Jay's foot in slow circles.

"To have the devoted attention of such a special woman, hmm? She must think highly of you indeed."

Henry kept up a soft stream of praise, soothing Jay with his voice as she bathed him from head to toes. Running her hands over his body reassured her more than words and images ever would. His skin soft and slick. His muscles hard beneath. Whole and healing under her fingers and Henry's voice. Comfort for them all.

Afterward, they settled him onto the bed naked, his shoulders and head propped on three pillows to prevent trouble with his breathing. She climbed onto the bed, but Henry didn't join them. She had her instructions. If he needed to take care of other things while he had the opportunity, she wouldn't take his distance as rejection.

"You know, if you wanted me to blow you again, Jay, you didn't have to go to all this trouble with the delivery truck and the hospital." Mouth perched above his groin, she felt at home. "You could've just asked Henry."

He chuckled, but the way he stared at her mouth made his preoccupation obvious.

She took her time. He'd been excited from the bath and the toweling off, but his interest had flagged when they coated the worst of the road rash with antibiotic cream and replaced the bandages. Planting her hands on either side of his hips, she kissed his stomach and thighs. Every patch of bruise-free flesh she found.

The attention worked to arouse him, but not her. This wasn't for her own gratification. She did it because Jay needed to feel included, and Henry had asked her, and she wanted to please them both.

So even though she wasn't aroused, she didn't rush. That wouldn't be fair to Jay. He deserved to feel good. She didn't drag things out, either. That would've left his muscles strained and tense for far too long. Henry's reasoning for the bath and blow job both had likely been to relax Jay, to encourage him to fall asleep without pain.

Taking care in how she held his hips down, she allowed him the freedom to shift and thrust rather than pressing on his bruises. She didn't tease. She brought him gradually along until he gasped her name and his climax spilled over and ran down her chin.

"Alice." Henry called to her with little more volume than Jay had.

Releasing Jay, she eased back.

Beside her in an instant, Henry tilted her face up. He wiped her mouth and chin with tender strokes of a washcloth, kissing her forehead and offering her a bottle of water.

He bathed Jay with the cloth while she drank, offering the water to Jay next with two small white pills. Painkillers. He kissed Jay's forehead as well.

Henry prized balance. Kindness. Part of his performance? He never made her feel unwanted or less important than Jay, except when he'd made his point tonight. If he limited his willingness to make the effort to a few hours every other week, she wouldn't begrudge him the rest of the time.

"Wait here a moment, Alice." He departed with the washcloth and the water.

Twice in a row now, he'd catered to them rather than the other way around. Jay's injuries gave him cause, but she might be missing a deeper point. He hadn't told her to dress. He'd let her stay, even after she'd failed at submission.

Jay beckoned her toward him. "Thank you, Alice." He seemed more coherent, less like an overexcited child, as he waited for his pain medication to kick in.

She leaned in and kissed him near his ear, far from the bruising across his eyes. "I'm glad you enjoyed it."

"No—I mean, I did, but I mean thank you for worrying. And caring. And taking care of us. I know tonight was hard." He bit his lip. His whisper came to her ear in a frantic rush. "Would you stay and let Henry make love to you here? He needs you, and I want to feel close to you both tonight, and I, I don't want to be alone."

Her heart broke for him. She stilled her tongue from spitting out the words crawling through her brain. *We don't make love, Jay. We fuck. At agreed-upon times.* If she let herself forget the difference, she'd only get hurt.

But he'd pinpointed Henry's needs. After two rough days, Henry deserved comfort, and sex was her only way to offer it. And she wanted to offer it.

She kissed Jay again and whispered, "I'll see what I can do."

Sitting back, she pulled the sheet over his hips and chest. The silk-soft cotton covered his bruises as she tucked it under his arms. Henry didn't want to be vulnerable in front of her, not like Jay. He wanted to be in control. "But you have to promise to try to sleep, Jay."

"An excellent idea." Henry strode into the room. "It's time for you to rest, my boy."

Jay pleaded with her in silence, the brown depths of his eyes a well of strength and need. He depended on her.

"Henry?" God, this was hard.

"Yes, dearest?"

She'd never asked something of Henry when she couldn't chalk it up to orgasm-deprived begging as he teased her body. This was asking when the answer wasn't guaranteed, when he'd barely touched her and didn't seem inclined to, despite Jay's assertion.

"Can we . . . would you . . . take me now? While Jay's awake to enjoy it?" Good. Make it about Jay, and Henry would let her comfort him and herself.

The tape on Jay's arm had peeled up at the edge. She pressed a finger on the corner and smoothed it. Up. Down. Silence. The waiting blasted her ribs like an industrial freezer. Her nerves thrummed as she craned her neck.

Inscrutable. Henry, master of the expressionless face.

"I sense a conspiracy here." He started unbuttoning his shirt from the top. "It's a wonder I imagine myself in control of anything at all."

She rolled onto her legs in Jay's favored pose. Kneeling near the center of the bed, she bowed her head toward Henry. Imitation. Jay ought to be flattered.

She meant to show perfect submission, naive innocence and a soft voice to match, but her stare refused to leave Henry's chest. Lust spilled over, filling her with the need to have his body bared to her. The flat nipples waiting beneath the edges of his shirt. The scratchy-soft patch of hair where she rested her cheek when he cradled her to his chest. "You're in control of me now, Henry."

He paused at the final button. White folds of fabric sloped toward the last point of tension, a rushing river leading to his waist. He spread the tails wide and shrugged free. The shirt fluttered to the floor. Bare flesh. All hers tonight.

"Lie on your side, Alice, facing Jay." His commanding voice made her tremble. He, too, felt eager. Engaged. Present in the moment.

Obedience was a gift she could offer him. One she owed without question during these hours, as much as she was able. She sank into the sheets, lying on her side, giving up her beautiful view of Henry's chest.

The rustle of his clothing tempted her as he undressed. The bed dipped behind her. His body warmed her naked back, and his head nestled behind hers on a single pillow. Heaven.

"Tell me your safeword, Alice."

As he led her through the familiar ritual, her body relaxed, comforted by his voice and his touch.

"Feel, Alice," he murmured. He brushed aside her hair with his nose. His exhalations puffed against her neck. "Just feel."

Her eyes fell closed as he stroked her skin. Her body a canvas, his hand the brush, the sensation rose in her like an electrical impulse. Her stomach, first. Expanding to graze the undersides of her breasts and the tops of her thighs, slow and steady and firm, until she trembled with need.

Caressing her breasts, he teased her nipples into tight peaks. He raised her leg and parted her lips. He skimmed her clitoris, and she cried out.

Body arching, she pressed her shoulders and hips into him as her spine pushed forward. And still he didn't stop, didn't hurry. He stroked her at the same slow pace no matter how she squirmed.

"My sweet girl, tell me how you feel, hmm?"

"Good." She hardly had breath to speak, not with his fingers moving over her. "So good."

"Only good?" His voice teased and coaxed as his fingers did.

"Better." Incredible. Indescribable. Floating on the edge.

His mouth rested against her ear. "Not feeling unwanted now? No, not my sweet Alice. The center of the world. Jay can't take his eyes off you, dearest."

Jay's sleepy gaze, hazy with drugs and adoration, pulled a moan from her throat. She let her eyes slip closed again as Henry's voice lulled her with its rhythms.

"And I can't take my hands off you, can I? You feel it, don't you, Alice? How much my body wants to touch yours?"

She rocked against him, the two of them sealed together all along each other's bodies in a hyper-aware coupling. She relished the roughness at her back, the hair on his chest, down the center of his abdomen, and surrounding the thick heat of him.

"I feel it," she answered.

"Good girl." He kissed her neck below her ear.

His breath on her neck made her want to beg for the sound of his voice again, but he stayed silent, focused on his fingertips. Her orgasm seemed endless, a full-body climax with no peak. A blissful plateau sustaining itself when his fingers left her and his hips tilted away.

His movements and soft grunt spelled condom. He'd fuck her now. She pulsed with anticipation.

When he pressed against her once more, he spread her lips and buried his cock in one thrust. He rocked with minuscule motions.

"Nothing too vigorous, my dear," he whispered. "We mustn't jostle the bed too much, hmm?"

Not too much. They didn't want to hurt Jay.

"You're still feeling for me, aren't you, Alice?" He took slow, small thrusts, barely pulling back at all. Thick. Solid. Sunk inside her to stay. "Tell me about this feeling. Do you know it? Have you felt it before?"

The night in November, when she'd tried to cancel at the last minute, and he hadn't let her. He'd fucked her slowly then. Tonight he'd tried to cancel at the last minute, and she hadn't let him, either. Yes, she'd felt it. The closeness. Being special. Cherished.

She'd learned her lesson from Christmas. She needed this. Before Henry, she'd never felt it, not like this. "I, I know it. S'good. Want it. Need it. Feel it. Only . . . only with you."

He groaned and covered her neck and shoulders in tiny kisses, nips of his teeth, swipes of his tongue. All the while, his fingers moved over her clit, coaxing her to orgasm in a series of shuddering waves as he thrust inside her. "Sweet Alice. So deliciously wet, so beautifully trusting."

Finally. She'd missed his voice in the silence. She gave herself over to him.

"Your eyes closed, your body open, admitting your need. So close . . . you're so close."

A steady flow of low, groaning words sank into her ear as he sank into her again and again. "You'll feel it. Want you to feel it. You'll get there."

The combination brought her to a higher peak and took him with her, the two of them quaking as he thrust a final time and stayed deep within her when he came. "I promise you."

Chapter 3

Alice strolled back to awareness, enjoying the warmth of the room and the softness of the sheets and the low rumble of Henry's and Jay's voices. In no hurry to move, she soaked everything in. Perfection existed right where she lay, sprawled across half of Henry's bed.

She'd be sore later. Worth every second.

The suede flogger was possibly the object she loved most in Henry's arsenal. He wielded the tails with such confidence and care. Even lying on the dresser, her suede lit a fire under her skin.

Jay had enjoyed it this time, too. No panic, no special-exception rules, no tears. Something had changed for him. Henry had alternated striking her body with the flogger and dragging it over Jay's skin while she recovered from the sting. He never struck Jay, but he stroked Jay's back with the tails and asked him to describe how they felt.

He hadn't needed to ask her. Between the begging for more and the string of orgasms, her enthusiastic response defied misinterpretation. She'd been mid-climax when Henry had laid the flogger aside and pulled her onto his cock, finishing with a shout, his hands curled around her hips.

She'd drifted in that special kind of hazy bliss, unable to hold a thought as Henry urged Jay to his knees on the bed. Kneeling behind him, Henry had wrapped his hand around Jay's cock. Jay had splashed his thighs and the sheets and Henry's hand sliding on his flesh when he came.

No self-handling allowed yet. Not with the supportive wrap on Jay's wrist.

After two weeks, the bruises from his accident had faded, and the stitches had come out of his leg. He'd shown her the leg at their regular Tuesday lunch with pride. Layered patches of fake skinlike stuff protected the almost-healed road rash. He'd complained in jest about Henry's insistence that he wear the wrist wrap for another week.

All of which had made Jay more observer than participant tonight, prohibited from putting much weight on his right hand or bending his wrist. Not permitted more than the lightest brush of suede on his skin. If he even wanted more. From his reaction the last time Henry had used it on her, months ago, she wouldn't have expected Jay to want it touching him at all.

Her sister's voice floated up from memory, last week, their most recent video chat. *"What's the deal with your not-boyfriends? Are you still letting smoldering art guy hit you? Don't you want to tell him to stop sometimes? Do you get to hit him back?"*

She'd laughed off Olivia's questions. It wasn't as if Henry hit her with things every Friday they spent together. But the questions played in a loop now, because the answer was no.

No, she hadn't wanted to tell him to stop. She'd wanted him to keep going. If he'd threatened to stop, she'd have begged him not to.

That was weird, right? They'd been in this arrangement for six months, and she only spoke her safeword when Henry asked her for it. Confirming she knew how to stop. Never using her escape clause.

What did that mean? Did it have to mean anything? Was Henry just that good? Was she that messed up? Shit. She fumbled for the euphoria slipping away.

"You're tense again, Alice."

Henry's hand came to rest on her head. He sat with his back against the headboard, beside where she lay on her stomach. She pressed against the reassuring presence of his leg. Jay lay on his other side, an unseen bookend.

"We three put a good bit of effort into relaxing you this evening, an endeavor that seemed a screaming success, no?" His voice teased.

He lifted strands of her hair as he soothed and petted. "Yet here you are, tense once more."

He'd ask her the cause if she didn't answer his indirect invitation to talk. His control was never heavy-handed—mmm, no, she'd loved the heavy hand he'd used on her tonight. But he never started with a heavy hand. He'd rather they came to him first. A demonstration of trust? Loyalty? Lo—affection? "Is it weird I haven't used my safeword yet?"

The hand in her hair stopped moving. Fuck. Her brain should've thrown the mouth-override switch.

"Have you wanted to, my dear?" Deliberate and bland.

She might've angered or upset him somehow with the question. But he took so much care to emphasize safeword use, so why—oh.

"No." If she'd wanted to but didn't, he might consider it lying. "That's the thing. Is it weird that I haven't wanted to?"

His hand relaxed on her scalp. "Everyone is different, Alice. The fact that you have had no cause to stop events could mean any number of things, not all of them about you."

"Yeah," Jay said, his voice muffled. "It could mean Henry-the-dominant is a sex god."

She half laughed, half snorted. "I know that."

"Shameless flatterers, both of you. I ought to take you over my knee next time."

She wriggled and stretched. As a punishment, spanking didn't sound so bad. It sure as hell had made a fantastic birthday present.

"But Jay does, accidentally, I suspect, have a point."

The answer leapt to her tongue. "That you're a good dominant."

"That I pay attention," he corrected. "I enjoy it, and my role with you both demands it. That you have not felt the need to stop might indicate I have not yet discovered your limits or I have correctly gauged the depth of need in you and met it."

He brushed her shoulder, fingertips trailing fire across sensitized skin. "I admit, I'm pleased that our activities have neither hurt nor frightened you thus far. I hope I am able to continue satisfying you without doing so."

She rolled onto her side. He took the invitation, his hand following the top of her shoulder down to her breast and squeezing.

"Some submissives refuse to safeword, considering such behavior a point of pride. It's a dangerous practice, my dear, and one I will not tolerate." He tweaked her nipple with his fingers and soothed the sting away in a single fluid motion. "A dominant must be attentive to such things, to nonvocal cues from a submissive's body. Even the things they seek to hide."

She'd better not be giving off cues about things she wanted to hide. Things like wanting more than hot sex every two weeks. Like pancakes and laundry and arguing over whose turn it was to take out the trash.

Besides, trash duty would always be Jay's turn. She nuzzled Henry's thigh and tasted salt on his skin. Flogging her was a workout for him, too.

"To answer your question, Alice, no, your behavior is not 'weird.' It is entirely *you*. So long as you are honest with me when we play, it's fine that you have not used your safeword."

The conversation lapsed into silence. She refused to voice the obvious question. Whether Jay ever used his safeword wasn't her business. What he and Henry did on their time was private. She wasn't part of it. She might never be.

"I have," Jay piped up. "Safeworded, I mean. All the time when we started, just to be sure I could. I was . . . trust was hard."

"With good reason," Henry murmured.

"Is that why . . ." She paused. Pushing Jay without understanding what triggered his bouts of fragility might hurt him. But Henry rubbed encouraging fingers over her arm. Maybe talking would do Jay good.

Her back burned, muscles pulling where the flogger had danced, as she breathed too deep. "The first night Henry flogged me. You were upset."

The sheets rustled as Jay shifted. Henry reached out and stroked his back. A hand for each of them, now.

Jay started slow. An oddity, because words drained from his mouth in a steady stream, like sand in an hourglass. When he ran out, flipping him over and getting him going again took no effort. But not tonight.

"Almost five years ago. I was a year out of school, shy of twenty-five. MBA fresh in my hand. Working in insurance. Financial stuff. Suit and tie."

The idea baffled her. Kayaking instructor, sure. Camp counselor, absolutely. Fitness coach, no doubt. But financier? Jay?

"I hated it. Really hated it. But I didn't want to fuck up a job my brother got for me. So I worked these crazy hours with no way to blow off steam. The company had a whole pack of us guys. Full of ourselves, all swagger and stupidity. Don't say it, I know, I haven't changed much."

Not even close. Sweet swagger, maybe. Lovable goofiness, but never stupidity.

"Anyway, I started hanging with them after work. Bars. Strip clubs. Private parties. Hotel rooms. I met this guy. Cal."

The nervous discomfort in his voice, the flat way he said the man's name, suggested the word should never be uttered, least of all in Henry's bed, their safe place. Unless Jay only felt safe enough to talk about it here.

"The first time I saw him, he, umm, he . . . everybody in the room was watching him."

She curled closer to Henry, raising her head onto his thigh. Jay lay half buried, tucked against his other side.

"Be honest, my boy." Henry smoothed her hair from her face. "I don't believe you'll shock Alice."

"I'm listening, Jay." She made her voice quiet, easy. "To whatever you want to tell me."

Henry kept his hand in constant motion, slow strokes along Jay's spine as Jay described the scene. Disapproval didn't show in his movement, but the tightness at the corners of his mouth gave it away. Not of Jay—of the party. Of the presence of drugs and alcohol.

She'd never been served more than half a glass of wine on any contract night with them. Henry never drank more than that, either. Wits, sensation, response times—he wouldn't want any of them dulled while they played.

"There were maybe fifteen, twenty people. Cal, he put on a show. He, umm, had a woman tied up. Hog-tied, you know? Arms and legs behind her all roped together. Teasing her. Denying her until she begged, and then he . . . he pushed her knees wide and fucked her. She looked crazy-happy about it. Me and half the other guys in the room jacked off watching."

He sounded apologetic, like he regretted the experience, and she responded with lightness. "Henry's right so far. You haven't shocked me yet. I like to watch you jack off."

"It's 'cause I have such a beautiful cock." Trying for his arrogant charm voice, he fell far short.

Henry ruffled Jay's hair. "You do, my boy, but you also have a penchant for going off topic."

"Right." Jay took a deep breath and let it out slowly. "I saw him again later, same guy, in an armchair talking finance. He had this naked guy sucking his cock. That's when I knew. I didn't want to be Cal, throwing my weight around and making people obey me. I wanted to be the guy curled up against his leg. The one who got to please him."

"Okay." Curled up like he was now beside Henry, more or less. Easy to relate to that desire. "You wanted to play submissive games."

"Yeah. I didn't know the name. But my buddy from work, the one that brought me to the party, he sees me watching Cal and says I should try this club he goes to. A social club, he called it. His uncle had gotten him a membership. He says I'd be amazed at what some people would do for a pat on the head because they're so desperate for approval."

"He mocked them? For being submissives?" She fought the urge to pull the name from Jay's lips, find the asshole friend and deliver belated justice on Jay's behalf. Knocking his teeth out might satisfy her.

"I guess he thought I wanted to *be* Cal and not, you know, not like the ones pleasing him."

"A dominant who disrespects the gifts his submissives provide shouldn't be playing games with them." Henry's quiet tone made her certain he'd said the same to Jay many times. "Trust is a privilege."

"I know now. I do. I just learned the hard way."

"Someone broke your trust." Forcing Jay to talk about something that still bothered him, even if it had happened almost five years ago, smacked of kicking a puppy.

"Yeah. I was a complete novice. Hadn't done my homework. My buddy said Cal belonged to this club, so I agreed to go." He laughed, a pained bark.

"My buddy wasn't a Henry. I didn't have a Henry then. He set us up in a room with a couple of girls. Said they'd do anything we wanted. Half a minute, and I knew I didn't want to tell my girl what to do. I wanted her to tell me." Jay lifted his head onto Henry's thigh and rolled his eyes at his foolishness. Stupidity, he might've called it.

"I ask her what *she* wants, and she says she wants to please me. I didn't have the slightest clue. I had her pick a flavored condom from the basket and blow me. Simple, right? But it was, I mean, she could tell." He half shrugged, drawing lines with his finger on Henry's skin.

"If Henry treated us as indifferently and incompetently as I treated that girl, we wouldn't keep coming back for more, you know? So when it's over, she says something like 'You sure you wouldn't rather wear one of these?' and she tugs this green ribbon on her shoulder strap."

Jay closed his eyes. "I confessed I had no idea what she meant, because my buddy had handled the arrangements, and she got all horrified. She says, 'You don't even understand the rules? Your friend is an idiot.' I think she felt bad for me. Said I wasn't a top, and I should ask at the desk about getting a ribbon like hers. My buddy had gotten me a guest pass. He would've sponsored me if I wanted to join as a dominant. So I did pretty much the stupidest fucking thing a person can do."

"Jay, you're not that boy anymore." Henry's chide carried no more sting than the feathers. "You know better now. Your friend ought to have taken responsibility for you. To have dropped you naked in a new playground . . ."

Jay nodded and opened his eyes. "I know, Henry. You've said. And I believe you. I do. I just . . ." He stared at her as if willing her to understand. "I came into the club the next weekend when my buddy was on an out-of-town account, 'cause I didn't want him to see me being . . . submissive. I asked for a green ribbon, sure I was up for anything. Got offers for all sorts of things."

He grinned. "Turned out I had a real knack for sucking cock. Who knew?"

She laughed because he wanted her to, but her stomach flipped. His eyes wouldn't focus on hers. He'd hit the verge of whatever had made him safeword so often. Maybe she didn't want the image of Jay in pain in her head. Maybe Henry was wrong and she couldn't handle it.

"I had a blast for about three months. Or thought I did." He frowned, rolling his head. "I loved pleasing anyone who asked. Hardly ever turned anyone down. Then I finally saw the guy from the hotel. Cal. I went right up to him and waited to speak to him. We played a few times. It was good. I thought he . . . I thought we'd clicked. I stopped saying yes to other offers. I trusted him. But it was—I was . . ."

Henry smoothed Jay's hair and rubbed his neck and shoulders. "Take your time, sweet boy. Only as much as you're comfortable sharing, hmm?"

Jay took another deep breath. "It got out of control. With . . . with a whip. I was tied, I couldn't . . . There was nowhere to go. I was, umm, bleeding, and it hurt, and I, I used my safeword for the first time. But he didn't stop."

She slammed her teeth together to stop a shocked gasp from escaping. Not that Jay would notice anyway. His gaze went past her, or through her, or into his own head. If reality came anywhere near what she pictured, she didn't envy him the memory of it.

"I thought maybe he hadn't heard me. But then it was . . . I knew he wouldn't stop until *he* wanted to. I was, umm, crying, and shouting, I think, and he . . ." Jay cried silent tears, no sobs.

She ached to reach across Henry and touch Jay's face, but she feared his flinch. Her touch might be unwanted while these memories dominated him.

He cleared his throat. "That's when I met Henry. Heard his voice first."

She understood in an instant. "He stopped things."

"Yeah. I could've . . . it might've been bad. Really bad, I mean, if Henry hadn't insisted Cal stop. I got pretty fucked up. But that didn't— I was still healing when I went back the next week."

A breach of trust that had to have felt like a rape, whether it had been or not, and he'd gone straight back for more. Jesus Christ. Poor Jay.

"I was a pathetic mess. Physically, emotionally, whatever. Everybody saw it. Nobody would touch me."

"They were right not to, my boy." Henry rested his hand against the muscle sloping up toward Jay's neck. "What you needed wasn't something they could give you in a single night."

"I couldn't help myself, though. I practically begged for someone to let me please them." He'd hated himself. His voice bled raw contempt. He squeezed his eyes half-closed, and his lips curled like he'd smelled something foul. "It was disgusting. I was—"

"No." Henry wasn't to be contradicted. "You were neither pathetic nor disgusting, Jay. You were in need, yes, but the urge you have to please others, to seek their approval, is not wrong, my sweet boy. It's simply *you*. And you didn't know what to do with it because no one had taught you. That's all it was."

Doubt hung in the lines of Jay's face. Henry loved him and wanted him to feel good about himself. But Henry had such a dominant voice. Jay probably couldn't imagine Henry begging for anything. She sure as hell couldn't.

No matter how much Jay wanted to believe Henry, he'd never believe Henry understood his desperation. How much he'd hated himself for being weak. For not being the kind of guy who'd take whatever power submissive partners gave him and mock them behind their backs for it. The kind of man like Cal, who could beat Jay until he bled and call it a good time.

Until he'd met Henry, Jay would've wondered, wouldn't he? If those people he'd been having a good time pleasing praised him to his face and mocked him when he'd gone. If they were supposed to.

Henry could tell Jay—probably had told Jay—a million times that men like Cal and Jay's coworker were the wrong and disgusting and pathetic ones. Didn't matter. Jay'd only remember how they'd made him feel about himself. Victimized by the echoes of their cruelty.

"Do you . . ." Faltering, she grounded herself in the supporting presence of Henry's hand splayed wide across the center of her back. "Do you think I'm disgusting, Jay?"

"No!" Jay's gaze, wide and horrified, darted to hers. "Never— Alice, I'd never—"

"Twenty minutes ago, I begged Henry to flog me harder." She pushed herself to say the rest, to ignore her sister's voice in her head, because she refused to be ashamed of this, dammit. But, Jesus, if the struggle taxed her resolve when her sister didn't mean to make her feel bad, how much harder did Jay work to ignore those voices? "I wanted it, Jay. Hell, I can't even tell you how many times I came tonight because of it."

He jerked as if she'd hit him. "That's different. He's *Henry*. He wouldn't hurt you. I would've followed anyone."

Fine. He wouldn't believe it was the same thing, not now, but maybe she'd plant a seed. "Yeah? And less than five minutes after the first time you told me you and Henry wanted to fuck me, I let him bend me over a table and strip my underwear off and fuck me like I was the appetizer. And *I liked it*. If he'd told me to, I would've gotten on my knees and sucked him off afterward. I'm not ashamed of it."

Christ, she'd gotten loud. Henry rubbed her back.

Calm. Calm for Jay. "This guy, this Cal, you looked up to him and he took advantage of that to hurt you. He's the one who oughta be ashamed, but he won't be, because people like him never are." She stretched across Henry, touched Jay's fingers, sought a loose clasp when he didn't avoid her.

"You're not any more pathetic or disgusting than I am. You're playful and sweet and giving. You just needed the right person. The one who'd respect those things about you."

Jay stared at their entwined fingers and smiled. "Henry was the only person to approach me all night."

By design. She'd lay money on it. Henry answered her glance with a brief nod. He might've stood between Jay and potential partners like a guard dog for hours.

"He came right up and asked me to sub for him for the rest of the night. I said yes without even thinking. Without asking what he wanted from me. Even with what had happened, I just, I *needed*." Jay shook his head.

"Cal liked whips?" She couldn't snap her fingers and give Jay his self-worth back. He'd talk himself back into feeling ashamed if she let him. The feeling would be waiting for the next time he felt insecure.

"Yeah. A lot."

"Did you like whips?" That's why Henry was quick to praise him. To show Jay his approval. Make Jay feel safe to be himself.

"I liked pleasing people." Jay gave her a rueful smile. "How didn't matter so much. But I didn't dislike them. At least, not before."

She rubbed her thumb over his knuckles. They weren't so different. She enjoyed pleasing Henry in their games and his approval and praise afterward. Enjoyed the false feeling of closeness and intimacy that sex provided, the short-term rush.

"If Henry thought the others were right to stay away, why . . ." He'd approached Jay and asked him to play the submissive for him in such a fragile moment? Henry exercised dominance and control, but he wasn't a predator. He wouldn't have marked Jay's vulnerability and leaped for the kill.

"He didn't touch me." Right eyebrow raised, he smirked. "That first night? Never fucking touched me, not once. Too clever, right? He gets me to promise not to play with anyone else, and he takes me downstairs and makes me switch out my green ribbon for a red one, and that's that. He tells the girl at the desk she's not to give me anything but a red ribbon from now on and he's to get a phone call whenever I walk in the door. She looks at me, I nod like I know what the fuck is going on, and she makes a note. Done."

Henry's hand tightened against her back.

She pressed her head against his leg. The moment must've been comforting and terrifying. For Henry, not just Jay. To be able to help Jay, and to accept utter responsibility for him, too. Jay's protector.

She might not know ribbons, but she understood stoplights, and Henry had tied a big flashing one on Jay. Jay's eagerness to please made him a danger to himself.

"He took me upstairs, but only to the lounge. No sex. No shows, no demonstrations, nothing more kinky than people sitting around unwinding. We get juice—no alcohol at the club—and sit down, and he quizzes me for like four hours, and he sends me home with specific masturbation instructions. Homework!" He sounded more like himself now, with words bubbling out. Talking about Henry did that to him. He'd pushed through the hard part to reach giddy relief.

"None of the others . . . nobody had done that before. Tried to make it more than whatever they wanted from me for a few hours, I mean. I felt special. Because Henry gave me this task, you know?"

Responsibility. Henry's trust. She'd been intimate with that feeling.

"He wanted me to think about it, too, so I'd be able to give him a report the next week. *Next week.* That whole week, I was so damn happy. Not worried at all. 'Cause I knew I'd see him, and he'd listen to my report, and I'd have done such a good job he'd give me another thing to do."

"You wanted to make him happy, and he . . ." had made it easy. Given Jay a task he couldn't fail at.

Their first night together, he'd told her they'd have to correct her feelings of inadequacy. Jay had been a project for Henry. And now she was, too. A sex hobby.

"I enjoy teaching," Henry said with quiet patience. He'd seemed content to let Jay dominate the discussion, maybe because Jay didn't talk about his past often. "What Jay needed most at the time was a teacher to show him how to have his needs met in a safe way."

"Safe means *talking.*" Jay sighed. "That next night? Same thing. Except instead of sitting at a table, we walked around and watched some scenes. For every room, he'd ask what I liked or didn't like and how I felt watching."

Jay rolled forward, shifting his leg over Henry's and rubbing his foot against Henry's calf. "He was sneaky. Not in a bad way. Not a liar. That's not Henry." Jay's unblinking stare unnerved her. Brown depths she'd never feared before. "He's always honest, but what he did for me? He took it so gradual and subtle I didn't realize at first how safe I felt in his hands—and how different that was from before."

She flinched. Her fingers slipped free of Jay's. His words could've belonged in her own mouth.

"Six months later, I moved in with him. So I guess we'd better—"

"Pause to clean up and fetch a snack, yes, Jay. An excellent suggestion." Henry sent him to fetch washcloths and asked her to help replace the sheets for the night.

She couldn't help but count the months. She'd reached her sixth as a project on Henry's roster. She curled her tongue, desperate to keep her questions from spilling out of an unguarded mouth. Had Jay been about to make a joke? Confess fear that Henry would ask her to move in and displace him?

Henry might ask all of his submissives to live with him at some point. She'd no idea how many he'd trained. Was cohabitation in Jay's contract? Living together sure as hell wasn't in hers. She liked living alone. Being independent. Not answering to anybody.

Didn't she?

She was losing her fucking mind. Sex with Henry killed brain cells.

Jay brought back warm washcloths. Henry tenderly cleaned them both and himself before asking Jay to retrieve the arnica cream from the nightstand.

"Lie on your stomach, sweet girl. I want a proper look at your back."

She lay still, her face turned to the side. Henry's touch heated her skin.

"Does that hurt, Alice?"

She'd be red for a while. Her skin was too fair not to bruise no matter how carefully Henry distributed the flogger's tails.

"It burns a little." Too, she'd feel the pull in her muscles when she stretched. "Not badly."

But she wanted to keep that feeling. Like she carried Henry's careful attention to her needs in her muscle memory. She didn't have to leave it in this room when their time together ended.

Humming, Henry took the jar from Jay and handed off the wash-cloths.

Henry applied the cool cream with light, gentle strokes. She basked in the attention he paid to her shoulders and ass and upper thighs. He paused once, to kiss Jay and thank him for taking care of the washcloths.

Jay settled on the bed beside her and nuzzled her face as Henry finished his work. Replacing the cream in the nightstand drawer, Henry studied them. "Alice, please be so kind as to spare Jay's wrist and fetch the snack tray from the kitchen while the arnica settles into your back."

She slid off the bed and onto her feet. Henry laid his hand along her cheek and kissed her forehead. "Thank you, dearest."

She went willingly, damn sure the choice of tasks had nothing to do with Jay's wrist and everything to do with Henry needing a mo-ment alone with him. Praising Jay for sharing or warning him not to tease her about moving in, maybe. That lifestyle wasn't something Henry would offer her—or something she'd accept.

She wouldn't be where Jay was in four years. Henry had grown deeply attached to him. Loved him. Even if Jay had started as a proj-ect, he wasn't one now. Unless . . .

She stumbled over her feet and caught herself.

Henry had flogged her tonight. Jay hadn't been upset like he had in November. What if her presence belonged to a subset of Henry's project with Jay?

Henry wouldn't use her, but her contract laid out her consent. If Jay had been a broken machine, Henry might've needed to find a re-placement part or jury-rig a temporary workaround. Her.

Tray in hand, she ducked into the bedroom. Jay clung to Henry, resting against the headboard with their dark heads bent together. Comforting and comforted. She wouldn't mind some of that action. Wrung out physically and emotionally, she'd let her head tie her in knots. And not those nice quick-release ones Henry knew.

"Lovely, Alice, thank you." Henry gestured toward the nightstand, and she set the tray down. He patted the bed. "Sit, sweet girl, and tell me what's on your mind. You've been processing things, I'm certain, and you've no doubt come to some questions."

She passed Henry a glass of juice. He handed it to Jay to sip before taking a drink himself. Bringing the plate, she settled next to Henry and started to lean back.

He stopped her with a hand on the back of her neck, making her wait until he'd placed a pillow between her sensitive shoulders and the wood. He'd sent her out of the room to talk with Jay, yeah, but he'd also given her time alone to think, because he understood how her mind worked. So where to start?

"The games . . . the bondage, and the spanking, and the flogging. If it bothered Jay . . . was I . . . how could you . . ." She traced the edge of the square plate around a blunted corner. Three ripples decorated the gently sloping sides like a washboard. "Why?"

"Trust and desire, Alice." Henry handed her the glass of juice. "Sip. It was trust, and desire, and patience."

"It helped me," Jay blurted. "I want those things, Alice. I wanted them before and I still want them. I've just been afraid. Seeing you all confident and brave and satisfied, knowing you enjoyed every minute and you weren't scared or hurt after, it helped me. I don't want to be afraid. I hate it. I hate that panic, I hate that my body sometimes still reacts that way. I watch you and I feel like I can do it. Like I'm okay because you are."

"I'm . . ." *An example.* Nothing more. She dragged her finger across the ripples. Bump. Bump. Bump. He'd meant it as a compliment. "I'm glad I can help you, Jay."

Henry issued a quiet challenge. Not quite a hum, not quite a grunt, but something that disagreed without disagreeing. Lifting her right hand in his left, he pressed the back of her hand to his chest.

"Everything was carefully chosen, Alice, with an eye toward your enjoyment, Jay's fears, and my own skills." He pursed his lips and rubbed his thumb over her palm in slow circles. "Think back to our first nights together. You were pinned, bound by my body even then. I would not have added physical restraints if I hadn't been certain from your contract answers and your early responses that you would enjoy them."

"But if I hadn't, if I'd freaked out, it would've been a disastrous lesson for Jay." Massively fucking risky. If she'd had to pick words to describe Henry, "risky" wouldn't have made the top hundred.

"It would have been a *different* lesson for Jay, and for you. A lesson in using your safeword, and a lesson in how quickly I responded to your distress." He raised an apple slice to her mouth. "Eat. You need the sugar."

Jay had snatched pieces from the plate on his own. She'd gotten wrapped up in talking and thinking. And Henry still held her right hand pressed to his chest. She accepted the apple slice from his fingers.

Henry nodded. "The night with the cuffs, your first experience of true bondage—you tested the release and safety features, do you recall?"

He'd made her yank the strap free, and she'd been able to relax. She swallowed in a hurry. "I remember."

"The demonstration comforted Jay as much as you, my dear. He had direct control of the scene, the ability to stop at any moment and reassure himself that you enjoyed the attention and the restraint. You'll recall he was playing a role, Alice, imagining himself making a poor experience into a good one for you. A set task. He asked you several times if you were enjoying it."

True. Jay had asked, and she'd taken his questions and hesitations as role-playing. Maybe Henry's choices hadn't been so risky.

"So this whole time, all of it has been a lesson for Jay." Not the lesson she'd originally thought, not teaching Jay to please her. But her revised hypothesis matched. She was the temporary, jury-rigged solution to Jay's fears.

"For *him*, in some ways, yes. For *you*, these months have been an exploration of unexpressed desires. An opportunity to find more complete satisfaction. Something your life has been missing."

Missing? She wasn't missing anything. Her life was fine, thank you very much. *Orgasms, idiot. He means orgasms.* Well, that and finding out she liked some minorly kinky shit.

She cleared her throat. "And you like the bondage games and the discipline because you like control. You couldn't play those games with Jay." The conclusion bothered her. Hurt deep and twisted her with confusion.

"Alice. Look at me."

Instinct demanded she obey his command. Deep green eyes saw into her soul.

"Alice, you are not a substitute for Jay."

Henry's words landed like a blow under her ribs, stealing her breath. He'd named the fear she couldn't even speak. She nodded, three times, slow and deliberate, before trusting her voice. "Okay."

"Jay, the plate, please." Henry's soft voice promised understanding, and Jay leaned across him to lift the plate from her legs. Pale green ceramic floated away on Jay's fingertips, the near-emptied glass following.

Henry scooped her sideways into his lap, tucking her side to his chest. "On the nightstand for now, my boy."

Wrapping his other arm around Jay's back, he curled him into his shoulder. Bookends, she and Jay, their foreheads resting against Henry's neck. Jay smiled and whispered "hey" beneath Henry's chin.

"You are each unique." Henry spoke in a low-toned whisper. "I treasure each of you for the pieces of yourself you bring to our time together. If, on occasion, those pieces fit into a larger picture that benefits us all, that helps us confront and overcome fears, I treasure them all the more for it. But none of the pieces is lesser. Never *less*. Never *instead of*."

She shivered, and Henry cupped the back of her head. She wasn't *just* anything to him. She was Alice. He'd never treat her callously, never mock her needs or use her exclusively to fulfill his own or Jay's. Responsibility was Henry's watchword.

Even on their first night together. She'd told him afterward she'd trusted him, and he'd been upset by the idea that he'd taken her without explaining the rules of the game. And then he'd spent three months *not* fucking her. Atoning for his lapse.

Before he finally did fuck her, he'd asked her if she believed he could control himself. Understanding burned. Henry would be horrified if he occupied the space in her head Cal held in Jay's. Fuck.

"Henry?" His neck muffled her voice.

He scratched her scalp with gentle fingers. "Yes, Alice?"

"I know you'd never treat me like an object for your own gratification. And that you're not using me to help Jay. I *know* those things. I just forgot for a minute. I'm sorry I made it sound like you would do that."

Hand traveling down her spine, he tipped his cheek against the top of her head.

"My sweet, sweet Alice. Do not apologize for expressing your feelings. If they are happy, allow Jay and me to share in your joy. And if they are confusing or hurtful, bring them to me and permit me to help you. The trust between us underpins all we do here. I would rather you shout, and curse, and call me a monster a million times over than have you push *any* feelings down where they might fester. A fear confronted often enough with powerful opposition will fade until one wonders what made it so fearful in the first place."

Curled together, they fell into silence. She'd try harder to talk to Henry about her feelings. To expose what went on in her head. But for tonight, exhaustion won the battle.

She slept easy, lying on Henry's chest with an arm and a leg thrown across Jay beside him.

Chapter 4

Alice huddled deeper into her blankets. The apartment had been cozy when she'd gone to bed. Chilly now, though. The clock called it ten after midnight. At least the apartment had power, which was more than she could say for some sections of the city.

The snow had started coming down Wednesday afternoon and hadn't stopped yet. The forecast estimated something like three feet. A little much, even for mid-February in Boston. The storm battered the city like the winters of her childhood, the deep, sweeping drifts on the Dakota plains.

Comforter wrapped around her, she shuffled to the window. The cars in the alley had almost disappeared, rounded mounds of white glowing pale blue under the building's security lighting.

The view was beautiful, and so silent—wait, silent? The heating system should be rattling and clanking and hissing. She laid a hand on the radiator cover. Cold. Pulling the cover forward, she touched the pipes. Also cold. Broken. Dammit.

She added baggy sweats and her fluffy bathrobe over the top of her pajamas before rewrapping the comforter around herself. Debating the merits of suffering through the night or calling Mr. Nagel to report the problem now, she jumped when the knocking started.

"Alice? You awake? Alice?"

"Hold on, Jay." Awkward shuffling, hampered by her desire not to trip over the blanket, got her across the room. She unhooked the chain, flipped the dead bolt and opened the door.

Jay had on sweats, too, though his didn't come with a bathrobe and blanket. He took one look at her and laughed. "Cold?"

"Maybe a little. You have a reason for banging on my door after midnight?"

"So many reasons." He stepped forward, arms flung wide, and squeezed her in a tight bear hug. "But most important for you? Henry found out from Mr. Nagel the boiler's blown and they can't rig it to run. Roads are closed to all but emergency services, so we can't leave and the replacement won't be here tonight, which means *you* are coming home with *me* right now."

"I am?" She warmed in Jay's embrace.

"Yup. Henry says you're coming to bed. No excuses. C'mon." He started to lift her, and she swatted at him with blanket-covered hands.

"Henry didn't say that. It's not Friday." He never tried to dictate what she did outside of those five hours. He was hyperconscious of that sort of thing. Rules. Maybe he didn't want her thinking he'd try to control her without her permission.

"You think Henry doesn't care about you if it's not Friday?" Jay lifted her higher, ignoring her ungraceful squirming, until their eyes were level. "That's bullshit."

"No, I know we're friends, Jay. But it's not Friday. I don't belong in his bed."

Jay opened his mouth, closed it, looked away and shook his head. "You do tonight. Emergency circumstances." The seriousness faded from his face, and he broke out his most charming smile. "Besides, you didn't even let me get to the other reasons. I've got so many ideas for warming you up. Heat works fastest from the inside out, you know."

He kissed her jaw and breathed on her ear. It was practically the only skin she had showing, and his beliefs about heat were clearly false. Neither point stopped her from turning her face into his neck and inhaling woodsy Jay-musk with the faintest hint of Henry's leather and citrus. They must've been sleeping. Or enjoying other things.

"See? You like my ideas. Come to bed." He took a step forward, into her apartment, and another, carrying her with him. "Or we could try out your bed. That would be new and exciting, right?"

Have sex with Jay? In her bed? Leave Henry across the hall waiting and wondering—or worse, knowing—what they were doing? "I
don't think Henry would like that. And I'm sure it's not what he told
you to do."

"How about I show him what I have in mind and we let him be the
judge?" He nudged her with his hips, not that the force penetrated the
layers of pajamas and sweats and bathrobe and blanket. His
wheedling tone made her laugh.

"Put me down and gimme a minute, loverboy." She stuffed warm
clothes and toiletries in a bag for the morning once he set her on her
feet. "I swear you think about nothing but sex. How do you ride a
bike with a 24-7 erection?"

He shrugged and flicked imaginary lint off his shoulder. "Skills,
baby. I got 'em, you want 'em."

"You are the most ridiculous man. C'mon." She abandoned the
comforter and gestured him toward the door. "You promised me
warmth."

She stopped outside to lock her door. Her pause gave all the encouragement he needed to crowd behind her and throw his arms
around her.

"Hey, I deliver on my promises. Plenty of warmth. This is just the
start of my warmth." He shuffled her down the hallway, refusing to let
her go despite their awkward gait. Standing ajar, the apartment door
needed only her shove to open.

"Found her, Henry." Jay pushed her into the apartment ahead of
him, his arms still wrapping her in a bear hug from behind. "She's
freezing, though. I've got ideas for warming her up."

"I'm certain your furnacelike heat would be ample enough to do
so, Jay, but perhaps Alice is inclined to give you the opportunity to
demonstrate your ideas."

"Oh, I think she is. But she wanted to check with you first."

"Did she now? How lovely."

Had she pleased him with her desire to seek permission? If he saw
it as a sign of her growing comfort in submitting to him, that seemed
reasonable. What he wanted.

Henry kissed her cheek. "Welcome, my dear."

Sex with anyone else, even Jay, felt inappropriate without Henry
present. Not because of their contract, but because she didn't fuck
other people when she was in a relationship. Monogamy, even if he

hadn't asked it of her. Didn't want it from her. Didn't practice it himself?

No. He'd have said if he had someone else. The contract mandated disclosure.

He clasped her arms and rubbed her biceps. Jay encircled her waist as he pressed against her back.

Henry sported a proper pair of pajamas, a matching set in steel blue. The silky fabric rippled across his chest as he warmed her. She tried to push away the idea that he might not be satisfied with her. With her and Jay.

"It didn't seem right." What could be right about taking Henry's lover to her bed and leaving him alone across the hall? She disliked feeling excluded. She wouldn't impose it on Henry.

"You needn't seek my permission to indulge on our nights apart, Alice. Our contract does not stipulate that you abstain, only that you not engage in potentially dangerous games without my supervision, that you inform me afterward of any encounters, and that you practice safe sex."

"I know. But Jay is yours, and . . ." *I'm yours*, she dared not say. Even if she wanted to be, wanted the everyday intimacies Jay had, Henry hadn't claimed her. She couldn't be his if he wouldn't acknowledge it. She was every-other-Friday Alice.

Henry cleared his throat. The sound pulled her gaze to his. Revealed the weight of his steady stare and the slight quirk in his brow. Desperate hope that her longing hadn't been blatant on her face flashed through her.

"Come along to bed, my dear." Whatever his thoughts, he kept them to himself. "We'll all be warmer under the covers, I expect."

"Thank God." Jay, bouncing in place, prodded her back with one hand. "My toes are freezing. Somebody better have warm calves available or I might lose them to hypothermia."

She dug in her feet with playful resistance. "You? With cold feet, furnace-boy? Impossible."

"Careful, or I'll prove it to you. You're not afraid of the cold, are you? I could get some ice."

She squeaked and dodged away from his hands creeping into her collar as he pretended to drop ice cubes down her back. He chased her down the hall and tackled her on Henry's bed.

Henry followed at a more measured pace. Upside down to her

eyes, as her head hung off the side of the bed and she squirmed under Jay's weight, he filled the doorway. A commander inspecting his troops.

"No ice tonight, my dears," Henry declared, closing the door and shutting in any warmth they might generate. "Another time, perhaps." He shooed them out of their clothes and under the covers.

Jay hauled Alice over himself to drop her in the middle when Henry slid beneath the sheets. "You're the littlest."

"I'm not little."

"Are too."

"Am not."

"The least heat-efficient, if you prefer, Alice." Henry's calm broke their teasing squabble. "Lacking sufficient body mass to perform the function as Jay and I do." He nuzzled the curve of her neck. "Don't despair. You have myriad other charms. You must leave something for Jay and me to do well."

"You and Jay do a lot of things *very* well." She dropped her voice to a loud-and-proud whisper. "Don't tell Jay. His ego's already too big to fit in the bed."

Jay pressed himself against her. His cock formed a fiery impression along her hip. "I've got something that'll fit better and warm you up."

She rolled on her side, leaving him at her back. Henry's expression gave no hint of command.

"It's your choice, my dear. You're under no obligation, but neither are you under any restriction." He pressed a soft kiss to her cheek.

Carte blanche, in Henry's bed? The thought thrilled and terrified.

It excited Jay. She'd have sensed the eager anticipation in him even if his cock hadn't jumped against the base of her spine. But she ignored him for the inscrutable lines on Henry's face in the low light.

"No restrictions?" She doubted he meant she could go digging through the special dresser for toys. She wasn't confident enough to try it anyway. She couldn't do what Henry did. Not yet.

"Within your comfort level, Alice." With his back to the window, where snow drifted downward in a moonlit dance, Henry was shadowed and difficult to read. "It's not a challenge you must meet. I trust what you desire is not beyond your reach."

She drifted toward him, testing that the freedom he offered included access to not only Jay but himself as well. That he allowed it without taking control surprised her. She kissed him. Coaxed his mouth open. Stroked his tongue with her own.

Sliding her hand over her hip, she dropped it between her body and Jay's until her palm curved around his cock and her fingers cupped his balls.

"Fuck, Alice."

Jay's whispered words came as she let Henry's mouth slip away. She couldn't start with Henry. For so many reasons.

He intimidated her. No—the idea of being wholly in charge of pleasing him without his guidance intimidated her. And Jay would take her lack of attention as a rejection. He covered emotional fragility with sexual bravado.

Besides, Henry always made her wait. Fairness demanded she do the same. Dinner didn't start with dessert.

Her gentle squeeze made Jay jump. "Within my reach? Some very desirable things."

Imagining Henry meant more than this would be silly. He didn't know everything she desired. If he did, he'd tell her to stop entertaining schoolgirl fantasies of romance. The same advice she kept giving herself.

She turned toward Jay, letting go of his cock and pushing at the center of his chest. He rolled flat on his back. She kept her amusement to a small smile despite the laughter that wanted out. His hands rose to claim her hips when she straddled his stomach.

She pressed his hands back to the mattress. "Later."

She kissed him no less thoroughly than she had Henry. Sitting up, she let the covers fall. The chill in the air hardened her nipples into tight, tingling points.

Jay sucked in a loud breath.

She rose on her knees and scooted forward. "You promised me warmth, Jay, and we all know you're full of hot air."

His tongue greeted her with eager attention when she lowered herself to his face. She braced her hands on Henry's headboard and let Jay feast.

His hands crept up to caress her ass. She allowed the touch, encouraging him with wiggling hips and soft moans. His tongue swept between her lips and teased her clitoris. She pulled back before he could make her come.

"Good boy, Jay." She patted him on the head and returned his hands to the sheets. "I think I'm warm enough now. Got anything hotter for me?"

His abdomen strained beneath her as she shuffled backward across his chest and down his stomach. He thrust into empty air behind her.

"Down, boy," she murmured, and he stilled, his eyes intent on hers. "I'll tell you when it's time to thrust."

She moved lower yet, straddling his thighs, and stroked his cock in a firm grip. Damn. Condom. She should've grabbed one before she started. Now she'd interrupt the flow by digging in the nightstand.

Henry held out a foil square. Of course. Because he was Henry, and he thought of everything.

She opened the packet and rolled the contents on Jay's cock, slow and teasing, reveling in the trembling thighs beneath her as he struggled not to thrust into her hand. When she'd finished, she gripped him at the base with one hand and balanced herself over him.

Jay whimpered as she stopped and rose again, taking him a fraction deeper each time. As she sank down completely, his whole body shuddered. She walked her fingers forward to stroke his chest. To travel over the subtly defined muscles in his abdomen. The chill in the room no longer bothered her. Heated from the inside out.

She reached for his hands, lying flat on the bed where she'd placed them, and brought them to her hips. Bending forward, she kissed his lips.

"Thrust, Jay," she whispered, sitting up.

Her weight wasn't much for him to lift. His hands held her steady as his hips moved.

"Faster."

She rode his short, snapping motions like a wave, surging forward and back. She wanted hard now. Fast. It would be good for Jay, a reward for his patience. But she craved more.

She played with her breasts with one hand and sent the other lower. Fingers slid between their bodies as Jay thrust, gathering lubrication and circling her clit. He was close. She needed to match him.

There. Just like that. Her frantic fingers fed off his beautiful face, the tension in his neck, the flex in his abdomen as he tried so hard to please her.

"Alice? I . . . I'm . . . please."

"Almost there," she murmured. "You can wait for me. So good."

In the split second before his motion and her own set her off, the heady rush of control pushed her higher. "Now. Now, Jay. Come with me."

When she'd come down and the world lost its fuzzy haze, she leaned forward and kissed him, gentle kisses to his nose and cheeks and lips. She whispered to him of how beautiful he was when he was inside her and how well he'd pleased her.

The joy on his face floored her. He soaked up tenderness better than a sponge held water.

She eased off of him before the condom became a concern. Silence to her left. Atypical. Worth investigating.

Henry lay on his back watching them, one arm bent beneath his head on the pillow. He'd watched the whole time, surely. She'd put it out of her mind to focus on Jay. Maybe his eyes held hunger, but they revealed tenderness, too. Unguarded and loving.

Forget it. He meant the look for Jay. His actual lover.

Henry's gaze shifted to meet hers. In the faint moonlight, she imagined tenderness hiding behind his darkly possessive look.

His left hand rested at the base of his erection. He idly stroked himself.

Boldness devoured her doubts. He'd said no restrictions. Torn between the intensity in his eyes and the hard cock in his hand, she tried out her best seduction voice. "That for me?"

He gave himself a firmer stroke. "If you're not too tired to take it."

She wouldn't pass up that gift even if she were. "I'm never too tired to take what you have to give me."

Thank God for sultry, teasing tones. She managed to make it sound as if she were playing the game. As if she didn't want to fall asleep in this bed every night and wake up to a hard gift from her all-the-time lover every morning.

Far from dulling the edge of her desire, sex with Jay had whetted it for Henry. She rode an orgasmic high. She didn't crave control anymore. She wanted to be taken. She wanted the pleasure from Henry she'd given Jay. That feeling she'd had the first night with Henry pressed up behind her.

"On your knees, Henry." She waited, nervous, uncertain about giving him any sort of command, even one putting him in a position to dominate her. But he followed her instruction, kneeling near the headboard and watching her with a raised eyebrow.

She knelt in front, facing him, and reached past him for a condom lying on the nightstand. Ever ready. Thoughtful of him.

The movement tempted her too much. She surprised him in mid-stroke, wrapping her lips around his cock and chasing his hand toward the base. He thrust, and she hummed with pleasure. *I made that happen.*

Forcing herself to let go, she sheathed him in the condom. She knelt on knees and forearms. Wiggled her hips. He loomed tall and dark over her shoulder. "Fuck me?"

"You want hard and fast tonight, Alice?"

Damn straight. "You always make me wait. Don't make me wait?" *Oh sweet fuck.*

He pushed inside before she'd categorized the sensation. So fucking thick, and he was talking. Christ, she'd never tire of his voice.

"You were beautifully tender with Jay, dearest. And now so wanton and needy for me." His voice grew rougher as his thrusts gained speed. "My lovely little chameleon."

The sheets slipped through her clenching fingers. Her head grew heavy, dizzy, and her hair swept across her forearms. Her hips tilted, and he sank further on the next stroke. *Oh God.*

He rocked her with his force, flesh swinging forward to strike her clit on every thrust. She jumped at the contact and ground against him harder. This wasn't like being spread across his table. She had room to maneuver.

Her breasts and her stomach rapidly shifted as she panted with pleasure. Beyond, Henry moved even more rapidly. Disappearing. Reappearing. She moaned, low and needy.

"You're watching, aren't you, Alice? Watching me take you?" His voice deepened. Pauses punctuated his speech. "You do like to watch, my girl. Perhaps some night soon you'll watch me take Jay."

The image flashed in her head with startling speed. Her body shook and her mind buzzed and it took no more than that to tip her back into orgasm.

He drew her climax out with deep thrusts and fingers dancing over her clit. Even after he came, buried inside her and roaring, his fingers worked until she begged him to stop.

"No more, please. I can't." Her legs collapsed beneath her, carrying him down.

He pulled out with care and cradled her body with his own. "Shhh. No more, my dear, not tonight."

She shuddered against him, nerves firing beyond her ability to control.

"It's time to rest."

Now *that* sounded like a fantastic idea. The room had warmed. The still-functioning cold water allowed them each to make hurried trips to the bathroom before bed, on variously shaky legs.

When she closed her eyes and drifted off, she lay between her boys, with Jay clutching her from behind like a teddy bear and Henry's chest a more than adequate pillow for her head.

Chapter 5

Her name woke her. Or the cold. The lack of warm bodies around her. And Henry's voice somewhere behind her, near the bedroom door.

"Mmm. She is. Extremely, beautifully fuckable."

Happy delirium. Maybe she was still dreaming.

". . . crawl back in bed?" Jay's smirk imprinted itself on her eyelids.

". . . I'd prepare breakfast, my boy. Lunch, more properly, given the hour. You're staying with her?" Not angry, but confirming. As though Henry wanted to be certain she wouldn't be left alone.

She'd never woken alone here. They'd always been in the room, if not in the bed.

"I'll find a way to keep her warm." Oh yeah. Definitely smirking.

"Not unless she initiates, Jay." Henry's tone rolled out low, hard, and commanding. Dominant Henry.

She could get used to him acting that way every morning.

"She's not a toy for your amusement. I won't have her pressured. Her well-being is as much my responsibility as yours is."

A sense of being cherished that only he inspired washed through her. He fed her in body and soul. The notes on her door. The meals at his table. The nights in his bed. Maybe making a submissive feel like the center of his world was the trick to being a good dominant. *Thank you, Henry.*

Though Jay wasn't wrong either. Persuading her to replay last night's events wouldn't take more than a word or two.

"No, I know, Henry." Even subdued and contrite, Jay barreled ahead. "I'm too eager. You've said. I won't fuck this up, promise. It's just . . . it's Valentine's, and she's here—"

Shit, it was. She'd planned to spend the day alone after work. Find a distraction to avoid dwelling on Henry and Jay's holiday shenanigans. Thank God for city-paralyzing snowstorms.

Though she ought to give them their privacy. Henry probably had special plans for Jay.

". . . and you said I couldn't ask because it wasn't a Friday and she doesn't owe us anything, but she's here, now, and I just . . ."

"I know, my boy. But behave. Or you'll spend the holiday in a time-out while Alice and I entertain each other."

Silence. An empty threat. It had to be. Henry wouldn't do that, would he? Jay's soft moan teased the air. Kisses, probably.

"*Behave.* I'll return shortly. It will be a cold meal, I expect, unless I manage to work miracles with that camp stove of yours."

The electricity must've gone out. The broken gas boiler killed the main stove along with the heat and hot water, but the microwave would've worked, at least. Rolling over to check the bedside clock's functionality would be admitting to eavesdropping.

The covers shifted, and the bed dipped. A lean body, cooler than hers, pressed up behind her to snuggle. Jay nuzzled her ear. "Happy Valentine's Day, Alice."

Ignore his whisper, or dive into holiday festivities? Ignore Jay. Right. She hummed and stretched. "I'm not big on the hearts-and-flowers holidays. But I hope you have a happy Valentine's. Sorry for crashing the party."

"You're not crashing." Adorable astonishment colored his tone. "You're always welcome."

She doubted Henry would see it that way. If Jay liked the hearts-and-flowers crap, Henry wouldn't let the day pass without celebrating.

She wasn't about to stomp on Jay's sweetness. She'd slip away discreetly later. Turning in his arms, she pressed her forehead to his. "What's the situation this morning?"

"Let's see. Boiler's still out. Power's gone off 'cause ice snapped lines somewhere." He tapped fingers against her back as he counted the day's troubles. "Emergency traffic ban's still in place, not that you could drive down our street anyway, 'cause I don't think a plow's touched it yet. Umm . . . it's still snowing. Buuut . . ."

Jay loved an appreciative audience. She squirmed in his arms and mimicked his tone. "Buuut what?"

"Henry's making breakfast." He kissed her nose. "So the day's gonna be fantastic anyway."

He pulled back with an earnest, innocent expression. She laughed. Of course Henry fixing him breakfast made Jay's day perfect. Henry enjoyed cooking; Jay enjoyed eating. The definition of a symbiotic relationship.

They lazed in bed, Jay surprisingly quiet and no more sexual with her than on a contract night when Henry had granted them leisure time. Maybe he had. Jay's contract had to be more expansive than her own. Living with Henry, he didn't get days off, did he?

Henry'd called Jay's room the only place in the apartment where Jay didn't answer to him. He'd never said if a time existed when Jay didn't owe him some kind of obedience. Rude to ask, though, and Jay might not be allowed to answer anyway.

She crawled out from under the covers, instantly missing the warmth, and pulled her abandoned robe around her. Sixty degrees, maybe. Shiver-worthy in the nude.

Jay pouted. "You're leaving me here alone?"

"I'm not taking you to the bathroom with me."

He exaggerated his sigh. "Fine, but I'm not waiting here."

He swung his legs out of bed on the far side and stood. Bare-assed, he bent over and snagged a pair of sweats.

He had a sinfully round butt for such a narrow frame. The long muscles of his back stretched as he leaned forward, the sides of his ass tightening, the muscles of his thighs rotating out. *Mmmm.* If not for the damn cold, she'd feast on Jay's movements all day. Watching him warmed her right up.

Henry's words tickled her skin in an absent caress. If she initiated, Jay had permission to respond. A surprising, exhilarating, non-Friday power. Henry trusted her to treat his lover with care.

Jay snapped his waistband. "I know. You like what you see." He hooked his thumbs in his sweatpants and thrust his hips forward with a swagger. "I get that a lot. Women who can't keep their eyes off me."

"Yeah? What do you tell them, stud?"

Jay tilted his head. "That I'm a one-woman man."

Tension ratcheted and locked her in place. Click-click-click. Henry might be okay with Jay scoring one-night stands or whatever he'd meant last summer about packing a lunch. But that stood worlds apart from encouraging his lover to develop a long-term relationship with someone else. On fucking Valentine's Day of all days.

She forced a laugh. "I thought you were a one-*man* man."

She'd worried off and on for months Jay might fear she'd stolen Henry's attention from him. Not once had she considered Henry might need to worry about her stealing Jay.

"I am." His ease had to be real. Jay lacked the poker face to fake complete unconcern. "But that doesn't dissuade the ladies from looking."

He lowered his voice. "Some of them want to eat me up with a spoon. A spoon, Alice. I don't think they understand how sex works."

Oh thank God. He'd just played her longer than usual before giving the punch line.

Hysteria tinged her real, relieved laughter. She waved him off and sequestered herself in the bathroom. The cold water worked for now, but someone—Henry, probably—had planned ahead, lining up full buckets of water in case they needed them for tooth brushing or washing up or flushing the toilet.

She emerged to Jay heading in her direction carrying a tray.

"Henry says we're having brunch in bed. Too cold in the kitchen." He waggled his eyebrows. "We can shut in the heat in the bedroom."

"Does he need—"

"No, thank you, Alice." Henry, coming around the corner in pajamas and a robe, followed Jay down the hall. "All's well in hand. Back to bed, my dear."

She scurried in the doorway ahead of Jay and pulled the covers halfway back before climbing in and thrusting her legs beneath. The extra blankets and her two companions would make it snuggly and warm in short order.

"Whatever you made, it smells fantastic," she called to Henry.

"A bit of a mix," he said, shutting the door behind him. "It seemed best to use up the items in the refrigerator as much as possible, in the event the electricity remains off long."

He and Jay settled themselves on either side of her and pulled the covers up. Henry handed her a plate and fork.

"Are you kidding me?" Christ on a cracker. "A bit of a mix" in

Henry-speak meant enormous omelets with ham and cheese and peppers alongside a stack of blueberry-banana pancakes.

"You made all this without the stove?" The blueberries were *arranged*. Heart shapes. Jay's plate confirmed it. Every pancake bore a blueberry heart.

"I find creativity distracts one from the cold. And a camp stove is still a stove. A finicky one, yes, but still a stove."

They stuffed themselves with little talk beyond her and Jay's thanks and compliments to the chef, which Henry demurred with customary grace. Afterward, without discussion or direction, she and Jay carried the trays to the kitchen. Henry had done the cooking. The cleanup belonged to them.

The morning's nonsexual behavior continued after brunch, despite their silent mutual decision to remain warm by huddling naked in bed. She hadn't opened the overnight bag she'd brought for anything more than her toothbrush.

Henry made a single phone call, to check on the situation with Mr. Nagel, and reported the super expected a boiler replacement tomorrow if the city cleared the roads. Setting the phone down, he picked up a book from his nightstand. He removed his bookmark, laid it aside, and suggested she and Jay might entertain themselves with their cell phones.

Jay bounded out of bed to fetch them and came back insisting he was cold. He seemed plenty warm when he rolled under the covers alongside her and handed over her phone. Making few calls, he sent a slew of texts rescheduling regular courier runs. She checked work messages.

They lay side by side, hip to hip, elbows knocking as they played games (mostly Jay) and followed news of the snowstorm blanketing the region (mostly Alice).

Much as she enjoyed the time together, the lack of sexual tension struck her as strange. She lay naked in Henry's bed, snug between his hip and Jay's, and it felt platonic. Comfortably so. Like when she and Ollie were young and she'd take her little sister by the hand, both of them in their jammies, and they'd climb into their parents' bed while lightning and thunder rode the prairie.

Today the storm was snow, and the prairie the coast, and her parents and sister were Henry and Jay. Like a family. Where she belonged.

Special circumstances, that was all. What was the saying about houseguests starting to smell after three days? She'd been here half a day, and they'd slept for most of it. Besides, she'd bet Henry incapable of making a guest feel unwelcome in his home.

By midafternoon, Jay's fidgeting became all-out distraction. Inactivity made him restless. He hopped out of bed every ten minutes to stare out the window and give a report.

"Still snowing. Dunno where they're gonna plow it all."

"You know that red SUV that always parks by the corner? Completely covered."

"Kids. With a sled. We should go out. I bet we could get a snowball fight going."

His exuberance for the idea of playing in the snow died quick.

"We'd take too long to warm up properly afterward, my boy. Surely the snow will be waiting for you Saturday, when we might expect to have heat again."

Henry's gentle denial helped, but his offer to read to them sealed the deal.

Jay hurled himself under the covers at full speed, kissing Alice with giddy affection as she laughed.

"Henry has the best reading voice," he confided.

Story time. Okay. The adapted Kama Sutra for gay boys? Erotic poetry, probably. No, Jay was horny enough. He didn't need encouragement.

Something sweeter. Love talk. A Valentine's Day seduction she should distance herself from.

"Mmm. Thank you, my boy. I suspect you may be biased, however. As you've so much energy to burn, run and fetch the hurricane lanterns from the kitchen, please, and then settle yourself with Alice while I select something suitable."

Well, that decided that. If Henry planned to fill Jay's ears with Shakespearean sonnets or some other classical love poetry, she'd have to sit and listen. She'd call attention to her discomfort if she tried leaving now.

Jay came back with the lanterns. The old-fashioned style and soft yellow glow suited Henry's design sensibilities. Beneath the covers they were modern, battery-powered models rather than open flames. Much safer. That suited Henry, too.

The sun hadn't set yet—her phone showed just past four—but the sky presented an unforgiving gray, and night would fall soon enough at this time of year.

"Settling," as Jay defined it, involved piling the pillows at the center of the headboard, lying back against them, and pulling her between his legs. She leaned against his chest, her head tucked beneath his chin. Arms draped around her waist, he rubbed her stomach.

She resigned herself to listening to romantic declarations on a day she should've left to Henry and Jay alone. She'd tried apologizing to Jay, and he wasn't having it. If she tried to apologize to Henry, he'd say something gracious and ask probing questions and she'd blurt something stupid like "What am I to you?"

Her best bet would be to keep quiet, not ruin Jay's holiday, and watch Henry for the slightest sign to make herself scarce.

Staying focused while Henry walked around naked demanded more concentration than she managed to muster. Despite the chill, he offered plenty to look at when the book he returned with didn't block his assets.

Henry sat beside them, adjusted the covers and the lantern, and leaned back against the pillows. "Lovely work, Jay, thank you. Shall we begin?"

They both agreed he should. Her body rocked as Jay snuggled them closer to Henry. She wasn't sure what she expected Henry to say next, but it wasn't anything close to what he did say.

"This book came to me through my mother's mother. My mother read it to me many times before entrusting it to me." He opened the plain, dark green leather cover and turned the pages with care, smoothing them with his fingertips. "Chapter One: In Which We Are Introduced to Winnie-the-Pooh and Some Bees, and the Stories Begin."

Her shock leapt into his pause. A *children's* book?

Henry continued, his voice smooth and low. "Here is Edward Bear, coming downstairs now . . ."

Her surprise had just about faded by the time Winnie-the-Pooh discovered the bees and renewed itself when Henry sang Pooh Bear's little song in a beautiful soft baritone. If Henry's choice of book had shocked Jay, he hadn't given any hint.

Maybe they'd made reading together a regular thing. Or a special treat? Or—*or maybe we say fuck it to the questions and enjoy this.* Twenty years since anyone had read to her. Did she have to analyze everything to death?

Not this time. Analysis would wait. Enjoyment lived in the moment.

For the next hour or more, as the world outside the window grew dark, she lay silent in Jay's arms while Henry read to them from a beloved family heirloom. He even tilted the book to share the illustrations. She couldn't recall the last time she'd felt so peaceful and safe, her mind and body stilled, outside of Henry's company.

Don't question. Accept.

When Henry paused longer than it took to sip his water and reached for a bookmark, she stuffed unspoken pleas to continue down her throat. He tucked the book in the nightstand drawer, his broad back a temptation limned in lantern light. Turning, he pursed his lips and cupped her cheek.

"Don't look so sad, my dears. We're only halfway through. We must save something to read tomorrow, hmm?" He leaned in and kissed her, a slow, sweet nibble of her lips. Jay received the same treatment. "Time for a snack, at any rate."

He refused their assistance in the kitchen as he dressed. Something up his sleeve, no doubt. A Valentine's surprise for Jay. Biding his time, waiting for her to suggest she needed to go do something, anything, to keep her out of their bed for a few hours.

She excused herself to the bathroom and dawdled, spending more time than she needed to in the frigid air, planning to . . . *I have no idea.*

"Okay." She lowered her voice. "Analyze away." Best if neither of them heard her.

"Henry hasn't said anything. He might not have special plans. If he did, he might move them to another night. He expects me to stay, or he wouldn't have said he'd read to us tomorrow."

Situation defined, she squirmed at the answer the mirror reflected in the hurricane lantern's golden hue.

"It's me. I'm the one with the problem. This holiday makes me crazy. All that pressure and fake happiness. They're fine with me being here."

Her toothbrush stood beside Jay's and Henry's in the holder. She traced the raised roundness of the antique bronze chain climbing the Grecian urn design. Henry's decorating choices so often invited her touch. His artsy knickknacks. His soft linens. His Jay.

"Stop trying to outguess Henry. Trust he has this handled."

She grasped the lantern. Henry had taken the other to the kitchen. Every minute she stood here equaled one Jay spent alone in the dark. *Sorry, Jay.*

She returned to the bedroom calmer than she'd left. Jay took the lantern and disappeared into the bathroom.

Rolling over, she burrowed her face into Henry's pillow.

Losing track of time came easy in darkness. She dozed, her mind providing an image of Henry to accompany his scent in her nose. He beckoned to her, and joy tickled her ribs. She'd go to Henry if he called her, wouldn't she?

Her feet wouldn't move. She couldn't bring herself closer to Henry's image, and he wouldn't come to her. *She* had to be the one to step forward. But her feet wouldn't move.

Blood thrummed in her ears. Where was Jay? She needed him to push her. He'd make the first step possible, break her paralysis and bring her to Henry. *I need Jay.*

She shot up, the heat of the blankets suffocating, and shivered in the cooler air of the room, lost and disoriented. This wasn't her bedroom. This wasn't her bed.

She was alone.

Scrambling to free herself from the sheets and hunt down her men, she jumped as the door opened. The sudden light stung her eyes.

"Too bright? Sorry, Alice." Jay shielded the lantern with his hand.

Back from the bathroom or wherever else he'd been. In the kitchen, seeking out the privacy unavailable in Henry's bed?

Jealousy refused to rise to the bait. Their activities without her provoked happiness, not anxiety. What made Henry happy, what made Jay happy, those things intersected with her own contentment. Complementary. Odd. Warming.

"What're you doing without the covers?" Jay set the lantern on the nightstand. "That's silly. You'll get all cold."

Climbing onto the bed, he scooted in close. He surrounded her from the side, his legs folded up, one knee against her back and the other draped over her shins. Closing his arms around her shoulders, he dipped his mouth toward her ear.

"It's kinda obvious you're cold." His low voice teased. "I mean, I know I'm good, but I don't think I make your nipples hard from across the room in an instant."

At her laugh, he squeezed her shoulders and continued in a

louder, more thoughtful tone. "Henry might, though. I'll keep an eye on that."

"An eye on what, my boy?"

They turned their heads in unison toward the doorway. Henry came bearing a snack tray and the second lantern.

"Alice's nipples," Jay answered, with no discernible shame. She nudged his head with hers, and he pushed back.

"Has Alice agreed to be the subject of a study?" Henry balanced the tray and the lantern on the other nightstand.

The promise of a Henry-made snack had her leaning back for a glimpse. But he shed his robe and started on the pajama buttons, and no treat topped Henry. Solidly built, not so muscled as Jay, but an image that breathed masculine in her ears and other places. Broad chest. Strong arms.

Jay snickered. "We can hammer out details later. Maybe sooner. I'm gathering valuable data."

"Doesn't count," she murmured. Henry held her mesmerized, running his thumbs along the top edge of his pajama pants. "It wasn't from a flat start, and four feet isn't across the room. Science isn't your top field of study."

"Nope." He pecked her cheek, a brief kiss. "But you and Henry are. I'll just reenroll in this class every semester. That'll keep my GPA up."

His cock brushed her thigh on its way toward fullness. No surprise, what with watching Henry undress.

"It'll keep something up." She shifted her leg to rub against Jay. "I'm gathering valuable data here, too."

"I'm a fountain of valuable data."

Laughing, she buried her face in his neck. The mattress rocked. Henry closed in beside her, leaning across her shoulder, his hand moving in slow circles on her back.

"You want to be a fountain, my boy?" He wedged her body between his torso and Jay's. "I suspect we can arrange that."

The muscles in Jay's neck shifted under her cheek. Vibrations of almost subvocal whimpers tickled her as Henry kissed him.

"But first, a treat." Henry pulled away.

She followed his movement, the precise pivot, the beautiful slope through his shoulder blade as he reached for the tray on the nightstand. He presented them with a square red plate covered with a thin

layer of wax paper and a dozen chocolate-coated strawberries. Jay stretched across her knees to snatch one.

"Mind you don't make too much of a mess, my boy. The chocolate's just set."

Mouth full and moaning with appreciation, Jay nodded.

She hesitated. "You made those? Just now?"

"It's not so difficult, my dear. If the day weren't cold and powerless, we might have had liquid chocolate for other things." He handed off the plate to Jay, fingers brushing her arm, and she shivered at his touch. "As it is, hardening the shells seemed the better choice. Perhaps another day."

She didn't doubt his skills in the kitchen. Or the bedroom. *Yum.*

Her incredulity stemmed from the notion that he'd gone to the trouble. He could've bought them in advance from the party place in Coolidge Corner or half-a-dozen other shops within walking distance. Instead, standing in a cold, dim kitchen for the better part of an hour, he'd made a romantic Valentine's Day dessert himself.

Of course he did. That's why he's Henry.

"I apologize for the romantic trappings, Alice. I recognize your aversion to the . . . overblown falsity of the holiday, shall we say? But I cannot be faulted for the near candlelight in the room when the electricity is being finicky, can I?"

He winked and lowered his voice to a conspiratorial whisper. "And for all his bluster and charm, Jay is quite the romantic. A few sweet words and soft kisses, perhaps a special Valentine's Day dessert, and he'll tumble right into bed for me."

Jay looked up, accusingly, in mid-selection of another strawberry. "Lots of sweet words, thank you."

Sheer exaggeration. Henry could say one word—Jay's name, "bed," any of the thousands of words in the English dictionary. So long as Henry used the tone Jay's brain interpreted as lust or love or whatever he called it, he'd be naked and on his knees in two seconds, no question. As if she'd be any different with Henry seducing her.

Jay raised a strawberry and rubbed her lips. "Here, try it. You might like it, too."

She sucked the berry into her mouth and teased the tips of his fingers with her tongue. Sinfully sweet milk chocolate melted almost instantly in her mouth. A burst of sugary strawberry juice drenched her. Henry deserved thanks for his craftsmanship.

The hunger in his eyes stopped her. Why wasn't he kissing her, if he—

Unless I initiate. It's not Friday.

He'd laid out the rule for Jay this morning. He'd told her last fall he held himself to a higher standard, one even more important when he had no one else to enforce it.

"Have you tasted them yet?" Her voice seemed lower to her ears. She'd tried sultry with a boyfriend once and gotten laughter in return. She banished the memory, because Henry shook his head at glacial speed and locked his gaze to hers. Little more than a whisper emerged from her throat. "You should."

"Should I, sweet girl?" Curling his hand behind her head, he stroked her hair. "Do you know where I might find a sample?"

She pressed her mouth to his.

He nibbled at her lips, coaxed her mouth open, and thrust his tongue inside as if chasing the flavor of chocolate and strawberry. A season of growth, the freshness of summer in midwinter. "Mmm. A delicious suggestion, Alice. How thoughtful of you to offer."

A hand rose in her peripheral vision. Chocolate swept across her lips.

"You should have another." Jay's voice. Close. Intimate. The firm heat of his cock brushed her thigh. "I've been listening when you talk about science at lunch. One's not a good sample size, right?"

"Right," she whispered. "Excellent attention to detail, Jay."

His mouth touched her ear. "I'm a great listener when you're talking."

She sucked in the strawberry and its chocolate shell, twirling her tongue around Jay's fingers until he moaned. Drowning in the richness of the thick coating, she welcomed the splash of juice and sucked sugared drops from Jay's fingers.

Henry watched her. Her eyes. Her mouth. Jay's fingers.

Power consumed her. She licked her lips to savor the rush again.

"Another, Henry?" Her voice aspired to steadiness. Her body didn't make the effort.

Henry kissed her with more force. Pressing her back against Jay's warm chest, he seduced her with his tongue and tugged at her lip after. "Still delicious. Might it be impossible for our Alice to taste anything but sweet, my boy?"

"I can't say without more sampling. She'd tell me it's bad science."

"That's easily remedied, isn't it, Alice? You wouldn't want to teach Jay bad science, would you?" Henry shifted her easily, pulling her to his chest with a light touch and rolling her in his lap to face Jay.

She wiggled to assess the situation.

Henry laid his hand against her stomach, holding her firm. "An experiment of your own?"

Hard and heated, he thrust against her back. He swept her hair aside as he kissed her neck. Fuck, he delivered suction like he meant to pull her into his body and trap her there, the intensity a painful, pleasurable delirium.

Jay seized the moment to capture her mouth.

Kissing Jay back harder, she took control with firm lips and a stroking tongue. *She* decided when the kiss was over.

Henry paused his nuzzling at her neck. "What conclusions can you draw, my dears?"

Jay, biting another strawberry, offered an enthusiastic *mmm*.

"Jay's just as sweet," she affirmed.

"A challenge to your own sweetness for the crown, my girl?"

"Not a challenge." Henry sucked hard below her ear. She squirmed. He thrust against her back. She had to catch her breath, and Jay's attention fastened to her breasts.

"A mutual admiration society," she finished. "You should taste Jay, too. For comparison."

"Would you like that, Alice?"

"Oh yeah." She moaned the words, but sounding needy didn't bother her now. Not when Henry stretched out his arm and pulled Jay to him with a hand on the back of his neck.

"Alice says you have a beautiful taste, my boy."

With careful wriggling, she twisted sideways and slipped partway out of their embrace. Leaving her hips between theirs in Henry's lap, she toppled to her elbows for a better view.

Henry let her get away with it—a clear sign he wasn't strictly enforcing rules tonight.

He teased Jay with brief, fluttering movements. A kiss to his upper lip. The lower. The corner of his mouth, first one and then the other. A tug with his teeth. His tongue tracing the seam.

Jay whined, an urgent plea.

Henry nuzzled Jay's cheek. He dragged his hand across Jay's shoulder blades. "Open for me, my boy. Let me in."

He returned his lips to Jay's for a deep kiss, one lasting forever, renewing itself again and again.

She leaned her weight on her left elbow and idly stroked her belly with her right hand. The soft touch, up and down, grew firmer and spread until she found herself fondling her breast and pinching her nipple.

Which was, of course, the moment Henry and Jay ended their kiss and turned toward her. She flushed, fingers stopping in mid-motion.

"How *very* thoughtful, Alice." Henry's voice conveyed approval. "You see what a lovely treat she has for you, Jay?"

Jay slipped his legs free of their tangled bodies and lay along her left side, dislodging her elbow and leaving her torso flat on the bed. His mouth hovered above her breast. "For me?"

She let her fingers fall away.

He closed his lips over her nipple. His light, steady rhythm echoed the thump of need between her legs. Humming along together like precision-machined components. Gotta respect the master mechanic who'd put them together. Theirs had stilled, silent and intent, his hand warm on her calf and a fleeting smile crossing his face.

What is he . . .

Henry lowered her legs to the bed and stretched across Jay. On his return, he carried a berry to her lips.

"I believe I'll need another taste, Alice," he murmured. "Will you indulge me?"

Eyes on his, she nibbled at the chocolate shell. The sweet fruit. The tips of Henry's fingers. Chocolate melted as she dined. She sucked Henry's fingers clean and cracked the sticky-sweet dessert drying on her lips.

Jay tugged hard at her breast, an unexpected surge in his rhythm, and she arched into his pull, eager for more. Henry descended on her mouth, sucking away strawberry sugar and melted chocolate, dipping within to feast.

A hand cupped the inside of her thigh. Jay's, his fingers not so long as Henry's but equally firm. The pressure spread her legs wider. Jay squeezed her thigh as his leg tangled over the top of hers and he thrust, his cock rubbing low on her hip.

A second hand. Not Jay's.

Henry curved his hand over her breast, squeezing in a slow rhythm to match the stroke of his tongue against hers. She wanted him closer, but he kept his distance.

She squirmed, raising her hips and sliding her feet along the sheets as she struggled to touch him the way she touched Jay. To turn her aching anticipation into confirmation of his hard desire. Wet, needy heaviness pulsed between her legs.

Jay's hand migrated from her thigh to her sex, covering her, unmoving.

Henry kissed her jaw. "Will you offer Jay a true taste of your sweetness, Alice?"

The fingers covering her teased her lips. Rocking her hips, she tried to coax them into a firmer touch. Begged them to enter and give her some small measure of relief.

"Strawberry juice is a poor imitation for the wetness he wants coating his tongue, my girl."

Jay ground himself against her hip. He lifted his mouth from her breast, anticipation plain on his face and impossible to deny. "Please, Jay."

She floated with the sensations. Jay's mouth and fingers between her legs. Henry's mouth on her neck, his hand at her breasts. In no time at all her hips rocked steadily with the motion of Jay's tongue. Long, flat licks and a quick suck of her clit repeated with building speed and intensity.

"My lovely, lovely Alice." Henry augmented the pleasures of Jay's fixed attention with murmurs in her ear. "Will you come for Jay? Flood his mouth with your satisfaction? He wants dearly to please you. For me, my girl? I want you drenched and open when I take you tonight."

Sharp breaths burned her lungs, turning to pleasurable cries as they left her mouth. Intensity rippled through her, climax swift and sudden at Henry's urging.

She lay boneless afterward, shuddering with the heat of Jay's breaths across her clit a stimulating echo of his performance.

Henry pressed a kiss to her forehead and called Jay's name.

Anticipation embraced her. Fuck yeah, he deserved a reward. The sweep of Jay's matted hair departed from her slick thighs.

The bed shifted. A drawer opened. The nightstand. Condoms. First Jay, and then Henry, because hadn't he said he'd take her tonight?

But no eager, wiggling Jay topped her. No desperately thrusting Jay. The bed dipped to her left. Jay, his face inches away, his mouth wet and shining, lay calm at her side. Had he come on his own, and she'd missed it, wrapped up in her orgasm?

"Kiss?" he asked.

She stretched toward him, and he closed the gap. Even his gentle kiss held no hint of urgent need. Usually his anxious, eager attitude forced Henry to rein him in. But when their lips parted, he snuggled at her side, seeming content to wait.

Before she found words to tease an answer free, Henry rolled into the cradle of her hips. His hard cock slid between her lips. Not entering.

He moved over her sex with steady patience. Her labia parted easily, gripping him with a wet squelch. The sound of her body wanting his.

"You offered Jay a taste, Alice." Henry settled his arms to either side of her, one sandwiched between her body and Jay's. His weight fell lightly atop her. "Will you offer me more, sweet girl?"

His coaxing tone had her raising her knees before she'd even answered the question.

"Will you offer me your hidden depths, Alice?" He rubbed her clit with the head of his cock, bumping and catching with only a thin latex barrier between them. She tilted her hips toward him, a silent plea for his entrance.

"Yes, Henry. Please. I need to feel you."

The compulsion to phrase her answer as anything more than yes lacked logic. Need demanded his cock inside her. Feelings, beyond the physical sensation, had nothing to do with it. But his soft smile in return made her miss a breath.

"My magnificent girl. You please me so . . . very . . . much." He slid inside her as he spoke, one slow thrust to his full depth, her body open and welcoming.

She gripped his back with her legs. He took his time, slow thrusts as he watched her face. He leaned in to kiss her at intervals she couldn't predict. Satisfying a need of his own, maybe, or reading cues in her face. Did his purpose matter when he made her feel so comfortable with him?

"Two nights in a row," he murmured. "What a lovely gift you are, Alice. A special treat."

Three, unless he planned to reschedule their night tomorrow. Three nights in a row with Henry and Jay. *Don't get used to it.*

Even the nagging voice in her head couldn't touch her arousal now. Need wasn't a bonfire or a live wire or a storm raging in her. This grew gradually deeper, as if she'd dipped her toes in and found the water inviting. Arousal flowed up her calves and her thighs. Over her hips and waist. Deeper and deeper until she breathed her last rebellion and sank to the bottom.

She waited, breathless, her body rocking. Henry slid in and out, his mouth at her face, her neck, her collarbone. Eager for his lips and tongue, she bared more of her throat.

"That's it. You're almost there, Alice. I feel it in you, your body tightening, the tension where you grip me, the slick wash of your excitement flowing out around me with every push." He parted her hair, fingers lying over her ear. "Will you share this with me tonight? Come for me so sweetly?"

Palm cupping her jaw, he rubbed his thumb over her cheek. "You needed to feel me, my dear. Do you feel me? Will you let me feel you?"

Yes, yes, want to feel this, warm and tender and so good.

She might've told him so if she'd had the breath. But her throat tightened. Frozen in place, her chest strained. Her body coiled with energy in the darkness at the bottom of the water.

His hand gripped hers and pulled with strong fingers that wouldn't let go. She surged to the surface with desperate need, thrusting her head into the bright light above the water and calling his name.

Her shudders lasted longer, clenching around Henry's cock, hard and unmoving. He didn't chase a climax of his own. Did he find contentment feeling hers?

He kissed her and traced her cheekbone. Poised. Controlled. Waiting for her to settle, maybe. For her body to relax, for the last of her orgasm to slip away.

"All right, Alice?"

"Better than." Lazy satisfaction thickened her voice.

"Good." He kissed the bridge of her nose before facing Jay, who lay snug at her left side.

"Such wonderful patience you have tonight, my boy." Henry nuzzled Jay's cheek with his nose. "It ought to be rewarded, hmm?"

He kissed Jay, slow and lingering. Buried inside her, his cock throbbed.

She curved her hips to bask in the fullness. A good feeling. Special, to be part of the connection between Henry and Jay, to feel

Henry's desire for his lover. Jay needed to feel that. For all his flirting and sexual bravado, he lacked confidence underneath.

Henry gave Jay approval and unconditional acceptance within boundaries he needed. What he thought she needed, though . . . Six and a half months, and certainty eluded her. But she'd grown attached.

Emptiness entered her when Henry pulled out.

He rose and knelt between her spread thighs. Laying a hand on her hip, he offered a soothing caress before he stripped off the condom. Beautifully hard, his cock stood thick and dark, flushed with excitement. The thin ridges of veins formed a raised blueprint begging for her tongue to trace his lines and curves.

Maybe he'd used an unlubricated condom to avoid unpleasant aftertastes and he'd let her watch Jay suck him off. If Jay didn't come from that—he might, as much as he enjoyed it—Henry would give him manual assistance. Jay would come like a fountain then. Or Henry might let Jay take her afterward. He'd left her well satisfied, but she wouldn't turn Jay away.

Unhurried, Henry accepted a tissue from Jay. No commands, no praise, not for either of them. Just his silent attention as she and Jay lay on their backs side by side. Shifting to straddle Jay's leg, Henry leaned forward and planted his weight on one hand between her shoulder and Jay's. He tossed the tissue-wrapped condom in the bedside wastebasket, freeing his other hand to plant on the far side of Jay.

Henry knelt over Jay on hands and knees, their faces aligned. The intense kiss that followed didn't surprise her. But the slow lowering of Henry's hips as his legs stretched out. The way his cock brushed Jay's and both jumped. The low groan when Henry's weight settled on Jay. Those things were new. And not so much surprising as arousing.

Maybe she ought to have slipped away to give them privacy. But with Henry lying atop Jay and their mouths fused, she couldn't force herself to retreat an inch. She rolled on her side and propped herself up for a better view.

Henry's ass flexed as he ground his hips down on Jay's. His shoulders curved over and around Jay's body. Elbows holding his weight, Henry brushed Jay's hair off his forehead and traced the tips of Jay's ears with his fingertips.

Jay caressed Henry's flanks and moved up to grip his biceps. Henry nudged Jay's head with his own and descended on the offered throat he received in return, licking and sucking with surprising gentleness. When his mouth wasn't occupied, Henry crooned to Jay with patient, sweet words.

"My good, good boy. You've been working so hard to please me, Jay. And you have. Beyond even my expectations."

Jay squirmed beneath Henry, his hips rocking, thighs spreading, letting Henry's weight fall more securely over his groin. Not so different from her behavior.

"You've thrown yourself into your tasks with such joy, formed a beautiful new bond with Alice, hmm? It pleases me that you play so well together, my sweet boy."

Aside from Jay's constant stream of whimpers and moans and whines of Henry's name, of course. She tended toward silence. Although that seemed to be changing, the more time she spent in Henry's bed. *Must be Jay's example.* She stifled a giggle.

"You want more tonight, don't you, Jay?" Henry punctuated his words with a thrust of his hips, and Jay thrust up in reply. "What I've given Alice tonight? What I've saved for you, my boy?"

Holy fuck.

Henry and Jay kissed in front of her often. Jay'd blown Henry once in her presence. But she'd never been privy to more.

"Yes." Jay's answer came with a quiet whine. "Please, Henry."

Henry kissed him, slow and gentle. "Yes. You were eager for it, weren't you? That's why you emptied the nightstand."

He'd done what? Beyond Henry's body, the sheets resembled a makeshift workspace skewed by their movements. Small packets of tissues, plain and moistened. A hand towel. A black bottle. Lube, likely, though the angle obscured the label.

Beside her, their tangled legs, their subtly shifting hips. Flat torsos pressed together. Henry's strong back and arms. Their faces, intimate, touching.

"Yes, Henry. I want . . ." Jay's glance caught her gaze. He put his mouth to Henry's ear, hidden on the far side. His voice rumbled, low and indistinct.

Maybe her first instinct had been right. Selfishness motivated her impolite behavior. Her desperate desire to stay wasn't worth making Jay uncomfortable or inhibited.

Henry moaned. A quiet, almost hopeless sound.

"My sweet, sweet boy." He shook his head, a slight twitch. "I fear it's not so simple as that. But we know, hmm? And perhaps eventually we'll both see that wish realized." Henry rubbed his cheek against Jay's and kissed him again, a demanding kiss.

The moment Jay submitted fluttered in her belly as if he'd been her. Unhappy tension flowing out, happy tension flowing in. Henry's magic touch.

"I want you focused on *your* need, Jay. Relax for me. Think about what you feel. What you want." Henry pushed himself up and back, until he sat on his heels between Jay's legs. "How it pleases me to take you."

Streaks of pre-come dampened their stomachs. Jay watched Henry with absolute trust. Henry scratched his fingernails across Jay's abdomen and down, parting to avoid his cock. Too much stimulation, maybe. He teased up and down Jay's thighs.

Torn between such a beautiful vision and her concern for Jay's feelings, she wandered in an unfamiliar maze. Sought refuge in analysis. Jay's parted lips, his whimpering pleas and intent eyes, didn't scream upset or inhibited or embarrassed. Not even when Henry's hand slipped lower. He had to be teasing Jay the way he'd teased her last month, fingers stroking Jay's ass. He moved his wrist in slow circles.

Analysis ceded ground to arousal. Excitement quaked in her thighs. Merged watching with being. The phantom touch of Henry's fingers. In Jay's silence, she found Henry watching her.

"I will not attempt to force you to stay and watch, Alice." His voice rolled smooth and deep, a bottomless sea. "But Jay and I would both enjoy it very much if you did."

They wanted her to stay. Both of them. *Yes, yes, please.*

"I want to stay." Her answer emerged soft and breathy and wholly unlike her.

Henry beckoned her to him. She rose on her knees, and he pulled her closer. He kissed her, hard, nuzzling her throat afterward. "My lovely girl. Stay with me here a moment, hmm? See how beautiful Jay is in his need."

He lowered his hand and pushed Jay's thighs farther apart. Jay raised his knees.

His sudden motion exposed the tiny ring of flesh that hardly seemed an opening at all. If she were Jay, she'd be extremely fucking nervous right about now.

But Jay flexed his feet against the sheets and rocked his hips. His ribs expanded and contracted to the growing rhythm of his breath. Eager anticipation lit his eyes. Catching her gaze, he smiled and nodded as if to encourage her.

His enthusiasm emboldening, she trailed her hand down Jay's thigh when Henry leaned away.

Jay hummed. He tipped his hips upward, his cock swaying across his abs, and his ass tightened. She pressed harder, a light scratch like Henry had used, and Jay's ass lifted off the bed.

"Oh, *very* good, Alice." Henry kissed her temple.

Pleasure rushed down her body.

Taking good care of Jay, paying special attention to him, would always earn Henry's approval.

"Do that again for me, please, my sweet girl."

She swept her fingers down Jay's thigh toward his groin with a light touch and dragged them back with the heavier one. Jay raised up, chasing the pressure. Henry slipped the edge of the hand towel beneath him.

"Silicone lube," he murmured. "Terrible for the sheets. Excellent, however, for mimicking the slickness you produce effortlessly, my dear."

He unscrewed the cap on the black bottle and squeezed until the pads of his right thumb and first two fingers gleamed with an oily sheen. He rubbed them together. Thin and smooth, the liquid bore no scent.

Jay whimpered, watching Henry's fingers move, his hips shifting and straining.

"Gently, my boy," Henry chided. His lubed fingers pressed against the center of Jay's ass, the sheen making puckered flesh shine deep pink. Jay tried to push forward, but Henry slipped his fingers to the side, stroking around but not on.

Sympathy for Jay's frustrated whine engulfed her. That desperate need, the waiting Henry demanded of them, made sex so much better. No dispute. But being suspended in that moment, Christ. She leaned forward, silently urging Henry to give Jay what he craved.

Henry caressed Jay's thigh with his left hand, a slow and soothing touch. His right index finger rubbed a tightening spiral and pushed. His wrist turned in a slow circle as his finger disappeared, knuckle by knuckle. His other fingers curled in a fist, knuckles brushing Jay's skin, thumb rubbing alongside. Jay sighed, a happy sound, a relieved sound, even though Henry hadn't thrust.

The first sensation of fullness. When what she wanted was a hard cock, but what she had was her fingers. Get aroused and needy enough, even the substitution came as a welcome relief from clenching and feeling nothing in return.

At Henry's first slow thrust, Jay rolled his hips and pushed forward.

"You want more, my boy? Is that what you want to tell me?" Henry smiled at Jay's nod. "So sweetly impatient."

Henry circled his wrist again, wider. This time when he slid his finger inside, a second joined it.

Jay groaned. His legs tipped outward.

Henry's hand rested, unmoving, with Jay's flesh stretched around the base of his index and middle fingers.

She shifted closer, vaginal walls tugging at her. Did Henry's fingers feel the same to Jay? Would they feel as good to her if she let Henry touch her this way? The pain she feared didn't show on Jay's face.

Jay grinned, his eyes heavy-lidded, his cock bobbing against his stomach. His knee stood inches from where she knelt, leaning forward as Henry put on a show with his fingers. The swift beat of desire urging her on, she ducked her head upside down and kissed the inner underside of Jay's knee, sucking at the soft flesh. Hips thrusting, he groaned when his ass clenched around Henry's fingers.

Henry raised his left hand from Jay's thigh and tipped her chin. His eyes met hers.

"Playful," he murmured. "Lovely." He trailed his fingers over her skin and away. "Did you like that, my boy?"

"Yes, Henry." Jay's answer overlapped the question.

"Alice must be quite enamored of your beauty, hmm? Wanting to see your reactions to her touch? To mine?"

Henry rotated his hand until his wrist faced upward. He moved with such a short stroke it seemed more a flexing of his wrist than a thrust, but he repeated it twice. His fingers had to be doing more inside. Jay's cock stiffened hard enough to reveal every delicate line beneath straining flesh, and he whined as he dug his heels into the bed.

"But you don't want to come so quickly, do you?"

Jay shook his head with vigor. "No, Henry. With you, please."

He knew the answer would be yes, or he trusted it would be. A certainty she shared.

Henry withdrew his fingers and reached for a wet wipe. He cleaned his right hand and tossed the used wipe in the bedside trash can, delivering a thorough kiss to Jay, since he had to lean over him to make the toss.

Settling back, Henry lowered his ass to the bed and folded his legs to either side.

Jay raised his knees until his feet bumped his ass, which tipped upward.

Henry picked up the lube bottle and squeezed a few drops over Jay. The liquid coated his opening, pink and shining, eager and pulsing.

With his left hand, Henry gripped his cock at the base. To steady himself for penetration? To rein in his excitement?

She struggled to control her own.

Henry drizzled lube on the top of his cock and laid the bottle aside. Was he . . . he was. He teased Jay with the head of his cock, rubbing it against Jay's asshole, lubed and waiting for him. No condom with Jay. They'd be bare to each other. He might expect that of her someday.

Henry had shown her his disease-free test results and Jay's the day she'd signed the contract. Their tests had been dated two weeks earlier. She'd thought it coincidence. But now, understanding the detail he put into planning their nights together . . . he must've been expecting something. She'd had a battery of tests that week to fulfill his requirement for proof of her clean status.

Jay clutched at the sheets. The longer Henry teased without entering, the greater Jay's focus. He stilled, and Henry hummed approval.

He'd allowed oral sex without protection. But he hadn't once suggested fucking her without a condom, though he knew she used birth control pills. An extra precaution, or a concession to her comfort level? Or something he shared only with Jay.

Fascination pulled at her as Henry pushed forward. Such a tiny ring of muscle. The way it stretched around the head of Henry's bare cock seemed impossible, though she knew her own body capable of the same. But to be bare. *Naked.*

A shiver darted along her spine. She'd never experienced a relationship like that. Never trusted like that. But Jay allowed it. Didn't question it. Welcomed it.

"Beautiful, my boy. Tilt your hips for me." Henry grunted, his cock edging deeper. "Good, just like that."

Henry still gripped his cock. His fingers squeezed down tight, and he breathed out in an amused huff. "Impatient, are you, my boy? Or only proud, hmm? Proud of how tightly you hold me? Of how much pleasure you give me? Of how much you have yet to give?"

He had a lot left to give. Henry wasn't even half-buried in Jay yet. He pulled back, not far, and pushed forward again.

Jay moaned. He squirmed against the bed, his ass wriggling from side to side as if trying to pull Henry deeper.

His eyes were closed, his neck extended with exquisite tension. He breathed hard. The corners of his mouth twitched into a smile as Henry moved. Naked adoration softened his face, sculpting slender Jay-angles into open curves bent on Henry. He turned the same face on her, and warmth enveloped her as if he'd wrapped her in a hug.

He winked. "I'm fantastic, right, Alice?"

"Beautiful," she agreed. "Like Henry said."

Jay wasn't embarrassed to have her here, and he didn't have an ounce of selfishness in him. He took pride in sharing this with her, letting her see Henry claim him this way.

Henry still hadn't given him a full thrust. Hell, he hadn't even laid a hand on Jay's cock. But Jay's cock stood stiff, the ridge along the underside sharply defined and pre-come pooling in a wet patch on his stomach.

She wanted to run her tongue up that ridge, close her mouth over the head of his cock and suck while Henry fucked him.

"Beautiful," she repeated, holding back a moan.

"Even more beautiful in a moment, isn't that so, my boy? You've been very good today. It's been a wonderful day. You deserve to enjoy every inch I can give you."

"Yes, please, Henry." Jay pleaded with eyes wide and soft. "I can take it."

"I know you can, my sweet boy. I know." Henry rested his hands against the backs of Jay's thighs. "Nice and relaxed, Jay. Push for me."

Push? It sounded counterproductive, but Jay nodded.

Henry's low moan made her shiver as his cock slipped steadily inside. He rested flush against Jay's body. Neither moved beyond the rise and fall of their chests as they breathed.

Henry brought his arms around Jay's knees and ran firm fingers up and down the outside of Jay's thighs. "All right?"

Jay nodded. His smile became a smirk. "I give it two cocks up so far."

She stifled a laugh.

Henry shook his head, smiling. "My joyful comedian."

He pulled back and gave a slow thrust. Jay rocked with the motion, his cock stiff and his breath short.

"Let's see if I can't make you too distracted to joke, hmm?"

From the eager tilt of his hips, Jay didn't seem averse to the idea. Henry thrust again, deep and slow.

"Still . . . enough . . . breath . . . to joke."

Henry glanced her way. "My dear girl, would you be so kind as to put your lovely tongue in Jay's mouth? He clearly needs something to suck on."

She let her laugh out as she lay beside Jay and rolled up on her side. She kissed his shoulder first, a soft touch, and nuzzled his cheek, imitating Henry's treatment of him. She whispered to him, a tease in her voice. "You want my tongue, Jay?"

"If that's what I can get," he quipped. He moaned, his body shifting. Henry must've thrust again.

"I'm still hearing jokes, Alice." Henry's voice, too, teased. "Perhaps a more thorough application is in order?"

Seeking out Jay's lips, she sealed hers against them. He opened for her the instant her tongue touched his mouth. She tried to kiss him with the deep gentleness Henry often used. Jay moaned into her mouth, but his body didn't move. That moan belonged to her.

She kept up the kiss as the mattress swayed. Henry's arm brushed her breasts. His breath warmed her ear. "Beautifully done, my dear girl."

Shifting away, she accepted a kiss from Henry before settling in beside them.

He kissed Jay. He smoothed Jay's hair back, the shaggy black mop that never seemed to get cut but never seemed to grow, either. Their hips rocked. The muscles in Henry's ass flexed and released. He didn't lift far, didn't pull out much. Slow and easy. A nice, lazy fuck.

"I'm so very pleased with you, Jay." The low, intimate murmur came from Henry as he nuzzled Jay's ear. "My magnificent boy. Do you know how special you are to me?"

Their mouths met again, briefly. Jay tipped his head back. Henry's lips came down on the center of Jay's throat, sucking gently. Jay whimpered.

"Love you, Henry." His breath hitched. "I love you."

Jay tilted his head sideways, his face clearly visible. Beautiful. Terrifying.

How could he believe so deeply? Give without holding anything back. As if he didn't have the slightest fear. As if the feeling encompassed more than body chemistry.

Jay was either the stupidest person she knew or the bravest.

He's not stupid.

She shivered.

The men's chests separated as Henry rose over Jay, his arms extended and locked. He captured Jay's full attention. "As I love you, my boy."

Relief rushed through her. Jay hadn't been left without a response. She needed the certainty that Henry wouldn't do that to him, though she couldn't say why.

"Unconditionally, sweet boy." Henry lowered himself by millimeters. "With all that I am."

Their lips touched, and she almost looked away. The moment seemed so private.

Love.

Henry kissing Jay with slow, patient attention. Jay running his hands along Henry's sides, cuddling him close. They weren't mid-climax, throwing out words without hearing them. They weren't post-coital yet. Chemicals flooding the body failed as a satisfactory explanation.

This was making love. Sex wasn't just fucking for them. Henry's slow movements. The way his eyes fixated on Jay's face. His soft encouragement.

He'd done those things with *her*. She couldn't get a handle on the idea, couldn't find the edges and pick it up and examine it and see where it fit.

Did he mean to give her this? Her missing pieces, the way he provided unconditional love and boundaries for Jay. He'd pored over her contract answers. He understood she'd had sexual partners but never like this, never a lover. When he touched her, did he imitate the love he and Jay shared because he thought she needed it? Showing her what love looked like. Felt like.

For his effort, he received only sex he could find with any partner. Any partner who'd accept Jay, too. They rocked together, Henry pumping harder, Jay emitting a series of stuttering groans.

Henry's reasoning remained an undefined quantity making her heart race and her body tremble. Asking him . . . no. Too much like caring. She'd always handled her love life clean and neat. Short and sweet.

This arrangement centered on hot sex, not caring. And sometimes the chance to see two guys who happened to love each other also having hot sex.

Henry flexed his upper back, shoulder blades rippling with every thrust from his hips. Steady. Powerful. Capable of making Jay babble nonsense syllables and urgent whines.

If Henry wanted more from her, he'd order her to provide it on their Friday nights. If he told her to do something, she'd do it. If she couldn't, she'd use her safeword. What could he possibly need from her that he couldn't demand?

Nothing.

No reason to ask, then. Her panic lifted, the release of pressure leaving her light-headed. Off-balance and unsteady, she wanted Henry's touch, and Jay's, to ground her. To feel, for a minute, what made Jay declare his love and Henry respond in kind.

But they were wrapped up in each other. Jay's moans and whimpers gained volume as he got close, and Henry urged him on.

"That's it, Jay. Show me how much you love this." He thrust in short, rapid bursts. His voice became a low, guttural growl. "Show Alice, my sweet boy."

Body shuddering, Jay groaned. His surging hips lifted Henry with him.

"You want her to know, don't you? How you love this feeling?" Dropping his head, Henry buried his face in Jay's neck. His back arched in a bridge, hips pushing his cock deep. "How you come like a fountain when I'm deep inside you?"

Jay's cock lay half-hidden in the shadow of his upraised leg. As his groan turned into a tripping chant of *love you love you love you*, he came hard across his stomach and chest and to the edge of his jaw.

Two tiny streaks of fluid landed below Jay's right ear. Temptation skewered her, even when Henry in her peripheral vision closed the gap between himself and Jay. When his hips gave a final pump and he growled low and long with his own release. She zipped forward and licked Jay's face clean.

Eyes wide, he turned toward her, just missing her nose. She froze. She'd acted without analyzing. Without questioning.

Jay laughed and kissed her cheek. Henry raised his head, his gaze falling on them both.

She didn't want to steal Jay's experience, but she wanted to borrow it for a little while. To feel things and express them as easily as Jay seemed to. Unfiltered. Shut off the part of her never satisfied without determining how and why.

Jay didn't need those things. He didn't ask for them. He accepted. Felt. Laughed. Loved.

She closed her eyes. Maybe she could imitate the way Henry imitated with her. She could be Jay. Easy as pie. Jay. Free of worries, because Henry took care of him. At home in Henry's bed every night. *He tells me he loves me whenever I want to hear it. I love him back. It's a real thing. I believe in it. I feel it.*

She opened her eyes and pierced Henry with every scrap of Jay-feeling she could muster. Trust. Adoration. Love.

His eyes widened. Disbelief, maybe? He didn't want to play along?

Stop thinking. Be Jay. Feel.

She tried to deepen her belief, to allow herself to hope she'd gotten this right.

Henry groaned like a dam breaking. His lunge pushed her flat to the bed, her right shoulder clamped in his left hand. He pulled her in until she lay pinned so tightly beside Jay his ribs compressed hers when he breathed.

"My brave girl." Henry's low growl made her quake. "My Alice."

He devoured her, his mouth hard and hungry, and she let him control the kiss because she could hardly keep up. She whimpered, breathless, a needy, submissive sound. He lifted his mouth long enough for a harsh, guttural command: *"Breathe."*

She took a frenzied breath.

He refastened his lips to hers. Splayed across Jay's body, he half-covered her chest with his own. He pressed her deep into the mattress, keeping a fierce grip on her shoulder.

She trembled on the verge of something like a climax, but sex seemed somehow secondary.

Henry gentled the kiss and rubbed her shoulder as she shivered and moaned. He gave her one last kiss, an almost chaste brush of his lips on hers.

"It's all right, Alice," he murmured. "You're all right, my sweet girl."

She lay dazed as he kissed Jay's forehead and raised himself to his knees. His cock slipped free with Jay's sighing accompaniment.

Henry studied their bodies and made a wry declaration. "This requires much more than a washcloth."

No kidding. Drying ejaculate liberally coated his chest and Jay's, and he'd smeared some on her. Share and share alike.

Jay squirmed beside her, wriggling his arm free. Pushing it behind her back, he rolled her into a hug and squeezed. Words tumbled, rapid-fire, from his mouth. "That just makes it an extra-fantastic Valentine's Day, right, Alice? Making love with people who love us? It's worth the mess. I vote it the best ever. But next year—"

"Jay." Henry's quiet call halted the flow in an instant.

"Yes, Henry?"

Giddy, babbling Jay. Sweet Jay, who didn't have the slightest idea of the panic he'd inspired in her. She hadn't been in a relationship with anyone for Valentine's Day since college, and Adam had made a fucking production of it with that goddamn ring. They strangled the relationship between them in the months until he graduated. The day he'd gone for good had been a relief. She didn't want that memory in this bed, but her mind stormed along regardless, *no-no-no* as Adam produced that fucking velvet box.

"It's time for cleanup, Jay. Take the towel, please, and Alice and I will join you in a moment." Henry rubbed Jay's leg with short, quick motions. "Go on, sweet boy."

She sat up, freeing Jay to move, and curled her arms around her knees. The weight of his uncertain gaze pulled at her as he rose in her peripheral vision. She plucked at the sheet with her toes. Clench. Lift. Release. The image of the hurt on Adam's face when she'd told him marriage didn't interest her was enough. She didn't need Jay's, too. She'd had fun with Adam, but even after almost two years, that's all it had been to her.

Saying those things to him had been uncomfortable but true. Saying them to Jay would be heart-wrenching and maybe a lie. Being here had become a little more than fun. But love? And next year?

This arrangement functioned as a month-to-month lease. If she said so, she'd still hurt Jay and she'd make Henry the bad guy.

"Just a moment?" Jay, uncertainty written across his face, resembled a child in need of a hug.

Fuck.

"I promise, Jay." Henry cupped his cheek and kissed his forehead. "Do as I ask, my boy."

Jay left the bedroom faster than he wanted to, she suspected.

Henry sighed. "The day is simply a day, Alice. Different from other days in name only."

He touched her ankles, fingers trailing over the top of her feet. "Do we become different people on this day? Or are we the same people we always are, enjoying the same things we often enjoy? Is it the day that gives these acts meaning, or is it ourselves?"

Every second she spent untangling her nerves was one Jay spent alone and missing them. Ruining his night because she couldn't keep her shit together wasn't fair to him.

"What we do . . ." wouldn't end with a ring on her finger or even an offer of one.

Valentine's Day wasn't the problem. She hadn't been in love with Adam. If he hadn't proposed, she'd have found another way to end things. But that wouldn't happen here.

Henry wasn't Adam. Jay wasn't Adam. They wouldn't demand over-the-top commitments she couldn't meet, even if Jay sometimes seemed adorably confused on that point. She didn't have to avoid the entire day because she'd had a bad one once. And Jay had been right about one thing—best ever.

"You're saying it doesn't have to mean anything more than we want it to mean."

"Yes." Henry lifted her hand and kissed her knuckles. "It means precisely as much as you wish it to mean, sweet girl."

She could live with that. Some days, it would be just fucking. And sometimes she'd practice this love thing. She'd never have a long-term, stable relationship without it. Never be an adult until she conquered this.

The lesson was Henry's gift to her. Showing her the way to handle love like a grown-up. So when she found the perfect guy, she'd know what to do. What love felt like. What it should look like.

"Thank you, Henry." She worried he'd interrogate her the way he had before she'd signed the contract. The way he sometimes did on their nights together.

She wasn't ready for that, not now. Raw and exposed, she struggled to wrap her head around the idea that real romantic love existed. Even if most people in relationships faked it or fooled themselves, Henry and Jay truly loved each other.

Henry led her across the bedroom without questioning her. He carried the second lantern in one hand, with hers clasped in the other. His quiet laugh startled her. She'd missed the joke, and his face gave no answer.

"The shower," he murmured.

The shower had come on after the toilet flushed. Her ears worked fine. But what—a yelp from the bathroom, and she covered her mouth to stifle her chuckle.

"He forgot about the boiler." Despite the extra buckets of water sitting on the tile, despite the lantern Jay had taken to the bathroom, he'd turned on the shower and been greeted with frigid water.

"Distracted," Henry said as they exited the bedroom. "Or he didn't consider how cold the water would be."

"Think we should go rescue him?" A cold shower lacked appeal, but some places cried out for a good washing.

Henry squeezed her hand. "He does need a fair amount of looking after."

"Jay's worth it, though." She squeezed back. "And he always appreciates everything you do for him."

Henry pushed open the bathroom door and ushered her inside, setting the lantern beside Jay's on the counter. A large, lidded stockpot sat on the other side of the sink, a bath towel wrapped around the base. She touched the metal. Warm. Not hot, but warm, at least. Magic trick?

"Easy enough to warm water alongside chocolate, Alice, particularly when one wishes for a double boiler."

Of course he'd warmed water for cleaning up. Kept the water near boiling and left it in the bathroom before bringing the strawberries to the bedroom. She pressed her lips together to avoid laughing. Henry nearly set her off anyway, calling to Jay over the sound of the shower.

"How's the water, my boy?"

"Cold. So cold. I'm never having sex again."

"Never?"

"Never until the hot water is back."

"If you'd waited for us a moment, my boy, you'd *have* warmer water."

The shower turned off. "What?"

"I heated water on the camp stove, Jay." Henry lifted the lid from the stockpot and pushed three washcloths into the water.

"This is a lesson in patience, isn't it." The shower curtain opened on a naked, dripping Jay with a slight pout. The woodsy scent of his bodywash hit her nose. The boy made for one sexy drowned rat.

"The cold water hasn't hurt you. And you'll warm up in bed soon enough." Henry reached into the pot and pulled out a washcloth, wringing it out and tossing it to Jay. "Finish with this, my boy. I believe you'll find it much nicer."

Jay's exaggerated moan mimicked orgasm. "Oh, glorious warm washcloth! The greatest of all the gifts Henry provides."

She laughed as Henry laid a towel across the side of the tub and urged her to sit. It wasn't until he touched her with the warm washcloth that her laugh turned into a moan.

"Ha, see? You agree with me." Jay stepped around her and out of the tub. "The warm washcloth is fantastic."

"I don't *disagree* with you, Jay."

Henry kneeling naked in front of her and gently washing between her legs made keeping up her end of the conversation impossible. His hand rested atop her thigh, fingers idly rubbing. When he finished, he folded the washcloth and used the clean side to wipe Jay's ejaculate from her chest. The touch was hardly less distracting.

"Henry has great hands."

Jay laughed, and she blushed at her unintended oversharing.

"He has great everything," Jay corrected.

"He does," she agreed, her eyes on Henry as he ran the washcloth over the top of her breasts.

He lifted his head, smiled at her, and kissed her cheek. "All done, my girl. If you're cold, take one of the lanterns and go burrow under the covers. Jay and I will be a moment longer."

So clean he squeaked, Jay didn't need to stay, either. But he'd given her and Henry a moment to themselves when Henry told him to. Henry's command to her was less direct but still recognizable.

She placed a hand on Henry's shoulder to get to her feet.

"Take your time. I might be asleep when you get to bed," she teased. "I've had a big day."

"Is 'day' a new word for Henry's cock? Because I've had a big day, too." Jay smirked from his spot beside the sink, one towel wrapped around his hips and another rubbing his chest.

She stepped forward, stood on her toes, and delivered a firm, affectionate kiss. "Sure, why not?" She waggled her eyebrows. "Remember that at our Tuesday lunches when I ask you how your day is."

Henry's bark of laughter echoed off the tile as she sauntered out the door.

She recapped the lube and put it and the unused tissues back in the nightstand drawer. Straightened the sheets that had gotten kicked to the bottom of the bed and reclaimed the extra blankets that had tumbled to the floor.

Crawling under the covers, she settled on the far side of the bed. Leaving space for Henry in the middle seemed right tonight, and she didn't question the impulse. *Go with it. Jay would.*

Her eyes were closed, her thoughts drifting when they slid in beside her. Henry's voice came softly to her ears. "Not too cold, my girl? You don't want to be in the center?"

She half slapped her face against the pillow twice and curled her body into Henry's.

"Sharing you with Jay," she mumbled. "Like he does for me."

She yawned and scooted closer. Henry lay on his back, and his shoulder made an excellent pillow. His arm curved behind her, his hand sliding down her spine.

"All right, Alice." His lips brushed her forehead. "You're better at sharing than you realize, dearest."

She dropped off to sleep with the indistinct, low-toned lullaby of Henry and Jay's conversation in her ears.

Chapter 6

*H*enry.

His scent surrounded her. Not the citrus and leather she associated with him—just him. Warm, thick, sleeping maleness. She'd stayed pressed against him all night, and he still slept. Jay, too, his breathing steady and even on Henry's far side.

She inhaled, an attempt at classification and memorization. Who knew when she might need to identify Henry while blindfolded in a room of strangers. She could get used to this.

Whoa.

Back up. Temporary. Imitation. This was a testing phase to see if the design worked. To root out the flaws. When she came off Henry's production line, she'd be ready for anything. But finishing might take a while.

Jay'd been with Henry for more than four years, and he sure sounded like he'd started as a project, too. When had Jay stopped being a project? When had they fallen in love? If Henry had met her first, would—

Do not do that. You don't want to do that.

Jay wouldn't be jealous of her if their situations were reversed. He wouldn't resent her for having Henry's love.

But if this feeling she had for Henry was like love, an imitation of Jay's love for him, and if Henry used his love for Jay to make his

nights with her fantastic, maybe that explained why her previous relationships hadn't worked out. She'd found it so easy to kick men out
of her bed. They'd never satisfied her.

If love was the difference, what if she couldn't find it again? What
if she only touched the echoes from Henry and Jay and never felt it
herself?

She squirmed out of Henry's embrace in a rush, rolling face-to-
face with the pale blue of the alarm clock. Electricity. That was
something, at least.

She slipped on her robe and grabbed her cell phone off the nightstand, carrying it with her to the bathroom. A companywide voice
mail urged employees to stay home Friday. The company campus
hadn't been plowed and wouldn't open until Monday morning.

Another day to spend with her boys, unless she wanted to say
she'd tired of their company—a lie—or they wanted to kick her out.
Doubtful, since Henry had said he'd finish reading to them today.
Was it wrong to be as excited for story time as a kindergartner?

Fuck it. She felt how she felt.

If Henry wanted to help her recognize or understand or just *feel*
her feelings, she'd give it her best shot. So once she'd used the toilet,
washed up, and brushed her teeth, she headed straight back to the
bedroom to crawl under the covers until the boys woke up.

A golden light flashed through the window. Faint beeping penetrated the glass. Pulling back the curtain, she scanned the street. Plow
truck. Finally. Heaping snow even higher on the parked cars and side-
walks, but clearing the road. The boiler might get replaced today.
Heat. Luxurious heat.

She shed her robe and got into bed, shivering. The air had been
colder beside the window. Heat loss. Poor thermal insulation in older
buildings. She should mention it to Henry, have him get Mr. Nagel to
caulk the windows or add weather stripping.

"Alice." Henry's quiet voice surprised her. "Come   dear
girl. I feel you shivering from here."

"I'll make you cold," she objected.

"I'll make you warm," he countered. He stretched
stroked her neck. "Wouldn't you like to be warm?"

Hell yes. She rolled into his embrace, snuggli
as she had all night.

He held her tight, his hand on her back pulling her half atop him. His lips brushed her forehead.

"What discoveries have you made this morning, my dear?"

Keeping her voice low to avoid waking Jay, she told him of the electricity and the plow, though he likely saw the light from both himself, and of her day off from work. The back of Jay's head lay undisturbed on the pillow beside Henry's cheek. He must've sprawled on his stomach during the night.

"Delightful," Henry responded to her recounting. "If that's the case . . ."

He laid out his plans for the day, and she agreed when asked for input. She liked lying beside him, listening to his voice and the soft snuffle of Jay's sleeping breath, his face half-buried in the pillow. Participating in things like they were a family, like her opinion of what they did today mattered. With her parents in South Dakota and her sister at school in California, she didn't have that feeling often. Not in the decade since she'd left home for college.

The day went precisely as Henry had suggested.

Oatmeal with strawberries for breakfast. A call to Mr. Nagel afterward. Yes, he expected the boiler replacement to be completed today. Story time, with Alice and Jay snuggling beside Henry as he finished reading *Winnie-the-Pooh*. Venturing out, bundled in winter gear, to find a warm place to eat lunch, browse at the few open stores and replace groceries spoiled during the power outage.

The only hiccup came when Henry suggested they pick up a few things for her refrigerator. She sheepishly informed him of her fridge's emptiness. She might toss out a half-finished quart of milk, a couple of eggs from a half-dozen carton and a container of tuna salad.

His frown matched the one he'd given her last month when she'd confessed to spending Christmas alone, and his nod was short. "I suppose it isn't as enjoyable to cook for one, and in such cramped conditions as a studio apartment. I haven't the authority to force you to eat homemade meals when freezer items and takeout are more convenient."

"You should give him the authority," Jay said, manning the cart ⸺ted they take. He maneuvered around corners and popped wheelies like a bored kid. "Henry makes great meals for me. It could be like a CSA farm. You could buy a share of dinners. We'd vote on stuff. You'll second my motion on the more cookies proposal, right?"

She laughed, and the conversation moved on. Let Henry cook for her. As if. Too weird. To have her neighbor—friend—sex partner—was there no single word that fit? To have *Henry* cooking her meals all the time. She'd never even had a roommate who cooked meals for her on a regular basis. Or any basis. Asking Henry for that would be like saying she wanted to be part of his family.

They walked home just shy of six, Jay carrying the lion's share of the groceries. A cheerful Mr. Nagel directed action in the lobby, overseeing the departure of the plumbers.

"Heat's back on," he called to them. "Hot water's in demand at the moment, but give it time to run and it'll be there."

Without Henry's early morning talk, she might've panicked. Worried whether she should grab her stuff and head back to her own apartment. Heat on, crisis over: Bye-bye, part-time partner. Instead, she helped Jay toss spoiled food and put groceries away while Henry started dinner.

When seven o'clock came and they sat to eat, she didn't question Henry's authority. She answered the ritual questions between bites, and Jay did the same. As simple as that, Henry had taken the reins for the night.

At eight, she and Jay squared away the kitchen. Henry awarded praise, kisses and fondling for good behavior. Their activities felt nothing like a month ago when Jay had been injured. Doing household chores fueled pride and arousal when Henry expressed his pleasure at their work.

He ordered them to the shower, undressing them both himself and testing the water. The shower wasn't designed for three, but the tight fit and the bumping elbows didn't detract from the experience. She ended up clean, smelling like Henry, and wet in a way that had nothing to do with water.

She was ready for more than teasing, and so were they. She appreciated the view as Henry and Jay dried her first, and she and Henry dried Jay, and she and Jay dried Henry last.

He chivvied them into the bedroom ahead of him, ordering them onto the bed and directing them until he had them positioned to his liking.

She shivered with anticipation. He'd chosen a position new to her, but Henry calling the shots covered familiar territory, a comfort after two nights of stressful decisions and confusing emotions.

"I saw the hunger on your face last night, my dear Alice. And Jay had such difficulty stilling his mouth." He spoke from everywhere and nowhere, invisible but omnipresent. "You'll both benefit from tonight's arrangement, hmm?"

With her head lying on Jay's thigh, his hard cock and the roundness of his balls beneath short black hair filled her vision. He lay on his side with his lower leg pushed forward as her pillow and his upper leg pulled back to give her room.

The weight of his head on her lower leg and the warmth of his exhalations against her sex caused shivers. The gentle push of his hand kept her upper leg bent and raised, foot resting on the bed behind her other leg.

Henry directed them, having them trade licks, speed up or slow down. His voice rang loudest when he stood near her at the foot of the bed and quieted as he circled. Eventually he ordered them to continue on their own.

With her ear pressed to Jay's thigh and her focus split between his cock in her mouth and his tongue in her pussy, Henry's words faded in and out.

Henry murmured of art, maybe, and balance, or philosophy, male and female, dark and light, yin and yang, indivisible. The bed shifted, and he said something to Jay. ". . . unflavored, but safe to enjoy."

He lay down at her back, heat and pressure, the best kind of anticipation. She held the base of Jay's cock in one hand to give herself the best angle while she sucked.

"Beautiful." Henry kissed her cheek. "You don't mind if I join the fun, do you, Alice?"

He pushed forward, and Jay spread her lips for his entry. She sucked hard and popped her mouth free.

"No, Henry." She licked the tip of Jay's cock. "I'm looking forward to it."

"Mmm. Good girl. My lovely Alice." He pushed inside, a slow thrust.

Pulling Jay into her mouth tugged a moan free. Jay fell upon her again, too, licking at her and Henry. If finding that hot was wrong, sign her up for a spot in hell.

With Henry inside her and Jay alternately sucking at her clit and lapping at her flesh where Henry's cock parted it, she climaxed in what seemed seconds.

Henry clamped his hand over hers on Jay's cock. They weren't done yet. He allowed her a pause. Henry stopped thrusting, and Jay kissed her thighs and belly.

When her quivering ceased, Henry nipped her ear with his teeth and thrust. "Back to work, Alice. You're doing a wonderful job. Can you hear how appreciative Jay is? Or perhaps your sweet depths have muffled his enjoyment too much for you to hear, hmm?"

He stroked Jay's thigh as she sucked Jay's cock and listened for his moans. Hearing mattered less than sensation when he tongued her. The vibration in his mouth rippled through her as he sucked on her clit. She basked in the warmth of his powerful exhalation between her lips when he licked Henry's cock.

She refocused her efforts on Jay, using her tongue along the underside of his cock.

"That's it, sweet girl. Nice and slow." Henry whispered in her ear, his hips moving against hers. "Our Jay enjoys the teasing, hmm?"

His arm moved in her peripheral vision. She closed her mouth around Jay, sucking in the head of his cock, rolling her tongue over the edge.

"He enjoys your mouth on him as much as you enjoy his. As much as I enjoy sinking into you and soaking up your heat." Henry's hand reappeared on her breast, squeezing and holding her tight to his body.

"It's about balance, Alice. And right now that's *you*, dearest." Henry thrust faster, and she adjusted her mouth to match his movement for Jay. "Beautiful. You are the perfect fulcrum. Keeping the balance. Pleasing me. Pleasing Jay. Three forces acting on each other in harmony."

She moaned. Henry spoke science. Physics. Engineering. Her language. His voice tipped the scales, as it so often did for her. Body shaking, she broke the machine, upended the balance, the vibration of her moans taking Jay with her this time without Henry's hand to still him. Henry's climax seemed more deliberate, a choice to follow her, to come while she clenched around him again and again.

They lay together for long minutes catching their breath. She pressed her cheek to Jay's thigh, rubbing with catlike affection. Henry stroked the side of her breast with his thumb, his hand cupped firmly around her. Jay sprinkled kisses on them both, playful pecks at her sex and thighs.

"Jay, turn and join us up here, please."

Up was a relative term. Technically, she and Henry lay with their heads near the foot of the bed. But Jay scrambled around, managing not to kick her as he adjusted his position and flopped on his back in front of her. She needed no urging to reach out and scratch his chest, running her fingers over him in long, slow strokes. He breathed deep, his chest expanding under her touch, and Henry's hand left her breast to join hers. He splayed his palm flat across Jay's stomach, covering his navel and patting gently.

"You've both done wonderful work tonight, my dear ones. We've earned a rest, haven't we?"

Jay yawned as he nodded, his head nudging toward hers.

He'd agree to whatever Henry suggested. If Henry said they'd lie quietly for half an hour and go again, Jay would be up and ready for it. Hell, if Henry told Jay to run out for pizza, he'd do that, too. But she'd bet her annual paycheck Henry never did anything, never said or even hinted at anything, without giving thoughtful consideration to the repercussions for Jay.

"And you, my sweet girl? You're quiet. The night featured a new experience for you." Henry pressed his lips to the back of her head, a forceful kiss against her hair. "A pleasant one, I trust."

"I, yes, Henry. It was..." Something she'd never fantasized about, because the idea hadn't occurred to her. But now she had something new to fantasize about on the nights they spent apart: The quickness of Jay's tongue and the hardness of Henry's cock working at her in concert while her mouth and Henry's hand kept Jay's cock occupied.

She'd had both of them in her at once. Not the way Henry intimated last month, but still, the three of them had been together. Connected, with her as the connection point. A heady sensation.

"Memorable," she concluded. The word didn't cover the half of it. Three consecutive nights of memorable moments. Would Henry ever want that from her? Maybe not three nights, but two. A whole contract weekend, from Friday evening to Sunday afternoon.

No. She'd be asking too much. Infringing on his time with Jay.

Her hand settled, ending its wandering tour of Jay's chest over his sternum. She splayed her fingers like Henry's, the littlest one brushing his thumb.

"It's not something I'll ever forget," she said. Unforgettable. Not only this night or the newest sexual position in her arsenal but all of it. The whole arrangement. If she lived to be a hundred, her dreams, sexual or otherwise, would still be populated by Henry and Jay.

"Don't worry, Alice." Jay covered her hand on his chest with his. "If you forget, we'll be here to remind you."

He gave her a sly smirk. "Anytime you want my cock in your mouth, you just let me know."

She laughed, and Jay's grin widened. "I figure you don't have to let Henry know when you want his cock, 'cause you're like me—anytime is a good time for that."

She laughed harder, and Jay joined her, and even Henry chuckled. The light mood carried them through cleanup. Everything in its place.

She and Jay tucked themselves against Henry's side, playing lazy, teasing games with their fingers across his chest until sleep claimed them.

Alice wasn't surprised Henry had exercised his option to keep her overnight. Staying had become such a normal part of her weekend routine she no longer questioned it. She'd have counted it odd if he'd sent her home Friday night.

He always released her from their games before noon, though she took care not to make afternoon plans on the off chance he'd keep her. But she didn't expect Jay's plea.

After a satisfying round of morning sex with them both and a filling brunch, Henry thanked her, kissed her, and freed her to spend the rest of the day as she liked. She'd gone to the bedroom to pack up her bag, and Jay followed a few minutes behind.

"You're going to build a snow fort with me, right?"

"I—what?" She zipped her bag.

Jay leaned against the door frame. "I'm going out to the park to enjoy the snow. Maybe find a snowball fight to join. C'mon. You know you wanna build the fort. It's all engineer-ish."

She did, actually. She hadn't built a snow fort since she and Ollie were kids. Before Dad's accident, when he'd still play with them. The last time, she'd just turned thirteen. Acted too old to be out in the snow with her ten-year-old sister. Dad had sent Ollie off to pack snow blocks in bread pans and taken her aside.

"You were ten not long ago, and you loved playing with your baby sister. Now she's ten. Do you want her to remember good times playing with her sister or how her sister didn't want to play with her?"

The stuff she'd wanted to do had lost its vital importance in that moment. Gratitude tinged her memories now. The fun Ollie'd had bossing her around and deciding how the fort would be built and which scarf the snowman would wear. How Dad had helped them lift the last snowball on top of the snowman. How a few months later he'd gotten hurt at work, and making sure life ran smoothly for her little sister became her top priority.

Was anything she wanted to do today more important than playing in the snow with Jay? "Let me put on warmer clothes, and I'll meet you outside."

Jay whooped and lifted her off her feet. "Excellent."

He disappeared into his own bedroom. God only knew how he'd find proper clothes in that mess. She headed for the door.

Henry stood at the window in the living room.

"Staying in, Henry?"

"Pleading age and infirmity." He turned and winked.

Yeah, right. "I don't think you can get away with that excuse."

"Perhaps not." His lips twitched in a brief smile. "Have fun playing in the snow, Alice. Don't forget to dress warmly."

The tip of her tongue begged her to suggest he oversee the dressing process before reason intruded. Freedom. Boundaries. She was his friend this afternoon, not his submissive. No time for inappropriate flirting with Henry.

So she assured him she would, and she dressed in her own apartment, and she spent the afternoon in platonic games with Jay.

They defended their well-constructed snow fort against all comers until darkness fell, and they walked home together on the hard-packed snow in the middle of the street. He clasped her hand in his. She followed along, up the stairs, into the apartment. Henry took one look at them and prescribed warm showers, dry clothes and hot chocolate.

Shrugging out of her coat, she trudged down the hall after Jay, exhausted from hours of hurling snowballs. Simple thoughts, simple motions. Undressing. Stepping into the shower. Standing under the spray.

Her brain warmed up in front of Jay's bare, soapy chest.

Oh fuck.

Raw panic immobilized her. Hot water beat down on her back. Confusion seeped into her head. Henry hadn't stopped her. Hadn't taken her arm and steered her across the hall.

Jay treated her presence like a normal occurrence, chattering about the structural integrity of their fort and their snowball-fight domination of a group of college kids. He didn't try to start something, though she'd barged into his shower. If his eyes strayed to her breasts and his thawing body managed enough heat for an impressive erection, he didn't say a word about it.

He understood the difference between playtime and friend-time. She'd been the one to forget. *Sorry, Jay.*

The shower curtain shifted with a wave of cooler air.

"Fresh clothes are on the counter for you both. Kitchen when you're done, please." Henry didn't sound upset, but maybe he'd discuss it with her when she wasn't naked.

He hadn't stayed to oversee things, though. He must trust them to behave. Jay, at least. Plenty gracious, considering she'd trailed his lover into the shower like she belonged.

Her clothes turned out to be sweatpants, a T-shirt, and a sweatshirt, all similar to Jay's and appropriately oversize. She tucked the shirts in—both of them—and rolled the pants at the waist so she could walk.

Jay laughed. "You look ridiculous in my clothes."

She stuck out her tongue. "No, you look ridiculous in your clothes. I look fabulous."

Henry probably hadn't been willing to root in her pockets for her keys and rummage through her clothing drawers to bring her something of her own without asking first. He respected boundaries. Unlike her, Miss Waltz in Like She Owns the Place.

She followed Jay to the kitchen.

"At the counter, please," Henry directed them.

They sat side by side at the breakfast bar. Mugs waited on the far counter, steam rising. Chocolate sweetened the air.

"Did you have fun?" Henry kissed Jay's cheek and swiveled his chair sideways.

"Tons of fun." Jay launched into a description of the afternoon as Henry rolled thick socks onto his feet. Henry, listening closely, asked a bevy of questions Jay was only too happy to answer.

She sat straighter as Henry came around to her side.

"I hope you won't object to accepting some socks today, Alice." He unfolded a clean pair of heavy-duty tube socks in his hands. Jay's, probably. "If you'll allow me?"

Thankfulness left her mute and nodding. Henry wasn't fussing over her faux pas. Wouldn't mention her gaffe at all, it seemed.

He cradled her feet and slipped on the socks. She wiggled her toes.

"All right, Alice?"

"Perfect fit," she teased, laughing at the rings of cotton surrounding her ankles. "I might pull them up to my knees. Over the pants."

"An interesting fashion statement." Henry studied her with narrowed eyes and a small smile. Fetching the mugs, he set them in front of her and Jay. "Sufficiently cooled now, I expect."

Jay lifted his mug and drank deep. She cradled the warmth in her hands and sipped. Hot chocolate, like she'd assumed, but thick, creamy, *chocolatey* hot chocolate. "Is this real chocolate?"

"With milk, yes, and a dash of cinnamon." Henry leaned against the breakfast bar across from them. "Is the flavor not to your liking, Alice?"

"It's amazing. I'm used to packets. You know, water, microwave, powder, stir together . . ." She trailed off at Jay's horrified expression.

"You've never had real hot chocolate? Never? That's a crime against humanity."

"It's not—I mean, my mom just didn't make it that way." A rush of defensiveness overtook her twinge of guilt. So what if she hadn't had homemade hot chocolate? She hadn't been deprived. Her childhood had been just fine. Worse than some, maybe, but better by miles than others.

"I'm pleased to introduce you to something new, Alice." Henry's soft voice soothed. His hand twitched, a gesture that might've commanded Jay's silence. "Tell me, did you have a favorite meal when you came in from the cold?"

She tilted the mug, swirling the liquid chocolate round and round. Jay'd been teasing. She was being oversensitive.

Her distress owed nothing to her family or Jay's, or how they'd grown up, or the hot chocolate they drank. Jay could request hot chocolate whenever he liked, and Henry would happily provide it at his discretion. She dwelled in borrowed time, her status more tenuous. Contingent upon Henry's desire and her good behavior. Although he hadn't scolded her about the shower mix-up.

"Grilled cheese." She followed the row of buttons up Henry's shirt to his gentle smile. "With tomato soup for dipping."

"Then we have our menu for the evening." Henry began opening cupboards. "Jay, if you'll set the table, please." Jay jumped up and pulled open the silverware drawer.

"You'll stay for dinner, won't you, Alice? I must apologize for the lack of advance notice. But sometimes a spur-of-the-moment impulse can be highly rewarding."

She squeezed her mug. The men had their backs to her, pulling cans and plates from the upper cabinets. But understanding Henry's meaning didn't require rocket science. He'd punished himself, but he wasn't sorry. He didn't regret taking her across the dining room table nearly seven months ago. He found their friendship and their contract arrangement rewarding. He enjoyed teaching her new things.

"I'll stay." She sipped her hot chocolate. Just right. "Anything I can help with?"

Henry set Jay to mashing canned peeled tomatoes—the flavor being more consistent in the winter than fresh, he insisted—and taught her to cut an onion under running water and grate fresh garlic. In less than thirty minutes, they sat down to bowls of creamy tomato soup and grilled sandwiches oozing with spicy Colby jack.

When they finished eating, Jay drew her into a discussion of Hitchcock. Henry was in the middle of introducing him to the director's films, and staying for *North by Northwest* wasn't optional.

"A spy film. Action and intrigue! Henry promised I'd like this one." Jay tugged her toward the living room. "You know you want to see it."

Somehow, she ended up sitting beside Henry on the couch with his arm around her shoulders. Jay curled up on Henry's other side, his head propped on a pillow in Henry's lap. For more than two hours.

They talked about the film until midnight, resurrecting her days of hanging out in college dorm rooms, spouting crazy theories and following winding trains of conversation without any destination.

Only later, when she snuggled into her pillow and shifted irritably on her futon, did the truth threaten her sanity. She'd gotten comfortable in Henry and Jay's bed. In their daily routines. In their lives.

I am so fucked.

Chapter 7

The door opened to Alice's knock at seven PM, but no one stood on the other side to greet her. She stepped inside, craning her neck in a hunt for Jay or Henry and scooting forward as the door started to close.

The doorman was revealed as Jay—an expected occurrence.

An absolutely bare-ass naked Jay. An *un*expected occurrence.

No wonder he'd stayed behind the door.

When he turned and reached for her wrist, her inaccuracy glinted. Not naked. A dark-green ring circled the base of his erect cock. Utterly fuckable.

Henry's thirty-ninth birthday was two days away. Maybe he'd planned a special game tonight to celebrate.

Jay led her to Henry's bedroom without speaking. The mystery and anticipation enhanced the foreplay and her excitement. They stopped in the doorway, Jay's halt so sudden she almost walked into him.

Beyond his shoulder, the bedroom lights spotlighted an area away from the bed. The two metal brackets in the ceiling, the ones she'd assumed to be hooks for plants or model airplanes or any number of innocuous items, held a metal bar between them. From the bar descended a short length of rope.

She touched Jay's back in an instinctive quest for reassurance. Warm skin. Connection.

"Bring her in so I may see her, Jay."

Henry's voice, though she couldn't—oh. He occupied the leather chair on the far side of the room, shadowed and indistinct.

Jay led her in and stood her in the light. His hand dropped from her wrist as he stepped away.

"Turn, Alice. All the way around, please."

Her slow turn rustled her dress against her knees. The deep blue heavy-knit cotton with a square bodice and an empire waist wasn't fancy, but Henry assessing her body in it seemed to make it the sexiest thing she owned.

"Lovely," he murmured, and she flushed with the praise. "Perhaps we'll think on the possibilities of blue for another night. At the moment, I wish to see something more pink. Jay, if you would."

Jay returned to her, his hands skimming up her back over the dress and grasping the zipper. He lowered it with a slow pull until the track ended at the upper curve of her buttocks. His fingers pressed into her skin. Hands sliding upward, he parted the back of the dress, pushing the straps down her arms until the fabric slithered off her body.

The undergarments, a gift from Henry, nearly matched the dress. His pleased hum raised goose bumps on her skin. Jay's cock twitched with appreciation above the edge of her panties. "Tell me, Alice, do you enjoy wearing the clothing I've chosen for you?"

She'd worn Henry's gifts on most of their nights, but he'd never said a word on the subject.

"Yes, Henry." Putting on the bras and panties, knowing he'd pictured her and found her desirable in the clothes, excited her. She didn't fight feminist principles over it. Her turn-ons were her own. She refused to feel somehow less for having and indulging them.

"Do you only wear them here, for me?"

Uh-oh. Was she supposed to wear them only for him? The bra-and-panty sets he'd gotten her weren't blatantly erotic—not see-through, not covered in annoying lace, not uncomfortably cut and made to be worn for five minutes.

"Or do you wear them when you go out into the world?"

He'd given her tasteful pieces with high-end quality, and she hadn't for one minute considered not wearing them elsewhere.

"I wear them out." On their Fridays, especially, she wore them under her work clothes to remind her of what waited for her at the end of the day. As if he created the fabric's supportive embrace with his hands on her instead. "To work."

"Because they feel good against your skin?"

"Y-yes."

"There's more, isn't there, Alice? Tell me truthfully, now."

"I . . . wearing them reminds me of you. That I, that you . . ." Oh God. She couldn't tell him it made her feel like his lover. Jay was his lover. What she had with them was an amusement, an imitation of the real thing.

"Mmm. You sit in an office environment surrounded by men all day, don't you, Alice?" Fabric shirred against leather. Henry moving. Standing? "And you wear the intimate pieces I've chosen for you, and you imagine, perhaps, that these men sense my claim on you? That they know how you belong to me?"

"Yes, Henry." She squinted, trying to pierce the darkness beyond where she and Jay waited, illuminated for him.

"The bra first, please, Jay."

Jay worked the clasp with expert precision, removing the fabric without touching her breasts. Maybe he wasn't allowed, the way it seemed he wasn't to speak. Her nipples hardened as the air hit them, their puckering excitement beyond her control, less a chill than her awareness of Henry outside the light, seeing how he affected her.

His controlled breathing, deep and steady, with a hint of vocalization on each exhale, woke her fantasies. Imagining he held himself in check by a thin margin, she wet her lips hoping the provocation might unleash him.

He spoke. "Jay."

Fingers at her hips pulled her underwear down her body as she struggled to penetrate the darkness. Hands lifted her feet and swept away her sandals, her dress, and her underthings. A shiver ran through her. She was nude now, as nude as Jay—no, more so, because he proudly bore his ring in the color of Henry's eyes, and she had nothing.

"Do you know, Alice, there is a lovely daylily variety called Painting the Roses Red whose beauty I sought to capture on canvas one summer in my family's garden. Day after day I mixed my paints, and day after day I failed to encompass the exquisite shades, the tiny folds, the crinkled edges, the play of light and shadow. But you, my dear, you do so effortlessly every time you flush with desire." Henry stepped into the light. "Perhaps I'll manage to match it today on your skin, dearest."

He exuded masculinity in a three-piece suit. Black pants, black vest, black double-breasted coat. Pristine white shirt. His tie and pocket square matched the deep green Jay wore around his cock.

He extended his arm until his knuckles brushed her cheek, and she whimpered with want. Not only for sex, but for belonging.

"I have something I want you to wear tonight, Alice, though you won't be able to wear these to work, I'm afraid."

He delved in a pocket on his suit coat, emerging with two bands of material connected by a short chain. Her inhalation roared in her ears.

Handcuffs.

Silver metal attachment points dangled from brown leather straps dark as a liver chestnut and loose-wrapped in deep green silk. Green like the cloth peeking out of Henry's pocket. Green like Jay's cock ring. She bounced on the balls of her feet, giddy with relief. These cuffs were hers. She belonged.

"Do you remember your safeword, Alice?"

"Yes, Henry." *Yes, yes, I know it, please put those on me.*

"Tell it to me now, please."

"Pistachio." *I won't need it.*

"Good girl."

She struggled to restrain her impatience under his thoughtful gaze.

"Hold out your arms for—"

Thrusting her arms forward, she offered her hands side by side and loosely fisted.

"—me."

Henry raised his hand until his palm brushed her fingers where they curled under her hands. He bent at the waist and bestowed two gentle kisses, one to the back of each hand. He revealed a slight smile as he straightened. "Your eagerness pleases me. Perhaps it's been too long for us."

Always. Two weeks of waiting and wanting, and such a short time when fulfilling her sexual desires became a joyful hobby for him. He'd taken a year to make the decision, to agree to invite her into his relationship with Jay. How hard had Jay pushed to make that happen?

Gratitude flooded her, both for Jay's interest and Henry's willingness to play along.

Henry slipped the cuffs on her and tightened the straps. The silk slid over her skin. Two inches of chain separated her wrists. Henry lifted them over her head, extending her arms until the stretch hurt before lowering them a smidge. "Is this position comfortable, Alice? Be truthful, or our time together will end early tonight."

Jesus. Was he trying to scare her? His voice held a sharp edge of command. A safety reason, muscle strain, probably, had to be the cause, but to threaten to end the night early . . . "It pulls a little on my shoulders, but it doesn't hurt."

He lowered her wrists another fraction of an inch. "Better?"

"Yes, Henry."

"Good. Be still for me."

She complied while he made adjustments above her. Metal spun, whirring like the screw locks on the carabiners Jay used when they climbed.

Henry backed away to the edge of the light. "Relax your shoulders, Alice."

She lowered her shoulders as best she could and shivered at the secure grip of the cuffs around her wrists.

"Rotate your hands for me. Wiggle your fingers."

She obeyed without question. His safety concerns were for her benefit, and she wouldn't interfere no matter how desperate she grew to feel his touch. Having the length of his body grazing hers as he'd held her arms above her head hadn't helped. Holding still had been difficult when she'd wanted to rub herself against him like a cat.

He circled her, always at the edge of the light, prowling. Jay stood somewhere in the darkness, his role in this game as shrouded as his body.

"You're a very good girl, Alice." Henry spoke in conversational, relaxed tones. He stepped in front of her, a foot away, and unbuttoned his jacket. "I want you to understand that now, before we begin. You haven't displeased me in any way. Do you understand?"

He held his coat out behind him, and Jay stepped from the darkness to take it.

"Yes, Henry. I haven't done anything wrong."

Henry unbuttoned his shirt cuffs and rolled his sleeves to the elbow.

"Correct." He leaned in and kissed her, hard, one hand on her chin holding her in place as he nipped at her lips. "This is not a punishment but a pleasure."

Her whole body trembled. He hadn't even done anything yet. Anticipating Henry's attention made for the best sort of torment.

He stepped around her, an invisible presence, though his breath ghosted across her ear as he grasped her hips. The brief press of his clothed body to her nude one made her gasp.

Hard and trapped in his dress pants, he strained against the fabric. Either what he intended to do or the expectation that she'd enjoy his game excited him.

He moved away.

She waited.

His hand fell, a sharp smack against the left side of her ass. She jumped at the sting. The sensation repeated on the right. Afterward, he massaged her buttocks, slipping between her legs and stroking her lips. He nudged her feet apart.

The placement and the pauses between varied, making predicting where and when his hand would fall impossible. But after every three or four strokes, he cradled her and rubbed his palm over her gently, crooning to her, tracing her labia.

The sting grew sharper as the burn spread. Her body became heat, throbbing heat, and his hand the center of it.

He slipped his fingers inside with ease, her own wetness a surprise to her. How aroused she'd become from the alternating harsh and gentle touch. She pushed toward his fingers, trying to force him deeper.

He removed them without a word, ignoring her whimpered plea, and rolled his slick fingers over her clitoris. Her bucking hips jerked the cuffs at her wrists and bathed her in fearful excitement. He cupped her sex from behind, fingers flexing and rubbing. His fingertips dropped away from her clit.

Slap.

She jumped away, in startlement rather than pain, but the cuffs wouldn't let her go far.

He rested a hand on her hip, holding her in place.

"Pleasure, not punishment, Alice," he whispered in her ear as he massaged her clit. "Let yourself feel it."

He slapped her again, a darting sting, three times in succession, and then he massaged.

Trembling, she rose up on her toes, uncertain whether to get away or extend the sensation. An edge of fear coursed through her. But this new game was Henry, with his hand between her legs. Nothing wrong could come of that.

Though something right could.

She widened her stance, an inch at most. Enough, she hoped, to convey her acceptance to Henry, who recognized her responses better than she herself did.

The slaps came quick and solid against the fullness of her sex. The burning grew hotter, better, at the center of her desire. So close to a conflagration. She moaned as he massaged her, as his fingers sank into her and emerged coated with her need.

Dizzy panic took her as he moved away, but he didn't go far. He stood before her, his hand returning to her sex. Looking past her, he called to Jay before his gaze returned to her face. He kept up a steady massage, easing the burn.

"I'm going to slap you, Alice. Harder this time. You're a good girl, and I think you want to come for me. You do, don't you, dearest? You've been very close to the edge of it. I'm going to slap you, and you're going to come for me, and then I'm going to fuck you."

He thrust his tongue in her mouth like a brand. When he pulled back, leaving her breathless and leaning toward him, he slapped her vulva with unexpected force.

She sucked in air and endured the sting as he did it again, and again, and again. Each slap created its own sensation that rolled through her, a ripple interrupted by the next slap and the next. The ripples struck a wall and turned, crashing back against their successors and churning her arousal in a frenzy. Obedience demanded her surrender.

His hand came down, and she shook in orgasm. Senseless to all but the emotion flooding her, she lost her footing. The silk-lined cuffs tugged at her wrists. Eyes squeezed shut, back bent in a painful arch, she shattered. Whimpers and cries and moans echoed in her ears, all hers as her body attempted to process pleasure and pain into something coherent, something understandable.

Coherence hung out of reach when her body floated, when her

legs lifted of their own accord to settle around soft fabric, her thighs spread wide. Finally, a familiar sensation: Henry, hard and thrusting, inside her before the ripples quieted.

He was forceful, driving, and when physics didn't deliver the expected equal-and-opposite reaction, the solution presented itself as easily as laying her head on a waiting shoulder. Jay stood behind her, bracing her for Henry to fuck. He laved her neck and followed up with hard, sucking kisses as Henry murmured encouragement.

The pressure on her left knee disappeared. Chasing the reason led to teasing distraction, Henry's pants gaping open beside the shirttails hiding his cock from her on each withdrawal. He curved his arm under her leg, reaching. The brush of his fingers reignited the burning aftermath of her spanking as he grasped . . . *oh.*

Not all of that burning heat came from her. Jay, his hips bucking against the base of her spine, drove her onto Henry's cock as Henry stroked him.

She'd have helped, but the restraints trapped her arms above her. With her legs flung around Henry's hips and her body exhausted from the spanking and the orgasm and the rapid approach of another, she moved only as their bodies moved her between them.

Pressure and need built until Jay gave a hoarse shout in her ear as he came in Henry's hand. The slam of his hips forced her hard onto Henry, hard enough for her swollen clit striking him to send her spiraling into climax. Taking Henry with her, maybe, but the blur of sound and motion and sensation overwhelmed her.

Separating the feel of hands on her skin from her skin itself seemed an impossible task. She didn't try. She drifted.

She drifted as her arms sagged, no longer held above her head, and as she floated with dangling legs, and as the world tipped on its side and cool sheets greeted her back. Familiar sensations followed. The warmth of a washcloth between her legs. The touch of hands on her own, turning and stretching and wiggling her fingers. The sound of Henry's voice as he inquired after her health and comfort.

"M'good. Snuggle?"

Jay's quiet laughter heralded a reply. "I think you fucked her brains out. But she's got the right idea, finally."

Uh-huh. Naptime. Great idea. *Come snuggle, Jay.*

She patted the bed beside her, or attempted to. Her tired arms weighed her down, and the signals from her brain lagged. *Fucked 'em right out. Thank you, Henry.*

"Gently, my boy. Let's not wake the analyst, hmm? Lie down, and we'll snuggle with our sleeping beauty."

M'not sleeping. Speaking would've been too much effort. And the warm bodies cradling her now pulled her deeper under.

"Happy birthday, Henry." Jay's voice, followed by the soft sounds of lips sliding over each other.

"Thank you, my boy. You did a wonderful job presenting your gift." Henry cupped the back of her head, tipping her forward and bestowing a gentle kiss. Musky, masculine contentment flavored the air between them.

"Would've done it sooner."

A long, slow sigh from Jay—no, maybe a yawn. Opening her eyes wasn't worth the trouble, not when sleep called her name and Henry's scent filled her nose.

"But you wouldn't let me."

Wouldn't let Jay what?

"Some things take time, sweet boy. We mustn't rush them."

Slow and steady. *S'why Henry wins all the races.*

She woke to warmth and wetness at her breast.

Moonlight filtering through the shades illuminated the sheet draped over her body and the outline of a head beneath. The sleeping man sprawled to her left proved more enlightening. For once, Jay wasn't the one with the breast fixation.

She shifted her legs, restless, and hummed quiet encouragement to Henry. He stroked her inner thighs, his fingers long and firm. The extent of her body's arousal became clear with a pulsing thump and a wet rush.

Henry probably could've slipped in with ease minutes ago. A good dream. But now she was awake, and wanting.

She reached unthinkingly beneath the sheets, sliding fingers through his hair and tugging.

And he moved. The sheet fell back as his shoulders lifted and his face emerged over her own. He bucked once, aligning their bodies. She'd given his cock an eager welcome, her legs folding and wrapping around his, before the presence of protection registered.

He must've put the condom on as she slept. He'd intended his mouth at her breast to wake her. He'd been waiting on her, arousing her in both senses of the word.

"Nice and relaxed, Alice." He nuzzled her face, pressing gentle kisses against the corners of her mouth. "Slow, my sweet girl. These last seven months have been your birthday gift to me this year."

He could've demanded something for his birthday. Breakfast in bed. A blow job.

"You've given yourself over to my tutelage again. We may have left the museum behind, but the delights are no less artistic this year, dearest."

Something centered on his pleasure. Every last one of her previous partners would've. Not Henry. No, he lay with his cock unmoving inside her and kissed her.

He pinned her arms in a frame around her head, elbows out, but gently. He gripped her wrists, but his index fingers stroked her palms.

He scared her with how easy he made this seem. How quickly, now, she called up the emotional bond between them, as if their fucking deserved parity with the lovemaking he and Jay enjoyed.

The fear hit her especially when he took her this way, eyes staring into hers and cock thrusting with deliberate slowness. When he increased the pace steadily and kissed her with patient attention. When he murmured in her ear of how her body tightened around him and her muscles tensed beneath him.

When she couldn't stop his name from spilling out as she came, quaking under his body, and he whispered endearments and encouragement that brought her there again before their hips slowed and stopped.

She'd fallen in over her head. Sex had never held this kind of meaning in her life. Never been so attached to a specific person or feeling. Sex had been the expected thing, a sometimes fun, sometimes frustrating way to kill an hour. But not the way Henry did it.

Maybe his skills weren't what made the sex amazing. Or not only his skills. If the emotion played a role, too, could she duplicate that with another lover? Or could she only get that from Henry?

He kissed her forehead and thanked her for providing him with a lovely birthday memory. Her body warmed to his praise.

Discarding the condom, he rolled her onto his chest and pulled the sheets around them. He spoke of his plans for the morning, of the birthday breakfast he'd make after they woke Jay and showered. She lay content to enjoy the fantasy, to imagine this life, one in which she kinda sorta wanted something she'd never wanted, and with not one but two partners.

Love.

She almost asked him about the intense emotions. The confusion twisting her thoughts.

But he'd told her that was normal. At the beginning, he'd warned her confusion could happen in this sort of arrangement. Going to him with it, she'd dig herself in deeper. Play codependent girlfriend instead of a trusted friend who appreciated the nuances of what they had together.

She needed to depend on them less, not more.

Her sister's voice whispered in the back of her head, a remnant from their most recent talk. *I'm not saying you're not having a good time, Allie. I'm just saying where's the future here? They have each other. Don't you want that, too? You gotta go out and look for it.*

Chapter 8

About the time someone ordered a fourth round of drinks, Alice decided she should've gone home after dinner the way the family-having members of the team had done.

They had spouses and kids waiting. No one had thought it odd that they'd skip out after the celebratory supper their team leader insisted on buying them all for their elegant solution to a thorny design problem. Happy client, happy company.

Their eight-person engineering design pod, minus the two who'd gone home, stumbled far along the road to sloppy drunk, with a free Friday off to boot.

Partying should've been fun after eight months without a single night out. Not because she couldn't, but because she *couldn't*.

Awkward discomfort had held her back. The whiff of betrayal. Cheating. She didn't need another guy to satisfy her. Hell, she was more sexually satisfied now, with Henry and Jay, than she'd been in her entire life.

So why bother sitting at a table with five coworkers—five male coworkers, because she was the only woman on her team—at quarter to eleven on a Thursday night throwing back Black Castles and Black Barrels and black-fucking-anything because the guys loved their Guinness?

Beer made her horny and maudlin, a bad combination for sure. But having her at the table meant the guys claimed more numbers mastered than an MIT grad reciting pi, and they didn't want her to leave yet.

She served as bait. A statement that at least four guys at the table were unattached, but friendly enough and not so rowdy that a single girl couldn't feel safe. Nice guys. The kind of guys girls gave their numbers to or gyrated with on the dance floor or took home and fucked, depending on their own rules about sex and romance.

Right now, she wanted to go home and get fucked.

Thursday. Fuck.

Tomorrow she'd be in Henry's hands. A guaranteed good time. She pressed her legs together under the table. Waiting until tomorrow might be optimistic.

Her coworkers wandered off to dance and flirt or step outside and acquaint the gutters with their stomach contents. Had she been less drunk, she'd have chased off the newcomer.

As it was, he claimed the chair next to her with quiet stealth. She raised her half-filled glass in a salute. Round six. Maybe. Counting had gotten harder.

"You're not dancing." He leaned in as though he knew her.

Or wanted to know her. She laughed.

"That's funny? I'm a comedian, sure, but it usually takes some warm-up work before I get the ladies laughing. I'm Scott. Since you've already got a drink and you're lacking a partner, you wanna take a spin on the floor?"

His slick patter failed beside Jay's charm and Henry's elegance. Comparing every guy she met to them was probably inappropriate.

They didn't own her. They didn't want to own her. They wanted to fuck her. Sometimes. Not tonight, though.

She slugged back the rest of her beer. She didn't want to wake up in a strange bed. Just Henry's.

"Thanks, but I'm seeing someone." Okay, two someones. Whom she wasn't exactly seeing at all. She had two friends. Every other Friday, she fucked them.

Allowed herself to be fucked, mostly. Because even if she wasn't perfectly submissive, she hadn't taken a dominant role, either, which suited her fine so long as Henry anticipated her needs. He'd probably intuit when she wanted to be more active.

"I'm not seeing anyone with you now." The stranger flashed a charming smile.

She couldn't tell this guy any of that. It was private. Not because she was ashamed, but because talking about her relationship with Henry and Jay meant *talking* about her relationship. With Henry and Jay. To define it beyond the boundaries of her contract and rock the boat. She liked the ride the way it was, thank-you-very-much.

"You sure you don't want to dance?"

She pretended Jay sat here with her, playing a new game for Henry, who watched them from across the room.

"I do, actually." She stood. "Let's dance."

She led him to the floor. The fast music meant she didn't have to touch his sweaty hand or the rest of him for long. Not skin to skin, at least. Their bodies brushed often.

Turning her back to him made it better. Easier. Let her pretend.

He crowded her more with each song. Warning bells played a tune smothered by alcohol and wishful thinking. She gave off the wrong— right—*wrong*—signals. His hand rested on her hip after the first song. His breath warmed her neck after the second.

The tables near the second-floor railing teased her after the third, promising a man who wasn't present, the one she wanted watching her. She closed her eyes through the fourth song and said nothing when the hand at her hip curved around her, splaying out over her stomach.

Mmm, Jay.

He'd go for her breasts next. He loved to play with them. In his hands, in his mouth. Henry, in a playful mood, might duck his head and suck on a stiffened nipple. He'd tug at her until the world narrowed to nothing but slick, throbbing skin and the aching need between her legs.

The body behind her shifted closer, the firm ridge of a denim-covered erection grazing her back above the curve of her ass.

A voice whispered in her ear. "You wanna get outta here?"

Oh, fuck.

She stumbled forward, out of the embrace. That wasn't Jay's voice, and it wasn't Henry's voice, and she'd been practically fucking a stranger on the dance floor.

"I can't—I'm late—he's waiting for me at home." She turned, flashing an insincere smile. Best stick with the lie, get the fuck out and go the hell home alone. "Sorry. Like I said, I'm seeing someone."

"Someone who lets you go out and rub up against other guys for fun? He sounds like a real catch. Whatever." Face hard, the guy stalked toward the hall to the bathrooms. "Fucking cocktease."

Her heart hammered. That could've gone way worse. *You are so fucking lucky, Alice Elizabeth Colvin.*

She called for a cab and grabbed her coat from the check girl on her way out the door, standing in the circle of light near the club's doorman until her ride showed. It was fucking freezing, cold enough that her breath formed fog in front of her. The temperature shock after the heat of the club gave her a headache. It'd get worse when alcohol dehydration set in.

Fifteen minutes later, she stood outside her door. Her key ring carried two house keys, and one would open the door across the hall. Even at one in the morning. Even eighteen hours before her . . . appointment.

That's all it was to him, wasn't it? Satisfying sex, but no more than that. He didn't want to intrude on her relationships. He'd said so. Made it clear in their contract. She could've gone home with whatever-the-fuck-his-name-was, and it wouldn't have meant shit to Henry.

Her key was for emergencies only. Friend emergencies. It wasn't a license to walk in and slide into bed with Henry and maybe Jay as well, because who knew where he slept? Not her, not on nights she wasn't there. Maybe he slept in Henry's bed every night and kept his own chaotic bedroom as a formality and dumping ground. God. She wanted to know so badly. Wanted the right to know.

The mocking key ring didn't offer any answers. She laid her forehead against her door. *Work it out, Alice.*

Step one: Define the problem.

Horniness. Massive horniness and a huge fucking heap of loneliness.

Step two: Hypothesize a solution. Best-case scenario.

The key took her to Henry, and he gave her orgasms until she passed out.

Step three: Test the solution.

Fuck if she'd try that just yet.

Step four: Analyze the findings.

Potential for failure—laughably high. Likelihood Henry would be disgusted by a drunk and horny Alice in his bed—high. Likelihood he'd pour water down her throat and be a great caretaker for burdensome neighbor—high. Likelihood he'd reevaluate the status of their arrangement and end the contract—high.

All bad outcomes. Making herself a nuisance and losing Henry's respect. Drunk and horny wasn't an emergency situation or a friend situation. Henry didn't owe her anything tonight. He was on his time, not hers.

Step five: Present answer.

Home. Alone. She'd get off by herself and leave Henry and Jay out of it.

She shoved the key in the lock and stumbled through bedtime rituals, not bothering with the lights in the main room and blinking at their harsh glare in the bathroom. She chugged a glass of water, hoping to stave off her looming hangover.

She burrowed under the covers. Her arousal had waited for her. Time to test the best-case scenario.

She fumbled in the nightstand drawer for her vibrator. The toy hadn't gotten much use in the last eight months. Batteries still worked. Good.

She tried to keep her thoughts from straying to Henry and Jay. Tried hard. But no one else featured in her fantasies.

Desire sent her to their door. Using her key. Leaving her shoes by the door and a trail of clothes down the hall to Henry's room.

The door would be partly open. She'd push it the rest of the way, and he'd be sleeping. Vulnerable. Lying on his back in the center of the big bed, his arms flung out to his sides, the sheets draped tantalizingly over his legs, outlining his body in a feast for her eyes.

She circled the vibe around her clitoris but not over it. Not yet. She'd take her time, let the fantasy play out.

Fantasy-Alice ghosted across the floor and pulled the sheets back. Henry slept in the nude, as he did on his nights with her, those special nights when he allowed her to stay. When he wanted her there to fuck again in the morning.

The vibrator parted her lips as she squirmed. She'd been worked up since the third dance. This wouldn't take long. Not nearly long enough.

So fantasy-Alice didn't spend much time memorizing Henry's body, though she loved being able to ogle him like this. His relaxed, sleeping face, his strong arms and broad chest with its dark hair and the narrow line directing her to his flaccid penis waiting for her touch.

She crawled onto the bed. Her advantage would be lost once his eyes opened. But she wasn't about to deny herself. She knelt and lowered her face to his groin, inhaling his clean musk before she took him in. Even soft, he was a mouthful.

Working him with lips and tongue wouldn't be enough. She added her hand at the base as his interest grew, firming her grip and sliding her mouth along his length.

His cock stood fully erect and beautiful. Her mouth left him wet and shining in the stray bits of moonlight dancing across the room. His color deepened along the thick, textured ridge from base to tip and in the flared head. An organ designed to give her pleasure, attached to a man who wielded it with skill.

He pounced.

Fast, faster than she'd have expected, he toppled her back to the bed and pinned her beneath him. With her hands alongside her head and her legs spread wide, he pushed her open for him with his thighs and parted her lips with his naked cock.

He didn't ask what she intended in his bed. He didn't ask permission. He thrust rough and deep. He drove into her, and she matched his force with her own.

Fantasy-Henry growled at her, a low rumble. "You're going to come for me, Alice. Your pleasure belongs to me, and I want to see you come while I fuck you. Your pleasure is mine, and your body is mine, and *you* are mine. *Mine*, Alice. Come for me. Give me what's mine to take."

They did.

Fantasy-Alice and real-Alice both called his name in a single breathless gasp that became a quiet cry. But fantasy-Alice still had fantasy-Henry inside her, and his arms around her, and the comfort of his bed.

Real-Alice had a purring vibrator, sticky thighs and an empty bed. One even emptier when she silenced the vibe and set it aside. The shudders racking her body weren't the pleasant aftershocks of orgasm but the beginning of sobs.

She slept late Friday, stumbling out of bed several times to use the bathroom and drink another glass of water but always crashing again.

Even no longer tired, she drooped from fatigue. Mentally and emotionally drained. Getting out of bed seemed an insurmountable obstacle.

For the first time, as the hours ticked away toward evening, anticipation didn't gather in her gut at the promise of herself in Henry's hands for the night. Uneasiness blossomed. Fear. Dread.

He would know. Somehow, he'd intuit what she'd almost done, how she'd nearly crept into his bed like a thief and stolen the affection that belonged to Jay.

She curled her body in a tight ball around her pillow. The clock on her nightstand read five PM. Two hours. If she wanted to be on time, she ought to get up and shower.

She hadn't eaten all day, and the suggestion nauseated her. Her puffy, swollen face suffered from the dehydration caused by alcohol and tears. Henry wouldn't fail to notice, no matter how many ice packs she piled on her eyes now.

He might declare her an unfit companion for the evening. Or tell her he'd been wrong, that she was too immature to handle their arrangement if this was the result. Break things off for her own good.

He'd be nice about it, too, and that would make it worse. The reason she always ended things first, before emotional shit got attached. She'd given up way too much control here.

She spent an hour or more standing in the shower beneath the hot spray, until the water ran cold and her body shivered and her numb fingers turned off the tap. The towel became a weapon in her hands, rough and chafing, drying her with fierce intensity. She yanked the comb through her hair and blow-dried it. Brushed her teeth. Ignored her makeup options. Pointless. Henry would see through any mask.

All she wanted was to get in the door, get naked and get fucked until she couldn't hold a thought in her head. Henry could do that. As long as he did *that*, she wouldn't worry about *this*. Easy as pie. Problem, meet solution.

But at one minute to seven, her mind a jumble of contradictory advice and ominous warnings, her hand poised to knock, she battled the urge to pass out instead. Her knuckles thudded against the wood twice. A firing squad waited on the far side, and she'd given the signal for her own execution.

Jay opened the door with a stutter in his smooth pull. Wide-eyed, he gave a soft whistle. "Jesus. Are you okay?"

Fuck no, she wasn't okay. But she wanted them too much to admit that now. Needed them too much.

Despite the terror of presenting herself to Henry like this, she hadn't been able to make herself stay home. She wanted to be in Henry's bed, cuddled between him and Jay as she'd been the night the heat had failed. When it hadn't been a contract night and they'd sought her out anyway, invited her into their bed and let things happen without any trappings, as if they had a real relationship, all three of them, instead of her being added spice in theirs.

She stepped past Jay with a nod, not answering in words because she doubted he'd been instructed to ask. When Henry wanted her to speak, he'd tell her.

Jay took a long moment to close the door, only jumping into motion as Henry crossed the room to them.

Henry grasped her chin and tipped her head up. "What's happened, Alice?"

Was that real concern for her in his tone or irritation that she'd appear in front of him with bloodshot eyes and puffy cheeks? She wearied of trying to guess. Couldn't he just give her this? Tell her, instruct her, and not ask questions of her?

"I drank too much." Truth.

"Mmm." He prodded her cheeks with his thumbs. His fingers rested along her temples and across her ears. He stared into her eyes. "And why did you do that?"

"Work. We were celebrating at a club." Still true. Still not lying to Henry. Still ignoring the nagging voice in her head that accused her of adhering to the letter of their contract rather than its spirit.

"Is that all that happened? An excess of celebratory behavior?" His voice dug at her. Closed, clipped, suspicious, and she didn't blame him for it. "You're certain there's nothing else?"

The truth too much to speak, a lie unthinkable, she tugged free of his grip. Jay gawked at her with drawn brows and parted lips.

Henry frowned. Deliberately, formally, he asked a familiar question. "Are you ready to play, Alice?"

"Yes, Henry." *Please. Give me this, these hours when I'm yours. Make me forget all the hours when I'm not.*

"Sit on the couch, Alice."

She went to the couch and sat, nerves jumping faster by the minute.

She still had her clothes on. He hadn't sent her to the bedroom. Heaviness tightened her chest. Made breathing a chore. Did a panic attack feel like this?

"Tell me your safeword."

Good. A command she could follow. "Pistachio."

"Good girl." But still he frowned. "Would you like to use your safeword now, Alice?"

"No, Henry."

"Do you understand you may use your safeword for any reason? That you needn't explain, and you are free to exercise your right to stop at any time?"

"Yes, Henry." *Please stop asking me.*

"All right, Alice. Then tell me what else happened last night."

The fuck? This wasn't sex. It wasn't even foreplay.

"Anything I demand, unless expressly forbidden in your contract, Alice." Henry chided her with kindness, his voice soft. "Even if it's simply sleeping on the sofa for the night while I watch over you, remember? Either provide the answers to my questions or use your safeword, my dear."

His voice hardened. "Now, tell me. What else happened last night, Alice?"

"I . . . met a man."

"Did you fuck this man?"

"No."

"Did you want to fuck this man?"

"No. Not him."

"But you wanted to fuck."

". . . yes."

"This desire, it was overwhelming?"

"Yes."

"Yet you didn't come to me."

"No." Shame overtook her. The reasons she hadn't lost meaning when Henry beheld her with such disappointment.

"You felt I wouldn't understand?"

"It was late, and I was drunk, and things were . . . I was . . ."

If he didn't stop asking these questions, she'd cry. Not the delicate, girly, manipulative sniffles suggested by women's magazines and terrible advice books, but bone-racking sobs because it hurt so damn bad.

She'd disappointed him by not coming to him, but she'd have horrified him with her drunken neediness. She'd wanted him inside her, nothing less, and her disengaged babble filter would've had her spilling clingy demands for a relationship he wasn't interested in providing.

She couldn't win. This game she'd agreed to play had no winning move, not for her.

"You were drunk, and vulnerable, and aroused."

It wasn't a question, but she nodded in obedient agreement. The silence stretched. The coffee table's surface accused her with its clean perfection.

"You feared I would take advantage of you in that state?" His voice held a sharp edge. "That I could not care for you properly?"

"No!" God, she'd explained everything all wrong. Now he thought she considered him a letch or user or . . . or rapist. Way to go. How many ways could she fuck up the best relationship she'd ever had?

She wanted to stand, to move, but he'd ordered her to sit, and she wouldn't disobey him. She rocked with fierce denial, hands gripping the couch and knees bouncing from the motion of her feet.

"You shouldn't have to take care of me like that. It's not your job. I'm not, this is, this whole thing . . ." She waved her arm between them and toward Jay, who watched her with undisguised shock. "It's just sex. That's all it is, right? I can't expect you to hold my fucking hair back while I vomit because I go out and drink too much. Or take me to bed for a hard fuck because I get all worked up grinding against some stranger on the dance floor."

Henry's face formed an impenetrable mask. He turned away as though she sickened him.

"Yes. It's simply sex, Alice." Shoulders stiff with tension, he spoke with polite, cold indifference. "If you've satisfied your need for it, give me your safeword and go."

No. No-no-no. Please don't send me away. I'm sorry, Henry. I'll remember it's just sex. I won't try to make anything more of it. Please.

"Nothing? No safeword? Are you certain, Alice?"

"Y-yes." She managed a shaky whisper as panic beat at her.

"Then take off your clothes. We've wasted enough time this evening on your emotional issues, haven't we? When all you require here is a good hard fuck?"

Her fingers shook as she gripped the edge of her sweater and hauled it over her head. She fumbled at the clasp of her bra.

Henry glanced at her over his shoulder. "Jay. Help Alice with her clothes. This is my time, and she's shown enough disrespect for it this evening."

Jay knelt in front of her, eyes wide as he unhooked her bra and slid the straps off her shoulders. Shoes and socks next, everything set neatly to the side. Her arms rested alongside her thighs, useless, as he reached for the front of her slacks.

"Quickly, Jay. Alice is waiting for her good hard fuck, and she won't be getting it if she's still wearing her pants."

Jay hesitated as he slipped the button and touched the zipper. He whispered to her, his voice urgent and pleading. "Don't do this. Use your safeword. Please. He doesn't want this and neither do you."

"Jay." Henry's sharp tone hadn't softened. "Alice is an adult. She knows perfectly well that she may use her safeword at any time. Your sympathy is not required. She's here for sex, nothing more."

"Henry—"

"The pants, Jay." Henry turned with a blank expression. Either he didn't care about her, or he was doing a damn fine job of pretending not to. "Alice. Tell me your safeword."

"Pistachio."

"Do you wish to use your safeword now?"

Jay wrestled her pants down her legs and laid trembling hands on her hips, the top band of her underwear at his fingertips.

"No, Henry."

"You want this."

"Yes."

"Whatever I choose to give you."

"Yes."

"Was that what you wanted last night, Alice?"

"Yes."

She pressed her back to the couch cushion as Jay lifted her hips and pulled off her underwear. His eyes pleaded with her to stop this.

"Bring those to me, Jay. Alice won't be needing them again."

Jay stood and turned away, her underwear dangling from his hand. He clenched and unclenched, again and again. She ached to reassure him. Henry would only be giving her what she asked for. He'd given her soft words and kisses when called for, and now he'd give her hard and angry and taking. Because she needed it so bad. Because she wanted him to claim the right. To call her his.

Jay handed her underwear to Henry. She kept her thighs together, her nudity a discomfiting imbalance. Neither Jay nor Henry had removed a single stitch of clothing.

"Jay, pull back the table, please. I don't want anything interrupting my view."

Henry settled himself in the chair across from her, leaning back, his legs spread, knees wide. He raised her underwear to his face, inhaling, watching her over them.

"You're hiding from me, Alice. Spread your legs. You haven't the right to deny me what's mine unless you speak your safeword. Do you want to do that now?"

"No, Henry." A shudder rolled through her as she followed his instructions. Put herself on display for him. Spread her legs and waited. He wasn't in a hurry to fuck her. The knowledge oddly calmed her.

He wasn't angry or impulsive, no matter how his actions appeared, no matter how his words sounded. Henry was still Henry. He'd take care of her. He would've taken care of her last night if she'd come to him as she should have. Her fear and dread lifted.

"You denied me last night, Alice. You've said you went out and found another man to arouse you—"

"No! That wasn't, he didn't, I was, I was thinking about you." That the contract allowed her to pick up a stranger and give herself to him if she wanted didn't matter. Proving to Henry that she belonged to him and him alone mattered now. Even if she didn't always want to want that. Even if wanting it terrified her.

"Were you? Tell me."

"He asked me to dance. I . . ." Nerves seized her throat and dried her mouth. "I pretended he was Jay, that you'd told him to get me wet for you. So I could imagine you were watching."

She was whispering by the end of her confession, heat in her face and a mixture of shame and relief in her gut at telling Henry the truth.

"Yet you came home alone."

"Yes."

"Needing relief."

"Yes."

"Knowing I have told you to come to me *at any time* if you need something from me."

"... yes."

"Yet you chose to deny me that. Tell me, did you deny yourself? Or did you touch yourself?"

"I touched myself."

"Still thinking of me? Of Jay?"

"Yes."

"Perhaps you ought to be punished for that, Alice. Taking for yourself what should have been given to us." Henry cast his gaze left.

Jay stood by the coffee table, uncertainty writ across his features.

"Jay."

"I'm not . . . I can't, Henry." A shamed whisper. He sounded broken.

"No, I know, my boy. I wouldn't ask it of you." Henry stretched out his hand. "Come here, Jay."

Rather than making Jay kneel by his feet, as he'd done many times before, he pulled Jay into his lap. Curling an arm around him, Henry kissed him. A slow, romantic kiss deepening the longer it went on.

Her muscles pulsed with desire, and jealousy twanged in her chest. If Henry wanted to punish her, he couldn't have picked a better method.

Breaking off the kiss, he snuggled Jay closer and stroked his hair.

She waited, alone and silent. The space between them, no more than six feet, seemed a vast gulf.

"Touch yourself, Alice. Show me what you were doing last night when you should have been in my bed."

Oh God.

"I used my vibrator last night." Dissuasion. Evasion.

"You'll have to work harder tonight with your fingers, won't you?"

Tactical failure. Her hand hovered over her stomach. He really meant to make her show him this.

"You came home from the club. You lay in your bed, aroused. Imagining something more arousing than a solo session. Did you come to me in your fantasies, Alice?"

Her stomach muscles jumped as her fingers met skin.

"I used my key," she whispered.

"You wanted to slip inside unnoticed, didn't you? To be a naughty girl, climbing into my bed. Thinking I wouldn't know you were there, perhaps? That you might get away with something?"

Her fingers slid down, into her curls, curving around her sex. He knew her so well. Showing him this engendered no shame.

"I wanted to watch you. To touch you. But I knew . . ." She parted her lips, finding the slickness his voice inspired.

"Knew what, Alice?"

"You'd know I was there, even if you pretended you didn't."

"You know you can't hide from me. Not the sound of your breaths, coming faster, calling attention to your lovely breasts. Not the sweet scent of you, open and needy, as you are now."

She pushed a single finger inside, pumping. Added a second, a poor imitation of the fullness when his cock parted her.

"And what did you do to me, Alice, as I lay in my bed last night?"

"I pulled off the sheet to look at you." She unleashed her free hand in ceaseless motion, cupping and squeezing and tugging at her nipples as the need struck her. "And I touched you."

"With your hands?" His casual, curious tone held a hint of awareness. He didn't need to ask. He likely did so just to make her say the words.

Jay had relaxed into his embrace, Henry's hand sliding up and down his back in steady, soothing sweeps. They both watched her, Henry her eyes and Jay her fingers.

"With my mouth, first. I wanted . . ." She squirmed, a touch of embarrassment leaking through. Sliding her thumb across her clit and rolling her hips gave her the confidence she needed. "I wanted to feel you in my mouth, to feel you getting hard for me."

"You wanted to be in control."

Her admission came in silent agreement, the words too much. She'd wanted to prove she could have him, could make him want her and force him to accept her at any time, not only during the hours he'd allotted her. That if she came to him outside those hours it was not a burden on him but her right to do so.

"And were you, Alice? For how long?"

"Only until you were hard." Her fingers moved faster, dipping inside and slipping back to circle her clit, the pressure firmer, her hips rocking. "Then you, you pinned me down and fucked me. Told me I belonged to you. That I was gonna come for you."

Oh God. Thinking about it now, his voice saying the words, her fingers in frantic motion against her clit, she teetered on the edge.

"You are. You're going to come for me now. Show me. Show me you know you belong to me, Alice. Come for me."

Her back arched. Her eyes slammed shut. The next brush of her finger sent her over the edge, a half sob of his name pouring from her mouth.

Shuddering, she drew out her pleasure with her fingers.

Hands gripped behind her knees. Henry pulled her body down, twisting her until she lay on her back, her ass raised over the arm of the couch. He threw her legs over his shoulders as he pushed her hand aside and entered her.

He thrust hard, deep, not checking her readiness or asking how she wanted it or whether she did at all. She thrust back at him, reaching for his hips, desperate to pull him deeper.

Stroking her thighs where they pressed against his chest, he paused to grip her wrists. "Take these, please, Jay. Enjoy yourself."

Her arms were pulled over her head and stretched along the couch cushions. Jay licked her fingers, closing his mouth over them one at a time, sucking with enthusiasm.

A hard, abrupt thrust called her attention back to Henry. He held her legs tight to his chest.

"Was that gasp a request for more, Alice? Can you take more? Can you take everything I have to give you?"

"Yes. Yes, Henry, I can take it. Please. Please."

He bent forward, forcing her hips to tilt further, her body leveraged above her head, above her shoulders, and her vision filled by his looming form. She might black out from the intensity, but no fucking way would she stop this now.

"Was this what you wanted, Alice? What you needed so badly last night?"

With her knees nearly over his shoulders and his hips snapping against hers in a punishing rhythm, getting the breath to answer him proved impossible. Only a thin whine emerged, a wordless plea for more.

When she came, she couldn't manage even that.

A soundless scream shaped her mouth. Her body shook. Henry thrust through her release and beyond, coming with a bellowing roar that set her off again.

She lay dazed and happy as he kissed her calves, twined around his neck.

He released her thighs. She'd have bruises across the tops in the morning. He'd given her what she'd asked for. Claimed her. Marked her.

And he didn't seem angry at her neediness, even if he thought she only sought more frequent or more possessive sex. The day had ended up a hell of a lot better than it had started. She hadn't fucked things up beyond repair.

Henry pulled out and lowered her legs to drape over the side of the couch.

Jay kissed her palms. The goofy grin on his face probably had a twin on hers.

"I believe it's time to revisit your contract, Alice." Henry-speak for "we need to talk."

She froze. She'd given a breakup speech often enough to recognize one. Occasional muscle tremors still rolled through her thighs. Sated and hazy bliss dissolved into panic.

"Your needs are not being met by our arrangement. It's no longer capable of providing what you require."

How could he sound happy about something so terrifying? This was the thing she'd feared for months, the dread she'd labored beneath all day. She'd gotten emotionally wrapped up in this thing with her neighbors, pretended it was more than great sex.

"Would you agree that that is the case, Alice?"

Shit. She couldn't lie to Henry. Not because of the contract but because he was her friend and he hated lies.

In truth, the current arrangement didn't meet her needs. She needed something emotional he couldn't make himself feel for her. Something he'd taught her to feel so she'd have better relationships going forward.

She'd graduated from the Henry school. Time to thank him and get the fuck out. "Yeah, it's, um, not working for me."

She rolled off the couch and onto her feet without waiting for permission. Her legs wobbled. The sex worked. The sex worked great. The rest was the confusing part, and that was her own damn fault for not paying attention to how entangled she'd gotten. No breakup blow jobs this time. She'd wrap it up fast and salvage some dignity.

"It's been great, you've both been great, but, you know, people change, and move on."

"What? Alice? But—" Jay looked like she'd kicked him in the nuts.

Oh fuck.

"Jay, patience, please. Alice, might we make a specific adjustment to accommodate your desires?" Henry spoke in slow, measured tones. Unaffected.

He didn't feel anything. This conversation wasn't a reason for him to panic but a business decision. Practicality. If the form didn't fulfill the function, sometimes you threw out the design and started somewhere else.

"Something I have misjudged? Has something caused you to mistrust me? There's something else you need from me, perhaps?"

"No, I, you haven't done anything wrong." He had more experience making those mental adjustments. "It's just difficult." Separating the friend from the sex partner had grown harder for her the longer the arrangement lasted. She wanted both halves as a lover. "More difficult than I thought it would be."

She slipped into her pants and pulled her sweater over her head, forgoing the bra and underwear in her rush to cover herself. Naked vulnerability sucked when the games were over.

Henry sure as hell wasn't smiling now, and one eyebrow seemed fixed in what-are-you-doing position. Shit. Still on his time. She should've asked before getting dressed.

But what did he want from her?

If she'd come over last night for sex, that wouldn't have been part of their contract. Except it had to be, didn't it? Sex-related things were contract-related things, and they needed to stay in contract hours. If she hadn't been horny, if she'd needed a friend, she wouldn't have hesitated to text Jay and see if they were awake.

"Tell me what's difficult, Alice."

Except . . . the night the heat went out. When they'd invited her into their bed and let her play without rules. When Henry had made it her choice.

An emergency. A special case. Her *friends* had worried she'd freeze. As if she could've expected to sleep next to Jay and Henry all night and not end up fucking them.

"Tell me why you're pulling your clothes on as though you intend to leave us early tonight." Henry refastened his pants, too, without even discarding the condom.

Good. Less distracting. Less of a reminder he'd just fucked her senseless.

But what he asked of her—no, demanded. He demanded she make herself vulnerable, admit her need for him. He could make that demand of her, and he didn't have to offer her anything in return. Her heart pounded.

Why? Because she was a goddamned coward, that's why. Because trying to remember how to be herself around men always led her back to him. To him, and Jay, and how they were so fucking in love with each other they made her believe in it. Made her want it. Made her think she might be falling in love with them both.

How could he show her that? Why would he do that to her? She'd been fine—not happy, okay, but fine before, and now wanting more made her ache every damn day. How the fuck had she let this happen?

"Pistachio."

Jay choked, surprise blatant on his face.

Henry's reaction cracked her heart in her chest, the flicker of hurt, the pain in his eyes before he controlled his expression. He backed away from her, three steps. "All right, Alice."

Oh no. Using her safeword had been a mistake. Raw terror had pulled it out of her. But she couldn't force the word back in. She couldn't pretend she wasn't more afraid of this feeling than she'd ever been of anything in her life.

Henry flogging her for hours wouldn't hurt half as much as telling him she was maybe falling in love with him. His rationalization of her response would kill her. Flattering, he'd say. Proud of her for being able to say it, he'd say. He wasn't in love with her but helping her understand herself, and she'd mistaken attention for love, he'd say.

But her fear was a betrayal. With one word, she'd told them she didn't trust them to be gentle with her heart. She wanted to curl in a ball on the floor and sob. Dread descended. The numbness it brought mimicked relief.

"No, it's not all right." Anguish twisted Jay's face. "This is definitely not all right. It's totally wrong."

"Jay." Henry's hard look said he'd best listen and obey. "Alice has every right to use her safeword. I know you wouldn't wish to deny her that. Perhaps a break is in order. Some time and space for all of us."

A break. Right. The pretty words amounted to a concession to calm Jay. The time and space would grow, and scheduling wouldn't work out, and finally they'd abandon the idea altogether.

If she had exceptional luck, a year from now she'd be able to eat lunch with them as friends and not obsess about the tangled joy she'd found in Henry's bed.

Maybe she should've lied. Told him their arrangement wasn't hurting her.

Maybe not. Better to let it end before she made a bigger fool of herself.

"Sure. Some time and space to think about things." Her sweater scratched her breasts. Her pants clung to her wet thighs and groin. No washcloth tonight. No snuggling and talking in Henry's bed afterward. No possibility of waking up there. "That's a nice thought."

Henry nodded at her, his face resigned. As though he'd expected things wouldn't work out, and he knew, as she did, that "some time" likely meant "never again."

"Very well, Alice. If you'll let us know when you feel ready to discuss—"

"No way." Panicked anger overtook Jay's voice. "No. If you don't set a time for this talk now, you won't ever do it, and you'll both let everything fall apart. This is a stupid idea. You both, you're so, argh!"

He waved his arms in nonsensical gestures, frustration and fear bleeding out of him. "Just stop this, please. Please?"

She couldn't make him feel better about this. *She* wasn't ready to feel better about this.

Henry tugged Jay closer, wrapping an arm around the younger man.

Naked want for the security of that embrace chewed a hole through her. Henry would comfort Jay however he needed tonight.

"I realize this is difficult for you, my boy, but I'm certain it's not easy for Alice, either, and it's not where I would have preferred the night end."

"It's *difficult* 'cause you're both walking on eggshells." Jay pushed away Henry's arm.

Jay. Rejecting comfort. From *Henry*. Not possible.

"If you'd stop scaring each other and me with this overly polite concern bullshit and just say what you want, things would be fine. We all want the same thing, or close enough."

Even Henry had no reply to that.

"Fine. I'll go first." Jay blew out a breath. "I wanna keep fucking. A lot. Not just on special nights. Hell, I'd like it if Alice moved in and wanted to cuddle every night. She's family, Henry. She's yours as much as I am. We're both all yours if you'll have us."

The suggestion stunned her.

She'd suspected Jay had grown attached to her, more than with any of the women he'd "dated" with Henry's permission. But for him to be willing to share Henry's attention with her on such an intimate, day-to-day level?

God yes, sign her up.

"You've discussed this behind my back?" Henry's voice bit deep, a sharpened knife.

"What?" Jay shook his head. "No, of course not. I haven't talked about it with Alice, but I think *you* should."

"You're impatient, Jay. Reckless. To dangle the possibility now . . ." Frustration soaked Henry's tone, that and what sounded almost like hurt.

Because Jay didn't have the authority to make those decisions? To offer her something Henry didn't want to give?

"Henry's right, Jay." She chimed in more gently and spoke words it pained her to say, despite their truth. "We've had a super-emotional night. It's not the time to make big decisions. We should step away and calm down and come back with clear heads."

Jay groaned. "You two are so much alike. It needed to be now. When you're calm, you won't say what you need to say. You'll talk yourselves out of it. Your brains get all chatty and your mouths clam up. If you'd let every thought fall out of your mouth the way I do, and not analyze it eight ways first, we could've had this conversation months ago."

What? Henry had wanted to end things months ago?

Impossible. Counterfactual. Jay didn't want to end things. If he'd wished for this talk sooner, he believed something better waited on the other side of it.

Maybe the things she wanted weren't so far out of reach.

"Let's set a date." Eagerness curled in her stomach. "For the talk. That's a start, right, Jay?"

His wary nod conceded the point.

Henry cleared his throat. "By the current contract, we have two weeks before this becomes an issue. Shall we say the Monday after next? That will give us ten days in which we may each consider what we want from this arrangement and most of a week to make any necessary adjustments afterward, whether that involves allowing for more nights or fewer, or more frequent overnight stays, or perhaps including more activities outside the bedroom."

Overnight stays? Activities outside the bedroom? That sounded like *dating*.

More of her tension slid away. "Sure. Monday after next."

"Excellent." Warmth had returned to Henry's voice. "We'll say seven, as usual, to allow you time to gather your thoughts after work, Alice. I'll make dinner."

"Great. We'll talk then." She held her arms out to Jay, and he jumped at the invitation to hug her. Reassurance. His uncomplicated affection was something she needed, too.

"We'll make it work," he whispered in her ear as he squeezed her tighter.

"Jay. Oxygen. I need it to live."

He let her go with a smile.

She turned to Henry. Press her body to his? When hers vibrated with the ache of the emptiness he'd left behind? No. She'd beg him to let her stay, and that would embarrass them both.

"So, I'll see you Monday." Casual. As if she wouldn't fixate on him and Jay every waking moment in between while the imprint of his fingers faded on her thighs.

Henry frowned. Letting her leave probably clashed with his ideas about responsibility and his obligation to her as his contracted submissive.

"You'll contact me sooner if you need anything—want anything—from me," he corrected. "Even if you feel it's not worth my time or attention."

Green eyes studied her, made looking away impossible. "That decision is mine to make, Alice. I cannot properly provide for you if you don't come to me when you are in need. If nothing else, I would hope that after this evening you understand that much."

A peek at Henry's needs. A sign of his trust in her. "I do. I promise I'll give it a lot of thought." She wouldn't let him down. "I'm not used to leaning on someone so much."

She kissed his cheek. Something she wouldn't have considered doing before, not without his indication that he wanted it from her. A light kiss. An almost-friend kiss.

She walked out the door.

Chapter 9

Alice managed to go an entire week without running into Jay or Henry.

She didn't contact them, and they didn't contact her, and even going in and out of the building and stopping to collect her mail never seemed to turn them up. By the time she got home from work Friday evening, she suspected Henry had instructed Jay to leave her alone to think.

A protective gesture. Henry wouldn't attempt to sway her opinions about what their arrangement should look like. In the last eight months, he'd taken exceptionally good care of her. Physically, for sure. If he hadn't done so emotionally, well, the truth was she hadn't told him what she needed. She'd refused to entertain the idea. She'd feared her growing feelings, the overpowering nature of her desire for Henry and the almost maternal affection building on her attraction to Jay. Feared Henry hadn't wanted it too, that he wasn't feeling more for her.

He'd pretended, at least, on their nights together. Treated her with tenderness. Unless he hadn't been assuming some polite fiction as a dominant to give her only what she needed and not what he wanted. Unless that's what Jay knew that she didn't. That Henry did want more.

Fuck. Had she screwed up so colossally?

Monday. She'd ask him Monday at dinner. No backing down. She hadn't been on a single date in eight months, and they hadn't either. They would've disclosed it to her if they'd slept with anyone else. The contract's safety clauses required it. None of them had wanted more than each other. An exclusive relationship, by definition.

They had the friendship. The sex. The commitment. They just hadn't put all of them together and said the words.

Not true. Jay has. He's braver than we are.

She tossed two weeks' worth of laundry into the basket and headed down to the machines on the first floor. Throwing on pajama pants and an old T-shirt to do laundry on the Fridays she didn't spend with Henry and Jay had become routine. The activity kept her from sitting in the apartment wondering what they were doing across the hall. Those Fridays had to be Jay's, with Henry taking care of his needs the way he did hers on the opposite Fridays.

Jay had the added benefit of Henry's love and support every other day of the week. To talk about his day over dinner. To curl up on the couch together and relax. To lay his head down on the same pillow without needing sex as an excuse.

The empty laundry room boasted two spinning washers and a dryer of clothes waiting to be removed but plenty of machines open. She tossed in her washables, started the cycle, set her phone to give an alarm in an hour and crossed the hall to the community lounge to wait.

The blank television screen made an excellent listener for the things she would've asked on the day she agreed to the contract if their eventual importance had registered. Questions like "What happens if I want more than sex?" and "When you say I should come to you if I need you, what does that mean? What counts as a need?"

Her alarm interrupted. She dumped her clothes in a dryer and settled back on the couch. Jay still had a contract with Henry even though they'd lived together for years.

Having a contract didn't seem to mean they couldn't also have a relationship. The contract might spell out the amount of dominance she accepted or allowed or encouraged from Henry within that relationship. And he'd tell her she still had the control, wouldn't he? One word from her was all it took to make him stop, to back off and reassess.

Irritation blossomed with the soft *snick* of the door behind her. Interlopers. Maybe if she ignored them, they wouldn't drag her into small talk. She was busy wallowing here, dammit. But the long, lanky body swinging over the back of the couch and into the seat beside her chased irritation away.

"Hey, Alice."

"Jay? Shouldn't you be . . . I mean, why are you here?"

"Because you're here, obviously. It's your laundry night. Ergo and thus and other fancy-pants words, if I want to find you, I need to look here."

"You wanted to find me? Is something wrong? Where's Henry? Is he—"

"See, I knew you cared." He punched her shoulder, a gentle joke. "Henry's fine. Well, not fine, 'cause he's all worried about you, but otherwise, fine."

"Did he send you down here to check on me?" That didn't line up with her assessment of their distance all week. Or with the telltale wince crossing Jay's face. "Does he know you're talking to me?"

"Ah, no and no. But wait, before you give me some 'listen to Henry, Jay' speech like I know you want to . . ." He smirked, and she conceded the point, because he wasn't wrong. "Just hear me out."

Fair enough. She missed them. And Henry hadn't told *her* not to talk to Jay. "Go ahead."

"Watch a movie with me."

"What?"

"Movie night. Snacks? Soda? Laughter?" He grinned at her, his charming flirt grin. "It's a thing friends do. C'mon. We'll dump your laundry upstairs and pick a comedy and relax."

"You're serious."

"No, I'm funny. But I'm serious about the movie, yes." He grabbed her hands and stood with a playful tug. "Up, let's go, your clothes are almost dry anyway."

"What, you're a dryer psychic now?" She let him pull her to her feet. "How do you know my clothes are almost dry?"

He stood inches from her, clasping her hands. She fought the urge to lean into his strength.

"I recognized your green shirt tumbling around. You wore it yesterday. And I've been standing in the hall watching you for almost an hour."

Oh. He'd caught glimpses of her all week, maybe. Deliberately watched for her.

"One movie." She made her voice firm. "And only if Henry doesn't object."

"Deal."

He rushed her through getting her laundry and insisted on carrying it upstairs. She left the clothes in the basket as he dragged her across the hall.

"In a hurry?"

"Don't want you to change your mind."

"I'm not . . . Jay, you know I . . ."

"I know. I just want you to be able to say it to Henry sometime." He pushed her toward the living room. "Go, sit. Pick a movie. I'll make popcorn."

She sat. The closed door to Henry's studio taunted her. Henry in a painting frenzy might explain why Jay was at loose ends and seeking her out for companionship.

Jay brought the drinks and the popcorn bowl out, and she started the movie.

He found half-a-dozen excuses to touch her in the first ten minutes. He brushed her fingers when he handed her a drink. He leaned across her to grab the remote and adjust the volume. Impressive patience and self-control for him, though. He hadn't grabbed her in a bear hug yet. He stuck to fidgeting. A lot.

"I was sitting downstairs for a while, Jay." An olive branch they both desired didn't seem over the line. "I'd rather lie down, if you don't mind."

In five seconds, he had them both lying on the couch, her back to his chest, his arm in a secure grip around her stomach.

"No problem, Alice. We can do that."

They stayed that way until the credits rolled, and still the door to Henry's studio didn't open. He must've heard them laughing. Either he meant to allow them an awful lot of privacy, or he wasn't home.

"Is Henry at a gallery opening or something?" She succeeded in keeping her voice casual. Enough for Jay, anyway. "You didn't feel like going?"

"Oh, no, he's at a club." He looped a strand of her hair around his finger as she slid onto her back. "It's not my scene these days."

Clubbing didn't sound like a Henry activity. She'd sooner expect Jay to go out and leave Henry home. Maybe he'd gone to a jazz club? A poetry club? A men's club with brandy and cigars?

She wrinkled her nose and teased him with an elbow in the gut. "Since when does Henry like dancing and techno music more than you do?"

He laughed. "Hardly. It's way more tasteful. Classical music, mostly, and very little dancing, unless you count the naked and horizontal sort. Although vertical's pretty popular, too, come to think of it. And now I'm definitely thinking of it."

"He's at a *sex* club? Having sex with other people?" Shrill to her ears, her voice still didn't convey the depth of her confusion and horror. Was Henry at the place Jay had gotten hurt? No fucking wonder it wasn't Jay's scene. How could Henry go there?

"He's at one, yeah, but I doubt he's having sex with anyone."

Jay didn't seem troubled by an idea that didn't even make sense to her. But maybe Jay's experiences made it more complicated. The place he'd been hurt was also the place he'd met Henry. Maybe he still had that desire, but he didn't feel able to go. God, that must crush him. Like the way he didn't mind watching Henry flog her anymore but he wasn't begging for it himself.

"But he could be." Henry might be meeting a new submissive right now. Jay would miss her, but he'd have Henry to talk him through it.

"Sure. He could be."

Pleasing Henry came first. He'd transfer his affection easily enough if handled the right way. Hell, maybe he'd done it before. Maybe she'd been the replacement for someone else. Her stomach flipped.

"But if he is, he'll be safe about it. You know he wouldn't do anything to put us at risk."

Physically, he meant. Medically.

That wasn't what she meant at all. Didn't Henry feel an emotional connection to them? Fidelity? Or had this whole time, months of her life, just been fucking.

Playing.

God, being upset with Henry made her an unfair, hypocritical bitch. She'd said she wanted nothing more than fucking from the start. She'd lost her shit last week, proved she wasn't cut out for their arrangement, and he'd gone out tonight searching for her replacement.

She closed her eyes, cutting off the sight of Jay's earnest stare, his open, trusting expression. He had a hell of a lot more right to be upset than she did, but Henry's behavior didn't bother him in the slightest.

Henry would always come back to him. *He's the bride. I'm the stripper at the bachelor party.*

Shit.

All her thinking this week wouldn't change that. Somewhere along the line, their arrangement had gone from playing to serious for her. But not for Henry, not if he'd gone out to fuck other people.

Jay nuzzled her ear. "If you want help taking care of things, I'm here. You're here. The bed is here. We can play without Henry, as long as we keep things vanilla."

She pushed herself away from him, off the couch. "Sorry, Jay. I'm, I think I'm just gonna turn in. Get a good night's sleep."

He gained his feet in an instant. "Alice?"

Avoiding his gaze, she took a few steps toward the door. "Yeah, no, it's fine, I'm—"

"You're upset. I fucked up, didn't I—Henry is so much better at this than I am." He brushed her arm. "He wouldn't let you leave like this. So you can go, and I'll call and interrupt his night, or you can stay and we can go to bed—no playing, I promise—and I won't call."

"Anyone ever tell you you're really dominant for a submissive?" Her jab lacked punch. She didn't truly want to cross the hall to her empty bed. But she didn't want to talk, either.

"Ah-ah-ah—I'm the senior submissive here. In Henry's absence, you report to me."

"My contract doesn't say that."

After they talked on Monday—renegotiated—who knew what her contract might say? Assuming she still had a contract. Henry and Jay had been fine as a twosome before she'd come into the picture. They'd be fine afterward, too. And apparently Henry had plenty of people waiting in the wings.

"Alright, you've convinced me." Jay smirked. "I'll have to call Henry for an interpretation and a ruling on that."

God, no. Showing Henry what a pushy, whiny, needy submissive he'd contracted sure as hell wouldn't make him inclined to extend her greater participation in their relationship. Arrangement. Whatever the fuck she should call it now.

Jay'd do it, too. Not to piss her off, but because he hadn't been able to fix the situation himself and he'd rely on Henry to know what to do. "Stop that. I'm coming to bed."

"No more arguing?"

"No more arguing." She didn't want to leave him alone anyway. Not if Henry had gone to the sex club where he'd met Jay.

"No more clothes?" His hopeful voice teased. His best puppy eyes pleaded with her. If her laughter sounded forced, he didn't mention it.

"No more clothes."

Zipping forward and down, he wrapped his arms around her thighs and lifted her over his shoulder. He took a playful bite of her ass through her pajama pants as she hung upside down. She slapped his ass in retribution.

"Caveman style, really?"

"I caught a feisty one. If I don't carry her off quick, she might leave me."

He could've carried her to his room, to his bed, but he passed his own door and stepped through Henry's at the end of the hall. Maybe he missed Henry tonight more than he would say. He just buried it under his familiar happy-go-lucky demeanor.

She let his exuberance lift her mood, cuddling and teasing in the big bed. When he would've disappeared to handle the results in the shower himself, she stopped him. Pushed him back against the pillows and delivered a hard-and-fast blow job that had him calling her name as she swallowed. Licking him clean, she traced his disappearing veins and the wrinkles reforming as steely satisfaction retreated to sweet sensitivity. The closeness, his intimate vulnerability, all heavy-lidded eyes watching her and fingers curling softly in her hair, made her ache.

"C'mere," he murmured. "Sit on my face. I'll make it good."

His softening cock slipped from her mouth. She pressed a kiss to the crease of his thigh where it would settle. Sliding upward only far enough to lay her body alongside his, she tucked herself against his boneless warmth.

"I know you would. I'm just not in the mood." Partly to ease the sting of rejection for him and partly to ease her own loneliness, she added, "Hold me?"

He rolled on his side, pulling her back against him, and dropped his arm over her stomach. Head dipping, he sprinkled kisses on her back and shoulders. "S'good?"

"S'good," she agreed. "Sleep, Jay."

He hugged her tighter. Eventually, his relaxed stillness and steady breaths signaled his successful arrival in dreamland.

She drifted on the border between sleep and waking for hours, gaze continually flicking to the bedside clock. Nearly two AM, and though Jay's long form remained curled around her back in slumber, no head occupied the pillow in front of her.

Henry was still out with someone else, surrounded by beautiful men and women, ones trained to perfect submission, and she lay in his bed, imperfect and unwanted.

The tears she'd held back in front of Jay clogged her nose and dripped to the pillow. She stifled her sobs. No need to wake Jay with her weakness and insecurity.

He seemed to take it as a given that Henry would go out and leave them behind. Did not asking questions make Jay a better submissive? Was that what Henry hoped to get from renegotiating their contract?

Above Jay's soft snores came a new sound. Footsteps on hardwood, soft padding thuds. Henry. He'd have left his shoes at the door to avoid waking Jay. He wouldn't expect her here. He might be angry.

The door pushed open.

Henry stepped inside by moonlight. She'd run out of time to wipe her face in the pillow to hide the tears or sniff to clear her nose.

He stood near the door for a long moment. Stripped off his tie and rolled it neatly, unbuttoning his shirt one-handed as he moved to the dresser and laid the tie atop it. His watch and cuff links followed.

Pulling his belt free of his slacks, he coiled it and set it aside before dropping his pants. Those, he folded over his arm and hung on the back of the chair beside the dresser. Boxer shorts and socks were draped on the chair seat.

She let her eyelids drop fully closed as Henry approached the bed in the nude. He was unaroused. Had he found satisfaction at the club?

She waited for the bed to register his weight, but instead his voice rumbled in the silence.

"Were you lonely, dear ones?" A musing question, a hint of curiosity and compassion.

He'd gotten it right, too, without even knowing. Half a sob hitched in her throat before she could call it back.

"Alice?" The bed dipped, and a quiet *click* heralded the coming of muted light, a brighter shade of blackness inside her eyelids. Fingers touched her cheek. "You've been crying. Why?"

The pillow rustled with her movement. She didn't want to talk about her overblown fears, least of all with Henry.

"I require an answer, Alice. Open your eyes, now, please." He typically reserved that commanding voice, quiet but firm, for scenes.

Would he punish her for refusing? They weren't technically playing, but she lay in his bed. That was as good as consent, an invitation, the implicit understanding that she'd be guided by his voice.

He might reject her. Replace her. As much fun as she'd been having, as emotionally entwined as she'd gotten, Henry considered her a temporary plaything. He might've found a woman tonight he'd rather have in his bed.

She squinted at the light and blinked until her vision cleared. The bedside lamp silhouetted Henry's form but hid his face from her.

"Much better. Now, why have you been crying?" His firm gentleness urged her to let go. Let the words tumble forth before she could lose her nerve.

"Are you ashamed of us? Of me?" Her tears had thickened her voice. It didn't matter. He'd seen the evidence on her cheeks. "Is that why you go alone?"

He flinched, his head jerking away. "Oh, my dear girl, no."

He brushed her hair aside with his knuckles and stroked her cheek. "Would you like to go? Is that something you desire? Are you ready for all of the eyes staring at you? To follow my instructions exactly and perform for a crowd? To have them see you in such an intimate moment? Or is that something you would prefer to share only with Jay and myself for now?"

She squirmed, wanting to please him but not wanting to be so exposed. Not yet, at least. "No, you, you're right, I'm not ready. But if I was..."

"I would take you with me in a heartbeat, dearest. I will be delighted to show you off, if and when we both agree it suits your needs. Until then, I will go alone."

"But..." In matters outside the bedroom, she wouldn't have hesitated to question him. But sexuality was his territory. He made the rules.

"It's all right, Alice. Ask your question."

"I get why you didn't take us with you. But why did you go at all? Aren't we enough for you?" Didn't he want her? Had she fucked up beyond repair?

"More than enough." He chuckled.

"I go because I enjoy observing and for . . . continuing education, you might say. To help me keep up with the two of you." Cradling her face, he stroked her lips with his thumb and caressed her ear with his fingers. "I'm not so immune to the same fears you battle as you might imagine me to be, Alice. Someday, you and Jay may decide to move on. I would very much like to postpone that day for as long as possible."

His naked admission of vulnerability wasn't something she'd considered. The fault of her own selfish blindness, or his expertise at concealing himself behind a composed, confident exterior? He wrestled with doubt. Worried her affections might turn.

That was silly.

Like her fears.

She should . . . let them go. And help him let go of his.

She raised her hand to his where it grazed her cheek, holding him still and turning to press a kiss into his palm. "I don't want anyone else, not as a dominant and not as a lover. Just you and Jay. Let me show you?"

Henry's hand slipped away as he stood.

She lifted the edge of the blankets, the oddity of inviting him into his own bed while another man slept at her back a piercing note of uncertainty shrieking at her. But he settled on his side, facing her, without evidence of hesitation or concern.

His hand brushed her stomach. With a gentle touch, he unwound Jay's arm from her body. Trapping her gaze with his, he spoke in his low, commanding tone. "Jay. Roll over."

The warmth at her back disappeared.

Past her shoulder, Jay sprawled on his stomach on the far side of the mattress. He seemed asleep yet, despite the bedside light and their voices. Maybe he slept as deeply as she often did in Henry's bed. Obeyed Henry's voice on instinct. Would she do that? Had she?

Henry and Jay might've made love as she slept beside them. Fearing they'd left her out would be a step backward. If they had, she wouldn't begrudge them. If they hadn't kicked her out, her waking to find them together didn't concern them. She was welcome here. She belonged.

Henry touched her cheek, turning her to face him. "All right, Alice. Show me, dearest."

She shoved the covers down past their hips, her eagerness to explore him the way he explored her pulsing with every heartbeat.

Running the back of her hand over his chest, she memorized the smoothness of his skin and the not-quite-roughness of his hair. She treated his body as if every inch were new. It *was* new, the idea that he wanted to keep her here, contented and in his bed, so much so he'd seek out new activities and games for the three of them. Had he planned to bring a promise of more adventure to their negotiation Monday?

She turned her hand over and traveled the same expanse with her palm, the familiar firmness of his chest and softness of his stomach with a hint of roundness. Whatever might've gone on at the club, she'd damn well reclaim anything that—

"So serious." His voice soothed.

He flattened her hand beneath his, against his sternum. With his fingers shielding her own, she seemed to disappear into him.

"No one has touched me tonight, Alice. Not even a kiss of greeting or a clasp of hands. Only you."

The tightness in her throat eased. Leaning in, she kissed him, tentative and searching. As if it were their first kiss, as if he'd walked her to her door and might expect to be sent home with nothing more than this.

She pulled back long enough to drag air into her lungs and kissed him again as she pressed her weight against him, her hand firm on his chest. She couldn't push him over without his cooperation, but he followed her silent signal. His arm came around her waist to rest on her spine when he allowed her to tip him onto his back.

Now she had both hands free to stroke his arms, his shoulders, his neck. To cup his face as she kissed him, to run her fingers through his hair, nails dragging over his scalp.

He kneaded her back and buttocks as she squirmed atop his thigh. She bent her leg to better straddle him and his cock hardened in response.

This was making out like she'd never done it in high school.

Henry's bed offered infinitely more comfort than the bed of a pickup with a sleeping bag thrown open. His devoted attention made her proud to share her body, and he wouldn't be apologizing in five minutes for coming in his jeans.

The highlight of those experiences, when second base was the best her boyfriend could hope for, had been the forest of stars above her and the cool breeze washing over her. They'd have to try it sometime, the three of them. This summer. Jay had camping gear. He'd expected she would join them. She'd suggest it to Henry. Later.

Right now she busied herself staking her claim to his neck. Nudging his face to the side, she sampled the spice of his skin, the savory hint of leather akin to the scent of her flogger, the citrus zest as sharp in its perfection as the meals he served her. She nibbled on the cord of muscle leading to his shoulder. Taking her time, she pleased herself, gratified when his breath caught or a moan rose from his throat or his hands clenched on her ass.

She moved leisurely down his body. The muscles of his neck and shoulders. The hollow of his throat. The line of his collarbone. All became well acquainted with the suction of her lips and the stroke of her tongue.

His cock stood hard and ready for her long before she'd finished her attentions to his chest, the slopes of his ribs and the softness of his stomach. When she knelt between his legs and covered the points of his hips and the creases of his thighs with nipping bites and teasing kisses, he groaned low and thrust at the air.

"Punishment, Alice?" Strain deepened his voice. "For all the times I've made you wait?"

He held her entranced, eyes dark and bottomless as a sea of pines. She shook her head in slow, rolling denial. "Pleasure. For all the times the wait was worth it."

Lowering her mouth, she took him as deep as she could, using her hand to make up the difference. She moved in unison, lips and tongue and fingers and palm, a twisting slide up and down. How odd that an action little connected to her own body's pleasure centers nevertheless made her throb with need.

She'd given previous partners an uncounted number of blow jobs, but never had one given her such a deep sense of satisfaction and arousal. Hell, she'd given Jay one a few hours ago and it hadn't made her feel so joined. Maybe because she hadn't used one to communicate her appreciation and affection before.

Henry's hand came to rest on her head. He stroked her hair without attempting to control her movements. Vivid recollection brought her the sight of Jay kneeling in front of him on a rainy morning. She shuddered with pleasure, understanding now why he so enjoyed worshipping Henry in this way.

Their service exposed trust and acceptance and something her mind shied from naming. But the power of that nameless thing spurred her to ignore Henry's murmured warnings and refuse to remove her mouth. She hummed encouragement, hovering on the edge of orgasm herself when he climaxed, his hips bucking once as she swallowed. His fingers tightened in her hair, and a fierce growl of her name broke the silence of the room.

She reluctantly allowed his cock to slip from her mouth, tonguing him as his harsh breaths echoed in her ears and her body throbbed. For about ten seconds.

Gripping her rib cage, he hauled her bodily up the bed. He rolled the two of them toward the center, one knee dropping between hers and spreading her legs. Driving three fingers into her, he pressed his thumb hard on her clit.

She came on the second thrust, as his tongue swept into her mouth and surely found his own taste. When her trembling subsided, he pulled his fingers from her and savored them, too. Shifting his weight to both arms, he rested his body fully over hers and pressed soft kisses to her neck and chest.

She lolled her head to the side, obedient to his desire for access, and buried her nose in the pillow, in Henry's scent.

Jay startled her as he blinked, his face inches from her own. She and Henry had rolled clear across the bed.

The corner of Jay's lips, askew through her one eye above pillow level, turned up in a smile. "Want a washcloth?"

She didn't have to answer. He climbed out of bed, Henry calling after him. "A bottle of water as well, Jay. Alice may be dehydrated after her emotional evening."

Henry adjusted his body and her own until he half sat, propped against the headboard and pillows with her reclined against his chest. Arms encircling her, he cupped her breast in a possessive hold.

"You asked me to let you show me, Alice." His breath washed over her ear. "Shall I tell you what you've shown me tonight?"

A glimpse of his wisdom and understanding? Yes, please.

"You value these nights together more than you have admitted to me. You've been struggling with emotions that overwhelm you, and you've feared to bring them to me. But you seek comfort in my bed. You find your own pleasure in pleasing me." His arms tightened around her. His voice dropped to a whisper. "What am I to do with you, my sweet girl?"

Her heart hammered. Her throat rivaled the Sahara. A tiny croak emerged. "Keep me?"

His lips brushed her temple. "Did you imagine I would give you up?"

They sat in silence as Jay returned bearing a warm washcloth and a cold bottle of water.

"Well done, my boy, thank you."

Henry held the bottle for her to drink as she rested on his shoulder. Once she'd had her fill, he drank before trading the bottle to Jay for the washcloth to clean the stickiness from her sex and thighs, briefly sliding her forward to do the same service for himself. When Jay reclaimed the washcloth, Henry pulled him in for a gentle but thorough kiss before sending him on his way.

"Perhaps you don't realize how special you are to us, Alice—how much of a departure from the norm." Henry idly stroked her stomach, a pleasant distraction.

"What, you don't normally go for blondes?" She shut down her joking tone when he squeezed her breast in warning. "No, I know. I mean, Jay thought I was hot the day we met. I get it."

"*Jay* thought." Confusion sounded odd from Henry. "And do you suppose I made him wait a year to approach you in order to teach him patience?"

"A thousand years couldn't teach Jay patience." Jay smirked at her from the doorway. She stuck her tongue out. "I figured you didn't want awkward hallway conversations every time we ran into each other. Or you wanted to make sure I wouldn't freak out or tell the super you were harassing me."

Having this conversation came easier without looking at Henry. Maybe he'd considered that when he'd settled them as he had.

"Or Jay wanted to fuck me and you didn't, and you eventually let him convince you." Revealed now as an incorrect hypothesis, because Henry would never let Jay convince him to do something if he didn't want it himself or believe it necessary for Jay's well-being.

Which explained her? Necessary for Jay or wanted by Henry? Was wanting to be both wrong?

The silence lasted as Jay approached the bed. Finally, Henry spoke.

"I made both of us wait for you because I wanted to be certain of success, Alice. Because you were not simply a borrowed female submissive for a hotel-room rendezvous. Because the longer we knew you, the more emotional the need for you became." Henry stroked her breasts and belly, his arms enfolding her. "One night would not have been enough. You are the only woman to have been invited into this bedroom, Alice. You're certainly the only person with an open invitation to come and go as you please."

Tears threatened. An unexpected unknotting in her chest stole her breath. She wasn't a replacement. There hadn't been a woman before her. And Henry hadn't been out looking for her replacement tonight. Relief overwhelmed her.

He tipped her sideways and studied her face, his own relaxing.

"You are not a toy, Alice. You will not be discarded, no matter how perfectly trained the participants at the club. You are here because you are *you*. No replacement exists for that."

Jay flopped onto the bed and rolled on his side, his head propped on his hand near their feet. "Yeah, if Henry were the type to shuffle through submissives like a deck of cards, he'd have dealt me to someone else years ago. I'm a problem child."

She giggled at the unrepentant pride in his voice. He squeezed the arch of her foot and kissed it. "Besides, you've got it all backward. Henry's the one who brought up the idea of extending an invitation to you."

Disbelief fastened her attention to Jay's face. Smooth. Calm. Not hiding a punch line. But Henry was a meticulous man, not an impulsive one.

"You think I'm teasing, but it's true. Not that I wouldn't have suggested it—I mean, if I hadn't wanted to see your reaction, I could've found something besides my wadded-up shirt to prop the door that first day." He flashed her his most charming smile. "But Henry beat me to it that night. Wanted to know if I'd feel slighted."

"Do you?" She'd never asked, though she'd worried. A submissive rivalry equivalent of sibling rivalry might make them compete for Henry's favor, and Jay had been here first. He deserved the lion's share.

"Nope." Jay bolted up, leaned in and kissed her. Sweet at first, but with growing possession, even as Henry embraced her and his breath warmed her ear. Jay drifted back.

"I'm the youngest of five. Knew how to share before I could walk. And Henry's good at balancing personalities and needs. I bet he could tell you why we work."

Her silent inquiry received a light kiss on the tip of her ear in reply.

"I enjoy staging and direction, observing often, participating less so. Having two actors to instruct is more satisfying." Henry shifted behind her, the brush of his soft cock as perfect in its own way as his arousal. "Jay enjoys pleasing others and being surrounded by people. The opportunity to bring you pleasure while pleasing me is a double joy for him. And you, Alice . . . you enjoy giving up control to me and being the central focus of our attention. That is why we 'work,' as Jay says."

"I just thought you were hot. Teasing you was fun. You got all flustered first, and then you teased back." Jay shrugged. "Henry's the one who said you 'showed promise.'"

What could she have done or said—oh. "My roommate and her boyfriend?"

"You didn't blush, my dear. You weren't ashamed. You were comfortable with sexuality and sexual acts happening in front of you." Henry paused to run his thumb over her nipple, coaxing it to harden. "But no, it wasn't merely that. It was a culmination of many things."

She pleaded for clarification, a wordless hope that understanding what had drawn him to her might shove her insecurities out the door.

He gave her rising nipple a teasing pinch. "You're a needy, greedy girl, Alice. But as I enjoy indulging you . . ."

He looked down at her face, eyes narrowed and distant. Picturing her as she'd been that first day, maybe. "The way you reacted to Jay's body, to my nearness and voice. The way you allowed me to coax you into relaxing and accepting assistance, the trust you showed despite the brevity of our acquaintance. The way you attentively listened and participated in every conversation, whether the topic interested you or not, and the way you fell naturally into teasing us both."

Too much to take in, a revelation to the horizon of her understanding.

"Verbally, that is. I'm certain you were not, on that day, deliberately teasing us physically. But you gave as good as you got. A great number of things added up to a desire to show you pleasure."

Twenty months since the day they'd met, an enormous block of time. So much she'd missed or misinterpreted or ignored.

"Your loveliness and sexual compatibility, though highly enjoyable, are not what have kept you in our bed for the past eight months, my dear. The emotional bonds run deeper than that."

Jay's hand wandered along her thigh and Henry's, an oddly grounding touch. Gazing above her, at Henry, he tilted his head like a puppy. The warm pleading in his eyes could've melted an iceberg.

Henry sighed with exaggerated amusement. "Perhaps now would be a good time to open the discussion of your contract, Alice, instead of waiting for Monday. We might contrive something with more flexibility."

If Jay had a tail, he'd be wagging it.

"I think I'm plenty flexible." She curled her shoulder into Henry's chest and gave him her best innocent smile.

He breathed out slow and steady, his eyes dark. "And I think I'll demand a demonstration soon. But not while this conversation remains unfinished."

She shivered at his tone. "Are you going to be inflexible about the flexibility?"

"You don't want more flexibility in our arrangement, Alice?"

Her second chance. She'd be fucking brave this time. Tell him the truth. Trust him.

"Less." She worried for Jay. Her truth would affect him, too. But he flashed a thumbs-up and a wide grin. "I want less flexibility. I want more time with you both. Guaranteed exclusivity. No potential encounters with other people. No dates with them. Because that's, that's not okay with me. I know you haven't taken advantage of that clause, 'cause you would've told me, but I don't like knowing it's an option. I don't like having it as an option. I'm not out looking for someone else. And I don't want to feel like I should be. I like what I have here."

Henry's smile held a predatory edge. "Agreed. Your pleasure belongs to me. I will provide it more frequently, in ways sexual and nonsexual. I have no objections to those conditions, dearest."

One down, one to go. She couldn't impose exclusivity on Jay, and he'd dated other women with Henry's blessing. He shrugged, his grin morphing into a smug smile.

"I already begged until Henry changed that in my contract. In August. It used to say I could have vanilla sex with any woman I wanted, as long as I kept him informed. Now it outlaws that, by *my* choice." His bragging dropped to a teasing whisper. "But it got a new Alice subsection. You fill up three whole pages."

August. The month they'd started this. She had no words. Her entire contract would fit in a subsection of his—and his included that many rules pertaining specifically to her. Rules he'd asked for. Given up other women for.

Jay laughed like a delighted child. "Twice! Twice in one night." He fell to the bed, his laughter becoming a chortling snort. "God, Alice, I can't even . . ."

"Easy, my boy." Henry twitched his lips, a single break in his calm, steady voice. "You'll make Alice believe you're laughing at her expense."

Jay's laughter cut off. "No . . . no-no-no. Alice, you know I'm not, right? I'm just so fucking happy. You, this whole time, you were shocked. Like you couldn't believe Henry wanted you from day one. Like you can't believe I'd pick time with you over dates with random women who make my dick twitch. Being with you and Henry is off-the-charts better, trust me."

The contract discussion lasted another hour before Henry insisted she demonstrate her flexibility. That discussion lasted much longer than an hour and featured much less conversation.

Chapter 10

The awkward adjustment period Alice dreaded never materialized. No nagging voice urged her to give up indulging in a fantasy of a relationship and take life more seriously.

She tangled her life with the one Henry and Jay shared, her contract broader in scope but weighing no heavier on her than the original. Their Friday schedule unchanged, she submitted to Henry's whims in those hours, bearing a responsibility to be obedient to him.

Her submission remained more casual than Jay's. A choice. The contract additions had been less sexual and more personal. Emotional.

Henry expected her to attend dinner each night. She might make excused absences—a phrase that brought to mind school and doctors' notes and made her laugh at the idea of requesting a note from her boss to present to Henry. "Please excuse Alice from dinner this evening, as she is needed for overtime on the McGinty project."

But barring emergencies or the occasional desire for solitude, which any affected party might voice, Henry put dinner on the table at seven, and she wasn't to treat the evening as playtime. He insisted she not think of sex as the only reason they brought her into their home.

So she arrived by seven, and she helped Jay set the table, and she listened as Henry explained the dishes and the techniques used in their preparation. Her new normal. As if they were a family of three.

She'd given up too much of their friendship in the last few months. Feared to intrude on their lives outside contract hours and missed out because of it.

Now she didn't have to weigh whether they desired her presence or what signals she sent by knocking on their door on a Tuesday night to watch television with Jay or listen to music with Henry. She used her key on every night but Friday. On those nights, she knocked and waited on Henry's pleasure.

She'd gained girlfriend privileges. Sitting on the counter and reeling Henry in for a kiss while the salmon baked. Tossing a pillow at Jay so he'd take the invitation to push her down on the couch and kiss her until Henry called them to the table.

Her boys walked her home. Never later than eleven o'clock, because Henry insisted she have a full night's sleep during the week. The walk measured all of ten feet down the hall, okay, but they alternated nights and kissed her at her door.

The Alice subsection in Jay's contract had probably gotten longer. He delivered precise good-night kisses. No lower body contact, no roaming hands. Jay's tender kisses were the opposite of Henry's.

The other night Henry had pinned her body to the door with his weight as he suckled and nipped at her neck. When she was panting and wet with desire, he'd growled in her ear.

"I want you thinking of me when you touch yourself tonight, Alice. Will you do that for me, sweet girl?"

She'd lacked breath for more than a whispered promise. "I would've thought of you anyway, Henry."

He'd kissed her once more, firm, and stepped back. "Go inside, Alice. Go now."

She'd imagined him standing outside listening. Her climax had been swift and sudden.

Their awkward adjustment period had passed. Unrecognizable from the inside. The wrongness she'd struggled with for almost nine months. In reconciling the friendship half of her life with the sexual arrangement half, she'd come close to fucking up both.

For once, her response wasn't thank God for Henry—it was thank God for Jay.

He'd been open about his needs. Dropped hints for months that she meant more to Henry. Demanded she rely on Henry to fix things.

If she hadn't been waiting in that bed when Henry arrived home, their contract renegotiation talk would've gone a hell of a lot differently. He would've worn a mask of politeness, she would've let insecurity best her and Jay would've been devastated by them both.

And she wouldn't be in Henry's bed now, enjoying the full attention of his tongue working between her legs.

Her arms lay behind her head, palms tucked beneath to elevate her view, at his direction. He'd wrapped his arms around her thighs, though at times one hand would slide upward, over her stomach, across her ribs, until his arm stretched out along her body and he stroked the fullness of her breast.

He'd bade her raise her feet until they crossed tailor-style atop his back. Then he'd begun his torment, with a full arsenal of weapons. His breath. His lips. His teeth. His tongue.

She hung suspended in pleasure, never certain whether he'd tug at her lips with his teeth or plunge his tongue into her or send a heated breath across her clitoris.

And the sounds. He wielded them as a weapon all their own. Not only flesh on flesh but also his appreciation of her. With his mouth full, his articulation suffered, but she had no complaints.

He hummed encouragement at every jump of her hips even as his arms halted her motion, kept her pinned and open for him. Made her submit to this pleasure, to the repeated climaxes he gave her. Their groans mingled in the heated bedroom air as he lapped at her sex.

Centered between the slopes of her breasts, down the length of her belly, he moved in exquisite harmony with her need. Every so often he'd lift his head. Tongue extended, flicking her clit, he locked his eyes to hers. Pleasure tore her free, incoherence and darkness and surrender an intoxicant carrying her away.

Her haziness lifted in minute increments. He'd stopped. Her legs had slipped from his back to the bed. She hugged his rib cage with her calves. He lay with his head near her hip, his nose nudging at the short golden curls above her sex.

"Tell me what you're thinking, my dear."

"That you're sinfully good at that."

"Particularly for one who doesn't practice often, hmm?"

Embarrassment heated her face. He'd grasped her thoughts with exactitude. He'd only been with her and Jay in the last nine months. Jay had been his primary partner for years. He'd indulged with women at the club and in hotel rooms, and those seemingly rarely.

Lacking the necessary partner, he couldn't have practiced this skill often.

He kissed her stomach, a line along the cradle from hip to hip.

If only he'd kiss her harder. Leave a ring of tiny bruising reminders like a belly chain of hickeys. Marks proving she belonged to him, that she allowed his ownership and he claimed it with pride.

"I was quite enthusiastically bisexual before I began devoting so much attention to Jay, my dear. I don't expect I've forgotten the basic idea . . . or lost the taste for it." He lifted his head and smirked at her, his eyes laughing and dark.

"The basic idea? I'm sure you've taken an advanced course." Of course, her experience of receiving oral sex was limited to Henry and Jay. Somehow she'd always picked guys who wanted to get straight to their pleasure and skip right over hers. Not anymore.

"Mmm. I did train rather extensively."

"Tongue exercises?"

He tickled her ribs as she twisted and giggled.

"One of the ways a dominant may learn to handle submissives is to assume their role in the games." He reached for a condom packet on the bed. She curled her toes with anticipation. "I learned to please women before I learned to dominate them, my dear."

"You were a submissive?" Henry, open and vulnerable, naked and kneeling at his master's feet? Impossible.

"Part-time, for two years, yes. I don't make a particularly good submissive." He pushed her legs to her chest and covered her body with his own. "But understanding those desires is important." His voice slipped into silky seduction. "You understand them, don't you, Alice?"

Hips rotating, he slid his cock forward to brush her sex.

"You know the eager grip of anticipation." He lowered his arms, resting more of his weight on her legs. "The helpless vulnerability of being pinned and spread open."

He thrust his hips and drove into her. Desperation and desire urged her to meet his thrust with her own, but he'd immobilized her.

"The need for more, and the satisfaction when you receive it." He raised up on his arms, allowing her legs freedom to move. "Grip me, Alice. Hold tightly."

She spread her thighs and wrapped her legs around Henry's back as he lowered his head and sucked at her breasts. He spoke between kisses.

"You enjoy knowing you need ask for nothing—that you, in fact, often *cannot* ask—but that I will provide precisely what you require. Because I know *you*."

He nipped his way to her neck, and she rolled her hips against him. He still hadn't thrust. Unmoving inside her, he remained a constant presence and a promise.

"Your body tells me what you want." He dragged his hips back, and she lifted hers, chasing his cock. "Patience, Alice."

His shallow, teasing thrust wasn't even so deep as his tongue had been. Her hips stirred upward again in reply, but he merely pulled farther away.

"Be still, dearest. Wait. Feel. Anticipate."

He teased her again, and this time she managed to hold herself still.

"Good girl." A deep thrust, and she moaned. He pulled back. "Imagine the sensation. You know what but not when. You remember how it feels, don't you?"

He thrust hard, three times, leaving her panting. Need spiraled up in her.

"You feel the emptiness, the waiting, and you remember the fullness you crave."

Thrust. Again. His mouth on hers, swallowing her moans.

"And I give you what you crave, don't I, Alice?" Teasing, seductive, he whispered in her ear.

Thighs trembling, she clutched him, her body pining for his.

"Please." Strained and breathy, her voice sounded unlike her. But he made it happen effortlessly. "Henry, please."

"Yes, *please*. That is precisely what I intend to do, Alice. Please you." He moved his hips in a teasing circle, and she fought to keep herself still. "My good girl. You needn't chase after anything. I'll bring it right to you, if only you listen to your body and wait."

Frustration burned in her at his shallow thrusts. But he leaned his weight forward over her, and every stroke pressed hard against her clitoris. No matter how much oxygen she sucked in, her breaths fell short of her body's need.

"Hen—Hen—"

"I know, dearest." Even Henry strained now, his voice rough and low. "I know you. Let me know you. Let me wring the last drop of pleasure from you."

Another swivel of his hips and a true thrust, hard and deep, filling her as she began quaking around him. His breath washed hot over her ear. "Let me in, Alice."

And she was gone. Pleasure rolled through her, grounding his final thrusts as he groaned in her ear.

Her legs dropped to the bed.

He rolled their bodies to leave her sprawled atop him. The position wasn't as nice as being sprawled beneath him, shielded from the world by the breadth of his shoulders and the press of his hips, but it had its own joys. When she shifted just so, his heartbeat thrummed beneath her ear. Her torso rose and fell with his breathing, long and deep as he recovered his calm.

Eventually he tipped her to the sheets and left the bed, returning sans condom with a washcloth in hand. Sitting beside her left hip, he leaned across her. With one hand planted alongside her right hip, he dangled the washcloth in the other.

She yearned for the words. He pursed his lips in a knowing smile.

"Spread your legs for me, Alice." He spoke in a tender tone utterly distinct from the one he used when he wanted her to open for his pleasure. Both tones made her shiver.

She spread her legs, and he applied himself to the task of bathing her with thorough, gentle motions. The way he cared for her seemed almost ritualistic. "Why do you do that?"

"Bathe you?" Continuing his work, he glanced up and she nodded. "Do you dislike it, my dear?"

"No." Dislike the soothing comfort he offered? God no. "I just wondered. I mean, I could do it myself."

"You could, yes. But you've granted me any number of rights to your person, Alice. You may be sore and uncomfortable. If I send you off alone to wash up, what message does that convey, hmm? That what we've shared is something dirty or shameful? That whatever occurs afterward is your responsibility to bear alone? That you matter nothing beyond your ability to induce an orgasm?" He shook his head. "If instead I make a ritual of your comfort, it encourages me to be mindful of your physical and emotional health. It extends our contact. It deepens our bond, the understanding of the roles each of us will play here." He smiled at her, suddenly less serious. "And, of course, it pleases me to touch you."

"Was it your teacher, I mean, the woman you, um, did she make you do it for her?" Smooth. Someday she'd graduate to complete sentences.

"Not specifically, no. But we talked a good deal about scene dynamics. She believed the most satisfying scenes came from a place of comfort and trust." Henry nimbly folded the washcloth into a square. "Short-term liaisons like the experiences one often finds at clubs provide it only in the most superficial way. Building a long-term association makes the experience more gratifying for both parties."

Her curiosity grew stronger than her nerves. Perhaps his touch made her bold. "Would you take me sometime? To your club? Not, not for . . . just to watch? To see the superficial rituals?"

The expanded contract, what he'd called less freedom and she'd called more, diminished her fears. She wasn't replaceable. He'd initialed the blueprint for their relationship. Her right, her responsibility, to seek him out and ask for what she needed. His right, his responsibility, to determine her readiness for it. Need prodded her to understand what drew him to the club. To discover how it differed from what he shared with Jay and with her.

He traced the seam of her lips with what seemed thoughtfulness rather than intent to arouse.

"Soon, Alice. The social club I attend has more stringent codes for behavior than those to which you're accustomed. And there are other considerations." He bent over her and chastely kissed the line his thumb had traced before he sat up. "But we were speaking of our own rituals, my dear."

"What makes them different? More . . ." What was the word he'd used? "Gratifying."

"The nature of the rituals depends upon the individuals, in some ways." Moving his hand to her thigh, he stroked her skin and met her gaze.

"You enjoy a comforting touch, a reminder that you have not been forgotten once you've satisfied your partner, perhaps? I expect because your previous partners lacked even the courtesy to be certain you were satisfied, never mind providing emotional stimulation. Jay, on the other hand, enjoys verbal affirmations that he has done well and pleased his partner."

Henry had a reason for everything he did. They needed different things from him, and his gift was understanding the nature of those things. He liked that. Needed that? "You usually send him to fetch the washcloth." She'd assumed Henry wanted to be certain Jay understood his place as the junior partner, but maybe the action held more meaning.

"Interpersonal dynamics, my dear. It allows me to stay and provide you with the comfort of my touch—"

"—and when he returns, you can praise him for a job well done."

"I knew you were a quick study, Alice."

"You haven't said where he is." In all the months they'd been playing, tonight marked only the second one she'd spent alone with Henry.

"He is, rather unhappily, I might add, owing to having to miss a lovely time with you, participating in another ritual tonight. I'm certain his mood will have lifted by now." Henry pushed himself up and off the bed. "He and his siblings organized a special dinner for their parents' fiftieth wedding anniversary."

"Fifty years?" Unbelievable. Her own parents had been married thirty years, and even that seemed impossible. For half that time, they'd been unhappy. "How do you know you'll be happy with someone in five years, let alone fifty? That's a lot to live up to."

"I suppose it might intimidate someone considering marriage. Though it might also inspire."

His intent stare had her retracing her words. Shit. He'd given her an inch on developing a relationship, and she mimicked a woman taking a mile. A marriage mile.

"For Jay, I mean. If he ever wants to marry someone." Right. Because flirty, immature, man-child Jay screamed ready for marriage. As if. But adorable, vulnerable, hungry for affection Jay . . . yeah. He might want the security of marriage.

Why hadn't Henry asked him? Even if their marriage wouldn't be recognized in every state, it would here. Except now she'd thrown Jay under the bus.

"Not that he has to. Or is thinking about it. Or isn't. I don't know. He hasn't said anything to me." Christ. Could she fit any more feet in her mouth?

"No proposals?" Henry's lips twitched.

She bet the volume of laughter in his head rivaled the roar of a jet engine.

"It's quite the relief to know the two of you won't be eloping. Though you're good with him and for him. Kind. Patient. Playful. Forgiving."

He seemed to frown as he left the room, but no sign of one remained when he returned a moment later without the washcloth. The clock on the nightstand insisted it was ten minutes to midnight.

He lay beside her, pulled the covers over them both and wrapped his arms around her back.

"Comfortable, my dear?"

"Mm-hmm."

"Good." He grazed her throat with his lips. "You'll stay the night, Alice."

A demand she endorsed, even if tonight he merely missed Jay. His touch woke tingling hunger in her skin. Snuggling closer, she encouraged his renewed attentions. "Not expecting Jay home?"

"He's staying the night at his sister's home in New Hampshire. It's late, and he'll have been drinking."

"You told him he wasn't allowed to drive home tonight." Henry set limits for Jay. More than he did for her, but maybe Jay needed them more. Or maybe wanting them was a trait she and Jay shared.

"For his own safety, yes. It's a long drive, and he has already made it once today. I won't have him falling asleep at the wheel."

That was why. Not because she and Jay couldn't set those limits themselves. They were capable, when they wanted to be. But every time Henry set a limit, he showed them their importance to him. That he cared. If only she'd seen that sooner.

He kissed her mouth, and she leaned her body into his. He wasn't hard yet, but he would be soon.

Sleep took a long time coming. Exhausted and entangled, they stumbled toward it together in the hour before dawn.

Chapter 11

Despite their talk, the next time Henry invited Alice out, they didn't visit a sex club. His invitation was much more dangerous. An art opening. For his show. As his date. His and Jay's. Publicly.

Had he shared his plans before she'd knocked—seven PM precisely—she might've turned tail and run. But the way Henry had introduced the idea, every step seemed perfectly reasonable until the moment he asked Jay to go start the car.

Henry answered the door himself, Jay nowhere in evidence, though the patter of water on tile escaped from beneath the bathroom door as Henry led her to his bedroom. His hands lingered on her skin as he stripped her. He murmured approval at the citrus scent her shower had left behind. She'd chosen it with him in mind, to mimic his scent on her.

He stood behind her as he peeled her shirt away.

"You smell delectable, my dear. Alas, it's not in the script for the evening to eat you right up." He took teasing bites of her neck between his words. His hands, smoothing over the red silk of her bra, hardened her nipples as they passed. "I'll have to allow time for it later. I find myself quite hungry indeed."

She shivered at the promise in his voice, the low tone that crawled through her like an electric current. The slide of her pants, a controlled fall in his hands, sharpened her pulse's thumping rhythm between her legs. His proximity as he knelt behind her curled her toes.

He'd bade her leave her sandals by the door. When he lifted her feet and pushed her pants aside, she stood before him in bra and panties, the red set he'd given her.

"A bold palette this evening, Alice." He stood and pressed himself against her, a brief tease of his erection through his black linen slacks. "Feeling daring, were you? An auspicious beginning. Suitable. We'll see what we might match with it, hmm? Wait here, my dear, just as you are."

He stepped away. She waited, unmoving. He'd ventured into the closet, from the sounds behind her. A zipper lowered. His? No, the sound went on too long.

Henry returned and knelt in front of her, holding a circle of charcoal-gray fabric open for her. "Step in, please, Alice."

She followed his instructions to the letter, her arousal growing as he carried out every action himself, from sliding her arms into the sleeves to running a hand up her spine as he zipped the back closure. Pressure on her shoulder demanded she turn to face him.

Stepping back, he tipped his head. He motioned, a command for her to twirl. The sheath gripped her tight, stretching with her as she moved.

"Mmm. Not tonight, I think. Your curves are delightful, my dear, and tonight I desire to see fabric slide over them like water and imagine my hands following its path."

He unzipped her and removed the dress. More noise from the closet. More distantly, the sound of the shower cut off. Henry had closed the bedroom door behind them. Maybe her dress would be a surprise for Jay.

The unpredictability of where the game would go, of what would come next, excited her like nothing else. Henry never failed to take advantage of it on their nights together.

Their pantomime repeated with a second dress, though this time Henry paused to kiss her thighs before he raised the fabric over them. "Such exquisite beauty. It's almost a shame to cover you, my dear."

When she twirled, the hem flipped out and spun with her in a flirty dance. It continued swaying after she'd stopped, brushing high on her thighs where Henry's mouth had touched her. His quiet growl raised the tiny hairs on her neck and arms.

"I *will* take you in that dress, Alice."

Exultation entwined with giddy fear. She had no control here, none. He'd take her however he liked, whenever he liked. Her legs shifted without any urging. He could strip off her panties and take her now. She'd be ready for him.

"But not tonight."

Frustration gnawed at her. He enjoyed teasing her, getting her too worked up to think, putting her in the state of needy, wanton desire he'd declared he found most attractive on her.

Swift hands stripped the second dress from her body, though not so swift he didn't find time to swipe his fingers over her panties. She struggled not to squirm and press into his touch.

He stepped into her, allowing her to feel the strength of his undiminished erection. She moaned. He desired her with equal ferocity. He wouldn't make her wait long.

He kissed her cheek, as polite as if he greeted an acquaintance at afternoon tea, and stepped away. "You're such a good girl, Alice. So very enticing. I'll have trouble keeping my hands off you tonight."

Part of the game? He might make her come without touching her. If anyone could, it'd be Henry.

He brought out a third dress. Flowing red silk with a mandarin collar, sleeveless, knee-length, though the sides had slits cut higher.

He nudged her hair aside and kissed the back of her neck as he zipped the dress. His hands fell to her hips, stroking up and down over a few short inches of territory. Christ yes. Like sitting astride him, his cock buried inside her as she rose and fell in satisfying rhythm.

"Mmm. Perfection, dearest. This is the one."

Guiding her to the bench in the corner, he pulled a pair of matching red shoes from underneath and slipped them on her feet. Strappy sandals with a wedge heel.

He helped her stand, his fingers curling beneath hers as if he'd asked her to dance, though he stayed silent. The wedge brought her almost to his height. She flashed a bold look at him, a dare to take her now, on the bench. The dress rucked up around her waist, her knees along the outside of his thighs as he sat, his pants shoved open, her panties pushed aside . . . *yeah, just like that, harder—*

"You'll tell me what you're fantasizing about, Alice. In the car. Come along."

The car. Part of the game? She adjusted the fantasy, exchanging the padded bench for the backseat of Henry's car.

He tucked her arm around his and walked her down the hall to the living room. Jay, seated on the couch, stood at their approach. Well-dressed this evening, in sleek black slacks and a formal black shirt, he'd left his collar flipped up.

He whistled when he eyed her before his gaze moved to Henry. "The reds? You're sure?"

"I'm certain, yes, my boy. It's an appropriate statement."

Jay's grin split his face. He pulled two ties from a pile draped over the back of a chair. Red. To match her dress, it seemed, although why red made him happy remained a mystery.

He brought the ties to Henry, who made swift work of Jay's tie and fixed his collar before donning his own.

Amused, she nudged Jay with her elbow. "Can't tie your own tie, eh? Will you ever be a grown-up boy, do you think?"

Jay smirked at her, shaking his head. "Call it a renewal of vows."

A *what*?

Had he and Henry talked about marriage after she'd stumbled into the subject two weeks ago? Maybe they'd had a commitment ceremony before she met them and hadn't told her. No. Ridiculous. Henry would've disclosed that.

Jay's smirk grew. "Besides, he dressed you, too, didn't he?"

"You're telling tales out of school, my boy." Henry's mild tone didn't fool her, not when he raised an eyebrow and tugged on Jay's tie. "It's time to go. Do you have the keys?"

Go? Out? Together?

Jay pulled a set from his pocket and jangled them. "Ready and waiting."

"Go on and start the car, please. Alice and I will be down in a moment."

Jay departed. Not a joke, then.

"As you've undoubtedly surmised by now, my dear, we will be leaving the apartment for tonight's games." He swept her hair back with his fingers, his palm resting against her cheek. "You needn't be anyone but yourself tonight. You've been wanting something more, hmm? Something akin to a relationship? You'll have it tonight."

He leaned in, replacing his hand with his lips.

"I'll answer one question before we depart, Alice. I know you've several buzzing around in your mind." He pulled back and studied her. "Choose one only."

A dozen questions waited, and more arrived by the minute. But she trusted him to have her welfare in mind. She was content to wait to find out where they were going. Dinner. The theater. A concert. The possibilities were endless. What she really wanted to know, though . . .

"What statement are you making with the ties? How does it relate to what Jay said about the vows?"

Henry tapped her lips with one finger. "Those are two questions, my dear. I'm not inclined to answer either if you cannot follow instructions properly."

"It's a single question," she argued. "One question with a nested corollary for clarification purposes."

He laughed, a short but delighted bark, as he helped her into her coat. "Clever, Alice. Quite clever. I'm afraid it still won't provide the answer you seek, however. You'll have to phrase your question more precisely next time."

A challenge. Damn straight she would.

Taking her arm, he led her toward the door. "The only statement I am making with the ties is to match the red of your dress, my dear." He turned off the lights and locked the door behind them. "As for Jay's words . . . beneath his boyish charm beats the heart of a romantic. But I expect you knew that already, Alice."

How like Henry to give her no answers at all.

He escorted her down the stairs and outside in silence.

Standing beside Henry's car, Jay opened the back door. Henry helped seat her before joining her, and Jay took the wheel.

"Where to, good sir?" The rearview mirror reflected Jay's smirk as Henry rattled off an address. "Very good, sir."

Jay dug into the fun of playing chauffeur. Although he wasn't driving for the reasons she assumed, because Henry didn't make any sexual demands during the ride. And it wasn't as if he didn't have reason to. He ordered her to describe the fantasy scenario she'd imagined in the bedroom, which made Henry growl and Jay whimper, but he only kissed her cheek and commented that the idea had merit.

"Tonight, however, it wouldn't be appropriate to arrive at the gallery so mussed."

"We're going to an art show?" That could definitely be fun. Like a day at the museum. She'd always enjoyed her outings with Henry.

"We're attending an opening reception." Henry paused. "For my new exhibition."

"You have a new show?" A thrill danced down her spine. She'd get to see what Henry had been working on. "How come I didn't know about this?"

Jay laughed. "Knowing ahead of time only means you carry wood crates to the car and help deliver them to the gallery." He caught her gaze in the rearview. "I still don't know what the pieces look like, either."

Henry raised his hand to her jaw, his index finger and thumb tipping her face toward him. "Surprising you is an irresistible temptation, my sweet girl. One I hope you'll forgive me for, as I cannot promise to stop."

"You can't?"

"The delight on your face is much too enjoyable to witness. As bright as Jay's smile when he knows he's done well."

"Nothing's that bright," she teased. Joy unfurled in her stomach. She'd been part of his plans, not an afterthought. "Not even the sun on a clear day."

"We'll have to be certain to give our boy praiseworthy things to do when we arrive home this evening, won't we, Alice? So we might enjoy the sun's warmth after dark?"

Jay squirmed in his seat. He sat tall, his shoulders pushed back, and controlled the car with smooth confidence.

"He's an excellent chauffeur," she pointed out. "That's one praiseworthy thing already."

"Keeping a running total for the night, Alice? What a lovely thought. Jay will have to thank you for it when the night is over and he reaps the fruits of his good behavior."

Jay pulled into a parking space, turned off the engine and blew out a breath. He gripped the steering wheel.

"It's all right, my boy." Henry's voice soothed, though she couldn't for the life of her figure out why. "We'll wait until you've calmed yourself. Best for the artist to be fashionably late, in any event."

Calmed? *Oh.* Yeah, okay, Jay probably didn't want to walk into Henry's exhibit with his own exhibit going on in his pants.

Henry talked about the show arrangements and the tedium of the afternoon, when he'd been overseeing the installation with his agent, until Jay indicated his readiness to step out of the car. Henry sent a quick text to his agent, who met them at the gallery's back door.

"It's going well, Henry." The agent was a slender man, not slender-but-muscled like Jay, but more gaunt. "I have a woman interested in picking up one of the pieces, and I think you might entice her into taking a second, so we'll start there."

About her own height, which made him shorter than her in the wedge heels. And busy. Fidgety busy. Much too busy for Henry, but maybe he needed that in an agent to balance his own unflappable calm.

"Yes, thank you, Elliott." Henry slipped off her coat and handed it to Jay. "To the left, my boy, you'll find the manager's office. The coats will be fine on the chair. Elliott, you remember Jay, of course."

"Of course. Jay. Pleasure to see you in person again." Elliott nodded and turned toward her. "And this is your new muse? Wonderful."

"This is Alice, Elliott." Henry stroked the back of her neck, and she burned with pride beneath the possessive touch. "She's been quite the inspiration."

Henry wouldn't lie. If he said she'd inspired him, she had. Pride crossed the sound barrier, well on its way to transforming her body into shimmering light.

Elliott leaned in as he shook her hand. "Whatever you're doing, please, keep at it, Alice. Tie him to the canvas if you must. He's pulled together some beautiful new pieces for this show."

She edged closer to Henry's side. Wicked impulse made her speak. "Usually I let him tie me to the canvas. He needs his hands to paint."

"She's a quick one, Henry. You ought to let her do the talking." Elliott waved his hands in a flitting gesture. "Play up your enigmatic persona all you like tonight. I can make sales with this girl doing the rounds. Where did Jay run off to? He's good at parting the cougars from their money."

Jay mingled on his own while she accompanied Henry and Elliott, attempting to be witty but not embarrassing and charming without screaming to the unattached browsers that Henry was taken. They'd never turn into buyers that way.

The first hour passed in a whirlwind of faces, and the second much the same.

The night was half over before she had a chance to stand in one place and appreciate Henry's paintings on her own. Elliott continued his schmoozing campaign alone. Henry left her to check on Jay, with the promise of his return.

Beautiful examples of Henry's work filled the gallery. Still lifes, mostly. Each painting took her deeper, a tour into his mind via the colors and themes and elements he'd highlighted. *Daylily* held her enchanted. Pink, rose and red petals spread, trimmed in gold, every crinkle and fold painted in delicate detail.

Stepping in close at her side, Henry swept his arm across her back and curled his hand around her opposite hip. "Have I done you justice, Alice? If I stripped your clothes from you right here, would the colors match?"

He wouldn't strip her in public. Doing so would force everyone in the room into their game without consent. He wouldn't do that to anyone, even if she wanted him to.

Not that she wanted him to. The notion that he could, though. Just because Henry was a painter and not a performance artist didn't mean he couldn't . . . *oh God.*

Arousal. The rush of heat prepared her body for him, flushed her pink and red with desire.

She slid her cheek against his in a nod, as close a caress to the one she wanted from him as she dared in public. "They would now."

He chuckled, low, for her ears only, and kissed her cheek. A flash went off as someone captured the moment.

"You're wonderfully responsive to my suggestions, Alice. I wonder, would you follow instructions here, in a public setting? Would you like that?"

Folds of flowers. Folds of skin. Both opened to his talents. Had he held a brush or his cock in his hand when he'd conceived this painting? Bringing her here tonight might be more than playacting. Not her contracted dominant supplying her with what she needed from him but her lover showing her he valued her.

Unless this show marked the culmination of his work, his nearly yearlong project, and he wouldn't need her afterward.

"It's a contract night, Henry," she answered him, her voice as light as she could make it. "You know I'll obey you if I'm able."

His fingers tightened on her hip, and he pressed his forehead to her temple, but he stayed silent. Maybe she'd misstepped, and he hadn't wanted to be reminded of contracts. Maybe he wanted to be free to enjoy her without the polite fiction that dictated their actions only because they allowed it to. Or maybe she'd projected her own desires onto him.

"Of course, my dear. How could I expect otherwise?" He grazed her cheek in a kiss, and his tone grew brisker, more focused. "Very well. Listen and obey, then."

She had nothing to fear. Henry wouldn't suggest anything obscene. Humiliation, public or otherwise, wasn't part of their arrangement.

"Have you ever played the game Simon, sweet girl?"

"Uh, sure." His conversational pivot had her scrambling for an answer. "Memory and pattern recognition." This was sexual how? "Flashing lights and sound."

"Precisely. I'm going to demonstrate a pattern on you. You're to seal it in your memory. And then I want you to repeat it on our boy."

"A pattern?" She rarely fell so far behind in discerning Henry's intention, but now she struggled to catch up.

"Of dominance." He drew teasing spirals in the small of her back. "A claim. A chance to play go-between." The heat of the overhead lights deepened his scent, mimicking the musk of arousal. "To share a taste of power." He licked his lips, the act slow and mesmerizing. "A kiss."

If he'd surprised her, it was only that reserved, private, practically-asexual-in-public Henry would be willing to give the impression. Although that, too, might be a bonus for him. The edgy and eccentric artist persona.

She shifted her weight, eager, anticipating.

"If the idea makes you uncomfortable, Alice, you may use your safeword at any time. You know that."

Uncomfortable, no. Or only in the best way. The one ending with her drenched panties on the floor in Henry's bedroom. "It doesn't. If you had your hand between my legs right now, *you'd* know *that*."

"What a lovely thought, Alice. I hardly needed the encouragement, but I assure you, I'm envisioning it now."

He kissed her mouth, greedy and demanding, a kiss that surely told everyone in the room what he'd be doing to her when the soiree ended. An extension of the game, no more, but he probably would do those things to her. Whether he would or not, these strangers would imagine he was. They assumed she was his, and he didn't object to them believing it. His possessive hold strangled her doubts.

He tipped his head as he pulled away. "Go on."

"Yes, Henry."

She skirted groups of chattering people, some gossiping about her. The evening's small talk had revealed Henry never brought a date to his shows. Well, that he always brought Jay, but he never treated him as more than a friend. He kept his sexuality as private as she'd assumed he did. Not tonight, though.

A cluster of beautiful, predatory women surrounded Jay. He played the charmer well. They might take artwork home in lieu of him.

". . . friends with the artist?"

"Henry? Sure, I've known him for years." Jay's grin broadened.

The women preened as if his smile were for them. Temptation begged her to tell them he wore his I'm-sucking-Henry's-cock-tonight face.

"He's a fascinating guy. Art really lets you get right into a man's head, doesn't it? Like you're touching his soul."

The brunette on the end smirked as if she'd like to be getting right into Jay's pants and touching his cock. *Not to worry, Jay. Henry has a fix for that.*

She circled behind the women, drawing Jay's attention, and slipped into the space he stepped back to create beside himself.

"Ladies, this is Alice, a very good friend of Henry's. I'm sure she'd agree with me. Right, Alice?"

"That what you see on the walls is exactly what Henry has on his mind? Oh yeah. I'd agree with that." Her tone oozed sex and confidence. Playing the role of a secure woman who knew her worth, she'd enjoy every damn minute of it. "In fact, I know what Henry has on his mind right now."

The brunette glared at her. "Well? Are you going to share?"

Alice turned her back to the women, laid her hand on Jay's chest and stroked his tie. She curled her hand loosely around it, fondling it like she would his hardening cock. Henry would be watching, but breaking her stare with Jay would disrupt the excitement of the game.

"Share. Funny. That's exactly what Henry told me to do. And I always do what Henry tells me to."

She tightened her grip around Jay's tie, holding him in place, and kissed him with the greedy, possessive need Henry had demonstrated on her. And kept kissing him. And wrapped her other arm around his back until her hand rested dangerously close to his ass.

Jay let her. He responded with enthusiasm but without trying to take control of the kiss.

When she let his mouth go, half of the room was staring sideways at them. The women he'd been charming had disappeared. Other attendees displayed shock, arousal and confusion as the rumor mill started its work. On the other half of the room stood Henry. The whispered chatter increased as he inclined his head and raised his wineglass in a salute to her.

"Jesus, Alice." Jay hadn't moved away, probably because he couldn't without displaying the erection pressed to her belly. "You're one hot switch."

"A hot switch? What, because I turn you on? Please. A stiff breeze could turn you on." She said it with affection, rubbing his tie between her index finger and thumb.

Jay laughed. "You do turn me on, but that's not what I meant. You're a natural switch. Submissive as all get-out for Henry but no trouble dominating me. I'd let you, you know. Henry could teach you. It'd be fun."

She stilled her fingers, her thumbnail a white crescent digging into the slick red tie bisecting his chest. Jay breathed charm on the surface and fragility underneath. Henry knew how to handle him, when to be delicate and offer comfort and when to demand and push him further than he believed he could go. "You'd trust me that much?"

"I *do* trust you that much. And Henry wouldn't let it get out of hand."

"I'll think about it." Excitement danced in her neurons. Like having a new puppy to play with, an already trained puppy, and the owner promising to show her all the commands.

If her dominance pleased Jay, that would please Henry, and the submissive part of her mind wriggled in pleasure. Dominating Jay would be one more way to tie herself to them, to make a place for herself in this relationship.

"C'mon. Let's look at the walls and play 'guess Henry's motivation' until he needs us. He said his agent wanted to pimp him around." She eased back, giving Jay room to breathe.

"Yeah, the art crowd likes their five minutes with the enigmatic artist before they buy. Henry puts up with it. I'm surprised the pimping doesn't bother you, though."

Her? She wasn't bothered. Not at all. What had he noticed? Her quick scan failed to find Henry but yielded face after face of people who'd never sampled his lips. Never lain beside him in the stillness of exhausted satisfaction. "He's not taking them home with him."

"Nope." He offered her his arm with a wink, a playful imitation of Henry's manner with her. "Just us."

They strolled around the gallery, ignoring—and sometimes laughing at—the whispers that followed them.

Peaches and Cream swamped her in lust and yearning and a grateful astonishment threatening to smash her into tiny pieces on the glossy mahogany floorboards.

A familiar orange plate graced its center, a glass tipped on the edge, spilling milk across the plate toward a ripe peach with a single thin slice missing. Beside it, *A Bountiful Feast* displayed one of the daylilies Henry envisioned as her labia. A fat bee hovered above the unfurling petals, the splashes of black and dark gold a match for Jay's hair and her own. The view was from above, the way Henry would've seen them as she writhed in his lap and Jay brought her to climax with his mouth.

Jay leaned in, his lips touching her ear. "We could re-create it when we get home. We still have the plates. And thinking about how you taste is making me hungry."

She didn't doubt their first night together had inspired the pair of paintings. The colors. The detail. The best decision she'd ever made.

Jay nudged her shoulder. "Need a minute?"

She executed a slow neck roll, dropping her gaze to his pants, and gave him her best are-you-fucking-kidding-me stare below her raised brow. "Do *you*?"

"More than a minute, I hope, but not just yet. I'm pretty sure that 'Henry, what do you say you guard the door and watch me fuck Alice in the manager's office? Can you work with that scenario?' would get a resounding, 'No.' But if you wanna ask . . .'"

"Not me, thank you." Intriguing variations skated through her mind. How thick was that door? "You want it, you ask for it."

"I think what I want is a trip to the bathroom to adjust things." He moved to a more proper distance. "Please excuse me." He rolled his eyes at her and headed off into the crowd.

Wandering on her own, she kept to herself. Henry appeared through gaps in the crowd, trapped in smile-and-handshake conversations with his agent and various strangers. The abstract piece before her married shadow-gray squiggles and red splotches in what resembled splashes of blood on rumpled sheets.

A man bumped her elbow. "Sorry about that. The crowd is pretty thick in here, don't you think?"

Ugh. Time to trot out an uninteresting reply to chase the pickup artist away. She had more important things to consider. Why Henry would display that night like a trophy. "Huh? Yeah, sure. No problem."

"So, artist, actress, or escort?" His smarmy tone intimated prostitute every time.

"Excuse me?"

He crowded her, forcing her back unless she wanted to touch him. His arrogant smile annoyed her. "What legitimate name do you go by, so I know how to bill for the business expense?"

"I'm not for sale."

"Right, right, you're working, you're on his time. But that performance earlier . . ." His gaze dropped to her chest. "Do you have a card?"

This loser would never believe she wasn't some kind of sexual performance artist. Kneeing him in the balls would cause a scene and distract from Henry's art. Lacking a drink in her hand, she couldn't go for the stereotypical female response and drench him. But she was still a woman. No reason not to use the jackhole's idiocy against him. Manipulation. Jay and his tie. She'd been in control then.

Dropping her voice, she aimed for thick and sultry. "Not on me, honey. But you stop by the coffee shop down the block tomorrow morning and we'll talk business, all right? If I'm not there yet, you just wait for me, sugar." She pulled a quick fake, waving to no one. "Oops, gotta go. I'm on the clock, and when I'm performing, I always like to give it my all."

He let her slip away without complaint. She doubted he'd be so calm tomorrow if he sat at the coffee shop alone all morning. Too fucking bad for him.

Across the room, Jay's face sported a mix of anger and panic. He strained like a dog on an invisible tether, ordered to stay while another made off with his favorite toy. Quickening her steps, she zipped to Henry's side and projected a bright smile to calm Jay. "They should weed out the pathetic jerks before they open the doors. I had to send that idiot packing."

"You see, Jay? Alice handled the situation on her own, quite capably. Had you interfered, bloodshed might have resulted. In this instance, Alice's method was much more effective." Henry stroked her back and kissed her temple. "Jay deserves a token for his restraint, though, don't you think, Alice?"

She pressed herself to Jay's side, unsurprised when his arm replaced Henry's, curling proprietarily around her back and squeezing her closer still. Her kiss grazed his cheek.

"I'm fine," she murmured. "I'll show you how fine when we get home, if Henry thinks you deserve it."

She took care not to show how she'd startled herself, calling it home. The apartment was theirs, not hers, and yet . . . home. Henry's bed redefined home. Hopefully Henry thought she meant the building and not anything more. Because Jay had said a month ago that he wanted her to move in. Impulse and panic might've prompted him to say it, but it still sounded awfully nice.

Henry, though, hadn't commented. He'd already conceded to nightly dinners. Who knew what he'd say if she presented herself as a woman picking out closet space every time she entered his bedroom.

Chapter 12

The metal oval left the door unmarked but for four initials and the street number. A man stood beside it in something like a military at-ease, feet spread and hands clasped behind his back. He watched them approach.

Henry stopped about a foot from the man, with Jay and herself just behind, flanking him. "Good evening, Marcus. Plus two tonight."

The man nodded and touched a cord running up his shirt. He spoke into a headset. "Number seventeen and two guests."

The door buzzed, and Marcus pulled it open. "Have a good evening, sir." Neither she nor Jay rated a greeting, apparently.

Henry led them down a short hallway into a larger space. A counter like a hotel's concierge desk arced outward in a crescent formed by a curving set of stairs wrapping above and behind it.

The redhead behind the counter seemed more hair than head. The weight piled atop her head in ringlets had to be headache-inducing. Freckles dotted her face and arms. Her jewel-green corset emphasized the spill of her breasts, though her nipples weren't showing. A woman calm, collected and halfway to undressed.

Comfort descended. Henry would never have put her in anything to be mocked, but her anxiety had lingered on the ride over.

"Hello, Tara." Henry's greeting held a hint of familiar friendliness.

He must've met her on previous visits. The redhead didn't sport a name tag, and the desk didn't have a placard with a name. He slid his phone across the counter.

"Good evening, sir. You're looking well. Any other electronic gadgets to check tonight?"

"Just the one tonight, thank you."

Alice had been instructed to leave hers at home with Jay's, owing to a rule against private photography at the club.

The girl locked the phone in a numbered box behind her. "May Emma take your wraps?"

"Yes, thank you."

High heels clicked on the golden granite floor. An older woman in a tasteful black dress moved toward them. Not *old* old, but older than Henry. She took the coat Henry held out. Henry nodded to Jay, who smoothly removed his own coat.

He unfastened her buttons himself, pressing a soft kiss to her cheek as he pushed open her coat and Jay pulled it down her arms.

"All right, dearest?" His whisper rumbled in her ear.

So far. Except for the hammering in her rib cage like an imprisoned bird bent on escape. "Yes, sir."

Henry pulled back and watched her for a moment. "Good." He turned his head toward the desk. "Two red ribbons this evening, please, Tara. I'm not in the mood to share."

Ribbons. He'd told them before they'd left the apartment. Reminders for Jay, but every rule and expectation was new to her.

The club's ribbons announced a submissive's status. Green signaled it was appropriate to approach and touch. Yellow meant the submissive could be spoken to, but touching would need to be negotiated. Red meant invisibility. Near nonexistence. Others could look, but addressing red-ribboned submissives or touching them in any way gave offense to the dominant who claimed them.

"The red ribbon by itself is not an indication of your novice status, Alice," Henry had explained, his voice warm and reassuring. "It might indicate a submissive with triggers the dominant does not wish tripped, or a temporary punishment, or a possessive dominant willing to show off his toys but not share them. You will likely see several red ribbons and fewer green than you might expect. Many will be club employees or those paying for their attendance through consensual service. Unattached submissives, those who attend without an established dominant, often wear yellow as a safety measure and an invitation to discussion."

She'd nodded to indicate her understanding, too focused on memorizing his words to speak.

"Once I've attached your ribbon, you will need to be on your best behavior, dearest."

Her, sure. No problem. But Jay? Fiddly, bouncing-his-knees Jay?

One corner of Henry's mouth lifted. "Yes, Jay as well. The two of you may freely converse quietly with each other, but neither speak to anyone else nor raise your eyes to meet theirs. Do not address me without express permission. When you do, address me as 'sir' at all times. If you need my attention, place a hand on my knee or shoulder and wait for me to acknowledge you."

He'd paused, his serious expression encompassing them both. "Although your sexual contact will be limited to only what I instruct, you may touch each other for nonsexual comfort as you wish. If either of you feel anxious or notice anxiety in each other, do not hesitate, am I understood? And if you wish to leave, at any time, we will do so."

She jumped at his light touch. He smoothed over the space between her exposed collarbone and the tops of her breasts. No coat now. Cool air kissed her skin.

Her own corset wasn't so concealing as the one the hostess wore. Henry teased her exposed nipples, raising them to tight buds with the pads of his thumbs before tying the red ribbon in a bow at the top of the corset.

Jay wore a red band around his right bicep. Pure stud. Utterly fuckable, shirtless, showing off sleek, toned muscles. His formal slacks mimicked Henry's, charcoal gray and well-tailored, but with a tighter cut and an easy-access snap front. One yank on the flap would spill Jay's cock into a waiting hand. Or mouth. He raised his eyebrows and smiled at her.

They had the elevator to themselves, and the door had no sooner closed than Henry swooped in and kissed Jay greedily.

Her mouth moved with sympathetic desire as they kissed into the infinite distance of the mirrored walls until the elevator car came to a stop.

"Good boy," Henry growled.

The doors slid open on the third floor. Henry wrapped her arm around his as though he escorted her to a formal function. He was dressed for it, and she lacked only the dress. Hell, the undergarments were formal enough to pass.

Jay fell in behind Henry's right shoulder like he belonged there. Maybe he did. She'd have to track how everyone else behaved. She took in everything, careful to keep her gaze below head height. Accidentally offending someone and forcing Henry to apologize for her idiocy wouldn't make for a fun night.

If she'd wanted a visual dictionary of the nude human form, she couldn't have chosen a better place to stand. Men and women, both obviously aroused and not, passed through her field of vision in costuming ranging from elaborate to nonexistent.

An excitement, an energy, clung to the air and encouraged her own arousal. Bedroom-sized rooms lined the hall on both sides, with three true walls and one glass one. Wanderers watched at their leisure. Henry strolled, stopping at each.

She grew accustomed to the rhythm. Henry slid his arm behind her back, pulling her in and settling her in front of him. Jay sank to his knees beside them. Scenes played out in the themed rooms. Classroom scenarios, so far.

"All right, my boy?"

To her right, a woman in a short uniform skirt and too-small blouse earned high marks on her oral exam.

Jay nodded, the motion rubbing against her hip. His fingers rested on her calf. "Yes, sir."

To her left, a man dressed as a schoolboy took a spanking across a teacher's desk.

"He appears to be enjoying his spanking, doesn't he?" Henry tousled Jay's hair and lingered alongside her panties. "His mistress is careful with him."

The woman, dressed in something like nineteenth-century schoolmarm chic, struck the man's bare buttocks with a wooden paddle. His hands lay flat on the desk. Bent forward but not pressed to the surface, he rocked and his erection bobbed as every blow landed.

The paddle would make it too much for Jay. For now, at least.

But merging the scenes, combining design elements for optimum performance, slicked her with greedy desire. The evolving image pushed her craving deeper, pressed her back to Henry's chest and intoxicated her with the rhythm of his breath.

"Alice has had a thought, Jay." Henry plucked at the corset laces from her breasts to her navel. "She's going to share it with us now."

She squirmed, and Jay wrapped his arm around her leg in a reassuring squeeze.

"You needn't be overly specific, my dear. But I want you to tell me, right now, which image aroused you."

Footsteps and low chatter surrounded them. A couple stood no more than five feet away.

"Both," she whispered. "Jay bent over while you wielded the paddle and I sucked him off."

Hand tightening on her leg, Jay nodded.

"Mmm. Yes, that's quite creative, isn't it, my boy? Alice wants to reward you for playing a new game." Henry's breath stirred the hair beside her ear. "Beautiful. We'll keep that in mind for a future night, shall we?"

"Yes, please, sir." She hadn't gotten the hang of calling him "sir" yet, but a thrill zipped through her every time she did.

They moved on. In a formal music room, a man wearing nothing more than a green ribbon around his cock feasted between the thighs of a woman sprawled across the top of a grand piano.

"A special treat for a good boy," Henry murmured. "He serves with such enthusiasm."

Jay swayed against her thigh with an inquiring whimper.

Henry clenched a hand in his hair. "But my boy would do a better job, isn't that so, Alice?"

"So much better, sir." Shoving aside her lingering discomfort with the audience watching beside them, she forced herself to speak up. "Like his tongue was made for nothing else."

Jay's straight back, his squared shoulders, made her slight embarrassment more than worth it. Her praise and Henry's possessive hold eased his tension and fed his pride.

She hadn't asked if he'd been to a club since Henry had pulled him out of his self-destructive spiral. Tonight might be a reintroduction for him, a setting as new and unfamiliar to him as it was to her. She should've raised the topic before they'd come here. Too sensitive a question for this public space.

Down the hall, more rooms, more scenarios, some arousing and others not, but nothing frightening. Nothing she wouldn't have been willing to try herself.

The lazy sheik sprawled on a nest of pillows elicited boredom, but his dancers boasted excellent muscle control.

She leaned into Henry's hand on her cheek, his knuckles grazing her as he twined strands of her hair around his fingers.

Gauze and silks and rippling bodies. Chiming bells on wrist and ankle cuffs. Henry liked to watch. Maybe he'd teach her to dance for him. Beckon to her the way the master called one of his girls to him with an outstretched hand.

Henry pulled away. "Em? There's nothing amiss, I trust?"

The coat-check woman from downstairs? A shiver worked its way across Alice's shoulders without Henry to warm her.

"No, no. All's well, Henry." The woman smiled, laugh lines deepening around her mouth. "No undesirables this evening. I've been keeping a close eye for you." She came surprisingly close. Laying a hand on Henry's shoulder, she lifted her heels and kissed his cheek.

Alice stood in mute astonishment.

"Merely my own curiosity." She stepped back. "I didn't want to disrupt your focus when you arrived, but I simply had to meet your beauties, if I may."

"Giving me the chance to strut?" Henry slid a hand beneath Alice's chin. "Look up, my dear. It's all right."

Nerves ate at her as she obeyed. How well did Henry know this woman?

The woman studied her for more than a minute. Two. Three. She couldn't have been much older than Henry. Five years, ten at the most. But her distant inspection sapped confidence and raised fears of meeting Henry's mother. Not measuring up.

Alice struggled not to fidget. She drew strength from Jay's weight and warmth against her leg. *I am not intimidated. I'm right where I should be.*

"You're right, Henry." The woman delivered a slow, regal nod. "Eager to please, with a spark of independence. You have your hands full, no doubt, but the reward will be worth the effort. She's lovely."

Henry kissed Alice's temple and nudged her head downward.

The woman circled to Henry's far side. "And young Jay. How wonderful to see him enjoying himself. I was so pleased you came in tonight. They're beautifully behaved. You've every right to be proud."

"They make it easy," Henry said in a mild tone that edged into humor. "When they want to."

The woman laughed. "I'm certain Victor said the same of me, many times."

"And he loved every moment." Henry resumed his caresses, outlining Alice's cheekbone, and she nuzzled into his touch. "We may have a bit of fun later. Shall I send a runner to fetch you?"

"I'd be honored. It's been too long since I've seen you direct, Henry."

"I hope to have the opportunity more frequently in the future."

"I hope you will as well."

She wished she could see their faces as they exchanged farewells. But not so much that she'd trade away the delight of Henry tracing a path from her ear to her collarbone and back again with slow repetition.

They returned to the rhythm of watching and questioning and touching. The elaborate trappings, the periods and styles of the rooms, from the excesses of ancient Rome to a Wild West saloon to the silver-washed space age, seemed to heighten the experience for many participants. Sensationalism and formality.

She didn't need a silly sham to put her in the proper mood. The familiarity and comfort of Henry's touch did that. The deep shades of his bedroom, the softness of his sheets, the warmth of Jay beside her. She found truth in those things. Here lived falsity and desperate play-acting.

The formalities seemed a protective ritual here, a necessity for allowing desires and vulnerability out in the open among strangers. At home with Henry and Jay, play had become a natural extension of their relationship, a deepening of their friendship. The reasoning behind Henry's long wait to make her the offer shone with clarity under this new light.

He delivered personal care and attention not limited to a function of his needs and her convenience. A dozen women and men in various states of undress engaged in numerous sexual and nonsexual activities around them, but he wouldn't trade her or Jay for any of them.

His gaze, cool and appraising, as he studied the players and their games, and its softening when he looked at her, at Jay, to gauge their reactions revealed the truth. He'd wanted her to see this. She understood the difference so much better now.

Her nerves stretched and knotted not because she doubted him but because these others would judge them the way the woman had. They saw in her a reflection of Henry and his skills, his mastery, and she yearned to be a credit to him and not a disappointment.

Jay fidgeted more than usual, from more than excitement. Expectation might hold sway over him, too. His eyes held a sliver of his desperate, wild look from the night Henry first flogged her. Facing demons.

Henry ushered them into a larger room with a central raised platform and scattered seating. He moved with purpose, hustling them forward.

"Excellent," he murmured, happiness or relief in his tone. "The perfect gentleman for Alice's introduction, and a familiar face for you, Jay. Best behavior please, my dears."

Henry waved. A few more strides brought her face to chest with a giant of a man. Tall, broad, and carrying more than a handful of extra weight. Dressed to the nines, though, his body language relaxed and easy.

Henry seemed equally relaxed, and her body took its cue from him.

"Henry, it's been ages. I've seen you, what, no more than three times in the last year, always alone, and now you bring two beautiful pets with you?" The stranger circled as if inspecting them.

She kept her gaze downcast. Jay stealthily enveloped her hand in his.

"The boy I recognize, but the girl is new." His formal suit resembled Henry's, but with whimsy in his tie selection—a swirling pattern of what seemed red roses. Upon closer inspection, they revealed themselves as red foxes chasing each other in circles. "Adding to your collection, or borrowing for the night? If she's available, do tell me where you acquired her."

"She is entirely unavailable, William, as is he. And, I think, both together are much too spirited for you to manage." An affectionate wryness threaded through Henry's tone.

The man snorted. "They seem perfectly docile to me, Henry. But you've always had that gentle way with the subs. You walk softly and they still want the big stick."

He laughed, a booming guffaw. Between the jolliness and the oversize gut, he embodied Santa Claus. "You're certain you won't loan me your lovely? She must make a cozy little lapwarmer."

Sit on Santa's lap? Oh God. She couldn't help the first giggle, and she couldn't stop the second. Her behavior would embarrass Henry if she didn't get it under control.

Henry tipped her chin up with his fingertips, and that was worse. Santa William sported a close-cropped blond beard and rosy cheeks.

She bit her lower lip in a desperate attempt to stifle the giggles.

"She does indeed," Henry said as he studied her face. Smiling, he kissed the tip of her nose. "But I wager at the moment she's considering her Christmas list."

Blushing fiercely, her giggles gone, she wished she dared squirm away from Henry's fingers and hide her face.

William barked out a sharp laugh. "She can call me Santa if she likes, Henry—so long as she's sitting on my lap."

Henry wiped away her embarrassment with a gentle hand traveling along her jaw, over her ear, and around the back of her head. He smoothed her hair with slow strokes. Jay's fingers, curled around her hand, made the same motion.

"Not tonight, Will. It's her first outing. The only lap she'll warm is mine."

"Aha! So this is your new project. I see why you've been spending nights at home."

"They do keep me pleasantly occupied." Henry gestured toward an empty grouping of chairs. "Shall we? Neil will be giving the shibari demonstration soon, and I'd like to study his technique."

The Japanese rope bondage? Henry wouldn't explore it with Jay. He shied from bondage games, with reason, even if Henry's use of them with her had increased his comfort.

"Adding something new to your repertoire, are you?" William took three steps and dropped into one of the seats Henry had pointed out, a plump, oversize chair with wide arms and a deep cushion suited to his bulk.

Henry intended to put rope patterns on her skin. Thrilling anticipation coiled around her. A fresh project with her at the center. One to inspire his next gallery show.

"Perhaps." Henry selected an armless chair for himself, a flowing seat that left him naturally reclined. "Jay, to my right, please. Waiting pose, relaxed." He stretched out his arm. "Alice, with me."

Jay sank gracefully to his knees at Henry's right side, sitting back on his heels and resting his head against Henry's thigh. He was all tumble-puppy at home, but when he put on his best behavior, he was a credit to Henry's training. The consistency, in love and in discipline, gave him the tools to be his best self.

Henry guided her to his lap. Settling her on his left thigh, he pulled her body against his chest.

She snuggled her face into his neck. Familiar comfort, his scent and Jay's sweet face. Jay rubbed his cheek on Henry's pants like a cat, and the hunger in his eyes hardened her nipples. Christ. Their first night together, the pleasure of Henry's fingers and Jay's tongue inside her. Her legs rested between Henry's. She shifted her weight in an attempt to ease her building desire.

Henry shifted in response, moving from rubbing circles on Jay's shoulder to cupping her sex and rubbing his fingers over her panties. She struggled to keep from thrusting into his grip.

"I do enjoy trying new things with these two," Henry said. Calm and conversational, even while he worked at her. "They're wonderfully responsive to touch and tone."

"Yes, I see." Henry's friend spread his legs. His seat on the far side of Jay no doubt offered an excellent view of Henry's fingers skimming over her panties. "Domestic training, too? You've had the boy for years now, haven't you?"

"I have, yes. He's a delight. Playful, quick, eager to please." Henry's answer made Jay smile. "Prone to impatience at times, but having a new playmate to please has tempered him. I'm quite proud of how he's grown in recent months."

Wide-eyed and beaming, Jay squirmed. The way he rocked his hips, he must've skipped interested and gone straight to full-on ready. Public praise from Henry might cause a spontaneous orgasm for him.

"But no, they aren't under strict domestic submission at home." Henry slipped his finger under the edge of her panties and traced her lips. Her burgeoning laughter at Jay's unabashed glee washed away under a wave of arousal. "I find it stifles their creativity, and I adore their spontaneity."

William sighed. "I envy you. My wife would never submit. You know how demeaning she finds the entire idea."

A Mrs. Santa William? Jay nodded against Henry's thigh. Maybe a lot of the people here hid their activities from spouses or had ones who knew but refused to participate.

"Heaven forfend I suggest bringing a true sub home, even for nonsexual play. Jealousy, you know. Very bitch in the manger. And you've somehow managed to find two."

God, being married to Henry, knowing he played fetish games with Jay, but refusing to take part or even witness it would be worse. Fearing he cared more for Jay, eaten up by jealousy and confusion. The emotional crap had almost driven her crazy before Jay had helped her find her courage. To be trapped in that confusion forever? What a nightmare.

"I'm lucky," Henry said, mildly.

Skilled, she mentally corrected. Henry made his own luck.

He slipped his index finger inside her and thrust. She shivered, whimpering when he pulled his hand out from beneath her panties and pressed his finger to Jay's mouth.

"Open, Jay. Suck." Obedience resided in hollowing cheekbones and an intent stare. "You see? They play quite well together."

"I do see. You pair them often?" William readjusted his position.

Pants getting tight, Santa?

She squirmed in Henry's lap. Being the focus of outside attention induced more arousal than fear. She'd expected watching others play would be fun, and it was, if not emotionally engaging. But she'd harbored concern she might panic if Henry tried to put her on display.

Unthinkable. She refused to disappoint him at a place where he'd earned respect among friends she'd never met. The potential mistakes here went beyond using the wrong fork or forgetting to say grace.

"When time and good behavior permit, yes." Henry traced the outline of her labia through her panties. She opened her legs, a request for more he wouldn't fail to understand. "They please me equally in their care for each other's needs as they do in their responsiveness and obedience to my own desires."

Jay's tongue peeped out from between his lips. Apologies on his mind, she'd bet.

Henry brushed a finger over her clitoris, and her hips rolled.

William laughed, soft and kind. "She's eager for it, Henry. The boy, too."

He wasn't mocking, not the way Jay'd described some dominants he'd met. Santa William's deep voice held enchantment. "If they were mine, I'd have set them to work by now. You always have loved putting on a show. As I'm benefiting from it, I don't suppose I'll complain too loudly."

"Complain all you like, Will." Henry slid his finger beneath her panties and thrust. She rocked her hips until Henry slipped his finger free again. "Your complaints have never changed my plans before."

Henry touched her nipple. Warm and wet, his finger circled with teasing pressure. "Jay, be a good boy and clean Alice's breast for her. She's gotten something on it."

Jay rose to his knees in fluid motion and leaned across Henry's leg. Tongue out, he licked and lapped above the edge of her corset. Raising her nipple to a high peak didn't require much work.

He closed his mouth over her breast, his moan muffled by her flesh as he sucked. Her own moans, a series of low, breathy sounds on every exhale, weren't so stifled.

"Listen to them, Will." Henry kissed her cheek. Slipping his finger into his mouth, he sucked it clean. "Aren't they lovely playmates?"

"Lovely enough that I'll need one of my own." William's voice had grown deeper.

He beckoned, and within seconds a green-ribboned woman scurried over and knelt before his chair. Her positioning matched Jay's waiting pose. He, too, assumed it once more, Henry having quietly praised his thorough cleaning of her breast. Her silent thanks earned Jay's sweet grin.

Henry nudged Jay to lie against his thigh and stroked his hair. The lights flickered twice. She sharply reminded herself not to look at the ceiling and accidentally stare at the wrong person.

"I'm in the mood for a quiet friend with a talented mouth this evening." William spoke almost inaudibly to the submissive at his feet. Alice strained to hear him. "Is that you, little one? Or will you need to run and find me another friend to play with?"

"That's me, sir." The woman had a soft, thin voice. Her pale pink corset and white stockings with garters, but no panties, revealed smooth flesh. "My mouth is yours, sir." Deep mahogany hair had been pulled into a tight braid and wound into a bun at the nape of her neck. "Green, yellow, red, sir?"

Temporary safewords. Henry had described them as a common code for players who hadn't played together before. The woman had initiated an abbreviated safeword ritual.

"Green, yellow, red," William repeated. "What are you called, little one?"

"Nina, sir."

"Give me your hands, Nina."

Their intimate interaction fascinated her more than the rooms had. What kind of man would Henry have for a friend here? She marked his words, his movements, to determine if he treated this girl the way Henry treated her and Jay. How submissive this Nina would be with a man she'd apparently never met. One whose pants she eagerly opened.

"I see you've found something to pique your interest, Alice." Henry spoke directly in her ear, and she'd have jumped if his arm hadn't been tight around her back. "Curiosity, is it?"

Bingo. That was all right, wasn't it?

"Good girl," Henry whispered. "I'm certain Will is happy to have an appreciative audience."

A louder voice came from the raised platform. Henry tipped her against his shoulder. They'd have an excellent viewing angle.

The girl with her head moving in William's lap seemed to pay more attention to the low murmur of his voice. Instructions or praise, maybe. A microphone amplified the voice from the platform, overpowering other sounds.

A small man in loose yoga pants introduced himself as Neil and his nude female partner as Danielle. He'd demonstrate some basic ties and some more advanced decorative patterns. Alice got that much from his opening speech, picking out meaning around the unfamiliar jargon and foreign words.

Jay knelt patiently beside Henry, facing them rather than the stage. Henry didn't suggest he move, other than to pull him closer so Jay's head and shoulders lay on his thigh. Jay nuzzled her knee. Henry stroked his hair and bid him close his eyes and rest.

Being here had to be more mentally exhausting for Jay than it was for her. But he wouldn't want to leave, either. He'd want to prove his readiness to handle it to Henry the way he had the first night Henry had taken the flogger to her.

Henry murmured something about speaking to Neil later to suggest he start off more slowly for a crowd of novices. Alice settled her hand on Jay's shoulder, and he burrowed against her leg in reply.

The girl on stage bore a beautiful pattern of bright purple rope against mocha skin, an X crossing between her breasts and multiple stripes around her upper arms.

"The rope is so thin," Alice whispered. "Sir," she added in a belated rush.

A slow turn showed off the girl's arms. Rope immobilized them behind her back at her waist, her forearms pinned.

"But quite strong, my sweet girl." Henry pressed his cheek against her head. "And soft, when it's been worked properly, stretched and oiled and cared for. Not unlike my pretty pets, hmm?"

She wiggled happily. Henry's friend must've been pleased with his pet, too. He'd draped her across his lap, facedown, and his hand moved between her legs. Had she been commanded to silence? Was this her reward for pleasing him? Had she chosen it or had William ordered her obedience?

Alice wanted to know. Not merely those things, but everything. In this place, in Henry's arms, she was a toddler discovering the word "why" for the first time. Seductive. Full of promise.

The rope demo bound her in intricate detail. The efficient, almost knotless ties perfected with speed. The warnings about proper positioning, blood flow, nerve damage. The body as machine and sculpture both, the surface pinned in place while the function continued unseen beneath, lungs expanding and blood flowing and muscles clenching. The decorative ties with precision knots spaced for maximum effect, rope sliding between wet lips and knots pressing sensitive skin as the model bent and turned at the ropemaster's command.

Henry's intermittent questions never mentioned the model. Only her. Would she enjoy. Would she feel. Would she submit. Christ, his hands running over her as he made her body match his own image of her. Sly man, with his pointed questions and his offhand remarks. The rope could be hidden under clothing, he said. Worn all day without anyone the wiser. Shivering, she bit back a moan.

"Only you and I and Jay would know, dearest. We might wander through galleries and concert halls with you bearing my designs in rope on your skin. Would you like that?"

Would she *like* that? She verged on coming right now, and might yet if Jay shifted his head and exhaled or she closed her legs for a few seconds. She gripped Henry's shirt convulsively.

"Yes, sir," she whispered, her throat bone-dry.

The performance ended with the woman in an elaborate pattern of rope crisscrossing her torso from neck to crotch, until it seemed . . .

"Like a honeycomb," Alice murmured.

Henry growled in her ear. "And when I wrap the ropes around you, sweet girl, will you be dripping with honey for me?"

Oh sweet fuck. Her hips jerked.

Jay lifted his head, a hound scenting his dinner, and Henry pushed her panties to the side. "Ninety seconds, my boy. Savor the opportunity."

The groups around the demonstration broke up with polite applause and a rising conversation level, but Jay's tongue diverted her attention. Pressing between her lips, he sucked hard at her clit.

Henry kissed her, a deep kiss that made her forget she might be ashamed to be so wanton in a crowd.

She'd been incapable of counting, but she'd have bet, after Henry swallowed her moans and Jay repositioned her panties and her legs stopped shaking, that it hadn't taken ninety seconds for them to make her come.

Maybe no one had noticed. They'd been quiet. The club didn't lack for other sights.

"Was that the appetizer, Henry?" William. Of course he'd noticed. "You've certainly whetted my appetite for the main course. The boy must have excellent technique to bring her off so quickly. Learned it from you, I suppose?"

"Mmm. Months of practice, Will. The benefits of having them at my fingertips so frequently. They're attuned to each other's responses."

William's chuckle might have hidden a yearning for the same sort of arrangement himself. "Next you'll tell me you've trained them to play piano four hands."

"Now there's a thought." Henry caressed her back. "All right, Alice?"

"Yes, sir." Her voice shook. She didn't want to give Henry the wrong impression. She wasn't afraid. Not even embarrassed, exactly. "Thank you, sir." So what if William had seen her? He'd gotten blown in front of her. He'd been kind and friendly. Henry wouldn't have sat and chatted with him if he wasn't. "I'm still feeling it, sir."

The "sir" rolled out with awkward uncertainty. She might be overdoing the respect by ending every sentence with it. The girl with William seemed to, but they were strangers, and maybe using the word codified and reinforced their temporary relationship.

She added frequency-of-sir to her mental list of questions to ask

Henry before their next visit. Next visit. Getting ahead of herself, was she?

No. Not if she'd pleased Henry and he planned to study the Japanese rope thing.

Jay laid his hand on Henry's shoulder. Henry patted the waiting hand immediately. "Yes, Jay?"

He climbed to his knees, and Henry leaned in. Jay spoke in his ear, his voice too quiet amid the chatter around them as people questioned the rope expert.

Henry raised his eyebrows. "You're certain you wish to do that, my boy?"

More whispered words. Henry cupped Jay's chin and studied his face. He kissed him, possessive but tender. If anyone watching doubted Henry's devotion to his subs, they wouldn't anymore. Henry whispered in Jay's ear before he pulled back.

"Go on, then. Stay close and don't dawdle, Jay. We might find an open room and give William and some others a more thorough demonstration of how well you and Alice play together when you return, hmm?"

"Yes, sir. Thank you, sir." Jay grinned as he stood. He grasped her hand and tugged.

Henry gave her a gentle push off his lap. "Go with Jay, Alice. Mind your manners."

Bewildered, she allowed Jay to lead her through the crowd. "Where are we going?"

"Bathroom."

"But I don't—"

"Yes, you do. Trust me. You've been here a few hours, you've been distracted and aroused, and you're not thinking about it. You get five minutes to relax and your bladder's gonna remember how nervous you were when you got here."

"That's . . ." Oh. Not a bad idea. And she'd have been embarrassed to ask. "Thanks, Jay."

"Hey, we subs gotta stick together. It's not like I can't be trusted to get you to the bathroom and back safely. I can do it."

He was testing himself. Proving himself to Henry. And Henry would reward him with some time with her when they got back. For overcoming his fears.

"I know you can, Jay," she said, nothing but confidence in her voice.

He flashed her a smile. She would've kissed him if they'd been at home, but here . . . rules.

"Besides, Henry would've taken us himself, but then he wouldn't have time to talk to William." They passed out of the central room and walked down a wide hall lined with benches, some occupied, some not, and rooms open for viewing. "They've been friends for years."

"A long time?"

"Since prep school, I think. William's wife doesn't like Henry, though." Jay wrinkled his nose. "We had dinner at their house once last year, and she totally lost her shit. Accused William of bringing 'those people' into her home, even though we were playing the just-roommates card."

Jay ducked into a smaller hallway on the left before the stairs at the end of the hall. It held two doors, both closed, and red lights glowed over the top of each. Jay swore.

"What, they're occupied? So we wait."

He shook his head. "The lights are linked to the showers. If they're on, it'll be a while." He blew out a breath. "There's another set upstairs."

"Henry said to stay close."

"He'd also want us ready for anything. We won't be if we're distracted by other urges, right? He wanted us to hurry back."

Needing to pee, she conceded the point.

"C'mon." Jay took her hand in his.

They joined the steady flow of people on the staircase. She was growing accustomed to the wide range of dress. Stylish suits like Henry's and corsetry like her own. Leather and buckles in infinite variation. Nothing at all. Well, nothing beyond a house ribbon, sandals, and, sometimes, a collar.

At the top of the stairs, Jay's hand tightened around hers.

She squeezed back. "You okay?"

"I, uh, I don't like this floor."

She eyed the corridor ahead. Unlike the floor below, the space wasn't open and bright. Down the narrow hall, under dim lights, closed doors and muffled sounds beckoned.

Jay cleared his throat. "Besides, Henry said not to leave you alone." He tugged her down the short hall to the right and into a spacious restroom.

"Jesus. It's like a four-star hotel in here." A basket of folded cloths and an array of miniature toiletries flanked a double sink on the counter. A toilet tucked behind a half wall, an oversize shower behind glass block, and a stack of towels on a wall rack with a hamper beneath filled out the rest.

"Benefits of a private club. The membership fee for doms is pretty high." Jay flipped the lock on the door. "It's supposed to keep out the riffraff. Doesn't always."

He made a shooing motion. "Go on. You first."

"You're staying?" She would not share a bathroom. Even one as nicely appointed as this one. "Uhn-uh. Nope. Outside."

"No can do. I'm supposed to stick with you." Jay shifted his weight from side to side.

He'd follow Henry's instructions, but this was something more. Standing outside the door would've stayed true to the spirit of the command.

He didn't like this floor. He didn't want to be alone in the hall. Only one conclusion made sense. This was where it had happened. Down that hall somewhere, some jackass had hurt him.

Her chest ached. Bringing the memory up would make him more uncomfortable. She feigned a deep sigh of exasperation. "Turn on the water. And hum something. And don't peek."

"You have more rules than Henry," Jay grumbled.

But he smiled as he turned on the faucet and faced the wall. He hummed the *Jeopardy!* theme song. She rolled her eyes.

She used the toilet quickly and washed her hands while Jay took his turn. He met her gaze in the mirror as he washed his own hands.

"What?" Asking was a formality. His intense stare and the beginnings of a smirk made the answer obvious.

"We need to expand the bathroom at home."

"Oh?"

"You deserve to be fucked on a counter in front of mirrors. Don't worry." He shut off the water and waved his hand in an airy gesture. "I'll mention it to Henry. He'll have contractors in by the end of next week."

She snorted. "He would. But only if *he* wanted to."

"As if he doesn't. Trust me, two words—'Alice. Mirrors.' If he doesn't have a vision for a scene within thirty seconds, I'll spend the next three hours licking your pussy."

"That's supposed to be a punishment?"

He grinned. "Nope. That's 'cause I want to."

Grabbing her hands, he bounced with excitement, his anxious mood lifted. "C'mon. The sooner we get back, the sooner Henry will have something for us to do. It'll be fantastic, I know it. He'll wanna make sure William has a good time watching. He feels bad for him, I think."

"Because of his wife?"

Jay unlocked the door.

"Yup." They stepped into the hall together. "Henry's finally got everything he wants, and his friend's trapped in a loveless wreck of a marriage."

"Were they ever..." Henry and William's past probably wasn't her business. *Everything he wants. Jay... and me?*

"I don't think so." Jay shrugged as they hit the stairs. "If they were, he's never said so to me."

They threaded their way through the people, avoiding contact, keeping their eyes averted, speaking only to each other. Wearing the red ribbon invited relaxation in its way. Private. No social pressure to greet strangers or interact.

"...something visual, I bet."

Whoops. She'd missed the start of Jay's giddy chatter.

"He'll want to put on a show. And you've got that gorgeous corset on. D'you think I could make you come from sucking your tits?" He came to a dead stop and stared at her chest, on full display above the edge of the corset. "I bet I could, if Henry talked to you. I bet anything could make you come if Henry were talking."

She blushed, but she didn't deny it.

"I *thought* that was my stray bitch. It's been so long since I've played with him."

Jay paled. His arm shot out in front of her, crossing her body and gripping her hip, pushing her toward his back.

"I wonder, does he remember me at all? Does he remember how much he wanted to please me? How he begged? He used to beg so prettily for my attention like the little cock slut he is." The strange voice was male. Mean. Snide. Legs circled in front of them, black pants with shiny shoes at the bottom.

Trembling, Jay backed away, forcing her to move with him, toward the wall.

She squeezed his hand on her hip. "Jay?"

No response. The pants circled in closer. Her chest tightened. Jay's anxiety bled through their linked hands and into her.

"Henry's waiting," she hissed in his ear.

He didn't react. That wasn't possible. Jay would never ignore Henry's desires.

"We should go. For Henry."

The pants moved closer, and the chest above them came into view. Bare. Waxed and muscled in the manner of a desperate man pretending he was still a twenty-two-year-old stud.

"Is his skin still as I recall it?" The stranger lifted his hand. "Does his back bear my marks yet? Perhaps he'll turn and show me. A good boy would."

Marks? Jay's back wasn't marked. Why . . . oh Jesus. The guy who'd hurt Jay. What the fuck was his name?

The hand drifted closer. This man could never be allowed to touch Jay. Henry would be livid.

She slipped out of Jay's grasp and slid in front of him, blocking the stranger's access.

"Oh, I see. What a treasure." The fingers hung in the air an inch from her breasts, from the red bow Henry had tied there.

She pressed her back against Jay's chest.

"My cock slut has found a kitten to play with. Perhaps this little pussy is as hungry for my cock as he is. Such . . . fair . . . skin."

The fingers skimmed through the air over her breasts. If she breathed too deeply, they'd brush her skin.

"I wonder, what would it take to split it open?"

Jay moaned, the pained sound of an animal caught in barbed wire and unable to yank itself free. Anxiety blossomed into anger. She shoved Jay back with a powerful hip thrust.

"Mmmm, delicious. He even lets the kitten push him around, does he?" The stranger followed them forward, reclaiming the space she'd gained. "Still the poor little lost boy."

Jay was pressed to the wall. She couldn't retreat further. No one passing paid any attention. Why would they? For all they knew, this stranger owned them.

"He needs a whipping to remind him of who he is. Upstairs. I'll finish what was rudely interrupted."

Jay shook at her back. The urgent need to get him away from this man pounded at her skull.

She tried to sidestep, tried to tug Jay along with her without letting the stranger touch her. She lacked the leverage to get Jay moving, and the stranger matched her movement. She growled.

"Adorable. The kitten, too." The stranger's voice lowered and took on a singsong quality. "If someone's a good boy, he can watch me fuck her after his whipping."

A steady stream of mumbling penetrated her ear. Jay, moaning the word "no" again and again.

God-fucking-dammit.

She needed help. She wouldn't get it so long as this man looked like a dominant playing with his own off-limits subs. Shaking with anger and fear, with Henry's explanation of the club's rules of proper conduct a clanging refrain in her mind, she lifted her head and stared straight into the stranger's eyes.

Pretty, in an overdone sort of way, he sported spiky black hair and trimmed eyebrows over cold blue eyes. She took the deepest breath she dared, given his hand lingering near her breasts, and raised her voice to cut through the chatter around them. "Our master is expecting us. You're in my way. Please step aside."

Heads turned in their direction. A man on a bench along the opposite wall put his hand on his partner's head, and the motion in his lap stopped. His gaze skated over her and Jay, but he didn't linger, and he didn't address them. "Those aren't your toys? The red-flagged pair?"

The jackass shrugged. "I know their dom." His tone conveyed arrogance and annoyance. "We go way back."

"Still. Talk to their dom. Not them."

"I wasn't talking *to* them. I was thinking aloud."

"Back up and think quieter before I send my pet for a bouncer."

Thank you thank you thank you.

The jackass stepped back, palms up in an I'm-innocent gesture. "The girl's the one who offended me. She's horribly trained. Clearly she doesn't belong here at all—certainly not wandering around without supervision."

Nobody's buying your act, you fucking ass.

She wrapped her hands around Jay's arm and yanked him along with her. He stumbled but kept his feet. She whispered a running stream of encouragement. "C'mon, you can do this, Jay, walk, please, we'll go see Henry—"

"Yes, let's go see your master. Perhaps he'll have me punish you for your insolence myself."

Jay shuddered under her hands. "Jay, you know that won't happen. Henry won't let it." She quickened her pace, dragging Jay in her wake. "Don't listen, okay? Just listen to me." The big room loomed in the distance. "Henry will make everything better, I promise."

There. That grouping of chairs, less than twenty feet now, and Henry stood at their approach. God, let his frown be for the man following them and not her.

He intercepted her hand on its way to his shoulder, clasping her hand in his and letting it drop. She hoped he recognized the fear in Jay's eyes. The jackass had stopped his loud muttering somewhere along the way.

"Jay, at my side, please. Waiting pose." Henry's voice seemed the key to unlocking Jay.

He dropped to his knees with painful swiftness and rested his head against Henry's thigh. His relieved shudder when Henry stroked his hair rippled through her. The familiar pose probably comforted Jay. But anxiety, anger and fear simmered in her.

"Alice?"

He'd make things better. She'd tell him, and he'd handle it, and she wouldn't need to do anything but follow his rules.

Rules she'd already broken.

"There's a man," she blurted. "He knows Jay somehow . . . from years ago."

She kept her suspicion to herself. Henry would read between the lines anyway. "I broke the rules, sir. I'm sorry. Jay got upset and I didn't know what else to do."

"Did you touch the man?" Henry scanned the room past her head.

"No. But I spoke to him. And I raised my eyes. Sir."

"Is that him?" Hand under her chin, he turned her face gently.

The jackass had stopped about ten feet away.

"Yes, sir."

Henry sighed. "One would hope he had sharpened his skills in the last five years, but perhaps he's only sharpened his cruelty."

He trailed his fingers down the side of her neck in a soothing caress before his palm landed heavily on her shoulder. "He'll wait to see that you're disciplined for it. If I don't handle it, he'll report it as an infraction to be handled through mediation, which could result in a recommendation that he deliver the discipline himself."

Frowning, he bowed his head. "I won't allow his hands on you. Not either of you. Will you trust me in this, my dear?"

Considerate and patient, despite her fuckup. She could use her safeword, and he wouldn't force her to submit. Even if he'd lose respect here or face sanctions for her behavior.

His style of dominance channeled more caretaker than bully. His primary concern was her. Her health and safety, emotional as well as physical. If she couldn't do this, he wouldn't make her. But she did trust him, and she had disobeyed him.

"I knew the rules, sir. You were clear. I knew what I was doing when I broke them." She wouldn't shy from the consequences. "I'm sorry my behavior disappoints you and reflects badly on your training. I'll accept whatever punishment you think is appropriate."

Henry leaned in until his lips touched her ear. "You have not disappointed me, my dear. Quite the opposite. You protected your partner to the best of your ability and sought me out as quickly as possible. I'm very proud of you, Alice."

"She chooses to accept her punishment?" The jackass pandered to the crowd in a loud voice. "Does she choose to carry your balls in her purse, too?"

Seeking support. He might find it. He was a member, obviously a frequent guest, and she was a newcomer, a possible embarrassment to Henry in the eyes of the others here.

"You give your playthings too much freedom, Henry."

Henry nuzzled her ear, seemingly unaffected by the man's outburst. He threaded one hand through her hair, cupping the back of her skull and tipping her head toward him and down. Jay, pressed to Henry's side, received the same affection with the other hand.

A firm kiss landed on her forehead. Henry might be playing to the crowd, too. Staring the jackass down. Demonstrating control of not one but two committed submissives at his side.

"I give my *partners* precisely as much freedom as they require to enjoy our games." Certainty rang in Henry's voice. He knew without a doubt he pleased them both. His confidence in himself and his judgment gave her confidence in return, bolstered her trust in him. God, she loved him.

I'm in love with Henry.

Not an imitation. Not a lesson, not a game, not a chemical reaction. Love. The real thing. Holy shit. That wasn't supposed to happen. Distracted, she almost missed his next dig at the stranger.

"Perhaps your partners require less, or perhaps you're unable to read their needs. Is that why you're alone tonight?" Henry dropped his hand to her back and pulled her closer. Preemptive comfort, or possibly a ploy to make her appear vulnerable. He had knowledge she didn't of what the people here would expect. Of her . . . punishment.

A snicker sounded to her left, and a woman mumbled. ". . . most nights, he means."

"Not everyone needs to drape himself in pets in an attempt to look like a real man, Henry. Some of us prefer variety."

"Mmm. Or can't play well enough with others to keep them coming back, I suppose." Henry delivered the words with casual disregard, as if he hadn't addressed the jackass. "I wouldn't have expected to find you on this floor. The amusements here are too tame for your appetites, aren't they, Cal?"

Cal. Jackass suited him better. She resettled her face sideways against Henry's shoulder for a better view of the room.

"We can't all be as soft as you, Henry." Jackass Cal stayed well out of Henry's reach. A jackal, snapping and retreating, with a chair between them.

Give me a whip, you fucking bully. She'd whip him twice for every time he hit Jay, and a third time for every insult to Henry.

"I thought I saw something that belonged to me on the stairs."

Henry's hand tightened on her back. "You were mistaken, I'm sure, as there's nothing here that belongs to you."

"No." Cal spat the word. "Only stolen property and a kitten who imagines herself a lion. Your pet needs corrective training, Henry. A session upstairs will take care of the matter. I'll demonstrate, if you haven't the stomach for it."

"Corrective training?" William scoffed as he stepped alongside Henry. "The girl what, said a few words and accidentally caught your eyes? A minor infraction. The attention probably flustered her. She's little more than a child here."

"All the more reason to correct her harshly before she develops bad habits. A proper submissive is obedient above all else." Cal thrust his arm out, his finger pointing at her. "She looked me in the eye, bold as brass, and insisted *I* move out of *her* way. If her behavior isn't corrected now, it shows a blatant disregard for the rules of this establishment."

"You've had run-ins with the rules a time or two yourself, Cal." William's sly tone insinuated all sorts of things.

But whatever Cal had done, even the things he'd done to Jay, his behavior didn't excuse or erase hers. She'd chosen to break the rules, and someone had to answer for that. Either she submitted to Henry's punishment, or Henry submitted to the club's judgment because he'd vouched for her conduct. His personal ethics wouldn't permit less.

"And she doesn't owe her submission to you," William added. "It's a courtesy only."

He sounded as if he enjoyed goading the jackass. She approved.

Cal dismissed William's words with a wave. "She owes it to every dom she meets in this establishment to be silent and respectful. Or would you propose we have the inmates run the asylum?"

"They already do, Cal." Henry's voice was quiet but firm. "What you fail to understand, what you've always failed to understand, is that their submission is a gift. It can be revoked at any time, with the utterance of a single word. Those who don't recognize that are not dominants but abusers."

"Slander," Cal all but shouted. "You've led a campaign against me for years, Henry. Perhaps your kitten isn't so innocent. You set her on me deliberately, hoping to provoke some infraction from me you could take to the board. It didn't work out as you hoped, though, did it?"

"Often the ones who see such plots lurking are the ones most familiar with their uses."

Cal smiled, a thoroughly insincere expression. "Quit stalling, Henry. You know what I want to see. I demand satisfaction for the insult."

Had Henry been stalling? That didn't seem like him, and yet talking to Cal wasn't necessary. It wouldn't change his mind. She'd already agreed to accept her punishment.

"Of course, Cal. And you'll have it."

"Upstairs, then."

"No. Here." Henry still stroked her spine. Standing next to him, enveloped in his touch and scent, calmed her fears. She'd bet his touch calmed Jay, too.

Oh. Of course. Henry would stall because he cared more about making sure they were all right than placating the jackass.

"Upstairs," Cal repeated. "I'd prefer to see her on an x-frame. Say, twenty lashes? I have a lovely coachwhip."

A whip to split her skin, to leave her a sobbing wreck as he'd done to Jay. Disgust and panic curdled in her stomach. An objection from her would undermine Henry's authority. She had to let him handle it. Trust him.

"Here, or not at all, Cal. I'll accept a suspension of privileges before I let you tie an unprepared submissive to a frame and whip her bloody. I've seen the results of your handiwork before."

William jumped in. "Surely bent over a chair here would be suitable enough. A heavy flogger, perhaps? Buffalo?"

Henry hadn't yet used the one in his bedroom on her. What aroused her at home sickened her now. Not a flogger, not her suede or any other. Not with the jackass watching her.

"No." Henry shook his head. "I've plans for her, and I won't have her first experience with a buffalo flogger associated with punishment in her mind. It sets a bad precedent and instills a fear of trying new things."

"A riding crop?" William's continued suggestions made her wish he'd stop. "The sting is short but sharp, certainly an appropriate punishment for a moment's lapse."

She trembled in fear. Henry had promised never to use the crop on her again, but that was for pleasure and this was for pain and maybe he'd have to do it anyway.

"No, not the crop, either," Henry answered. "The short sting teaches her nothing and it's too easy to mark her with it. She's quite fair."

He breathed deeply, his chest rising against hers. A man at a decision point. Cal wouldn't wait much longer, and Henry would have to choose whatever punishment he found least offensive to himself and least damaging to her.

"She'll receive a spanking. Ten strokes. Her actions were those of a defiant child, and her punishment reflects that. She's familiar enough with my touch that fear will not distract her from her corrective instruction. Because the goal, of course, is not to make her fear me but to obey me." Henry gave a pointed glance to the obnoxious jackass. "If certain others cannot understand that lesson, they do not deserve the trust and affection of trained submissives."

"Pathetic." Cal's tone made his sneer obvious. "No wonder they run wild, if that's the sort of so-called dominance you provide."

"Think what you like, Cal. The responsibility to punish her is mine, and I will fulfill that duty. If you choose to take issue with how I do so, ask the board to cite me for it." He removed his hand from her back. "I'll need a moment for instruction and positioning."

His voice changed, softened, as he looked down. "Jay. Up, my boy."

Jay obeyed. He'd stand at Henry's command even if his legs were broken. He was still pale, though, his eyes wide and his face vacant.

"Alice. Follow." Henry took Jay by the hand.

She followed along behind, her head down. She ought to seem chastened, she supposed, not angry at the whole situation. Henry led them to a bench seat and placed Jay in a waiting pose on the floor in front. Then he sat, knees spread, and called to her.

"Come here, Alice." He took her hands, guiding her to stand between his legs. "Look at me, please."

Odd. Backward. Henry's face didn't belong below her own.

"Cal implied he saw you both on the stairs. Did you go upstairs, Alice?"

"Yes, sir."

"Why did you do that, Alice?" He kept his voice neutral, but their action must've confused him. Jay wouldn't have revisited that floor on a whim.

"The bathrooms on this floor were in use, sir, and Jay didn't want us to dawdle."

Only after she'd said it, after the muscle twitched in Henry's cheek, did she want to kick herself for echoing his instructions to them. In attempting to defend Jay, she'd made Henry keenly aware that trying to do what he'd asked of them had brought them to Cal's attention. *Fuck.*

Henry closed his eyes, briefly. "And it was when you returned to this floor that you encountered Cal?"

"Yes, sir."

"And you looked him in the eye and spoke to him."

"Yes, sir."

"Should you have done that, Alice?"

"No, sir."

"No. Tell me, in your own words, what you've done wrong tonight."

She'd let that man taunt Jay. Hadn't taken the chance to kick him to the ground and stomp on his balls.

"I shouldn't have strayed by going up the stairs without asking your permission. I shouldn't have spoken to another dominant. I shouldn't have challenged him with my eyes."

"Thank you, Alice."

Henry reached for the sides of her panties, and she barely managed to avoid flinching as his intent revealed itself. "Ten strokes, on your bare bottom, will remind you to avoid such childish behavior in the future. I don't expect you'll find the experience arousing, but should you do so, you are not to come. You'll count after each stroke, loudly enough for the man you've offended to hear. You may cry out as needed. Do not hide your pain out of misplaced stubbornness or pride. You have none now, do you understand?"

She offered mechanical, empty agreement, her mouth dry. "I understand, sir."

Courage deserted her. Exposure disturbed her more than she'd expected. She fought the urge to cover herself as Henry lowered her panties to her thighs.

"A true blonde? What a novelty. Is that why you don't shave her smooth?"

She refused to give Cal her attention. Only Henry mattered. But prickling awareness crawled along her nerves. A dozen people or more hovered on the periphery. William, in his familiar dress slacks, stood a few feet to Henry's right.

Probably not the show Henry had wanted to give him. But was it the sort he'd enjoy? Discomfort nagged at her. She was Henry's good girl. His eager pupil. Proud to be shown off with Jay. Not to be disciplined, to have made a bad impression with Henry's friend.

Henry turned her over his left leg and clamped his right leg behind her thighs. He pressed her back flat. Her fingers grazed the floor. Her head hung down. Jay, still vacant-eyed, knelt alongside Henry's feet. He wouldn't want to see this. Not here.

I'm so sorry, Jay.

Henry's left arm formed a solid weight on her back, his elbow resting between her shoulder blades, his forearm running down her spine, holding her in place.

The spanking wouldn't hurt too badly. She'd been turned over Henry's knee before and felt his hand turn her skin red. She'd taken more pain from the suede flogger and reveled in it.

But what struck her now wasn't simply the weight of his hand or the sting it left behind as she choked out, "One!" in response to his demand that she count.

This was punishment. Her spanking wasn't a prelude to soothing intimacy or a good hard fuck. It didn't further bonds of trust or affection.

Their games at home didn't revolve around punishment. She and Jay rarely misbehaved, and Henry had little desire to punish them when they did. Correct them with his voice, yes. But with force? No. That sort of dominance wasn't necessary. It wasn't what any of them desired.

And what they did at home stayed private. Here, as she called out, "Two!" in an unrecognizable voice, people murmured around her. They commented on Henry's technique and on the red color blooming on both sides of her buttocks. Questioned the offense she'd committed. Used her as a training exercise, a reminder to behave.

Cal's shiny shoes circled around her, around Jay, a danger she could do nothing about.

Henry's hand fell again, and she stuttered. "Th-three."

As she counted four and five, she cried for no reason. Irrational tears. The spanking didn't hurt that much. She could take it.

Her body felt differently, and her mind spun in a jumbled mess. She hadn't angered Henry or disappointed him. He'd told her so himself. But whatever his words, his hand bore the weight of judgment. Feeling became everything. Nothing existed but the short sting and the long burn and the way her ass throbbed with pain.

She stumbled through counting six and seven and for one panicked moment couldn't remember the word for eight.

She'd disappointed Henry. She'd let Jay be hurt. She deserved this punishment. She should be grateful for this punishment. If she took it well, Henry wouldn't end their contract.

"Nine."

He wouldn't, would he?

"Ten."

He might.

She sobbed with a child's lack of control, unable to breathe through her nose and forced to an openmouthed pant. Fucking pathetic. Snot stuffing her nose and tears leaving an itchy trail to her hairline and everyone watching her failure. Dangling like a sack, Henry's thigh a bar under her stomach. He was right to be disappointed in her. Disgusted with her.

The murmurs around the room thinned. Behind her, Henry's friend William said, "Oh, well done. She colors beautifully."

Henry didn't respond. She struggled to raise her head. Henry's elbow dug into her shoulder blades, and she emerged face to groin with *that man*.

The one who'd taunted Jay and landed her in this position. He stood a foot away, stroking the bulge in his pants. She shuddered and dropped her head, a fresh round of sobs clogging her throat as she squeezed her eyes shut.

"She's delicious in pain, Henry. I bet you don't take her to the edge nearly often enough to showcase it."

"Leave off, Cal. She's had her punishment for her misdeed."

"She hasn't apologized yet. I can think of a dozen ways for her to do it. You don't even have to move her. Be a good boy and pull her up by her hair, would you? I'll fuck her mouth while she quivers in your lap."

She was quivering, that was true. She couldn't seem to stop.

Henry's legs tensed on hers. His hands tightened on her back and thighs. He drew his spanking hand back, and fear rippled through her. Would he hit her again, or let this stranger—*no. He wouldn't. He promised.*

He leaned into her. The stinging pain didn't materialize.

"No, Jay. I have a task for you." Henry rubbed her back. "We're leaving, my boy. You'll carry Alice to the car. Pick her up now, please. Gently."

Her panties were pulled up. Her body was rolled away from Henry's lap, turned over and deposited in Jay's arms. He cradled her to his chest, his grip firm around her back and beneath her knees. She tried to focus on his touch, a distraction from her throbbing discomfort.

"If you persist in this behavior, Cal, you may be assured I will push for your expulsion from this establishment." Henry stood. He glanced at her, at Jay, and his lips formed a hard line. "Permanently, this time."

"Your punishment, if it can even be called that, is barely adequate." Cal stepped closer and lowered his voice. "You're not the only one with friends on the board, Henry."

She doubted anyone beyond their tight circle—herself, Jay, Henry and William—could hear him now.

"I could have fucked him in the hall. He wouldn't have stopped me. I could have taken him back upstairs, and the girl too, and they both would have learned their place. If they offend me again, the board's censure won't deter me, Henry. I'll be convincingly remorseful, of course, but the marks will be on them. And every time you touch them, they'll remember me."

The silence frightened her. Henry, her patient, calm Henry, radiated rage and revulsion under thin control. So still he seemed a sculpture. The barest hint of a flare in his nostrils. A trace of narrowing in his eyes, skin pulling tight beneath them. Even so provoked, he'd prize self-mastery. She lacked a reference point for an uncontrolled Henry. What he might do. The tension thickened.

William guffawed. A hearty, forced, loud laughter that turned heads. As if Cal had been making a joke and not threatening her safety and Jay's. "Cal, let it go. The girl's been punished for whatever imagined slight you fabricated. Really, on her first night out in public? Henry's hardly going to bring his lovelies for a return visit if you put her off the entire idea the way you did the boy. He won't let you fuck either of them. He's already said they'd both be collared if he didn't dislike the way it breaks the aesthetic beauty of the neckline."

Henry said *what*? She struggled to control her breathing. Collared. Both of them, not just Jay. A definite, unmistakable claim.

Had he said that to keep from being bothered about borrowing them, or had he meant it? Maybe she wasn't crazy to love him, even if he'd physically abused her in public.

Not abuse. She could've stopped it. Maybe she wouldn't have been allowed back, and maybe he'd have been embarrassed, but she could've done it. One word, and he would've stopped.

"If his pets aren't ready to be out in public, he should keep them home." Would that man never shut his mouth? Every time he spoke, Jay tensed.

She turned her face further into Jay's chest and nuzzled him. She would've placed kisses against his skin, but they might count as sexual contact. She wasn't about to break another rule. Not tonight.

"Otherwise, they should accept the consequences of their misbehavior."

Henry ignored him. "Jay. To the elevator, my boy. We're going."

Jay's shoulder made a woodsy-scented pillow as they left. Jackass Cal wasn't following. William provided a sturdy bulwark, penning Cal in the way the jackass had done to her and Jay. She found a grim satisfaction in it. Santa practiced more than comedy. If it weren't for the stinging pain, she'd ask Henry if she could sit on Santa's lap and thank him.

They rode the elevator to the first floor. Henry rattled off instructions about their coats to Jay.

Would it be wrong to ask Santa to hold a man down so she could cut off his balls?

She giggled as Henry tucked her coat around her. Frowny-face Henry. Tight lips. Pinched eyes under lowered brows. Maybe because he wouldn't get to ask Santa for anything? He didn't have to worry. She'd ask for two presents. She couldn't stop giggling long enough to get the words out.

Henry said something, and Jay picked her up again. The stars outside blurred, the world spinning too quickly and faster-than-light travel dangling a nanosecond away.

Henry used his spanking hand on the car door. Open sesame. The same hand that often brought her to orgasm in his bed. Made her dinner. Dried her tears and cradled her on special nights. She couldn't meet his eyes. Not now. Not when she was scattered and shattered and her mind shouted at her in a million voices and her ass throbbed with pain and everything circled back to the same point of confusion.

I love Henry.

He hurt me.

But I love him.

"Jay, you need to let go. Put Alice in the car, please."

Jay folded himself around her, ducking to lower her into the seat. He clasped her with care, eyes wide and fearful. When the seat brushed her ass, she gritted her teeth and forced the cry in her throat to come out as a hiss of air. She twisted her body to avoid more contact.

Jay's hands shook as he let go. He sobbed, and words poured from him even before he'd backed his head and shoulders out of the car. "I'm so sorry, Henry, it was all my fault. I heard his voice and I froze. It was like it was happening again, and I couldn't, I couldn't, if Alice hadn't stopped him, God, I would've let him 'cause I couldn't move, and she, he would've hurt her, Henry, he wanted to, I heard it in his—"

"Jay." Henry sounded sharper than a diamond-tipped carbide drill bit carving with precision. "Alice needs you. Focus, Jay. Alice needs you to help her. You can help her now, Jay."

Curled in the backseat, she started at the hard tone, the utter lack of sympathy in his voice. He wouldn't blame Jay, would he? She was the one who'd fucked up, missed finding a better way to handle things. The right answer refused to appear. How she could've gotten Jay moving and kept them both safe. And Jay couldn't do anything about it now.

"I can help her. I can help her." Jay calmed, his voice evening out with each repetition. "I can. Tell me what to do, Henry."

"Get in the car, Jay. Sit with Alice. Dry her tears. Tell her about your bike trip to the state park. I don't believe she's heard about it yet, and I'm certain she wants to. Right now, Jay."

Who cared about a fucking bike trip? That jackass in the club had been the one who'd abused Jay, who'd betrayed his trust, and now Henry shut him out and denied him comfort. He had to see how broken Jay was. Hell, even she saw it, and she had Grand Canyon-sized cracks herself.

Sliding into the backseat beside her, Jay raised her head and shoulders into his lap. He used a handkerchief that had to be Henry's to wipe tears and snot from her face.

His hands were gentle, tender. He watched her with such intensity, the broken bits of his emotions hiding around the edges.

"It was Sunday," he started, as Henry got in the front seat and pulled the car away from the curb. "I went up with my mountain bike early. Still dark. The sun was coming up when I finished my pre-ride checks. You should come sometime. I have that old mountain bike in storage that I haven't used in . . . years . . . it's . . ."

Losing focus, he hovered on the edge of a breakdown. Rattled herself, she huddled closer, as if touch might fix him. He stroked her hair like a beloved pet's fur.

"The sunrise, Jay." Henry's stern command flowed from the front seat. "Tell Alice about the colors."

"Yes, Henry."

Jay had never sounded so subdued and submissive, not even the first night Henry had flogged her, when panic had seemed poised to drive him from the room. Of course, he'd never lost it this completely in front of her, either. Tonight had been so much worse.

"I rode up the mountain, and the sun came to greet me. It was . . ."

She tuned out his voice, because his eerie, even tone, so unlike the enthusiastic chatterbox he'd been before they'd seen that man, deepened the pain and she'd run out of space to hold any more. She should've hit that fucker. Knocked him down and kicked the shit out of him while Jay watched.

She vibrated with anger, her whole body a blazing wire of rage.

". . . and my tire got stuck in the—Alice?" Jay lost his monotone. Her name was a panicked squeak. "Henry? She's shaking, I don't know what to do. What should I, what should I do?"

Fuck. I'm scaring him.

She reached for his hand, for the arm curled comfortingly around her waist, and squeezed.

"M'fine." Her voice sung out raw and unconvincing.

The car slowed. Henry changed lanes to the right. Pulling over?

She spoke through the burn in her throat the sobs had left behind. "M'fine, Henry. Just home. Please?"

She struggled to sit up. Jay didn't want to let her go and sitting hurt, but she needed to make Henry understand she was fine but Jay wasn't.

The light reflecting on the windshield turned red. The car stopped. She leaned forward, her weight on her elbows on the front seats. Jay steadied her as she placed her mouth at Henry's ear.

"I just wanna be home. Worry about Jay. He's the one who needs you, and you won't even tell him it's okay."

Henry's eyes briefly closed. "Now is not the time, Alice. Please be patient. Be patient, and stay with him."

What, it wasn't convenient for Jay to be needy now? *That's cold, Henry. Really fucking cold.*

She said nothing. Fighting with Henry wouldn't help Jay.

The light turned green, and she returned to Jay's lap before Henry had to tell her to sit back. She rolled to press her face into Jay's stomach. Wrapping her arm around his back, she hoped and prayed and gave a mute cheer when he mindlessly stroked her hair. He'd interacted, if only on autopilot.

They rode the rest of the way home in silence, without even music to accompany their thoughts.

When Henry put the car in park and turned off the engine, she scrambled out without waiting. No way would she let Jay carry her up three flights of stairs. Her ass hurt, sure, but she wasn't an invalid or a child.

He sat motionless in the backseat. She reached in and tugged on his hand.

"Jay? We're home. Time to get out."

No response. Henry came around their door and gently pushed her aside.

"Jay. Out of the car now, my boy. I want you upstairs in less than three minutes, am I understood?"

Jay didn't speak, but the command in Henry's tone got him moving. He swung his legs out and stood so quickly that Henry grabbed Jay's head to keep him from striking the top of the door frame. Henry herded them both into the building and up the stairs, his hand a repeated faint pressure on her back. One she welcomed, especially when it prodded her past her own apartment door.

Not that she expected he'd abandon her, but Jay's neediness screamed right now, too, and Henry hadn't done a damn thing but order him around. She wouldn't leave Jay alone to deal with this when Henry offered only silence and anger. Where had his tenderness gone? Where was the devoted man she loved?

Henry hustled them into the apartment and shucked his coat before pulling Jay's down his arms and off. She left hers lay on the floor because Henry had and he was already prodding them down the hall.

"Bedroom. Quickly, please."

She paused beside his bed, horribly off-balance. The night hadn't gone as she'd expected, and now Henry was . . . whatever he was. Her fault for asking to go at all. If she hadn't been so damned curious, they wouldn't have been at the club, and Jay wouldn't have run into his abuser, and Henry wouldn't have had to discipline her.

"Off." Henry tugged at the stays on her corset, his voice tight and angry. "All of it, right now."

He undid the snaps on Jay's pants himself, probably because Jay was gone, off somewhere in his head and unresponsive. Once stripped, Jay stood in silence, naked and waiting.

She struggled to get herself out of the elaborate costume, the lacing and the garters and the strappy sandals. Everything had too many clasps and knots, and her fingers didn't want to work.

Henry undressed himself with haste. He didn't place the pieces on the chair, either. They dropped to the floor around him, the suit coat in a pile, his tie half-knotted, the threads on the shirt buttons pulled loose from rough handling.

Naked before she was, he swore when he looked at her, shaking his head. Uncharacteristic impatience brought him to her side. In two years, he'd never sworn in front of her in anything but a sexual context.

Was he angry with her? She'd ruined the evening. She'd forced Jay to watch Henry hurt her.

Henry's motions, though quick, weren't rough as he extricated her from the constrictive clothing. He pulled the final stocking from her foot with gentleness. But his voice was short. "Get into bed, Alice."

He turned from her, pulling back the covers, obviously assuming she'd obey. Her own anger, all of that rage she'd wanted to unleash on Jay's abuser, wouldn't let her.

Henry had ignored Jay's emotional distress. He hadn't comforted Jay. Even now that they were home, he seemed short-tempered and disappointed in them both.

"No. I don't want to."

Maybe she could lead Jay to his own bedroom and take care of him herself. That would give Henry time to cool down, or whatever he needed to do.

"What?" Distraction colored his tone. He twisted toward her, his movements sharp. "Get into bed, Alice."

"I said I don't want to. Why are you being so fucking cold? Can't you see Jay needs you?"

A low keening made her jump. Jay.

Fuck. Jay, I'm sorry, I'll make things better in a minute, I promise.

She started toward him, intending to wrap him up in her arms. Henry was already there, pulling gently on Jay's wrist, guiding him to the bed.

"Come along now, my boy, lie down for me." His voice soothed and coaxed. "That's a good boy, just another moment, hmm?" Face turned down, he combed his fingers through Jay's hair.

She stepped closer to the bed. She needed Henry's eyes, some connection, instead of feeling like an emotional pinball machine on the verge of tilting.

Henry stretched his free hand toward her. "Alice." The soft tone, the one he'd just used with Jay. "Please. Come to bed. I can't . . ."

He raised his head, and the need warring in his eyes floored her. He wasn't angry. Or if he was, it wasn't with her or Jay. He'd been desperately trying to balance their needs, hers and Jay's, and she'd made his work more difficult.

Shame soaked her to her bones as she nodded her understanding.

He nodded, too, and lay on his side. Pulling Jay against his chest, he tucked the younger man's head into his neck and draped the top sheet over their bodies.

"All right, my boy. My brave, sensitive boy. You've done so well, Jay. I'm so very proud of you."

Embarrassment plucked at her. Her presence intruded on something private, something she'd nearly ruined by piling more guilt on Henry's shoulders with her careless words.

"You've held things together long enough, Jay. We're home now, safe in bed, where nothing can touch you without your consent. Do you feel the sheets against your skin, Jay? Do you feel my heart beating under your hand?"

Jay's mumbled response brought relief rolling through her like a flood. Adrenaline abandoned her, leaving her shaky on her feet. She leaned until the comforter brushed her legs and her weight started to shift against it.

"That's good, Jay. Very good. There's nothing to be afraid of here, my boy. Hmm?"

Jay mumbled again, and Henry lifted his head. His eyes found hers.

"She's here, Jay, she's fine, you haven't failed our Alice. She's getting into bed now, my boy. You want to feel her, don't you? To have her skin against yours and know she's well?"

She crawled up the mattress and slipped under the covers. Jay needed her. Henry needed her. She molded her body to Jay's back.

"You see, Jay? You haven't hurt Alice. Here she is. That's better, isn't it?"

Soft sobs. Jay trembled as she pressed her cheek to his back. Vibrations shook his torso, more suppressed sobs waiting to come out, as he spoke.

"I'm sorry, Alice. I'm so sorry." Muffled against Henry's chest, Jay's voice emerged thick with pain. "Your first night, it should've, should've been fun and I ruined it. I made Henry hurt you. I'm so fucked up. I don't, I don't deserve—"

He broke down, sobbing. Henry crooned to him, encouraging his emotional release. She snuggled closer. She didn't blame Jay, not for any of it, but she'd take her cues from Henry.

He knew what he was doing. He'd probably known from the moment he'd handed her over to Jay in the club. She'd been terrible to him. Untrusting.

Shame soured in her stomach. She should've known better. Would have known better if she'd been in any kind of state to think clearly. If Henry wanted her to verbally reassure Jay now, his commands would become part of the steady stream of comforting words spilling from his lips.

She lay still and listened, relaxing into Jay's body, trying to communicate her growing calm to him with her touch. It was obvious now how deeply Henry loved him. And how deeply *she* loved *them*.

Tears pricked at her eyes. She let them fall, silent and unnoticed amid Jay's emotional storm.

Henry's murmurs turned to kisses, a gentle rain on Jay's face, until the younger man's panic subsided. The trembling and sobbing tapered to a stop. He lay quiet between them, taking deep breaths.

"It's all right, my boy. You've had a difficult night. But you've done so well. No one blames you, Jay. You've done nothing wrong. You did what I asked of you. I'm certain Alice doesn't blame you for that. Isn't that so, Alice?"

She squeezed in tighter, laying her arm over Jay's side, her hand near his chest, avoiding any implication of sexuality.

"It wasn't your fault, Jay. None of it." She pressed a chaste kiss to his shoulder blade. "I'm not mad at you. I don't blame you. You didn't ruin anything. You deserve only good things, Jay. You're a good man. Such a good man."

She kissed him again, and Henry mirrored her action on his forehead.

"Rest, Jay. You've exhausted yourself." Henry's low, even tone might put her to sleep, too. "Eyes closed, that's it, good boy. I'll be here when you wake. I won't leave you alone."

She dozed, the steadiness of Jay's breathing and the warmth of his back combining with the soothing note of Henry's voice to make a concoction better than any soporific.

Darkness cloaked the room. She lacked any sense of how much time had passed. Henry's voice had fallen silent. Jay slept yet.

She started to ease herself out of bed. She needed to use the bathroom and maybe splash cold water on her face and check on her backside, which stung when the sheets moved against her skin.

"Alice?" Henry whispered to her from across Jay's body, and she shivered.

"Bathroom break," she responded, with equal quiet. "I just need a minute."

She moved without giving him time to object. The clock, visible as she stood, showed they'd been home less than two hours. Henry had been comforting Jay for at least half that. She hadn't slept long.

Emotional exhaustion, that was all. She still felt tired. Drained. More so than she'd been on any of the nights they had played together.

She closed the door to the bathroom behind her before turning on the light, not wanting it to spill into the hall and through the open bedroom door to wake Jay. She blinked owlishly at her reflection.

Luckily, she'd worn only the faintest touch of makeup. Her face wasn't terribly dirty or tear-stained. She'd sat on the bench in Henry's bedroom while he applied it to his liking before they left for the club. The counter in here wasn't large enough for her to sit comfortably. Maybe Jay would remember about the contractors.

A laughing sob barked from her throat, and she hurriedly used the bathroom before emotion swept her away. Sitting caused teeth-grindingly painful pressure. Henry's swats to her ass had been a choreographed show for their audience, and he wouldn't have been able to fake the results. He'd struck her with force.

She flushed the toilet and washed her face and hands before turning around and standing on her toes for a damage assessment.

Redness. It would fade soon. The tenderness would take a little longer, but then that too would be nothing more than a memory. Jay's damage would last a lot longer.

He'd had to face his demon before he was ready. He'd need support from Henry. Maybe even professional support.

The anger at Cal burned in her, and she forced herself to breathe through it. Was this what men felt when their wives or girlfriends or sisters or daughters were victimized by rapists and abusers? A horribly nauseating sense of not knowing how to fix things. A fear of saying or doing the wrong thing and setting back the recovery process. An anger with no outlet.

She had no experience with this, none. Maybe she ought to let Henry handle this. He knew what he was doing. Jay felt comfortable with him. Jay had been through the recovery process with him before.

Her presence might hurt Jay, remind him of his misplaced guilt. A complication that would slow his healing. But her absence might trigger fears of abandonment or be mistaken for anger. He already worried that she blamed him.

She gripped the edge of the counter, leaning in to bring her face-to-face with herself.

"Trust Henry. He'll know what's best. When you don't know what to do, ask him and he'll help you."

And if Jay needed all of Henry right now, his exclusive attention, so much that none was left for her . . .

She stared herself down in the mirror. They would find a way to make this work. She could wait.

She reentered the bedroom with caution in case the men wanted privacy. Jay slept curled around Henry's left side, snoring softly. Henry lifted his right arm and beckoned her toward him. She rounded the bed and slid under the covers.

"I'm sorry that you've had to wait, my dear." He spoke in a quiet undertone, his eyes on hers, easy to see after her vision adjusted to the darkness.

"Wait?" She had yet to determine how he did that. If their minds held such similarities that they traveled down the same paths. Comforting, if true. Jay had complained once about how alike they were, but the idea didn't trouble her anymore.

"For my care and attention. Jay's need was urgent, but you, too, have had an emotional upheaval this evening, in addition to the verbal and physical abuse. I have shamefully neglected my responsibilities to you, dearest. Are you in pain?"

Aftercare. Right. Because of the spanking. Even Henry's soft sheets chafed her skin, but the redness had nearly gone.

"Not really. I've had worse sunburns." Physically, at least. Emotionally, no sunburn could compete with the pain of having the man she loved punish her while strangers expressed amusement and arousal.

It had probably hurt him, too. He'd spent three months punishing himself for rushing things on their first night together. How would he punish himself now for taking them to the club, for exposing them to the possibility of harm, and for causing harm with his own hand? And how could she stop him from punishing himself unnecessarily?

"You've no bruising? Perhaps I should check—"

"I looked, Henry. I'm fine." She nestled closer, seeking out his side with her hand, hoping to reassure him along with herself. Stupid fucking Cal had hurt all of them tonight. "You didn't damage me. If anything, I damaged you by not understanding what you were doing to help Jay."

Her selfish blindness had made things worse. *Goddammit.*

"I should've realized when you gave us instructions for the night that you were concerned about how he'd react to being at the club. That's why you wanted him to look out for me. Not just because you knew I'd need it, but because he would, too. You thought he'd handle it better if he had me to focus on."

"Yes. Having a defined task calms Jay. You've seen that behavior in him yourself. I did not expect Cal would appear, nor that he would approach in such a bullying fashion after so many years." His face twitched as though the thought pained him. "He couldn't have been present when we arrived."

Maybe he needed to talk it out. Who did he have? Confiding vulnerability to Jay didn't seem Henry's style. He had to be strong for Jay.

She understood that impulse. Hadn't she been the strong one at home for Olivia? The one Mom depended on? She could listen. Finally, something she could do for him.

"No, Emma would have informed me, certainly."

She swiftly reviewed the night in her head. "The coat-check woman?"

"One of the founders, along with her husband," he corrected. "She keeps an eye on things, making sure the gatekeepers do their jobs, preventing intoxicated patrons from playing and so forth."

She tried, but she couldn't picture the woman. Older, in a black dress . . . *she kissed Henry.* Nothing else had stood out beyond her own nerves.

"We sit and chat on occasion, as we likely would have done tonight if the two of you hadn't been with me for the first time. Her voice is the only submissive's on the board."

"She's a submissive?" If Henry talked to her often, he did have a friend to confide in. She felt a mix of relief that he had someone and envy that it wasn't her. Had they ever . . .

Now wasn't the time to ask.

"Was. She hasn't played since her husband's death. But she has a head for business, and she gives excellent advice, and she never agreed with the club's treatment of Cal."

"What did they do to him?" If he didn't want her to ask, he'd say so. Speaking her mind was perfectly acceptable at home.

"Sixty-day suspension of privileges. A travesty. I pushed for a year and mandatory supervision by another dominant for a further year. Emma voted for a lifetime ban. She argued a safeword violation was insupportable. But Cal's father carried weight then. He was a board member himself. Sixty days, and not even an apology to Jay. I very nearly had to apologize myself, to Cal, for interrupting his scene when I had not first confirmed that his sub was in distress."

His voice was wry. She was horrified. Sixty days? How could anyone think that an appropriate punishment for what amounted to rape?

"Cal has clearly held a grudge, though I feel he has little cause, given the lightness of his punishment. His ego . . . Nevertheless. The error was mine, and you and Jay paid dearly for my misjudgment."

"The error was Cal's," she corrected. "He's a jackass. We'll be fine."

"Will we? Jay is drowning in guilt for abandoning you, for not protecting you, and the progress we've made in conquering his fear has been erased. I've guilt of my own for allowing such a thing to happen to both of you while you put your trust in my hands and for dealing punishment when you did nothing to deserve it. And you. My dear girl. How will you trust me, going forward? Cal misbehaved, and I abused *you* for it."

The uncertainty in his voice crawled under her skin. The edge of castigation, of self-flagellation. The same vulnerability he'd shown the night he'd brought Jay home from the hospital.

She'd managed to do everything wrong that night. Wrong enough that he'd hustled her out of the apartment rather than accept comfort from her. *Do not fuck this up, Alice.*

"You offered me the chance to stop it, Henry. You asked if I trusted you and I did. I still do. I haven't forgotten how to say pistachio. I *chose* not to."

"You flinched," he murmured.

"I'm sure I did." Actually, she wasn't certain of much. The experience had been overwhelming and even now remained hazy. Time and distance might make it clearer. "It's a natural response to pain. You know that."

"No. Afterward." His voice remained quiet, and she found it impossible to decide if it was only to avoid waking Jay. "I raised my hand to stop Jay from starting a brawl. You believed . . . you believed I would hit you again. That I wouldn't stop at ten as I said I would."

Lying to spare him pain, no matter how attractive, wouldn't make things easier.

"For half a second, yes." Better to tell the truth, to show him how much she still trusted him. "My body responded before my mind." She was here, wasn't she? Naked beside him in bed. "I wasn't in a thinking place, Henry. I was in a reacting place. If you raised your hand now, I wouldn't fear its fall."

Jay still clutched Henry's left arm in his sleep. She reached for the right, sliding her hand down Henry's forearm, giving him time to pull away if he wished.

Lifting the hand that had struck her with force mere hours before, she brought it to her mouth and pressed kisses to his palm.

"If you need my forgiveness, Henry, you have it. Circumstances conspired against us tonight. It doesn't make me question your judgment. Tell me . . ." She groped for words. "Tell me what you hoped tonight would be like."

"I had hoped it would be a pleasant experience for you both. You enjoy watching and being watched. Aside from the anxiety of being in a new situation, I expected you would do well, and having Jay at your side would provide reassurance, a familiar experience in an unfamiliar setting. Giving Jay the task of watching out for you, allowing him to focus on something beyond his own lingering feelings of discomfort, seemed a gentle way of giving him back something he once enjoyed."

Weary defeat invaded his voice, and she ached for him.

"It was working, Henry. You were right. His excitement was like a living thing in him. When we were heading back to you, before he saw Cal, he was so *Jay*. All that eagerness ready to play. He hoped you'd show us off in a scene. If we hadn't run into that man, it would've been exactly as you envisioned it."

She kissed his palm once more. Tears sliding from the corner of his eye past his temple astonished her.

"I forgive you, Henry. You haven't lost me, and you haven't lost Jay. We aren't broken. We're here, and we're whole, and we—"

She paused, the night's realization new and fragile and frightening. She'd never felt it this deeply and what if he didn't feel the same? But he felt something, or he wouldn't fear losing them. *Collared.* She pushed on.

"I love you, Henry. You and Jay both. I know it's not part of our contract and I know you're not obligated—"

He pressed his hand to her mouth, startling her and stopping the flow of words.

"You babble when you're anxious, dearest. You haven't any reason for anxiety in this. The sentiment is equally true in reverse. I love you, Alice. I simply didn't wish to put undue pressure on you. So many times, I was certain I had given myself away. Frightened you off with my feelings." He shook his head, as though he couldn't believe she hadn't known. "I think you already know Jay's feelings on the matter."

The utter sincerity of his words and the depth of love in his eyes stunned her into silence. Not only did he love her back, but he'd said it decisively. This wasn't something he needed to consider. It was something he knew. Something he'd known far longer than she had.

His quiet chuckle held a rueful edge. "I intended this conversation as a comfort *for* you, my dear, and yet I find myself utterly relieved and comforted *by* you instead. I'm hardly fulfilling my obligations to you."

"You have comforted me, Henry. Knowing you love me is all the comfort I need."

But it was still a contract night. Although witnessing sexual acts had figured largely into the evening, none of them had significantly engaged in any. She'd gotten the lone orgasm. Could she comfort him that way? Was that something he needed, something she could provide?

"Unless you want . . ." She trailed off as he shook his head.

"No, Alice. It's your contract night, and your right to ask for satisfaction. It's true I've provided little in the way of that this evening, another failure on my part." He frowned. "But no. Perhaps we need to look at things from a perspective in which comfort needn't be linked only to sexual acts. I would prefer to hold you close, my dear. Because I can, and because you enjoy it, and because you are far more to me than an outlet for sexual desire."

"That would be enough for you? Comforting?" She needed to know he was well, just as he always needed to know she was at the end of their nights. She didn't want him thinking of his failures. What *he* saw as failures. Didn't want him questioning himself or his judgment.

"Your presence itself is a comfort to me. You might have chosen to walk away. Tonight, these events, could have shattered everything. That they have not, that we have reached *this* point in time instead . . . I haven't even the words to express . . ."

Curling his hand around the back of her head, he slipped fingers through her hair. He guided her face to his for a tender kiss, all lips and no tongue. When he released her, she snuggled down against his side, her head on his shoulder, her body clasped to his.

"Sleep, Alice. In the morning we might discuss a new arrangement, if you're amenable. Something more long-term."

She wanted that. Wanted it like she hadn't wanted anything since she'd been a small child and everything that caught her interest had become an instant obsession. She wouldn't find a replacement obsession this time. She needed Jay and Henry in her life like she needed water and oxygen.

But she had Jay's needs to consider. And Henry's, though she wasn't sure what those needs were, even if they included her in some fashion. He was a difficult man to read.

"He'll need you, Henry." She forced herself to say the rest. "Maybe exclusively."

Jay's health mattered most. She needed to give Henry the option, to let him know she understood.

"You've been through this with him before. You know better what he needs." She could love him without being selfish. She could be generous. Like Jay. "If you need me to step aside, to make myself scarce so you can focus on helping him, I can do that."

It would hurt, but she could do it, so long as Henry loved her.

"No." Henry's voice was sharp, decisive. He took a breath. "He'll need you, too, my dear. He's been happier with you here than he has with years of casual encounters with women. He needs stability. Together, we can provide that, if you're willing. Or did you miss how desperate he was to help you tonight?"

He pushed her hair back, tracing the edge of her ear. "After I . . . hit you. When Cal suggested he would . . ."

She shivered, the image of that man stroking himself and idly suggesting fucking her mouth a too-fresh memory. Henry's hand tightened, clasping her to him, shielding her.

"Jay started to stand. Without permission. Moving toward the threat against you, toward the man he still fears."

Jay's victory registered, but her mind fixated on a single word: hit. Henry blamed himself.

"You mean spanked." She needed to make the distinction, for her own sanity. "With my consent."

The silence stretched. She waited. She would outwait him on this. He needed to know, to understand she understood.

"Do you truly see it that way, Alice? Can you? I've no doubt Cal manipulated the situation to provoke you—"

"He threatened to take us upstairs. To whip Jay. To rape me. To whip me until my skin split." She spoke in a deadened monotone.

Okay, maybe I'm not processing this well yet either.

At Henry's deep inhalation, she rushed onward. "It doesn't matter. I knew you wouldn't let that happen if I could get us back to you. So I did. And you didn't let it happen. What you did wasn't the same thing. It wasn't even in the same league."

She wasn't about to lie and imply the night had been easy. He'd never believe that, and she'd hurt him if she tried it. He wouldn't want her to hide from him. Above everything else, he needed her to let him help her.

"I'm not saying it wasn't embarrassing or that it didn't hurt. You know it was and it did. That was hard for me. Other than with you, I'm not really the best submissive, am I? Too independent. Seeing the submissives at the club—I thought Jay was, but . . ."

She shook her head against his shoulder. She'd need days to sort out the sights and the behavior, to assign everything a value and figure out what it all meant. Weeks, maybe.

"He just loves you, and he needs discipline and structure to help him focus. He craves it. And I love you, and I like how I feel when you're pleased with me. I need that approval. Being punished was feeling like I'd let you down even though you'd told me I hadn't. It messed with my head. But I know the difference between letting you spank me and being abused. And I need to know that you know I understand. Please, Henry."

He kissed her forehead, lingering, his lips promising protection and comfort and approval.

"I believe you, Alice. You understand the difference, and I . . . I haven't abused you. But what happened tonight will not happen again. If it means giving up my membership privileges, so be it. I will not punish you in public again, dearest. It doesn't suit either of our needs."

She squirmed closer, pressing her arm to his chest in a half hug. His voice turned thoughtful. "Perhaps I approached the night from the wrong angle. I intended for the red ribbons to protect you both, but the limitations hampered your ability to protect yourselves. Should you and Jay ever desire to return, perhaps it would be better if you had no ribbon at all."

"No ribbon?"

"No ribbon," he confirmed. "Had I brought you in as a dominant in training, you wouldn't have been in trouble for speaking to Cal. He and any others you saw while apart from me would have assumed you were Jay's mistress. He wouldn't have dared speak to Jay, directly or otherwise. He likely would have attempted to persuade you to share, but he would have had no leverage with which to do so."

"I wouldn't have known how to act. They all would have seen right through me."

"Ah, but that's the beauty of being the dominant half of the relationship, my dear. However you chose to act, it would have been the correct thing to do because *you* chose to do it. You needn't have explained yourself at all."

That fit the club atmosphere, the mix of dominants and submissives finding each other for the night, with no need for anything deeper. But the description didn't fit Henry. And it didn't fit her.

"I don't think I'd want to be that kind of dominant. I don't think you do, either."

"I have the luxury of being in love with my submissives, Alice, and knowing now that they both love me in return. My need for control grows out of my need to ensure the safety and happiness of those I love. Other people have different needs."

"I just need you," she said, trying and failing to stifle a yawn. "And Jay. I don't need anything else. Except maybe to cut off Cal's balls."

He chuckled.

"Go to sleep, Alice. As I promised Jay, so I promise you. I will be here when you wake. I won't leave you alone." He rubbed his cheek against her hair, his voice nearly soundless. "No more nights across the hall, my love. We'll set Jay to moving boxes in the morning. That, I think, will do more to raise his spirits than any amount of consoling."

Contentment. She drifted toward sleep.

"In the morning," she agreed. "Welcome home."

"Welcome home," Henry echoed. "Welcome home, Alice."

Meet the Author

Putting characters through the wringer hurts, but bringing them out stronger and more committed to their relationship on the other side feels damn good.

In writing *Neighborly Affection: Crossing the Lines*, M.Q. Barber discovered her characters are made of sterner stuff than she is. They demanded upset, confusion, and distress. She begged for fluff and tried to sneak some in by distracting Henry, Alice, and Jay with pretty words and shiny baubles. (They may have taken pity on her on occasion.)

When the author isn't tied down and held hostage by her demanding characters, she can be found on Facebook, Goodreads, and Twitter as M.Q. Barber. For updates, sneak peeks, and exclusive short fiction, sign up for her author newsletter at www.mqbarber.com.

If you enjoy the Neighborly Affection series, please take a minute to leave a review on Amazon, Goodreads, or wherever you prefer to hang out online and talk books. Alice and Jay are always excited to hear they've made a new friend. (Henry will launch his intent stare and nod in acknowledgment.)

Turn the page for a special excerpt of M.Q. Barber's

HEALING THE WOUNDS

When Alice leapt into sexual games with her neighbors Henry and Jay, she didn't plan to fall in love. She sure didn't expect she'd be the switch between Henry's commanding mastery and Jay's submissive playfulness. But now she's moving in with them, and she'd better figure it all out—fast.

Trouble is, she's never been a live-in girlfriend. The day after a traumatic first night at a BDSM club might not be the best time to start.

Struggling to find her place within the lifestyle, Alice seeks equality in a relationship built on surrender. Learning to lean on Henry challenges the foundation of her self-worth. He'll have to lean on her in return for their triad to find stability. But can her stoic dominant lover accept her as a confidante as well as a submissive? And will their love be enough to silence Jay's emotional ghosts?

On sale now!

Chapter 1

Alice sectioned her pancakes into a neat grid. Focusing on the spongy bounce in the stack kept her hands from trembling. Breakfast was the most important meal of the day. Especially when Henry served the living-together discussion as the main course.

A flip and sizzle sounded from Henry's spot at the stove. "I believe my studio might be repurposed."

"Your studio's already in the smallest room. Alice and I can share closet space. It's not like we'd sleep there anyway." Syrup dripped as Jay stopped his pancake-loaded fork halfway to his mouth and twisted around in his seat. "We won't, will we? You're not, I mean, your bedroom is—"

"Jay. Don't borrow trouble, please." Henry loaded fresh pancakes on the serving plate and turned off the burner. "I would not move Alice into my room and leave you alone."

"And I wouldn't let him if he tried." She shook her head at Jay as he swung around to face the table.

"But as Alice has a much more organized aesthetic, Jay, it might be best—"

"I can be neat and clean." Jay powered through without a hint of offense at being called a slob. Interrupting Henry right and left. Christ, he wanted this bad.

Not that she didn't, but displacing Jay from his room fell short of ideal. She refused to make moving in a panicked reaction to last night's disaster at the club.

"Jay."

Ouch. Henry's gentleness cut sharper than his command voice. Jay's suggestion would go down in flames.

"I can." Jay vibrated in his seat. "Put it in my contract. 'Keep bedroom to Alice's standards of cleanliness.'" His usually rich tenor bristled and cracked. "Add it. I'll initial the change."

He seemed manic this morning, and for once bereft of sexual innuendo. God knew he had plenty of material. Her sharing his bedroom, and he hadn't thrown a single suggestive remark.

Henry's expectant stare weighed on her. He didn't need her permission to alter Jay's contract, so why—she'd be acting in a dominant role. The woman who couldn't even figure out how Jay felt today.

Shoving aside her apprehension, she nodded. Serious responsibility came part and parcel with moving her relationship forward. She'd need to be consistent and set rules she could praise Jay for obeying. Make a ritual of checking the room so he knew she was paying attention to his efforts. Caring. One thing amid a sea of hundreds Henry handled. He thought that way all the time, for both of them.

Henry carried the serving plate to the table and set it between them. Taking his seat, he glanced at their plates before filling his own.

Jay stared, intent but restrained enough to refrain from asking again. She hadn't believed him capable of such impressive self-control. Although, when he wanted something enough, he always managed to surprise her.

Finally, Henry quirked one corner of his mouth in a smile. "That's a fine idea, Jay. We'll add it to your contract today."

Jay gave an exuberant shout. His fork clattered against his plate. He hopped up from his seat, rounded the table, and dragged her chair back.

Annnd there's the lack of self-control.

"You're done eating, right, Alice? We can go to our room and you can tell me what you want fixed and I'll—"

Henry's silent laughter greeted her pleading glance. She'd have to get him for that later.

"—and we can pack your stuff and I can move the boxes and—"

"I'm not done eating yet," she said, breaking into Jay's chatter.

Henry had warned her, while they lay talking late into the night and Jay slept beside them, that the new living arrangement would cause excitement.

"But I'm excited about moving in, too." And carried the teensiest terror of making a wrong decision. For Jay. For Henry. For herself. "How about if you start by, umm, dividing your clothes into piles for laundry and putting away."

He fidgeted with her chair. Henry would understand his anxiety without a prompt. *Okay. Unravel Jay-threads.* He needed to know she didn't blame him for his panic at the club or her public discipline. That she loved him. That she wasn't sending him off alone to punish him.

"I'll join you when I'm done with breakfast. We can work on it together all day, and by tonight—" She lacked the authority to promise her hope.

Henry tipped his head and nudged the tips of his fingers in a go-on motion.

"By tonight we can all tumble into Henry's bed together."

"For good," Jay said. "No more nights apart."

"No more nights apart, Jay." Henry's decisive tone formed the firm bedrock of their relationship. "Now, I believe Alice has set you a task regarding your shared room. Perhaps you'd best get started."

"Yes, Henry." Jay pushed her chair in and swaggered into the second bedroom.

"You did very well, Alice."

"I was terrified."

"Nevertheless. You found your courage, and you gave Jay the reassurance he needed. Thank you."

Cutlery clinked in their silence. Without Jay's chatter, the hallway and its open door—the bedroom soon to be half hers—spawned a whirling tornado of questions.

She wasn't a spontaneous person. She planned. Researched. Tested. Yet she hadn't run design models before agreeing to move in. Why the fuck not?

Henry, that's why. He whispered to her as he cradled her at night, and her questions and fears crumbled like improperly cured concrete. Love, that's why. As long as she loved them and they loved her, everything else was fixable. Open to negotiation.

"You know I'll never be as obedient as he is." Loving Henry and Jay didn't blind her to reality. Henry already knew. He had to. But saying the words mattered.

Henry laid his fork and knife across his plate.

Maybe he'd give her an answer key to this new world. The first time she'd been in love.

Henry's persistent stare and slow-spreading smile gleamed with a touch of I-know-something-you-don't-know smugness.

"What? You think living with you all the time will change me?" The first time she'd lived with a lover. Two of them. One who'd dominate her at least part of the time. Fuck, she didn't do things by halves. "Make me more submissive?"

"No, Alice." Chuckling, he clasped her hand in a comforting squeeze. "It might, as change changes us all, but no. What amuses me is merely that even *Jay* is not so obedient as Jay."

"He's been on his best behavior? For our nights together?" If he'd been trying to impress her, she didn't know the real Jay. She didn't know weekday morning Jay. Cranky, bad-day-at-work Jay. Or what Henry was like when a burst of creativity struck. If he disappeared into his studio for days.

"You believe Jay has never defied me in front of you?" Henry raised an eyebrow.

"No, I guess he has." Hell, Jay'd defied him at their anniversary dinner, moving things forward faster than Henry had intended. The very first night. In January, too, taking advantage of the relaxed rules granted for his injury. And the night she'd safeworded. He'd begged her and Henry both to listen to him. "A lot more than I realized. But he's so easygoing. Jay-like."

"He's happiest when he has a clear task to complete and unconditional affection. He can be quite stubborn when he's unhappy, for which I give thanks." Closing his eyes, he bowed his head. "Convincing him that saying 'no' or disagreeing with me in some way would not result in the loss of my love and approval took a long while."

"While I bulldoze ahead with my own two cents." She turned her hand in his, running her fingers over his palm. His hand delivered pain and pleasure both. She hadn't feared losing Henry's love and approval before. She hadn't known they were hers to lose. But she'd worried about losing her place in his life with Jay.

Now she'd traded the periphery for the center. No, not the center. An equally blended mix, one she wouldn't know how to create and could never replicate. Corinthian bronze. Gold, silver, and copper alloyed into a form beautiful and precious. Yes, now she had something valuable to lose.

"You know your own mind very well, dearest." He closed his hand, capturing her fingers and stilling their motion. "I don't expect that will change. You'll challenge me more often than he will. That, too, is a joy. You each complement the other in my heart, Alice."

"You're not expecting complete obedience from me? Even though we'll be living together?" A recipe for resentment and hurt feelings if Jay had to answer to Henry and she didn't. "Is that fair to him?"

"The question here is what's fair to you. Submission gives Jay a sense of security. It is not a burden to him. Its weight on him does not grow heavier if your share is lighter." Henry shook his head. "We'll find a proper balance, whether that requires continued restriction of the hours in which you answer to me or some other method. So long as I have you both with me and happy, the rest is a matter of fine-tuning details. We'll adjust as needed."

"We're going to memorize a table of on-and-off hours like a bus schedule?" A color-coded timetable on the fridge. Right beside the star sticker chart she'd never made for all the sex acts she success-fully tried with Henry and Jay. A snicker slipped out.

Henry's lips twitched. "If you'd prefer to expand your submission into something more akin to Jay's, though perhaps with less oversight outside the home, I've no objection. It's certainly something we may try. In that case, your safeword would take on a greater role. If you became uncomfortable with something—at any time, not only during a stated game—your safeword would instantly indicate such to me."

"Even when we aren't playing?"

"Even then. We would, in essence, always be playing. The games simply wouldn't always have the sexual emphasis to which you're ac-customed." He released her hand and gestured at the table. "If, for in-stance, I asked you to gather the dishes now, you might playfully protest. If you persisted, I might suspect you wanted to be commanded to do so or wished for more of my attention. But if you meant your protests in earnest and it seemed I had not recognized it, using your safeword would reset the conversation and our roles within it."

"But I don't have a problem clearing the table." Henry cooked nearly every meal they ate. If she and Jay helped under his guidance, they fulfilled a necessary function. Contributing as equals according to their skill sets was sense, not submission.

"My hope is that I will not ask something of you that you cannot give, dearest. But you may at some point have a conflict of which I'm unaware. Be unable to take care of the breakfast dishes because you must rush to work for an early meeting, perhaps. Or you may have bruised your arm on the subway ride home and prefer not to carry the supper dishes." He raised a finger. "In which case, I'll examine the injury before we play games of any sort. But the point remains. Your safeword will indicate to me the serious and sincere nature of your objection."

A safety valve. If the pressure of submission overloaded her tolerances, he'd adjust the flow rate to compensate and leave her the option to yank the emergency brake. "I'll keep alert for those T riders throwing elbows. I'd hate to miss out on a game with fun rewards because some jerk muscled past me during rush hour."

The hint of a smile accompanied his elegant shrug. "The real world must take precedence over my own control, Alice. Even when I have you firmly in my dastardly clutches every day."

She imagined him twirling a cartoon mustache, ridiculously oversize and sinister, as he tied her to a set of railroad tracks. Well. Maybe not railroad tracks. Maybe his nice big bed. "Got it. Good thing I don't like to eat pistachios. I'd hate for there to be any confusion."

"Shall we try it, then, my sweet girl? When you're in the apartment, you'll answer to me as Jay does, with the exception of the second bedroom, which will have its own rules."

A trial run. Fuck if she'd turn down a new adventure. "I'd like that. You want me to clear the dishes?"

"No, I'll clear today. If you've finished eating, I'd like you to come here and give me a kiss before you go and reassure Jay of the value of his labor."

She was up in an instant. "That I can do."

Henry kissed her, tender but brief. "Go on and make him work for it, then. The more instructions you give him—"

"The more I can praise him for following them to the letter."

"You see? No need for terror. You've thoroughly grasped the concept."

"Time to implement it." She preferred implementation over theory anyway. Moving in with her lovers. Practicing a larger submissive role with one and learning to take a dominant role with the other. What grander experiment could there be?

* * *

Alice's studio apartment almost matched the pristine whiteness of the day she'd moved in. Not much left. Not much to start with.

Fresh from hauling the vanity across the hall, Jay zipped through the door and thrust his arms out in front of her. "Load me up."

She hefted one of the waiting drawers. "You want 'em all now?"

"Do I ever." He rocked and sprang like a sweet, demented jack-in-the-box. "Gimme everything you got."

She laid the first drawer across his arms. Every one of Henry's handwritten notes to her snuggled beneath her pj's. "No peeking, stud."

Bras in the second drawer. "A girl's gotta keep some secrets."

Panties in the third, stacked beneath his chin. God, he'd get great mileage out of that.

"I'm trusting your discretion, here." As if he hadn't seen her in—and out of—more than half the dainty delicates safe in his arms. She flashed him her best winning smile and waited for the joke.

Blank-faced and blinking, he stumbled half a step back, caught himself, and zoomed toward the door. He nearly took out Henry coming the other way before he danced sideways and disappeared.

"Hey." She waved at Henry.

At least he smiled back. No unexpected dodging there.

"Almost done."

A scant two boxes of dishes and cookware had gone downstairs with one of towels and bed linens and another of assorted odds and ends. Clutter. The sort of thing Henry wouldn't appreciate in his apartment. Their apartment.

Her new home.

She'd spent almost two years in this apartment. Despite the thrill of having her own place, she'd never made the space hers the way Henry's apartment breathed beauty and elegance. Offered warmth and comfort.

Mmm. She'd awakened this morning wrapped in the circle of his arm, opened one eye, and gazed across his chest at the mop of shaggy black hair burrowed against his other side. Comfort for sure.

"Second thoughts, my dear?" Henry stepped beside her and rested a hand on her back. "This is not an insignificant thing you're doing."

Not insignificant, no, but not unwelcome. If moving in turned out to be a mistake, she'd learn from it and plan accordingly next time.

Except there wouldn't be a next time, because she'd make this work. "Not second thoughts."

She sagged into his side, and he shifted to cradle her. He understood how big a step she was taking today. A leap. A huge fucking leap. But she'd taken one last night telling him she loved him. And he'd caught her with a declaration of love in return.

"Excitement. Trepidation, a little." She nudged his shoulder. "And a big pinch of 'Wow, Jay works fast.'"

Henry chuckled and bestowed a light kiss on her hair. "He does at that. My eager boy."

"Somebody call for me? Are we giving out hugs?" Jay swarmed them, darting in front and throwing his arms wide. "The more the merrier, right?"

"Absolutely." She planted a loud kiss on his cheek. "We're admiring your work ethic while we stand around and slack."

Jay squeezed them hard and stepped back. "Gives me more chances to flex my muscles." He posed weightlifter-style, which emphasized his lean cyclist's body.

She tickled his ribs.

He yelped. "Flag on the play."

"Do they have flags in weightlifting?" She pulled her hands back. "I think the rib tickle is a legal move." They swung their heads toward Henry. "Ruling from the ref?"

Henry dragged his fingers up her ribs.

Senses alerted, muscles tensed, she slid a hand across his chest, fully prepared for a counter-tickling campaign.

But he flattened his hand and delivered a firm stroke. "Tickling, my dears, is enjoyable in small doses. Beneficial in some cases."

The feathers. Somewhere in Henry's special dresser lived the feathers he'd teased her with on the night she'd discovered the joys of flogging. An arousing night made more so by the faint tickle of the feathers between each new sensation.

Smack.

The sound crashed in her head, and it wasn't the paddle or the crop or the flogger. It was Henry's hand landing on her ass last night. Whispers and laughter and that fucking bastard Cal shoving his dick in her face. She sidestepped. A tiny shift. Nothing suspicious. Nothing calling attention to the narrow sliver of space she'd put between herself and Henry.

"But perhaps now is not the best time for play. If you wish to shower before supper, you'll need to finish up soon." Henry inhaled with ostentatious exaggeration. "And I do suggest a shower when you've finished moving furniture and carrying boxes, delightful as your musk may be."

"I always knew I was delightful." Jay sniffed under his arms. "You think we can bottle me and make a fortune?" He crowded forward, arms up, ducking his head and catching her eyes. "What do you think, Alice? Am I delightful?"

She fended him off, laughter sluicing fear from her mind and tension from her muscles. "Right now? You reek like a sweaty forest. Henry's right." Not much left to go downstairs but the futon. The lumpy, banged-up bed belonged to another lifetime. "We can leave this stuff for another day and you can hop in the shower."

Jay followed her gaze. "No, I can get it done. Today. Now." He hustled over and hefted the floppy mattress.

Bare, the frame revealed the long scrape where she'd lost her grip and dragged the damn thing on the pavement hauling it into her first apartment with no Jay to lend a hand. Exposing the bones of the bed the way Henry exposed hers, only he'd used gentle care and she never managed more than rough bluntness.

"Won't need this tonight." Jay balanced the weight on his shoulder. "I'll square it away downstairs. Come back for the frame." He rushed past them out the door. "I'll be done in time for dinner, Henry. Promise."

Footsteps echoed from the stairwell.

His bouncing between moping and mania nagged at her. "Does he seem off to you?"

"It's an exciting day." Henry lifted her hand and kissed the back. "And some small cause for nerves." He tilted his head toward the futon frame.

A lonely bed for a lonely woman who hadn't recognized her loneliness until Henry and Jay poured love into the layers they'd scraped through to reach her. She tried to see the bed as Jay might. More than a job to finish to please Henry. "An escape clause," she whispered. "He's afraid I'll back out."

"He'll settle down, sweet girl." Henry rubbed his thumb over her knuckles. "His behavior is neither a reflection upon the reality of your emotions nor a lack of trust in your love for him."

No fucking way would she let their love go. She'd rope herself to them and growl a warning at anything trying to send her back to that place without them. "I'm not backing out."

Henry pulled her to face him. "This is not a race, Alice. It isn't a test. It isn't a competition of any sort. Do you remember what I told you the night of your anniversary dinner? If events move too quickly, we will stop and reassess." He stood broad-shouldered and sturdy, his green-eyed gaze steady on her. "The words are as true now as they were then. You will never disappoint me by being honest with me."

"It's not too fast for me. The timing was a surprise, yeah, but I want this." She'd hit the right note. He didn't worry she'd back out. He'd have contingency plans for that. And everything else on the planet. Giddiness tickled her throat. "I want you. I want Jay." She stepped into his embrace.

He hugged her close. "Shall we give our boy a hand? The sooner your belongings are settled, the sooner he will be as well."

Alice wiped down the table while Jay carried the last of the supper dishes to the dishwasher with the flair of a court jester. Clearing her apartment hadn't slowed down her energetic lover. He'd start juggling plates in a minute if Henry didn't stop him. No sign of Henry down the hall yet, but he'd been gone mere minutes.

"Jay. Think fast." She tossed the dishcloth.

He snatched it out of the air left-handed.

"Hang that on the faucet for me, will you?"

He saluted and flashed a cheeky grin. "Day one and I'm already taking orders from my new roomie."

Shit. She'd meant it in fun, a little bit of practice, but she'd been ordering him around all day. "Jay, you know you don't have—"

"I'm not complaining. I swear I'm not." He draped the washrag in the sink and hurried around the island. "I love having you here." Close but not touching, he hovered beside her. "I'm happy to do whatever you want me to."

"Excellent." Brown accordion folders tucked under his arm, Henry strode into the room. "Then you'll be quite pleased with what I have here. If you've both finished your tasks, would you join me in the living room, please?"

"*Yes.*" Jay sprinted past her. "Contract time?"

"Contract time." Henry sat on the couch and laid the folders on the coffee table. "Alice, come sit, please."

She settled in next to him.

Grinning like a fool, Jay bunched up on the floor in a loose waiting pose and crossed his arms over Henry's knees.

"Our contracts are in those?" They hadn't made an appearance last month when they'd added exclusivity and nightly dinners to her contract. Even with the additions, hers couldn't total more than a dozen pages. The thinner folder was half an inch thick.

"Among other things, yes."

"Other things?" Notes? Sketches? His insights on their likes and dislikes? He'd stacked his attention so neatly. The full extent of the seriousness with which he treated their needs.

Henry kissed her temple. "Other things. Now, I've drafted an addendum concerning the second bedroom and the responsibilities the two of you will share in regards to it."

And she'd thought Jay worked fast. Henry must've been busy while she and Jay had organized the bedroom.

Henry leaned forward, tousling Jay's hair along the way, and retrieved two sheets of paper. "I'd like for you each to read it over, and then we will discuss what changes, if any, you'd care to propose."

She accepted her copy of the proposal, and Jay took his. Silence descended as they read.

The morning's nerves melted away, absorbed by a growing sense of security and confidence with each line. Henry hadn't left her to muddle through on her own, to make a misstep and hurt Jay. Of course he hadn't.

Her responsibilities included conducting weekly spot checks at a time of her choosing. Surprise inspections. Jay would immediately correct any minor imperfections she noted. If she observed none or he corrected them to her satisfaction, she was free to praise him with whatever combination of verbal and physical affirmation she found appropriate. Excepting, of course, she wasn't to employ toys without consulting Henry.

Verbal and physical. A whistle echoed in her head. She and Jay had always been free to fool around, even without Henry, though they'd only done so once. Nothing comparable to her, in charge. A heady sort of power, but not unlimited.

Should Jay fail to meet expectations and require corrective action—discipline—she was to bring her concerns to Henry. The decision to determine and impose a suitable punishment would remain his alone. Likewise, he'd arbitrate any disputes. Otherwise, he'd allow their little game to proceed without interference.

Rights. Responsibilities. A clear chain of command.

"I don't have any objections, Henry." This challenge she could accept. Something Jay craved from her. Something Henry trusted her to accomplish. "The language is fine as-is for me."

Jay heaved a vast sigh and sagged against Henry's legs. "Me either. I was just waiting on Alice to say okay. She's the one who has to make time to supervise me."

How like Jay to think of the deal backward. He was the one promising to complete chores. To follow her directions. He'd keep their room clean, and all she had to do was praise him for it. Although the thicker folder had to be Jay's, and it neared three inches high.

"Jay, if you'll fetch a pen, please."

Jay dashed off to root in the kitchen junk drawer.

"Nothing so exacting is required, my dear," Henry said in an undertone. "It's best to start simply. You won't be required to make formal reports to me." He stroked her back. "Merely enjoy yourselves."

This experiment wasn't a project for work. Detailed notes might be overkill. Still. Picking up a notebook wouldn't hurt. She'd track what she'd asked Jay to do. How well he'd accomplished it. The rewards she'd bestowed and his general satisfaction level with them. "It'll be fun."

Henry chuckled. "An elaborate system is already taking shape in your mind, no doubt."

She tipped her head onto his shoulder. "You know me too well."

"Blasphemy." He nuzzled her hair. "I could never know you too well. Though you may be assured I'm making the attempt."

He thanked Jay for the pen, and the three of them signed. She resisted the urge to peek as Henry slipped the sheets into their folders.

Jay replaced the pen.

Henry left the room to put away the folders wherever folders went. The special dresser's drawers did have locks.

She sat alone on the couch. Saturday night. Not even nine thirty. Henry might expect playtime when he returned. She lifted her feet and curled her legs to her chest.

Last night had been fun until it turned into a clusterfuck. Could've been worse, though. The spanking he'd given her had probably been the bare minimum. It had been bare, all right. The entire room had witnessed her bawling like a baby. For ten swats.

As if she hadn't gotten three times that on her birthday. Although those had been for fun, with rubbing and touching between spanks and with her own arousal as the goal.

Henry emerged from the hall. He might ask now. Or demand. She'd given him that right. Her first real night with them as a full-time, live-in lover should be something to celebrate. She'd never told him no.

A drawn-out hum, descending, proved to be Jay yawning. Ever-fidgety, full-of-energy Jay leaned against the dining room table with drooping eyelids and a sleepwalker's posture. "Henry?"

"Yes, my boy?" He changed course without pause to stop beside Jay. "Is there something you need?"

"Just sleepy. I figured I'd go to bed early. If that's okay."

Henry laid a pale hand against Jay's tanned cheek. "Of course. You've worked hard today, my dear boy. Go on and get ready for bed, and Alice and I will join you shortly."

Jay squirmed, half nodding.

Henry studied him in silence for a long moment. "Perhaps it's a good night for story time. 'To me, you will be unique in all the world,' hmm?"

Jay's eyes widened. He grinned, head bobbing. "Yes, please, Henry." He shot a glance her way, and his smile dimmed. "I mean, if Alice doesn't mind having story time."

Pfft. As if she'd deny Jay something he so obviously adored. Besides, story time meant she wouldn't need to find a polite way to turn down sex. "I liked our last story time. It'll be tough to beat *Winnie-the-Pooh*, though."

Jay opened his mouth.

Henry tugged on his hair. "She'll find out soon enough. *The grain, which is also golden, will bring me back the thought of you. And I shall love to listen to the wind in the wheat.*"

The words weren't familiar. They both stared at her.

Jay kissed Henry's cheek. "Thank you for the wasted time, Henry."

"My responsibility, brave boy. Forever." Henry gave him a gentle push. "Off to bed."